MURDER
UNDER ANOTHER SUN

ALSO BY COLIN ALEXANDER

LEIF THE LUCKY NOVELS

Starman's Saga: The Long Strange Journey of Leif the Lucky
Murder Under Another Sun

OTHER SCIENCE FICTION AND FANTASY NOVELS

Princess of Shadows: The Girl Who Would Be King
Complicated: The Interstellar Life and Times of Saoirse Kenneally
Accidental Warrior: The Unlikely Tale of Bloody Hal
My Life: An Ex-Quarterback's Adventures in the Galactic Empire

MYSTERY NOVELS

Lady of Ice and Fire
God's Adamantine Fate

COLIN ALEXANDER

MURDER
UNDER ANOTHER SUN

A LEIF THE LUCKY NOVEL

For Cello, who somehow puts up with me.

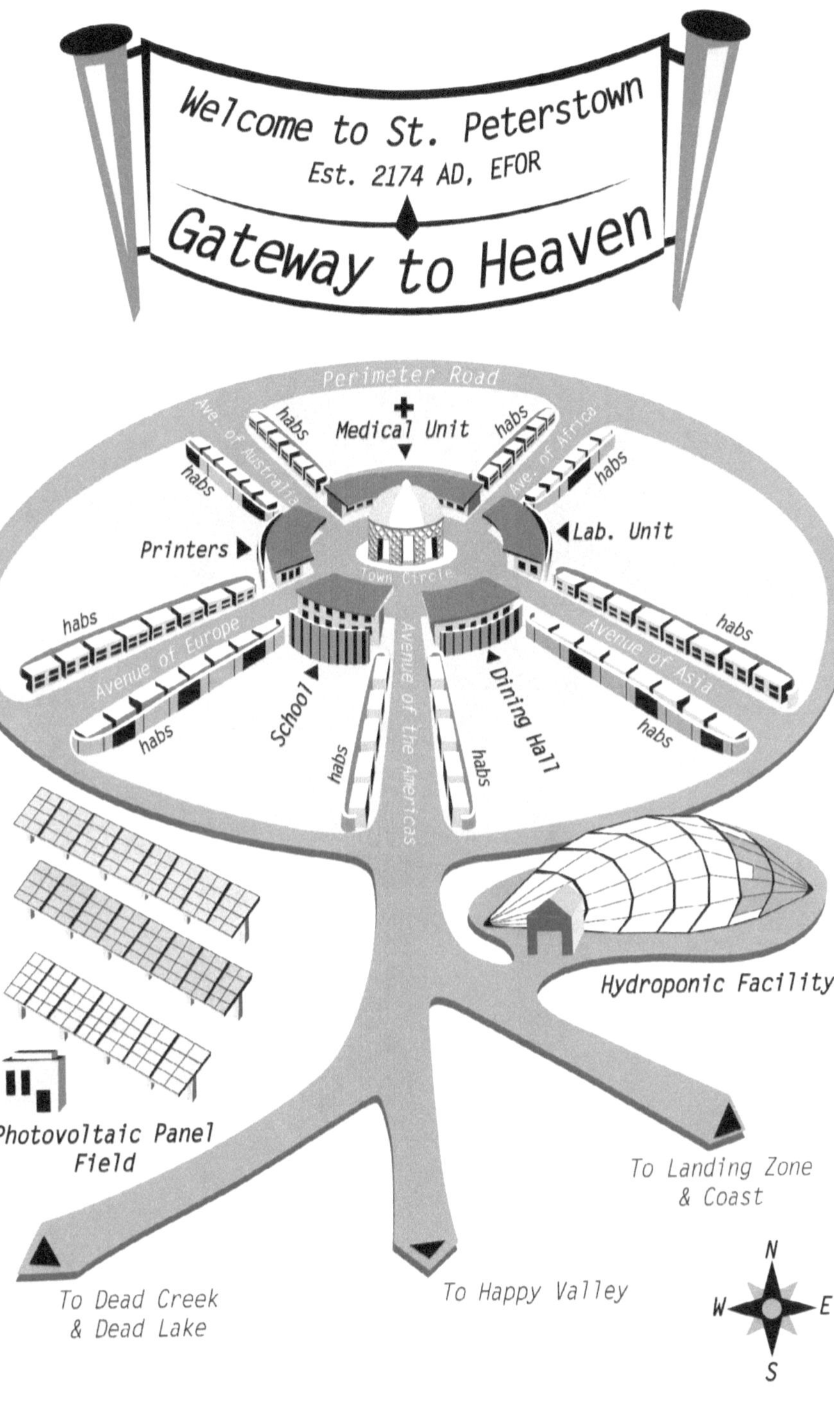

Welcome to St. Peterstown
Est. 2174 AD, EFOR
Gateway to Heaven

Perimeter Road
Medical Unit
habs
habs
habs
Ave. of Australia
Ave. of Africa
habs
Printers
Lab. Unit
Town Circle
habs
habs
Avenue of Europe
Avenue of Asia
habs
habs
School
Dining Hall
habs
habs
Avenue of the Americas
habs
Hydroponic Facility
Photovoltaic Panel
Field
To Dead Creek
& Dead Lake
To Happy Valley
To Landing Zone
& Coast
N
W
E
S

PROLOGUE

I'm not much for telling stories, even about murder, and that's what this was. Spinning tales isn't what I was trained to do. I joined the US Army out of high school in 2055, became a Ranger, and survived one deployment after another until the end of what we called the Troubles, in 2062. That's how I wound up being known as Leif the Lucky, but I don't talk about that. I left the army then, went back to school, and became a lab tech and a paramedic. Had no idea where I was going in life until I wound up becoming the International Space Commission's "Everyman volunteer" to the stars on the first starshot. I've told that story before.

When I decided to head back to the stars, it never occurred to me to write another story. After all, when you're the first to do something, when you lead the way, that's worth talking about. When you do it over again, who cares? I will agree that there is a mystery every time you venture somewhere new, to a planet no one has visited before. We may think we're really smart and can tell what's out there with our instruments in the solar system, but when you have boots on the ground, you find that reality is always different. Still, time, space, and relativity being what they are, who is going to read about unraveling those mysteries, and when are they going to read it?

On this trip, though, a dead body turned up. Make that plural: bodies. Now, there's nothing new about people dying; we had deaths on the first starshot too. But this wasn't combat, and it wasn't hazards of the unknown. Someone intended those deaths. That made me the first interstellar murder detective in the history of the universe. That's a title with a ring to it.

So, maybe it's only for my own amusement, but I've written down what happened leading up to the murders and how I solved them. With help from some friends, of course.

All the best,
Leif Grettison

HEAVEN
AD 2174, EFOR

PART I

All is for the best in this best of all possible worlds.
Voltaire, *Candide*

CHAPTER ONE

I was frozen. I was locked in a freezer and I was, literally, freezing. Before I wound up in that freezer, someone had sprayed me with water and I was encased in ice. I looked at my fingers. They were turning blue, the translucent blue of ice.

I woke.

I managed to unglue my eyelids and saw the top of my hib unit lifting up. The fluid from the unit's bath was draining away around me. A few drops of chilly liquid fell from the cover as it swung up, and they landed on me. I shivered. God, I hate the freezing dreams I get right before I come out of hib. I struggled to fight through the hib blur that fogged my brain, to make my eyes focus.

"How do you feel, Leif?"

It took a second for the voice to register. Charles Osborne. Our senior doc. Dr. Charley, as he preferred to be called. Yes, the ship's doc was supposed to be with you when you woke up, but this was the first time I had come out of a long starflight hibernation the way it was supposed to happen. I sneezed. Violently. That dislodged the cannula and knocked my mask askew.

"Here, let me help you," Charley said. "That's what I'm here for."

"I'm okay." My voice was a croak.

He reached over the sidewall of the unit, but I got a creaky arm moving to pull off my mask with the cannula before he could do it. Then I removed the port that connected lines to my vessels. "I'm good. I'm used to coming out of hib by myself. I'm the one who designed that port, way back when."

"I know that, but you don't have to be your normally stubborn and cranky self about it." Charley managed to look and sound hurt.

"Sorry."

"No worries. How about your OJ? Spiked with sugar, of course, just like the doctor ordered. Can you sit up on your own?"

"Yes." I wished my movements could have been as sure as my voice sounded. Every muscle felt like it had gone slack and atrophied, and every joint felt glued together. I was an iron suit of armor, left in the rain to rust. I braced one hand against the bottom of the unit and forced myself up.

Charley held out a glass of orange juice. I fought to focus on his face: dark brown skin, short black beard, kindly. His was the sort of face that could comfort a patient simply by appearing at the bedside. He had the gravitas of a doc who had been practicing for decades, although he was actually two years younger than I was biologically. He deserved a better patient than me.

"Thanks." I took the juice, chugged it, and managed not to cough. "How did we do?"

I saw a flash of surprise at the question, but then his face went back to friendly. "Your hibernation went fine. Four years, four months and change, SFOR. No problems anywhere. I'm up, of course, and Yang is on the bridge. She asked that the three of us be up a couple of days before we start the rest. I'm not sure why. Maybe because of that trouble you had before."

I grinned. We'd had a hib failure on humanity's first starshot, but I knew that had nothing to do with why Yong wanted to delay waking up the rest of the crew for a couple of days.

"Do you want any help getting dressed?" Charley asked.

"No, thanks. I've got it."

I wasn't being cranky or stubborn in refusing his offer of help. I'd been in hib over four years SFOR, which was our ship frame of reference, in a starship that had accelerated to relativistic velocities. The body didn't respond well right after wakening from that long a time in hib. I was going to be stiff, and my muscles would ache and have trouble holding me upright. That's why he offered to help me dress. But the thing was, my knee—the one that had been surgically repaired after I was wounded on Mindanao all those Earth years ago—would be awful. I didn't want him to see the trouble I was going to have. More specifically, I didn't want him to see me scream when I forced it to move. If I cried, and I might, that was going to stay private.

After Charley left, I managed to pry myself out of the unit, towel off, and dress in the ship pants and polo without crying. The polo was much like the one I had worn the last time out. The NASA insignia and my name, Grettison, were stitched over the left breast, and the starshot symbol, a suited hand clutching a star, over the right. The only difference was the embroidered STARSHOT XV under that symbol. Back on the first starshot, we didn't need a number to keep track.

I laughed when I saw the blister pack of "starflight laxative" capsules in the locker by my hib unit along with the clothes. One thing we had learned on the first expedition was that multiyear hib induced the worst constipation in the annals of medicine. The International Space Commission had heard that loud and clear in our debriefs. They'd also moved the locker inside the privacy enclosure around the hib unit so we didn't have to go padding out, naked and dripping, to get a towel and a robe. Maybe people did learn from experience.

I slipped the blister pack into a pocket and lurched toward the caf for more calories. The next stop after that would be the gym, where I would try to stretch and work myself into a semblance of a human before I went up to the bridge.

.   .   .

The former People's Liberation Army Air Force captain and now pilot-in-command of the *Dauntless*, Yang Yong, swiveled her chair around and stood to greet me when I entered the bridge. She was petite, literally half my size by weight, but her appearance belied her strength. There was nothing delicate about Yang Yong. Her face had that special tight little grin she reserved for me.

"It's good to see you, Soldier Boy." Her polo was decorated with the CNSA badge and her name in Chinese characters, but otherwise, the polo and ship's pants matched mine. Well, mine tended to look a bit rumpled the moment I pulled them on. She looked like you could take her image and drop it in a recruiting poster without any retouching. She always looked like that, even in the middle of chaos and impending disaster.

"Good to see you, too, Flygirl," I said. "It's only been, what, seventy-six years?"

Her grin broadened into a smile. Nobody else ever got that. "A bit more, according to the computer. Come, take the copilot seat and see where we are going."

I went for the seat on the right, but my thoughts were about us, not our destination. Our relationship had started off fraught—and that was the kindest way to put it. During the Troubles, a decade of fighting that had nearly wrecked the world, Yong flew attack planes for the Chinese while I fought in the US Army. On a steamy day in 2062, in the last major action of the Troubles, she had flown her superstealth J-45 against a position held by, among others, Staff Sergeant Leif Grettison and his platoon. She had blown the shit out of our position despite all our efforts to shoot her down. But while she was firing on us, our base missiled her carrier and killed her brother. We didn't know each other then, of course, and it's astonishing that we lived to actually meet, but when we did, on the first starshot in 2069, let me tell you: it was hate at first sight. She started out calling me Soldier Boy and I, naturally, retaliated by calling her Flygirl. Neither of us meant those names affectionately, not in the beginning. But somehow, in the process of saving that first mission—and each other—our relationship had changed. Now she was my Flygirl, and I would go much farther than the ends of the earth for her.

I smiled back at her, wondering what we were. Boyfriend and girlfriend? Too weak. The ancient term *significant other* didn't do it justice either. Naturally, neither of us ever used the L-word. I did know that I wanted to spend whatever life I had left with her, and she, obviously, felt the same way. She had made it possible for me to be on this mission.

I shook off thoughts about relationships and settled into the copilot's seat, reading the note our copilot, Jorge Olivares, had taped there before we went into hib. Jorge was a computer nerd in addition to being the junior pilot. His note read, in hand printed block letters:

JORGE'S LAWS OF COMPUTER SYSTEMS

ANY ELECTRONIC SYSTEM CONNECTED TO

A COMPUTER CAN BE HACKED

ANY SYSTEM THAT CAN BE HACKED, WILL BE HACKED
IF YOU THINK YOUR SYSTEM HASN'T
BEEN HACKED, YOU'RE WRONG!

Not out here, Jorge, I thought. Not out here. Melodrama in the middle of the blur that goes with coming out of hib is something I don't need.

The chronometer right above Jorge's Laws caught my eye. The glowing symbols read 23 OCTOBER 2174 on the screen labeled EFOR—Earth frame of reference. That was the date the computer calculated it was back on Earth now, seventy-six years since we had left. In our frame of reference on the ship, only four years and four months had passed. We had spent almost all of that in hib, where the combination of hib itself and a constant infusion of drugs kept our biological aging down to about four months. It was a weird universe Dr. Einstein had worked out for us.

I looked away from the clock to the screen labeled FORE, which showed the sky ahead. A bright yellow dot was centered in the middle of an otherwise normal starfield. There was no relativistic condensation of the stars; the ship had already decelerated dramatically from near light speed.

"That's our objective?" I asked.

"Yes. Class G2, very similar to our sun. Maybe a couple of hundred million years younger. Third planet out is the target. Mass very close to Earth and similar atmosphere, from the observations at Earth. Nearly a twin."

"And the mission plan is just to off-load the reinforcements—I mean, the additional colonists and supplies. Then we turn around and head back. Nothing has changed since we went into hib? We're not picking up any message?"

"No," she said. "The first expedition was four to seven months ahead of us, and it was their job to set up the colony. They had construction crew and bots for that. Our additional people and supplies will bring the place to a self-sustaining level. If they found a problem we have to deal with, they would have left a broadcasting buoy. Haven't picked one up. If ISC was completely wrong and the place is uninhabitable, they won't have planted a colony at all. Just left a buoy. They'd have gone back into hib and returned, and so would we. A wasted trip." She paused. "No other way to do it, though. We can't wait seventy-six years for a signal that it's okay to send reinforcements."

"I know," I said. "But it's boring."

I don't do boring very well. Nothing to occupy the intrepid exoplanetary scout, which was me. My position hadn't existed in the original mission plan, but ISC wanted Yong to pilot and she wanted me along, so they invented a position and I invented a title. It did have a certain cachet, even if there was no specific job. "Next time, let's go someplace brand new again."

Yong chuckled. I'm the only one who got chuckles from her. "Maybe they'll find monsters for you to kill. Or maybe they'll need you to take pretty pictures of different leaves. But I had little choice. My air force was not happy that I resigned, not at all, and this was the next starshot. It didn't seem like a good idea to wait for another one."

I gave her a laugh of my own. "You're figuring that when we get back from this trip after a century and a half EFOR, they'll have gotten over it."

"It's a reasonable bet."

Frankly, I hadn't wanted to wait for another ship either. I had been out of sync with the world after coming back from the first starshot. Nothing interested me, I didn't fit in, and I had been glad to leave.

I reached across the console between our seats and let my hand rest there. She put her hand lightly on top of mine. Her fingers curled gently around my fingers. We sat like that, wordless, and watched the starfield ahead of us. Her hand was small, made even smaller by comparison to mine. Her fingers were slender. Grip that hand, though, and it felt like steel rods and metal cable. That hand was like the rest of Yang Yong, nothing soft anywhere. Except when we were alone. Between the stars was a good place to be alone.

The gentle touch of her thumb rubbing the back of my hand was enough to send sparks and adrenaline coursing along every nerve in my body. We didn't do anything else, because the bridge was a public space, even if Charley was the only other person awake on the ship and wouldn't come to the bridge unless we called him. We didn't do anything else, because the bridge was a command post, an action station. Yong and I had both grown up in straitlaced societies, conditioned by the Troubles and by the crap that had happened early in the twenty-first century. In public, we were very correct.

"The ship will be fine with the computer in charge for a while," Yong said after several minutes. "We won't wake Jorge for two more days. Your quarters or mine?"

I had a coin we flipped for important decisions like this. "You call it," I said, and spun the coin into the air.

"Heads."

That's the way it landed. Relax, I told myself. Relax and enjoy the peace and quiet. This trip was going to be as challenging as driving a delivery truck.

Famous last words.

CHAPTER TWO

Jorge's hib unit clicked into wake cycle two days later, as planned. Charley got him up and moving. After a day to let most of the blur clear, he arrived on the bridge. He was a handsome Spaniard with a small multifaceted red diamond tattooed on his right cheek in the style of facial body art that had become popular in the 2090s. It stood out against his pale skin and I wondered if it would still be in fashion when we returned. His shock of black hair was combed straight back from the peak over his forehead to the nape of his neck. No way could that helmet of hair stay in place without products I would never take into the field, but he treated that hair like a prized possession. I think he believed it made women notice him. So I was surprised to see that his hair was not perfectly aligned when he entered the bridge. His hand was on his stomach, and he was moaning and groaning about the pain in his belly from the instant he was through the doors.

"Did you take Doc Charley's magic pills?" I asked.

"Yes." The answer was bitten off short. "Not that they've done any good. This constipation from hib is a bitch."

"Well, don't worry." I favored him with a smile. "This, too, shall pass."

He stopped behind the copilot's seat and put one hand on its back, bracing himself. "Not funny, Leif. Has anyone told you you're not going to win any awards for empathy?"

I admitted that had been said before. Once or twice.

He grunted and seated himself. Immediately, he and Yong launched into a conversation about deceleration vectors, fuel consumption, and estimated time until we made orbit. That was not a conversation I had any place in, and when it was time for business, Yong was all business. So was I, for that matter.

"Unless you tell me otherwise," I said, "I'll have Doc keep the wake-up schedule for the colonists. They'll all be up by the time we make orbit."

Yong nodded. She already knew that. Jorge grunted, which I assumed was an acknowledgment. I took it as my cue to leave the bridge.

.   .   .

Jorge's belly did not improve. He complained of it every time I saw him over the next three days, as though it were somehow my fault. Then, on the following day, a notification flashed at the periphery of my field of vision while I was having breakfast in the caf. I looked at it and it opened. Doc Charley wanted me in the Med Unit. Now.

I left my food and moved. Medical was one deck down, which meant I needed to wait for the lift. This could not be good news, but the sooner I got it, the sooner I could deal with it.

When I arrived, I saw Charley and Song Jing, who was our junior doc and his backup. Jorge was laid out on one of the beds, silent but awake, the mobile scanner next to it encasing his midsection. Jing bit at her thumb as she looked at the scanner's screen. She was sweet on Jorge and didn't hide it as well as she thought she did.

"Leif, take a look at that." Charley pointed at the screen. The image on it was a slice through Jorge's midsection, but I couldn't tell any more than that. What he was pointing at looked like a double-walled balloon.

"Charley, I was a paramedic after I got out of the service, not a doc. I can't read that."

"Sorry. Give me a sec."

Charley was looking off to his right and I knew he was reading through the output from our computer that his chip was projecting. Back when I grew up, we wore glasses that interfaced with our phone bases or implanted chips, and we read the projection by looking at the lens. While I was away on the first starshot, they improved the circuitry so that the chip handled everything at the neural interface, no need for glasses. I still found it odd when people looked away from me and off into space to read a message or something.

"What you've got," and Charley was talking to Jorge as much as to me, "is one piece of your small intestine has, like, telescoped into another section. It's called an intussusception. It's a kiddie thing, very rare in adults." He turned to face me. "Leif, that's why I wanted you here. Did anything like this happen on that first flight?"

"No. And I'm sure you've seen all the records and debrief."

"Unless it wasn't put in the records. There was talk that not everything was." Charley's face was as stern as I had ever seen it. "You were functioning as the doc by the end of that flight. If anyone would know if this could happen with multiyear hib, it's you."

I had been functioning in a lot of roles by the end of that flight, none of them planned. Charley was partly right; some things that had happened during the first starshot were buried deeper than the people they had happened to. This wasn't one of them.

"The answer is still no, Charley. But that doesn't tell you much. There were only thirty-three of us on that ship and five of us never made the trip back. If this only happens occasionally, that's not enough trips to know."

"Yeah." Charley put his hands on his hips. "Good point. Of course, by the time we get back, enough starshots will have returned that they'll know, but none of that does us any good now."

"So, what are you saying needs to happen?" Jorge said from the table.

"You need an operation," Charley said. "We need to straighten out your guts and, probably, clip off that piece that's stuck. I'll get the surgibot over here and we'll get started." He rubbed the fingers of one hand across his beard. "I'm going to message Yang. Leif, you can let her know that Jorge will be fine on the ship, after we're done, but she'll need to take the spaceplane down to the planet." Charley put a hand on Jorge's arm and smiled down at him. "And don't you worry about your laws of computer systems. Our medical equipment is up to the newest standards, with the latest and greatest in hidden security files. Unhackable and immutable. The secrets of your innards are safe with us."

"Like I care if someone hacks into a database out here?" Jorge said. "Just fix this, please."

Abdominal surgery in deep space. I'd rather watch it on a Hollywood vid.

.   .   .

Flygirl shrugged off the issue of Jorge's unavailability for the spaceplane. Literally. She shrugged. "The *Dauntless* won't need much from the pilot in orbit. In fact, we would probably be fine with only the computer, if necessary. It's no problem for me to do the flights to the surface, and I would rather be the one to do them. There may be a problem down there."

"What kind of problem?" Part of me was thinking that Flygirl would insist on flying the spaceplane if we were headed into trouble even if Jorge was in perfect shape. The other part of me was thinking that problems seventy-six light-years from any help were not a good thing.

"I don't know. That's part of it." Yong's fingers drummed on the armrest of her seat. "The colony transmitter responded to our arrival signal, so that means they are on the planet and set up, but listen to what they sent back." She tapped at the control panel.

A baritone voice that sounded vaguely British came out of the speakers. "Welcome to Heaven, where it's hotter than Hell." That's where it ended.

"Huh?" I said. Okay, that message was better than a frantic call for help saying they were under attack by aliens, but it was a pretty bizarre transmission.

"Yes, it's rather cryptic," Yong said. "The voiceprint identifies him as Jerry Whitehead, a colonist who came out on the first ship, the *Daredevil*. So getting a message from him makes sense, but the message doesn't. I queried him and got this back." She tapped at her panel again.

"We'll talk about it when you're on the ground," came out of the speakers.

"That's it?" I asked.

"I've sent another query," Yong said, "but given where we are entering the system, the transmission time is still about two hours each way. I don't know if he will expand on this."

I did some arithmetic in my head. All of this had happened since I was last on the bridge, most of it while I was in the Medical Unit, listening to the tale of Jorge's belly. A brand-new colony around a distant star was, in my book, the definition of a dangerous situation. When people in perilous situations were cryptic, they were usually hiding something.

"I guess it's a good thing the ISC sent us with more than a single rifle this time," I said.

"Maybe." Yong stopped there, because we heard the sound of the bridge door opening behind us.

I spun around, expecting to see Charley and bracing for bad medical news, but that wasn't who came through the door. This was Sonal Davis, a slender woman no bigger than Yong. She had straight dark brown hair that barely touched her shoulders and framed a light tan face whose artwork was a cluster of small hearts on her right cheek. Sonal wore her heart on her skin, literally. On Earth, her field had been organizational psychology, and officially, she was the unit leader for our colonist reinforcements. In my mind, I dubbed her the head counselor, although I knew better than to say that out loud.

"Leif," Sonal said, "I'm sorry to bother you and I know you have other issues, but could you come down to the caf? About thirty of our group are down there, and there's a bit of an issue."

"A fight?" Historically, that was when people called for me to get involved.

"No, no. Not yet. But it's getting heated." She pursed her lips. "It's about what we're doing. About the time change. You've been a starman; you've been out before. That's why I thought of you when the trouble started."

Lovely. I remembered sitting on the bridge with Yong, complaining that this mission would be boring. I had jinxed it.

CHAPTER THREE

Our colonists were drawn from the Pioneer Youth, a multinational group dedicated to helping people in impoverished areas or where a natural disaster had occurred. Now, apparently, they were tackling the task of colonizing the stars. We had 128 of them, half men, half women. When I met them for preflight training in the solar system, all of them seemed really nice and really earnest about what they were doing. They were also really young. Only Sonal and her deputy, Klaus Koch, were older than twenty-five. Of course, when I made corporal during Central Asia II, only one person in my squad was even over twenty-one—and it wasn't me—yet we were a bunch of hardened, kick-ass dudes. Our Pioneer Youth were different. They seemed like *kids*. I tried to imagine a brawl among them and couldn't. I didn't think they even knew how to fight. They probably thought soccer was a contact sport.

The doors from the lift to the deck that held the caf and the gym opened in front of me and Sonal. I braced myself for the raucous sounds of a fray. Instead, I got crickets. Nothing. Silence.

Inside the caf, a group of people were clustered by the wall across from the entrance. They all wore the outfit—a uniform, really—of the Pioneer Youth: baggy brown cargo-style pants with a wide opening at the bottom, which annoyed me because it could snag on something; a light tan, short-sleeved shirt; and a red kerchief. Some were sitting; some were standing. I saw no pushing or shoving. No one even had their hands up. All of them were staring at something on the wall.

I looked at Sonal. "This is heated?"

She had the grace to look embarrassed. "It was getting emotional."

Any less emotion, and we would need to check their vital signs to make sure they weren't dead. I shrugged and walked over to the group. As I got closer, I realized that they weren't silent. Someone was crying softly. Had a hib failed and someone died? Not possible. Charley or Jing would have messaged me. Still, I saw tears streaking young cheeks.

My mind focused on how young they were. Much younger than I was, even if you went only by biological age, which for me was between thirty-three and thirty-four, depending on how you calculated the effects of relativity, hib, and the drugs in hib. Whenever I saw the years they had been born in, I thought of them as children. That was a big change from the first starshot, when Yong and I had been the youngest on the ship. It reminded me of the difference between when I joined the army in 2055, a wet-behind-the-ears kid right out of high school, and when, as a sergeant, I dug in with my platoon along Camp Schwarzkopf's perimeter on Mind-anao. I was the old man of the platoon the day the Chinese assault killed every other man in it. *Get your mind off that!* I pulled my mind away from Mindanao and back to the starship *Dauntless* and looked over the kids in front of me.

It made sense that they were young. If you were going to settle a new world, and that colony was going to be isolated, the settlers should be in their prime reproductive years, capable of having lots of children. Humanity had plenty of experience growing animals from embryos in a lab, from chickens to cows. For obvious reasons, we had a lot less experience playing games like that with humans.

"All right. What happened? Who died?" Maybe my voice was a little harsher than it needed to be. Sonal winced.

A boy standing at the back of the group—I didn't recognize him immediately, and didn't bother checking his ident—simply pointed at the blank screen on the wall. He said nothing.

The screen was off, of course, although we could have put a starfield on it. Next to it was the chronometer with the date, now 30 October 2174, EFOR. Uh-oh.

"The screen's off." That was a young woman's voice. "The Community's off."

The comment triggered a cascade of voices.

"We can't check the Community anymore."

"There's nobody to send a message to even if we could."

"Everybody we knew on Earth is probably dead by now!"

"My family . . ."

Shit. The human psyche does not cope well with time shifts—thank you, Dr. Einstein and your damned relativity. Time traveler's remorse.

"Okay! Hold it down! Now!"

I have a voice that can squelch a grumbling platoon expressing its displeasure with the rear echelon. It shut down this group in an instant. They turned away from the wall and looked at me. Now it was time to play deep space psychiatrist, not the best match for my talents.

"Listen up," I said. "We all knew about this going in. Between relativity and hib, you haven't aged, but time went by in the rest of the universe. It's been seventy-six years and more on Earth. We went over this time and again before we left." That, and they had all been screened about their reasons for volunteering, and for any problematic attachments. So much for the vaunted psych profiles. Empathy would only get all of them bawling, so I reverted to Staff Sergeant Leif Grettison of the US Army Rangers. "I'm sorry if the reality hit you this way, but time only goes in one direction. We have a job to do and we need to march forward. I'm sure all of you have things to get ready, and you also need to work on your physical conditioning after hib. Put your minds on that and get them off an EFOR date that doesn't mean anything out here anyway."

"We were doing that," said the boy who'd pointed at the clock. "We were doing okay. But then she started it."

"She who?"

"Pennywise." He pointed toward the front of the group, but whoever was there was hidden from my view. A bunch of other fingers pointed there as well.

Pennywise? That rang no bells, and a quick check of the roster did not yield a match on my field. Regardless, we needed to break up this mutual pity party.

"C'mon, everybody," Sonal chimed in. "Let's get back to preparing for landing and working with the others coming out of hib. I'll make time to speak with each one of you."

"Everybody except you at the front," I said. Sonal would do the gentle empathy thing and make each person feel better, but if I had someone who was causing trouble, I wanted to have a different conversation.

Slowly, the group left the caf with Sonal, like a cluster of ducklings around the mother. Two people were left behind, one male, one female. One of them had to be Pennywise, the instigator.

The woman was small, maybe an inch or two taller than Yong. Her arms were a pair of pipe cleaners joined to her torso at angles twisted wire could manage. Narrow hips and narrow shoulders bracketed a narrow trunk with the figure of a soda can, making a skinny whole. Her face was a plain oval of olive skin with a generous nose. Brown eyes matched her hair, which was just long enough to be pulled into the stub of a ponytail, but not all the hair reached the band, so some of it stuck out in a curly spray. She was the girl in class nobody would notice except for her hand always being raised. I pulled up her ident on my field. PENELOPE PANAG-IOTIDIS, CUMBERLAND, MAINE. Somehow, she was twenty-two, although she could have passed for early teens. She went by Penny. Well, if my name were Penelope, I'd go by Penny also. I had no idea what Pennywise meant.

The other one who hadn't left was a young man. He wasn't tall, five-seven at most, but his was a face you would remember. He had a cleft chin and gray eyes under a mop of blond hair. I could see defined muscles on his forearms, and his shoulders were broad for his height. His shoes caught my eye, a garish gym shoe in red, white, and blue, with TEAM USA stitched on the leather. He had his hands on Penny's shoulders, kneading them. His ident read DUSTIN RUSSELL, MINNEAPOLIS, MINNESOTA, and it gave his age as twenty-four.

They were an odd couple. I would have preferred to deal with Penny separately, but Dustin showed no sign of leaving.

"All right, Penny," I said. "Would you care to tell me what you did and why you did it?"

Dustin answered before Penny could get a word out. "You're not the police," he said.

That put me back into noncom mode. I folded my arms across my chest. "That is not the point. Yes, all of you report to Sonal as the head of your group. However," I emphasized the word and paused to let it sink in. "My job is to do whatever I think needs to be done with regard to landing you, reinforcing the colony, and making sure it is ready for the *Dauntless* to leave. I have almost complete discretion." In a sense that was true, because my entire job description in the mission plan read, "as assigned by pilot-in-command."

"Having the lot of you pissing and moaning about what is now ancient history is not good for success, and that makes it my business. I wasn't asking you to comment." I glared at him, and I do a pretty good glare.

Penny brought a hand up to clasp his where it was rubbing her right shoulder. She turned to look at him. "It's okay, Dustin. I'm okay here."

At first, Dustin neither spoke nor moved. He kept his hands on her shoulders. I stared at him and said nothing. A minute passed. Abruptly, he raised his hands.

"Okay," he said. "Okay. I'll wait for you at my room. Just be careful what you say, Pennywise. I wouldn't trust this guy."

I watched him stalk off toward the exit from the caf. When he had gone, I turned back and found Penny staring at me, looking even more like a gangly teenager now that she was alone. She seemed to have trouble figuring out where to put her arms and hands.

"I'm sorry," she said. "Dustin is, well, protective, and that's sweet, but I'm okay talking to you. What can I tell you?"

"You can tell me what I asked about. Did you create that scene we just had here, and if you did, why? We drilled on this before we left, that focusing on the past after we come out of hib is a bad idea."

I didn't soften my tone, or my stance. I could see her trembling. She met my eyes briefly, then dropped hers to look at her feet. She didn't shrink back, though.

"I guess I did, and I'm sorry. I didn't mean to do it. We all came down here for a break and, well, the clock and the screen caught my eye. I tapped the screen—habit, you know—and I couldn't bring up the Community, of course, and that made me think of messages floating out in space that would never be answered and I saw the EFOR date and thought we couldn't know what our families and friends were doing for Halloween, but of course they're not doing anything, because of what year it is, and one thought led to another. I do that. With a lot of things. I thought

I was only thinking to myself, but I wasn't. I sort of do that too. Dustin is sweet about it, but the others aren't, which is why he doesn't want me off on my own. I'm sorry I caused a problem. I'll make a public apology, if you want."

"No. That will only make it worse." I thought for a moment. I wished we didn't need weeks to decelerate to the velocity that would let us make orbit. I wished we didn't need those weeks to get everyone out of hib and functional. "You know, I would let it drop. Sonal will talk to the others. Just don't do it again. Soon enough we'll be too busy to be thinking about it anyway."

"Okay."

I should have dropped it there, should have about-faced and left, but a question had been niggling at my mind almost from the day I met this crew. It was one of *those* questions, ones we were told were out-of-bounds, information you couldn't see when you pulled up someone's ident and checked their profile. But we'd already gone into that territory a bit, and I've had a tendency in my life to be impulsive.

"Mind if I ask you a question I shouldn't ask?"

"Ask away." She folded her arms across her chest and looked up at me. I wondered if she was mimicking me.

"Why did you—not just you, but your whole group—why did you volunteer for this? Back on Earth, everybody talks about it being the New Golden Age. I heard that nonstop after I got back from the starshot, that it was the best time in human history. I didn't fit in when I came back, but that's because I grew up in another time to begin with. But what about all of you? You grew up in the New Golden Age. Why did you leave on a one-way trip?" And then cry about it, I thought but didn't say.

"You mean why would anybody leave the BOT?" she said.

"I don't get the current slang," I said. "There are bots everywhere. What do you mean, 'why would anyone leave the bot'?"

Penny giggled. "Not *bot. B-O-T*: 'best of times.'" Her smile said she had a secret that she could finally share. "It's because we're all Agers."

"Yeah. New Golden Agers. I get that, but that doesn't make sense for an answer."

"No, no." The giggle became a laugh. "I said Agers. For *A-G-E*. It stands for Almost Good Enough. I made that up and nobody likes it, but it's true. We're the ones who started off well, did well, but then didn't make the final cut or get over the last hurdle. Take me. I studied agriculture. I got good marks and I like it and did well when we had our co-op farmwork practicals, although my parents thought it was awfully blue collar, but that farm was the only time I was ever away from home, and I get along well with plants and animals, basically, and my parents said it would be okay if I had a graduate degree, so I was going to go for synthetic biosystems and precision agriculture, but I couldn't pass the exams or the interviews." The smile faded. "My parents were so disappointed in me." She shrugged. "But Dustin loves me and he was a Pioneer and he was going. So I'm the sort who goes."

"And Dustin? What's his claim to almost fame?"

"Dustin's a gymnast. He was terrific in his teens; I've seen his vids. He made the national team. That's where he got his Specials, those shoes he always wears unless we're in zero gee and he has to use the StickStrips. I'd have been scared to talk to him then. Something happened to his wrist bones, it was like they died under his cartilage from too much practice. They fixed it, but he can't compete anymore, can only teach. So, same as me. Everybody has a story. All different, all the same."

That left one other question. "They called you Pennywise, not Penny. Where does that come from?"

She looked down at the floor again. "Well, it's better than PeePee, which is what kids always called me in school. I mean, that's my initials, although there was this really unfortunate day in fourth grade when I got scared and—"

I put my hand up. "Just about Pennywise, please. Not your life story."

"Sure. Dustin gave it to me after we started going together. You know the saying, penny-wise but pound-foolish? Well, my brain goes in a thousand different directions and I've got all sorts of details up there, but I miss the big picture a lot. Like what just happened here. It's probably why I blew the exams and interviews. Dustin thinks so." She looked up with a shy smile. "It's a good thing Dustin loves me anyway."

It was enough to melt my tone and make me wish I'd left well enough alone. "Maybe you should get back to your friends and your prep," I said.

"Dustin's my only friend, but he's enough. I will get back there and I'll watch my mouth. Best as I can." She stepped past me and walked to the exit.

I watched her go and turned over in my mind what she had told me. I was flying to the stars with a crew of the second best and second brightest. Not what I considered a rallying cry for launching into the unknown. And what about the settlers already on the planet, who'd come on the first ship? Were they also second best? Or third? Or somewhere else on a scale of one to ten?

CHAPTER FOUR

When I returned to my quarters, I found the Three Musketeers standing outside my door. All right, it wasn't Athos, Porthos, and Aramis. It was Bjorn Gudmundsson, Reality Busby, and Miroslav Petrovic, the leaders of the three cohorts of Pioneers. Sonal's crew of 128 eager Pioneer Youth was divided into three cohorts of forty-two, excluding Sonal and her life partner and deputy, Klaus. The three cohort leaders seemed nervous, shifting weight from one foot to another and looking up and down the corridor to see who might be coming. That was peculiar. No one had messaged me that they wanted to see me. I mean, it was a fair bet that I would eventually come back to my room and notice them, but this was an odd way to arrange a meeting.

I gave them a wave and sauntered over. I knew them, of course, from the training prior to our departure from the solar system. My bias was to think of them as platoon leaders, but that was an exaggeration of their role. They were more coordinators than real leaders, and none of them had the command presence I would expect from even a junior officer. They were kids playing a role. I knew them in a way I did not know all the other Pioneers because, as cohort leaders, they had the most interactions with the ship's crew.

All of them were dressed in the same Pioneer getup as the kids in the caf, with the addition of a red armband to designate their position as cohort leader. Their appearance probably would have provoked quite a reaction from anyone familiar with the history of the twentieth and early twenty-first centuries, but other than me, Yong was probably the only one who knew, and she kept any thoughts about it to herself.

They looked back and forth at one another as I stood there silently.

"Uh, Leif," Bjorn said at last. "Can we talk to you for a minute? Off the record? I mean, really off the record."

That explained why no one had messaged me. "Maybe," I said. "Some things can't be off the record, and you should know that."

"Yeah. This won't cross any lines. We're pretty sure of that." Bjorn scuffed at the StickStrips in the corridor we would use to anchor ourselves when the ship was in zero gee. He was a big man, six-five, with a big-boned Scandinavian frame to go with it. He was from Tromso, Norway, so we shared some genetics. I'm half Icelander. My hair is red, though, from my Irish mom, while his was light auburn. For all his size, he didn't impress me as a leader. Cheer captain might fit him better.

"Look," I said, "it's fine to talk for a minute, and let's say it's going to be fine to be off the record, but you've got to talk. What's up?"

"We want to ask if you'll do something about Pennywise," he said.

"You mean Penny Panagiotidis."

"Yeah, Pennywise." He repeated the nickname. "Look, we were checking off supplies in the spaceplane lander, but we heard about the scene in the caf. You saw it. It's always something with her, always trouble. We don't need a goddamn poinsie shooting her mouth off every chance she gets and making everyone upset."

Poinsie. I translated the current slang in my head into what had been used a generation before, when I was their age. Poindexter, an old term that had become quite common when I was growing up.

"You don't like her, because she's smart?" I put an edge in my voice.

"She thinks she is," Bjorn said. "About everything. And it goes on and on. She doesn't shut up. It's a problem for our whole team."

"It's a big problem for my cohort," Reality said. She was a Brit, with dark hair cropped short, pale skin, and a slight Yorkshire accent that I recognized from an SAS guy I had worked with. "If it hadn't been for her, my cohort would have beaten Bjorn's on efficiency scores during training."

Bjorn laughed. "That wasn't going to happen even if you didn't have Pennywise. You didn't have the leadership points, for one thing. Of course, if you could manage that many leadership points, you wouldn't be here."

"Hey, I didn't get pushed into Pioneer Youth like you did," Reality retorted. "I volunteered for this. Made my family proud."

"Yeah. That was about the only way you were going to do it," Bjorn said.

"Will you two give it a rest?" said Miroslav. He was a good six inches shorter than Bjorn, with a small mouth, rounded chin, and Mediterranean coloring.

I was aware that Bjorn and Reality had kept up an almost continuous competition during training—a competition their cohorts had joined, although with varying levels of enthusiasm from person to person. I had also seen enough instances to know it was not entirely friendly. Strictly speaking, this was Sonal's problem, not mine. However, while competition among teams to be the best could be useful, and could lead to people achieving more than they would have believed possible, if it got out of hand in the middle of nowhere, trouble would follow. I made a mental note to talk to Sonal about that.

"Whose team scored higher in training exercises is not the point of this conversation," I said. "I'll also tell you that what's coming up is real, not an exercise, and we won't be keeping score with points. We live well, or we don't, or maybe we don't live at all. Got it?"

They had the grace to look suitably chastened.

"Now, you wanted to talk to me about Penny. Beyond bitching that you don't like her, what did you want to say?"

"Uh, well," Bjorn said, "we wanted to ask if you would agree not to put her down with us. Just take her back with you."

I stared at him and he backed away. The other two did the same when I caught their eyes. "Did she ask to be separated from the Pioneers?" I asked.

Three headshakes followed.

"She tags after that Dustin like she's a puppy," Reality said. "God knows why he puts up with it, but that's his problem. She's got no other friends, I can tell you that. We won't miss her. Except maybe for Dustin, and he'll get over it."

I thought back to how many times I had someone in a squad, a section, or a platoon who was a problem, who didn't mesh with the others, who wasn't liked, sometimes for ridiculous reasons. My job had been to fix it so they weren't a problem, so they did mesh. I couldn't make people like each other, but it was for damned sure my job to see that they worked together as a team, the way they were supposed to do. One thing I didn't do was go running to the officer and ask them to fix my problem. I won't say I was always successful, and combat was a harsh environment in the best of circumstances, but I always did my job.

So I tried to tell the Three Musketeers, in fairly blunt language, what their jobs were. I'm not sure they got it, and they went away quite dissatisfied. I stood by myself in the corridor for a while. This wasn't the army, I told myself. It was more like a scout troop, and there was always one kid nobody liked, or so we'd been told in Hollywood vids from time immemorial.

I sighed. This is what your career has come to, Leif Grettison, decorated combat veteran. You're the leader of a scout troop on a camping trip. Or maybe only the bus counselor.

CHAPTER FIVE

For most of our journey between the stars, the *Dauntless* used a catalytic ramjet that sucked in interstellar hydrogen for fuel, which was there for the taking, and fused it to helium. In order to light that ramjet, though, we had to reach a velocity of 6 percent of cee, the speed of light. Antimatter rockets propelled the ship to that velocity. We used the ramscoop field as well, to brake us from relativistic velocities, but, as with the operation of the ramjet, it was effective only above 6 percent cee. So we also needed the antimatter rockets for the final deceleration into our target star system and the maneuvering to make orbit around our planetary destination. Unlike the interstellar hydrogen, the antimatter fuel had to go with us. We would need it for the return trip as well, so we were careful with how we used the antimatter. Fuel constraints were also the reason that the ISC sent two starships to set up a colony. Build a ship big enough to carry everything at once, and the ship would need that much more fuel to reach the magic velocity. And, of course, until it burns the fuel, there needs to be even more fuel to push the mass added by the extra fuel. The ISC could neither build a ship that big nor make that much antimatter fuel at once, so they sent two ships, one after the other. The first carried fewer colonists while being heavy on the building materials, infrastructure, and construction bots, along with construction specialists to set up the colony physically.

We were number two, with more people and additional supplies. I hate being number two.

It took a couple of more weeks after my heart-to-heart with the co-hort leaders for the *Dauntless* to decelerate to the point that she was able to match orbits with our target planet—which, we concluded from the brief first message, had been named Heaven. I would have liked a quicker rendezvous, but one gee was what the human body was designed to handle, at least for a sustained period. Add to that a trajectory that was conservative with our use of the antimatter fuel, and the timing of our arrival was dictated by physics.

Have I mentioned that I hate physics?

The leisurely approach did give us time to have all our Pioneers spend enough time in the gym to recondition. Sonal was in charge of seeing to that and did not bring any further questions to me. I heard no further comments about Penny or Dustin, which I assumed was a good thing, and I figured that the time traveler's remorse had run its course. I tried to ready myself for the tasks that would come my way on the surface, but I had no good way to do that. My job was vague, and in the absence of information from the first wave of settlers, it was impossible to guess what might be needed.

The continued silence from Heaven was more than simply irritating to me. It was against the mission plan. I won't say that I had never thrown out a mission plan—hell, no battle plan survives contact with the enemy, and I had been in enough of those situations to know—but I wanted to know *why* we were deviating from the plan. Something was wrong, and things that went wrong that you didn't know about killed teams. All we were receiving from Heaven was the steady beep of a transponder, which told us that it was working and where the LZ was located. I suppose that was better than nothing.

I was on the bridge with Yong when we made orbit around Heaven. Jorge was there as well, sitting in the pilot-in-command seat. His gut had recovered from surgery, but a heated conference involving Charley, Jorge, and Yong had affirmed Charley's original call. No one fresh off abdominal surgery was going to take the spaceplane down. Jorge had accepted that with ill grace, but we had enough risks without adding another one. He would stay in orbit as pilot-in-command while Yong went down. Sonal was also on the bridge with us, eager for a first look at the world before information started streaming back to her Pioneers.

The ship's telescopes fed images to our screens as the *Dauntless* approached. Heaven was mostly blue, with swirls of white clouds. It looked a bit like Earth, and I searched in vain for familiar continent outlines. I didn't see any continents at first, only blue ocean and white clouds. Then, as we circled the globe, I saw it. Heaven had one gigantic continent. It started under a bank of cloud cover in the high north latitudes, then extended south, going all the way to the south pole. It took up a good half of the hemisphere in the midlatitudes. The rest of Heaven was a globe-spanning ocean.

"Look at all the brown down there," Jorge said. "I'll bet most of the interior of that continent is desert."

"Plenty of green along the coasts," Sonal said. "Also in some inland valleys and as you get closer to the south pole. Where did they put the settlement?"

Jorge tapped at his panel, and a symbol for the LZ transponder superimposed on the globe. It was in a sea of green not far from the eastern coast.

"Seventy-one degrees south latitude," Jorge said.

"At least their pilot didn't put them down in a desert," I said. "I'd like to know more about what's down there than green and brown, though, and they're still not sending."

"I can display surface and atmospheric data," said a sultry female voice with a Spanish accent.

I jumped. The voice came from nowhere and everywhere. It was the damned computer.

"Don't you like the conversational interface?" Jorge asked. He had obviously changed the settings when he took over the pilot-in-command role.

"No!"

He shook his head. "Old-fashioned."

Yong's face wore one of her patented tight grins that meant she agreed with me. The generation before mine had played with speaking computers in the first two decades of the twenty-first century, but it went out of style around the time I was born. In my opinion, in pressure situations, you needed to keep your mind on the task at hand, and a computer that sounded like a woman trying to pick you up didn't help. I guess in peace-time, we could afford to play with talking computers again. What goes around comes around. I could only imagine what we would find when we returned home.

In deference to me and Yong, Jorge put the data up on the screens without having the computer read them off. We stared at the numbers.

"My God, it's hot." Sonal's voice was soft but did not hide her shock.

"That may explain the comment in that first transmission," Yong said. "That also explains why they selected a landing site at such a high latitude. The surface temperature is ninety-three Fahrenheit even there. I don't think the tropics are even habitable. We're showing temperatures up to one hundred thirty-four, one hundred forty there."

"Why not land even farther toward the pole?" Sonal asked. "It's going to be cooler."

"Axial tilt is about ten degrees," Yong said. "If they were much farther south, they would have days with no sun in the sky, like Earth above the Arctic Circle. From the green, there must be plant life adapted to long periods without sun, but the colony needs to generate energy from photovoltaics."

"Look at the ocean temperatures," Jorge said. "It's a hot tub." He was quiet for a minute as he looked at the readouts. "Something is odd." He sounded puzzled. "It's even hotter in the high north latitudes. That doesn't make sense. I'll check for a system error."

"Change our orbit," Yong said. "Bring us over the poles."

Jorge did and we waited for the *Dauntless* to fly over the northern hemisphere. As we did, we saw breaks in the cloud bank below. We gasped collectively at the view the cameras showed us. The landmass did go close to the north pole, and what we saw through the breaks in the clouds was an uninterrupted field of volcanoes. One right after the other, belching fire and lava, all the land we could see was covered in red-hot lava flows or cooled black ones.

"Oh my God." That was Sonal again.

"I think they did the best they could with the landing zone," Yong said.

"But still," Jorge said, "why so hot all across this world? The planet is farther from the star than Earth is from the sun, and the star isn't as bright. The insolation is less. It shouldn't be that hot; it should be chilly. Hell, we're prepared with all that cold-weather gear in the cargo." He pressed fingers against his temples. "If anything, the volcanoes would shoot dust and ash into the atmosphere and block sunlight. That should make the climate even cooler. That one in Iceland did it in the eighteenth century, although when it blew up again in 2046, back before the Troubles, it didn't do much."

I was there, back in 2046, even though I was still a kid. I don't remember anything about the weather, only that it ruined my school vacation.

"Let me see what we've got on the atmosphere," Jorge said.

We looked at spectra and numbers for a bit.

"Get Dr. Osborne up here," Yong said.

I fidgeted—hell, we all fidgeted—until Charley got to the bridge. He sailed in through the doors, taking advantage of the zero gee with us in orbit, then caught the back of Jorge's chair and anchored himself on the StickStrips. As he did, he was bombarded with a rapid-fire briefing from all directions at once until he finally held up his hands. "Would you all just shut up a minute and let me look at the screens? I can see the data." We did shut up, and he rubbed the beard over his chin as he studied the information.

"Carbon dioxide is about twenty-one hundred parts per million," he said. "We got into the mid four hundreds just before the Troubles on Earth, and we thought that was bad. No wonder this place is hot."

"Well, from the data we had on Earth, the confidence intervals on the gases in the atmosphere were a bit wide," Jorge said.

"What about living there?" I asked. "They put settlers down there and we're here to do the same. Is that level safe?"

I could see Charley look to the side, checking something on his field. We waited while he read.

"Yes . . . It should be." Charley let out a sigh. "Look, we haven't had people live all the time in that kind of CO_2, but what I'm pulling up says it should be . . . feasible. People should be able to adapt and tolerate it. Maybe some headaches, some drowsiness when you're first down there. I guess the air may seem stale, like too many people in a conference room."

"Even with a wind blowing?" I asked.

Charley shrugged. "I can't tell. Do you know what a paper mill smells like?" We all shook our heads. "It was something we studied when we learned about perception in med school. The old paper mills stank to high heaven. The air all around cities that had them, like Ticonderoga in New York, smelled awful, even at a distance. Everyone who traveled there found it revolting. People who lived there, though, didn't notice it. They were used to it." He rubbed his beard again and turned back to the screens. "I'd be more worried about the ozone," he said. "We used to have ozone holes in Earth's atmosphere in the late twentieth, early twenty-first century. The atmosphere on this planet is mostly ozone hole. Too much of the UVB will get through. Not good for the melanin-deficient among us." He pointed at me.

"Great," I said. "If I don't choke on the air, I'll get melanoma. What are you getting at, Charley? That maybe this place isn't habitable? That can't be. Why would they prerecord a message saying they'll talk when we come down if they're all dead?"

"Is the settlement there?" Sonal asked. "We should be able to see it from orbit."

"Sure. By now, we've stored plenty of images from the entire land-mass." Jorge changed a setting and gave verbal instructions to the computer.

The image of Heaven shifted, then zoomed in on one patch of ground near the LZ transponder. The screen flickered while the computer picked times when the cameras had clear skies over that area. The settlement was there. We saw a circle set into the green of a plain. It looked like a wheel, with five spokes radiating out from a smaller circle. I could see a circular structure, or the roof of one, at the very center, then five large buildings around the inner circle, and more buildings along the spokes. It matched the design in the mission briefing that I had studied and looked very much like the recon I would expect to see from an aerial drone over a target. Well, not quite. With an aerial recon, I would have expected to see people outside. The camera should have had the resolution to show shadows that people cast on the ground. Maybe no one was outside. Or maybe no one was there.

"Something else is wrong," Sonal said. "I don't see the photovoltaic array."

Jorge swiveled his seat to face her, then spoke to the computer. Mul-tiple images of the settlement and the surrounding land flashed up, one after another, at various magnifications. Sonal was right. An array of pho-tovoltaic panels should have been set up to provide energy, and it wasn't there.

"I don't understand," she said. "At the initial landing, they would have brought down a fifteen-megawatt nuke reactor. That's good for two hundred fifty years and would give them enough power for the settlement—even with our Pioneers too. But we're supposed to expand operations, start industry to make what we'll need, and grow to one thousand people as soon as we can. That's natural-born children and some from embryos. The plan was for the group from the *Daredevil* to set up a field of photovoltaic panels to give us more power."

Sonal was right. I had gone through the mission briefing book before we left and committed most of it to memory. I had learned never to rely on looking up what you needed. In a crisis, there might be no time or no data connection. The first crew down there should have set up those panels. The area had several fields that could have served; that was part of the criteria for picking the landing zone. My brain shifted into a different mode, one of planning for an airborne assault.

"That's not the only thing off," I said. "I don't see a structure that corresponds to the hydroponics facility. That's supposed to be up. I also don't see anything that looks like cultivated fields or areas prepared for planting. They were supposed to do that early in the settlement, create a hybrid ecology and grow food. Without the hydroponics and farming, they've only got ReadyMeals and they'll run out of those. They have bots to do that work. Those were part of the *Daredevil*'s manifest. But there's no sign of the ground being disturbed beyond the buildings. We'd see that from here, even if we couldn't see people or bots, but we should see them too. Is it possible the timing is off somehow? That they just got here and we just missed the other ship, and that's why none of this has been started?"

"No." Yong was definitive, as always. "I checked the time stamps from the transponder and listened to the two transmissions when they came in. The only way the timing would be off is if they falsified the data that were transmitted. Why would they do that?"

"No idea," I said. "So, our initial settlers aren't doing what the mission plan says they're supposed to be doing, they won't talk to us beyond a cryptic message we can't make sense of, and this planet isn't what we thought we were going to find. I suppose it's just as likely they've all been kidnapped by aliens."

That was rewarded with a rather forced laugh from the others. I guess alone and around a distant star, that didn't sound as absurd as I had meant it.

"Okay," I said, "Sonal, tell the kids to break out their sunscreen and beachwear. Let's get down there and figure this out."

CHAPTER SIX

The spaceplane we would fly down to Heaven was similar to the one Yong and I had used on the *No Name*, the ship we took to High Noon on the first starshot. It was stored in a large hangar bay that we entered through an air lock from an interior corridor of the *Dauntless*. That air lock kept the ship isolated when the bay was depressurized and opened to space. The bay even had the same cabling that looked like cargo nets, which I remembered from before. But that's where the differences began.

The spaceplane on the *Dauntless* was bigger, much bigger, than the one on the *No Name*. Where we had flown a research mission of twenty-five people down to the surface of High Noon, here we were landing 128 colonists who were going to stay. Where on the first expedition, the space-plane had carried a tiny reconnaissance jet for exploration and labs for research on the surface, this one was packed with supplies for the colony, everything from more bots and rovers to feedstock for 3D printers.

One day to go before landing, Yong and I stood in the bay anchored to the StickStrips and admired the lines of the spaceplane. We had con-ducted a careful check of the spaceplane and everything in it with our own eyes. Once we dropped, if we'd missed a problem, we'd have no way to fix it.

"Everything checks," I said. "The only items we haven't inspected are the Pioneers' personal packs."

"Those are their concern," Yong said. "They get two uniforms with general-issue boots, Pioneer rain gear, three outfits of personal clothing, and then miscellaneous items by weight. They can use that for anything from more underwear to a chess set. We don't check any of it."

"Not much to start off with in a new world."

"A lot of people have started with much less in the past." Yong's voice had a bit of an edge. "They have printers to make everything from knives to dinnerware, and textile recyclers for worn clothing, since clothes don't print well. The cell foundries can make most medicines. Refugees during the Troubles had far less."

"I know. I saw plenty of them." What she said was true, the same way it was true that many of our conversations came back to the Troubles.

Thinking of the Troubles brought my mind to one particular part of the cargo. "At least the ISC learned something from the last time," I said. "They gave us more weaponry this time."

Yong nodded. "If the issue is unexpected predators, as we found on High Noon, yes. If, however, you were being serious about the first crew on Heaven being kidnapped by aliens, I don't think eight M8s and these"—she slapped the holstered pistol at her belt that matched mine—"will suffice."

Flygirl did have a sense of humor—I had learned that—but I couldn't always tell if she picked up on mine. "I was joking about the aliens. I was joking. And this is limited, even for predators. I don't think they're going to be able to print a cartridge for the M8s, not anytime soon. The ammo will run out sooner or later."

"Then I'll have to see what I can do for air defense." She held out her hand to the spaceplane.

I looked for her little smile and found it. Yes, she was joking. So I laughed. "That's not going to fly like your J-45, you know."

"Too true." She paused. "My *Silent Dragon*. I loved flying that plane. I really did. Even though it was . . . I know you understand." She tugged at two fingers of her left hand.

"I do." I did, and I wanted to shift the conversation fast. Certain topics brought back too many memories, and those were dicey, even now. "What about the second run?"

"Yes." She let go of her fingers, I think as glad to have the conversation changed as I was. "The plan is to off-load as quickly as we can. I'll take it back up immediately and reload. That will take time, even if everything goes according to plan."

This was another difference from our first flight. The *Dauntless* carried extra fuel for the spaceplane. This time, the spaceplane would make two trips to the planet. As big as the spaceplane was, it couldn't take all the cargo in one trip.

"I think we should see what the situation is on the ground before you commit," I said. "A couple of planetary days one way or the other won't matter."

"Agreed."

A message from Sonal popped onto my field. LEIF, CAN YOU MEET ME AND THE COHORT LEADERS IN THE CAF? SOMETHING HAS COME UP.

I relayed that to Flygirl. She squeezed her lips together into something like a smile. "Maybe it's only a blocked toilet that needs your expert attention."

I should be so lucky.

.   .   .

The four Pioneer leaders were waiting for me in the otherwise empty caf. They were all spiffed up as if for a parade, kerchiefs tied just so with the knot on the left side of the neck, uniforms with creases that could have sliced bread. I don't think I ever looked that good, not even before my first deployment. I doubted they would ever look that good again.

"He started it." Reality had her index finger pointed at Bjorn and was talking before I reached them.

"Started what?" I asked.

"It's Penny," Sonal said. "Again. We had a formal D minus one assembly with everyone in the caf."

I stared at the three cohort leaders. They stared back.

"It's her own damn fault," Bjorn said. "Ever since we got the specs on the planet, she's been going off about sun exposure and UVB and protecting your skin. We've mostly tuned her out, but then, in the caf . . ." He started to smirk. It turned into a laugh. "It was a formal assembly, like Sonal said. Penny came in wearing the most ridiculous sun hat in history.

To make a point. Who would even take up space in their clothing allowance with something like that?"

"And you got everyone started making fun of her," Sonal said. "That's not my expectation of a leader."

Bjorn ignored her. "How could anybody take that seriously?"

"Bullshit!" Reality spat the word at him. "This was all about undermining my team's departure readiness, and you know it."

"I don't care about team scores," Bjorn said. "It's your job to deal with her. And it was too funny."

"It was not." Sonal turned to me. "Half the caf was singing, 'Pennywise, now she cries,' when she couldn't take it, and then she bolted off and locked herself in her quarters." She looked at the three of them. "You three are supposed to keep your teams together; that's how we keep our organization together. Picking on someone does the opposite."

"He keeps his team together," Reality said, "and works to fuck up *mine*."

"Enough." I put my hand up. Having these two going at each other did not bode well for the success of the mission, never mind how annoying Penny was. The third cohort leader, Miroslav, was looking on. Bored or interested, I couldn't tell.

I stared at Bjorn and Reality in turn. "I'm going to talk about you two in a second. But first, I'm curious. Where was Dustin in all of this?"

"Nowhere," Miroslav put in. "Oh, he was there, telling her it was really okay, that the hat was silly but she was making too much out of it. Meanwhile, he was telling us she didn't realize what she was doing, which he does a lot when Penny goes off on something. That was about it. He'll never really stand up for her. It's like he pretends he cares, but he doesn't actually help."

Great boyfriend she had. "Okay," I said. "I'm not much into talking things out, and we don't have time for that anyway. In one more day, you and your teams are going to be down on this planet. If you don't work together, well, God help you because I won't be able to. Trust me on that. I'm going back to Earth. You're going to live here with whatever mess you make. Think about that." My eyes were on Bjorn as I spoke, and I wondered if Penny would be able to live with whatever mess they made. Whatever I might do now or after landing, even if I took Bjorn aside and beat the daylights out of him, that would not be a long-term solution.

Maybe we should stick her back in a hib unit. Would that really solve anything? Or would Bjorn and Reality find something else to bicker about? I needed a crystal ball.

D-Day saw us back in the spaceplane bay. Sonal had her Pioneers organized and started them moving into the spaceplane as soon as the ramps were down to the floor of the bay. All of this was done along StickStrips. The last thing we wanted was a show-off who would try to use zero gee to fly into the spaceplane hatch, miss the opening, and make everyone wait until they caught the cargo nets on the walls and made their way back down or, worse, had to be fished out of the air and brought down.

I tried to guess what was going through their minds. Whatever their reasons for taking this trip, this was goodbye. I thought we should have had some stirring music playing in the bay. The only sounds were boots peeling away from StickStrips. I heard no chatter, no horseplay. I knew why. It had sunk in that they weren't coming back. Some smiled, some were impassive, some, frankly, looked scared. I tried to spot Penny and Dustin but couldn't. At least I didn't see a sun hat, ridiculous or otherwise. The lines moved steadily, with no interruptions and no outbursts. Whatever psych job Sonal had done seemed to have worked.

Yong and I took a separate small ramp up to the cockpit hatch. Inside, she took the left-hand pilot-in-command seat. I settled into the one on the right. Technically, that was the copilot seat, but the copilot was really the computer. The plan called for one pilot to stay on the starship and one to take the spaceplane down, but the standard design for a spaceplane had two seats in the cockpit, so there was one for me.

Once all the Pioneers were aboard and the indicators showed they were strapped down, Yong tapped at the control panel. I heard Jorge on our separate command channel announce the start of depressurization, and I could feel vibrations as the air was vented from the bay. The bay doors split open with a clank I felt through my seat but didn't hear, and then began to retract. When they were fully open, another set of bumps transmitted through the spaceplane. Those heralded the release of the wing and landing skid clamps. Yong manipulated the controls in silence—no stupid computer voice in this cockpit. Slowly, the spaceplane rose up in the landing bay, propelled by little thruster jets. As we emerged from the bay, I saw black sky dusted with a million pinpoint stars. Yong turned the ship and I could see the world called Heaven below us. It was gorgeous: blue and green and brown, with white clouds in the thin layer of atmosphere over the surface. I couldn't see enough of the outline of the supercontinent to tell me this wasn't Earth. There is something beautiful and awe-inspiring about seeing a living world from space. I had the same lump in my throat I'd had when I first saw Earth from orbit.

Yong oriented the spaceplane so that we faced backward to our direction of flight. Then she fired the SuperSabre engines in rocket mode to slow us and take us out of orbit. As the descent began, she pivoted the spaceplane so that we went down, needle-nose first. Shields covered the windows. We plunged from the sky.

Fire blossomed around us in the thickening air and showed as a yellow-orange glow on the screens in our instrument panel. I heard a bang as the first set of parachutes deployed to help brake us. The fire glow vanished from the screens. The shielding over the windows retracted and I could see out. The sky was still dark, very dark, but it was perceptibly turning blue. I could see white clouds far below.

"Switching to ramjet mode," Yong announced.

The engines outside roared, and the sound filled the spaceplane and assaulted my ears. We were no longer a spacefaring vehicle. We flew across the sky of Heaven like an airplane.

"LZ acquired." Yong's voice was flat, without emotion. She could have been announcing that she had acquired a target. In a sense, she had.

The surface of the planet came up to meet us. We were over the ocean at first, an endless expanse of blue-gray. A shoreline appeared ahead, then passed beneath us. Black cliffs rose up from the shoreline, tumbled rock at their base and flatland crowning their heights. We dropped lower, toward a green and flat stretch of high plains. We flew low enough that I could see dark dirt through the green ground cover. The plains were a man with thinning hair.

"Brace for landing," Yong said.

The ground rushed up to close the last small distance between us. The landing skids hit. The friction sections of the skids bit in and more parachutes deployed. Together, they brought us to an abrupt stop on the landing field. I looked at the empty plains of Heaven through the cockpit windows. The answers to our many questions were out there.

CHAPTER SEVEN

I surveyed our surroundings through the cockpit windows as Yong went through the shutdown procedure. Blue sky, speckled with some dark clouds off to the west, green—call it grass—stretched out in front of us on an undulating plain. It looked empty but inviting.

The hatch from the cockpit opened up and the ramp extended to the ground. We didn't worry about hazmat suits. The first expedition had the responsibility of establishing habitability. If we couldn't live outside without suits, the settlement wouldn't be here. I was headed out onto a new world in a short-sleeved polo and field boots.

I stepped through the hatch to the top of the ramp, and the climate of Heaven hit me with the ferocity of a boxer who sees blood. Sucking in a lungful of air was like breathing cotton candy. I fought on Mindanao during the Troubles; I've lived in Miami; I've roasted under the eternal sun of High Noon. This place was *hot*. The heat seared my exposed skin and made it tingle painfully. This heat was like being wrapped in wool blankets and then thrown into a sauna. Drops of sweat beaded on my back before I'd taken the first step down the ramp. A wind blew from distant mountains in the west and made the fabric of my polo flap. The wind was hot too. I wondered if rain would improve the situation, or only add steam.

At the bottom of the ramp, I kicked at the ground with my boot. Looked like ordinary brown dirt. Little green leaves sprouted out of the dirt and they did look like grass. For all I could tell, we had landed in Kansas.

I heard Yong coming down the ramp behind me, but I didn't look around, because at the same time, a rover rolled up out of a trough in the ground, a man driving it. Immediately, my mind discarded some of the scenarios we had discussed. The first settlers hadn't died. No aliens. All well and good, but then why such a mystery about the situation on the planet? Out of habit, my hand checked my pistol in my holster, but I didn't draw it. I waited for the rover to reach me. Yong came to stand next to me. Behind us, I could hear the ramps from the passenger compartment descending.

Some people go gray at a young age, and that must have been true of the man driving the rover. He brought it to a stop right in front of us and stepped out. His hair was almost pure white and blew across his face when the wind gusted, but the pink face below it was unlined. I doubted he was much older than my bio age, early thirties at most. He was slight of build with rounded shoulders and no more than five-eight. Not the standard image of a daring explorer.

"I'm Whitehead," he said, and wiped a sweaty brow with one hand. "Please call me Jerry."

This was the voice in the two brief messages we had received. I couldn't identify the type of British accent, although I'm pretty good with those. I filed that for later. I pulled up the listing of the first expedition through my phone and looked at my field. Jerome Whitehead, age thirty-four. That was it. Nothing else, no bio at all. A quick look told me that the same was true of the entire list from the first expedition. Names and ages. Nothing more.

"I'm Leif Grettison," I said. "I'm the exoplanetary scout, which means I'll head up exploration parties or do troubleshooting while we're here. Next to me is Yang Yong, pilot-in-command of the *Dauntless*."

"Leif Grettison?" he said. "The real, historical Leif Grettison?"

"You mean the one who did in St. Miles? Yes." I shook my head. How long would it take and how far would I have to go before Miles Richmond and I faded from memory?

Jerry was shaking his head. "I remember a bit—the furor with Militants for Miles when I was little, and then the craziness on the Community when you came back. That was right around when I volunteered for this."

"We don't need to rehash it." I needed to switch topics. "I have to tell you that all we've got in our system for you is name and age. Same for the rest of your folks. I'm sorry, but what do you do for the colony?"

He actually smiled. "So, they really did it. They kept their promise. I don't think any of us believed they would."

"What promise? I have no idea what you're talking about. There's nothing about this in the mission plan."

"They erased us." Jerry wiped off more sweat. "ISC promised we'd be erased from the Community, no links to any databases. That was the deal; it's why we volunteered. I mean, people might remember seeing my face on newsfeeds even without anything left in the databases, but you weren't on Earth for my fifteen minutes of fame. Or infamy. We're all criminals, you know."

"Excuse me?" I'm sure my jaw hung open. What had we done? Landed in some interstellar Botany Bay?

"You didn't even know that? That's brilliant. Oh, we're all nonviolent types," he hastened to add. "Nobody did anything violent, no sex stuff either. But, yeah, we've all been convicted for one thing or another, and you know how it is on the Community. Nothing ever goes away. People get shamed, their families get shamed, essentially forever. People kill themselves sometimes. Hell, I don't need to tell *you* about shaming on the bloody Community. So when they said that whoever went out as a colonist for this planet would be scrubbed from the Community and their families would have relief, people signed up. Isn't it the same with your crew?"

His words came to a stop. He was looking past me to where the other ramps had disgorged Sonal and her band of fresh-faced twentysome-things, all in their neat Pioneer Youth uniforms.

"They're all volunteers," I said, "out for adventure and world-building on the high frontier. Not a conviction among 'em."

My heart sank as I handed him the bullshit about adventure and world-building. How were we going to put together a bunch of big-time losers with a crew of second-besters and come up with anything that worked? Had anyone at the ISC or NASA, or any agency, thought this through? Did they even care? Or were they throwing as many colonies at the stars as they could, hoping that some of them would survive? The people who had made these decisions would all be long dead when we returned. The answers to my questions might exist only buried deep in some database, if they could be found at all.

Yong's face next to me was hard. I knew that look.

"Oh," Jerry said, and then stopped. The wind ruffled his shirt but he kept sweating. "Well, maybe it doesn't matter. I thought I would have a talk with the pilot first, but maybe it would be best to have everyone together. I'll call the Demos." He paused and I assumed he was sending a message on a different network than the ship used. "We'll go to the Community Dome, that's where we have the Demos meet. We're structured as a democracy, a true democracy. By the way, I'm the chief executive of our Town Council, although we've taken to saying that I'm the mayor of St. Peterstown."

I shook his hand, for lack of anything better to do. "And what is this mystery we need to talk about? Why wouldn't you send anything while we were coming in?"

"When we're all together," Jerry said. "We have a democracy here, we really do, so let's just get there and let everybody hear. It's not too far."

Jerry offered me and Yong seats in the rover and we both turned him down for the same reason. If our troop was going to hoof it in the heat, then we were going to do it at the front of the line. I hoped nobody got heatstroke before we arrived.

·   ·   ·

The hike to the settlement wasn't that long—the app on my phone, courtesy of the link through the spaceplane, gave the distance as a little over a mile—but the heat made it worse than unpleasant. I hoped that Sonal's Pioneers had paid attention to the reconditioning program on the *Dauntless*. Close to four and a half years in hib does not leave a body ready for extreme physical stress. There was no avoiding the march, however. Spaceplanes need lots of room for landing and takeoff, especially when they have to land on nothing better than an open field. Protocol dictated having the LZ at least a mile away from a permanent town. I also remembered the little river to the west of the town that we had seen from orbit. It made sense to put the town close to that river, as well.

I took the opportunity of the hike to study the land around us. The slice of terrain we were on was not very interesting, with almost no distinguishing features except lines of mountains at the western and northern horizons. A lone hill stuck up from the plain to the south of us. It wasn't a big hill, or even very high, but it was the only feature of note on the plain. The thin green ground cover stretched out in all directions. Spiky plants that looked like thistle with white flowers grew a couple of feet high at random locations amid the grass. I saw little pink and yellow flowers sprinkled in with the grass as well. I saw only one type of animal. This was a four-legged creature about the size of a Labrador retriever, with hind legs that reinforced the image of a dog. It had no fur; rather a turtle-like shell in mottled green and brown covered its back and head, and it chomped on the thistles, grass, and other flowers with a squared-off snout. It took no interest in us.

"We call them shellhounds," Jerry said through the open window of the rover when I asked. "Because of those legs. Dumb as dirt but edible, if you want. They're all over."

Flying creatures that looked and buzzed like insects clustered around the thistle and the other flowers. Other than the insects, however, nothing flew in the air, nothing that looked even remotely like a bird. I didn't see anything like a tree, either. The tallest plant came to about knee height. It was dull. Even duller than Kansas.

The settlement came into sight before I completely dissolved in sweat. The outer ring we had seen from the sky was, in fact, a perimeter road that separated the open plain from habitation. Hab units, all the same structure, were visible past the perimeter. Some were orange, some blue, and some yellow. The colors were probably supposed to create variety and be cheerful, but they provided a jarring contrast to the rest of the plain. A large sign, apparently made from salvaged packing crates, was planted just outside the perimeter road. Its hand-painted lettering proclaimed: WELCOME TO ST. PETERSTOWN, GATEWAY TO HEAVEN.

Sonal strode forward to come even with me, Yong, and Jerry's rover. I had never seen Sonal angry before, but it was plain on her face now. My mother always used to say she got her Irish up when she was mad about something, and while there was no trace of Irish in Sonal's ancestry, my mom would have recognized her expression immediately.

"I do not understand this, Jerry, Mr. Whitehead, Mayor, whatever. The mission plan was clear. You were to start the creation of a hybrid ecology here. We should see fields cleared and at least some planting. You had bots for that purpose in the *Daredevil* cargo. We saw nothing from orbit, and there's no sign of anything, now that we are on the ground. Unless you are going to tell me it's all on the other side of the town, you owe us an explanation."

"You will have the explanation." Jerry halted the rover and twisted in his seat to face her. "We will go through the situation at the Demos meeting and you will understand. We're going to head down one of the radiating avenues—we call the one we're coming to the Avenue of the Americas—and we'll get to the Community Dome. Just a little longer, please." He turned away from her and restarted the rover toward the perimeter road.

Sonal was not mollified, not really. If looks could shoot daggers, Jerry would have had several sticking out of his back.

It was obvious to me that Jerry wasn't going to say anything until he was good and ready, so I turned around and walked backward along our column to see how our Pioneers were doing. They were okay—only a few stragglers, and I figured those would come in under their own power, even if a little late. I did see Penny, fairly close to the front, in lockstep with Dustin, damned near glued to his hip. She had swapped the ball cap that went with the Pioneer uniform for what had to be the sun hat that had started the pre-embarkation ruckus. It was a floppy canvas hat in bright orange with green leaves and yellow flowers printed on it, fastened under her chin with a strap. It was enough to make me wince, although I supposed it would reduce the risk of ever losing her.

From where we had stopped, she spotted something off to the right, pointed that way, and yelled. I looked where she was pointing and saw a large, low structure, held off the ground by piers and struts. That had to be the hydroponic facility, although when I pulled up the mission plan on my field, it seemed way too small. That was probably why we hadn't identified it from orbit. Maybe it was only part of the facility. Okay, Sonal, they had planted something.

Penny's shout brought Jerry's rover to a halt again and everyone watched as she took off at a run to investigate, one hand clamping her hat to her head. I heard no catcalls and no laughter. Everyone was too hot and sweaty. When she got there, she let out another yell we could hear easily. She came sprinting back, directly to Jerry's rover.

"What is going on?" Penny got the demand out between gasps for air, but gave Jerry no chance to answer. "What are you doing? Those plants! That's a piece of the hydroponic facility, all right, but all that's in there is cannabis! How can that be all you're growing?"

Jerry started the rover moving again, but Penny stayed alongside. Frankly, I wanted to hear his answer also, so I jogged forward to come even with them.

"Cannabis is important," Jerry said.

"And what about corn, potatoes, legumes? I'd have to check what will grow here, but you should have done that already. And in the hydroponics, we need . . ."

Right. Penny's background was agriculture. And true to what I'd been hearing, she wasn't shy about saying what was on her mind. The only thing that stopped her from telling Jerry what we needed in the hydroponics was Dustin coming up and grabbing her arm.

"We have plenty of food," Jerry said while Dustin hushed Penny. "It's not a problem."

"But you can't do this forever," Sonal said from the other side of Jerry's rover.

"We really need to wait for the Demos at the Community Dome," Jerry said. "Everything will be clear. I promise you that."

CHAPTER EIGHT

I grew up around New York City—at least until I was ten; we moved the year after my mom died—and I still remember the Avenue of the Americas. It was a broad street of pavement, traffic, and crowded sidewalks. Towering buildings of concrete lined the way and, to a child's mind, reached all the way into the sky. The Avenue of the Americas in St. Peterstown was a dirt track. The thin grass had been cleared and the dirt had been packed down so the near-constant wind from the west didn't blow too much dust around, but it was still an unpaved road with no sidewalks and, when we walked down it for the first time, without any other evidence of traffic or even life.

The avenue was lined, from the perimeter road to the center of town, with the small, one-story habs we had glimpsed earlier. They differed from one another only in their garish colors. Up close, each hab looked like two cubes squashed together. I knew the interior layouts from the mission briefing. One cube held the sleeping quarters and bathroom for the occupants, the other a living area that contained desks, chairs, vid screens, kitchen, and other accoutrements of modern daily life. The intent was that the occupants of each hab would be a couple and that they would have children, who would grow up, eventually move out, form more couples, and occupy a different hab. The habs were all the same because they were all designed for bot-assisted self-assembly. All the transport crew had to do was see that the bots off-loaded the components in the correct place and the hab would, essentially, put itself together. Humans, working with co-bots, would come by afterward and install the details, down to the coffeemakers. In this way, a town with accommodations for a thousand people could spring up on the prairie almost overnight while the human crew spent most of their effort on the more complex buildings that had specialized functions. The thinking about the occupants of the habs was equally stereotyped, but building a town from scratch on a brand-new world was a lot easier if you didn't take any individuality into account. One thousand people was the population target in the mission briefing; that was as far as the planners had taken their scheme. After that, the town would be on its own.

St. Peterstown might have been built for a thousand, but at the time we entered—a few months after it had been built—the population was only the settlers from the *Daredevil* crew, a total of seventy-two. Even if the inhabitants had turned out to watch us arrive like some conquering army, the place still would have felt empty. However, no one was there to watch. We walked past a row of silent habs on each side of the street, not even a face at a window. With the wind blowing particles of dirt across the vacant Avenue of the Americas, it felt more like a postapocalyptic Hollywood vid set. This sense was heightened because each hab had a semicircular privacy screen of curved graphene panels that separated it from its neighbors. The space between the privacy screens of the row of habs on one avenue and the row on the next radiating avenue had been kept empty, a site for greenery or parks in the future. Right now, though, nothing was there except the original prairie grass and dirt.

The Avenue of the Americas, along with the other four radiating avenues—named with equal grandiosity the Avenue of Africa, the Avenue of Asia, the Avenue of Australia, and the Avenue of Europe—came to an end at an inner ring road with the imaginative name of Town Circle. Five large buildings sat on the outer circumference of Town Circle, in between the spokes of the radiating avenues. These were all central to the planned life of St. Peterstown. Unlike the simple cubes of the habs, these looked like real buildings, albeit overgrown samples from a child's Erector Set. All of them seemed to have been started as a frame of open beams, with the gaps filled in by panels and windows, leaving the beams visible. A flat roof had been dropped on top and overhung the walls on all sides. The design would have been really stupid in a place that got a lot of snow, and even here the shade from the overhang probably would not be useful for keeping the interiors cool. To our right on Town Circle, the dining hall was where folks could go to pick up their ReadyMeals and, in some future, to have locally grown food. We were bringing a larger stock of ReadyMeals to resupply the dining hall for the increased population. This would be important, since judging from the brief conversation with Jerry on the way in, locally sourced food would not be happening soon. I tried to do some mental calculations to guess if crops would come in before the ReadyMeals gave out. I couldn't do it. I had a suspicion Penny could, but I didn't want to start that conversation with her.

Across the Avenue of the Americas from the dining hall stood the school building, vacant for now. Then came the factory housing the 3D printers and the cell foundries, followed by the Medical Unit, adorned with a large red cross and equipped with surgi-bots, diagnostic instruments, and medicines. Last was the Lab Unit. This was a partial misnomer. It did contain analytical instruments and facilities for testing. A bigger portion, however, was devoted to the embryo and seed bank. Here were stored the terrestrial animals and plants the planners had guessed might be useful for the colony and might successfully populate the hybrid ecology the mission plan envisioned. Human embryos were stored there as well, in case population growth and genetic diversity needed help. The unit had its own artificial wombs to grow those embryos, human and animal, a delicate process under the best of conditions. From the relative scarcity of native life I had seen on the way in, I hoped those wombs worked. I saw no evidence the first wave had tried them. We had no puppies barking in the street, for example. Sonal's lips turned down in a frown as she stared at that building, obviously following the same reasoning I had.

At the center of the Town Circle, the very center of St. Peterstown, was the Community Dome. This was the large circular roof we had seen from orbit. It was more of a tent than a dome, however. Any side panels had either been removed or not installed in the first place. Only the open framework of graphene and woven carbon nanotube struts and beams was present. This allowed the breeze to blow through, although that failed to cool the place at all. I wondered how much power it would have taken to enclose the Dome and run an air system, although maybe the critical issue had been the work required to do it. I did not recall anything in the plan about this.

Under the roof was seating for one thousand. The seats were arranged in rows and in a semicircle, not much different from a typical auditorium. Facing the seats was a raised platform on which stood a plain, rectangular table with three seats. I made a quick count as we entered. Sixty-nine people occupied seats in the first three rows. Two women sat at the ends of the table on the raised platform. Jerry walked in, waved to everyone, and took the middle seat at the table. This was the Demos, the entire population of St. Peterstown and of Heaven, waiting for us.

The Pioneers filtered in and took open seats in no particular order, although I did not see any of them attempt to join the rows occupied by the first settlers. I walked to the platform and jumped onto it. There were no other seats there, so I stood to the side of the table, conspicuous and, for the moment, happy to be so. Yong and Sonal took the steps up to the platform and walked over to stand next to me.

"Jerry Whitehead, mayor of St. Peterstown." Jerry's voice carried across the audience without effort. The table must have built-in microphones. "The Demos has been called to meet the crew of the *Dauntless*, whose arrival we have expected, and to make them aware of the decisions we have made."

My ears perked up when he said "decisions." Something had been brewing. I wasn't sure I was going to like it.

"Vanessa Huggins, vice mayor," said the strawberry blonde to Jerry's right. Seated, she was a half head taller than Jerry.

"Ibiana Owusu, administrator and secretary." She was a compact Black woman in the chair to the left of Jerry.

"The officers of St. Peterstown are present." Jerry took over the speaking again. "By inspection, I deem that more than two-thirds of the Demos are present, the Demos being the current registered residents of St. Peterstown and not the newly arrived people from the *Dauntless*. Unless someone disagrees and requires a person-by-person count, I declare the Demos in session and open to address its business."

He waited, maybe for a heartbeat, then continued.

"With us on the platform are Yang Yong, pilot-in-command of the *Dauntless*; Leif Grettison, exoplanetary scout; and Sonal Davis, colony leader for the colonists of the *Dauntless*. The *Dauntless* is the reinforcement ship that was planned to follow us here and did arrive, as I assured all of you it would. In fact, it is here even earlier than we expected. Their colonists have taken seats with us in the Dome." Jerry encompassed the entire audience with a wave of his arm.

A few people turned around to look and to gawk at the Pioneer uniforms and the team leaders' red armbands. The original settlers wore a variety of clothes along the lines of denim shorts, polos, and T-shirts. I imagined that they had packed stuff of their own before leaving Earth. To this point, at least, everything Jerry had said sounded like a formula. Polite, but not very meaningful.

"I would like to explain the current situation to these people," Jerry said. "It is important that they hear and understand the decision we have made."

At last. I hate polite bullshit.

Jerry turned to face the three of us. The microphones still picked up his words. "You have seen a bit of this world. The climate is too hot, the carbon dioxide is too high, the ozone too low. The ground here supports only this thin growth of what we call grass. There are small trees up by the lake, but nothing that we could use for a reasonable source of wood. This world is marginal, barely habitable. The Demos has considered this and voted on it. We have voted to leave. We have voted to have you take us back to Earth."

CHAPTER NINE

"What!?" The word was out of my mouth before I had any idea what I was going to say next. Yong looked ready for combat; Sonal looked more like she was going into shock. I decided to keep talking and make it up as I went. "What are you talking about? Are you seriously telling us that you want to leave, and you didn't say anything until we were down on the ground with all our Pioneers? No, it's worse. You deliberately avoided saying anything until we were down here."

"That's true," Jerry said. "We had to consider that if we told you the situation here during your approach, really anytime before you landed, you might never come down. You might have gone back to Earth and left us here. The *Daredevil* crew did all the construction and setup for the town while we were still in hib. They didn't wake us and bring us down until the structures were in place, and when we started to raise concerns, they left abruptly. We weren't going to take a chance. Your spaceplane can make two trips. We know this. You can take us and also your—what did you call them?—Pioneers. No one needs to be left behind. We can leave this world to roast on its own."

"And what do you think you would do if you did go back to Earth?"

Jerry shrugged. "Whatever each of us did that ruined us and shamed our families will be so far in the past that it won't matter. We'll start new lives. Or go to another star, one with a planet worth living on."

I know wishful thinking when I hear it. In my experience, people who ran away from a mission because they thought it was too hard or too dangerous were not well received. They did not get a plum new assignment as a reward.

"It won't wor—"

"We're not all lazy cowards!" A man in the front row stood up and shouted at Jerry. He wore denim pants with a white T-shirt and had a scraggly beard. "We didn't all vote to run away!"

"The Demos voted!" A man in a plaid shirt jumped up and strode over to the first. "Leavers fifty-one, Remainers twenty-one. Majority rules. That's what it says in our constitution." He gave the first man a hard shove that propelled him into the laps of a seated couple.

White T-shirt struggled free, shouting, "That doesn't mean tyranny by the majority!" He ran at the other man and threw a punch.

I watched them inexpertly trade a flurry of blows with no real damage done. I love democracy in action.

While the fisticuffs were going on, a burly, heavily suntanned man from the second row climbed over the seat backs—some with people in them—to the open area between the seats and the raised platform. He had a shaved pate over a square face with a close-cropped mustache, and a tattoo in front of his left ear showing a sword crossed with an ax. His short-sleeved shirt showed thick forearms and bulging biceps. He reached the two who were now grappling, each trying to put the other into a headlock, and shoved himself between the struggling pair. With one arm, he forced White T-shirt down into a seat. He grabbed a fistful of Plaid Shirt and pulled him close, almost nose to nose.

"Do you want to have a go at me?" the burly man asked. "I'll do it, and then you can talk to the Public Safety Squad after, for all the good that will do."

The one in his grasp shook his head.

"Then sit your ass down." He pushed Plaid Shirt in the direction of an open seat in the front row.

The man stumbled, fell, then crawled and pulled himself into the seat.

The burly man turned to the stage. "For the benefit of our newcomers, and for the purpose of recognition, I'm Malachi Oates." His voice had a drawl reminiscent of the American South.

"You are recognized to speak, Malachi," Jerry said.

"Thanks. Jacoby was right when he said we voted, and he gave the count between the Leavers and Remainers correctly. But as you've also heard, it wasn't unanimous. There are twenty-one Remainers and I'm one of them. Sure, this place ain't what we were promised, but I say it's still better than taking a chance on what Earth will give us a century and a half after we left. They may not remember what we did without looking it up—and I'll bet it's recorded somewhere, promise or no promise—but that doesn't mean they'll care about giving us anything. Now, you've all heard me say this before, and the majority voted the other way, but the way you did this, Whitehead, you brought them down here"—he pointed to Sonal's Pioneers in the back rows—"and since they're here, maybe they should get to vote. We should have another vote."

Jerry's mouth moved, but no sound came out. Ibiana and Vanessa were looking at him, as were Malachi and the rest of the original settlers. That gave one of the Pioneers a chance to get out of their seat, scramble over legs to the aisle, and rush down to the open space in front. It was Penny, crazy sun hat and all.

"Okay, okay. Penelope Panagiotidis, Pioneers. I guess that's how you do it here. You may not know me, but I'm Penny." Despite the heat, she seemed to be shivering. "Okay. You should listen to Mr. Oates and you should let us vote. If the climate is bad, and I guess it is with how bad I'm sweating but that's not the point, but what is, is that I can tell you what will grow here and I'm sure I can find it in your seed bank, which I know is really comprehensive, and if the soil is a problem, I can analyze it and tell you what we can add or what will grow and if it's really, really bad, we can look for another place where it's better." She was forced to take a brief breath but she began again before anyone could shut her down. "I can do that analysis. I can work with the plantings. I think what you've done here is . . . is . . . garbage!" That seemed to be the strongest word she could bring herself to yell out, but she was red in the face and glaring at Jerry. "All you've done is sit here and grow cannabis so you can sit here and get high waiting for our ship. We . . . we . . . should get rid of you and have somebody else start over and run this place properly."

Dustin was at her side by that time and took her arm. "Easy, Pennywise, easy. They don't want a lecture on soil chemistry or root systems. Don't go off like a Roman candle. You don't know what's involved here."

He turned to face Oates, but kept a hold of Penny's arm. "Mr. Oates, Malachi, I'm with you. Whatever you need, you let me know. I'll get it done."

Mentally, I tagged Dustin as *suck-up.*

"Well, look," Jerry said, his arms spread wide as if to include everyone in the Dome. "If some of you are that determined to stay, you can. We're not forcing anyone to go back. If you want, we can have the Leavers stand on the right and the Remainers stand on the left, so we can get a count, but it's not a vote. You newcomers are not registered members of the Demos. The vote was taken and there will not be a revote."

"No!" Sonal shrieked, making Jerry jump. "You can't do that. We can't do that. You've read the mission plans, you must have. We need two hundred people to make this work. That's what we must have to do the work, assure genetic diversity—because you know we can't rely on transported human embryos—and to make up for, well, unexpected losses. There's not going to be another ship coming here, not for three years at least, maybe five; that's what ISC told us. If we lose any number of people, the odds against us go up. Lose too many, the ones here are doomed. We are all in this together. That's the only way."

"Then we should all leave together," Jerry said. "That's where I started."

"No. That will not happen." Yong's voice of command cut through the buzz that was building in the Dome, and she did it without a microphone. Everyone fell silent. I saw her give a furtive tug at the first two fingers of her left hand; then she assumed a rigid posture of parade rest.

"It is not possible to transport both colonizing groups on the *Dauntless,*" Yong said. "The ship does not have enough hib units, and that number cannot be changed."

"Then we can split time in the hibs," Jerry said. "Divide us into groups. Each group goes into hib for two years plus, then is awake for two years plus. Won't be fun, maybe, but we can do that."

"No. We cannot do that." A marble statue could not have been more rigid than Yong was. "The ship does not have enough food to sustain all of you for nearly two and a half years of awake time each."

"We can bring up the supplies we still have here and you have all the supplies the new group brought," Jerry said.

"Not enough," Yong said. "Even bringing up the remaining food here, there will not be enough. In addition, the ship systems for air and water will not handle that many people awake for that long a period."

"You haven't done any calculations," Jerry protested.

"I don't need to. I know what is carried in my ship. The colonizing groups do not bring food for that long. They are supposed to be growing food or eating what is on the planet in less time than that. You have already eaten months of the food you brought, so that is gone. And I will tell you now, I will not take any subset of people back and endanger the colony that is here. My mission is to leave a successful colony here and that is what I am going to do. This is my decision and I will not change it."

Jerry had a look on his face that said he'd thought of something she hadn't. "So, Pilot Yang," he began, "your mission, as you say, is to have this colony set up to succeed when you leave, and I can see that you will do whatever you need to in order to accomplish that mission. A noble goal. I would like to point out to you how you need to do that. Your colony leader, Ms. Davis, said that the number of people here was designed to account for some losses over time. Let's use blunter language. Accidents and illnesses happen and people can die. That's what she means by losses. So there is some number of people who could be removed from the colony, taken back to Earth, say, without endangering the colony. Is that one person? Almost certainly. Two people? Again, almost certainly. Is it all fifty-one Leavers who voted to go? Maybe. I will leave it to you to decide the number.

"But while you think about that, please consider something else. Your Pioneers are not yet registered as members of the Demos. To add access for a new person to our network here requires the approval in the system of me plus one of the other two town officers. I will not grant that approval until you agree to take some number of Leavers back home." He looked at Sonal. "Until that is done, Ms. Davis, none of your Pioneers will be recognized by our network. That means they cannot send a message in our system, they cannot draw supplies from our dining hall, and they cannot make a hab power on even for the purpose of flushing a toilet."

He paused. "If you want to complete your mission successfully, Pilot Yang, they will need to be able to do those things. And if you, Mr. Grettison, think to solve this the way history tells us you solve problems"—he pointed at my pistol—"let me tell you that the reactor here has an automatic shutdown program. The only thing that prevents that program from executing is in my chip. It's a deadman switch; I think that's the term. So you should decide how many you will take."

"You are evil!" The scream burst out of Penny, and she lunged forward. "You should die!"

Dustin caught her before she took her second step. That was probably the only thing that kept her from jumping onto the platform, rushing the table, and doing I-don't-know-what to Jerry Whitehead.

"Calm down, Pennywise," Dustin said. "You don't know what you're saying. This would be a bad time to do something foolish. Come on."

Dustin half walked, half carried Penny back to the seats in the rear row. She struggled in his arms and batted at him with her hands, with about as much effect as a kitten being carried to a box. I heard scattered nervous laughter in the Dome.

Jerry turned back to me, Yong, and Sonal. His face held a beatific smile. "Please bring me a number," he said. "This meeting of the Demos is adjourned."

Jerry made a quick getaway from the table and the Dome, with Vanessa tracking close behind him. It gave me the impression that he wasn't going to take the chance that someone more physically adept than Penny might put the deadman switch to the test. Everyone in the Dome looked stunned, albeit for different reasons.

In the first three rows, I was sure I could pick out the Leavers. Yong had pricked their pipedream bubble of returning to Earth; many faces were wet with tears. Other people—Remainers, I assumed—were angry. Our Pioneers looked as if they had been poleaxed. I searched the crowd for Malachi Oates and found him standing at the end of the front row. His face was set and determined, and he was in the midst of a rapid-fire conversation with a tall woman. I wanted to speak with him, but that would have to wait. I had to deal with 128 Pioneers whose world had just dropped out from under them. I touched Sonal lightly on her arm.

"We need to get your kids stashed safely while we figure this out. Can you get them outside to the circle? I'll meet you there and we'll work this."

I wasn't sure she heard me, but she nodded and moved off.

"I'll meet you in a few minutes," Yong said. Then she was gone too.

· · · ·

As I walked out of the Community Dome, I tried to sort out my own feelings. The pathetic faces of Jerry's Leavers stayed with me. I'm not given to feeling sorry for people who believe they are entitled to impossibilities, but those folks looked stricken. Life had just kneed them in the balls. They had been given a constitution for their colony that said they, as the Demos, could vote on issues and the vote would decide what would happen. Life didn't work that way, although I understood the mindset. I came from a country on Earth that shared much of that illusion. Unfortunately, the universe doesn't care about votes. We could vote to make pi equal three, but that wouldn't make it so.

Jerry's Leavers were stuck with the fact that we couldn't take everyone back to Earth. They were also stuck with Yong's refusal to endanger the Remainers by taking some of them, and Yong's determination was as inflexible as any law of physics. They would also have to grapple with the fact that, beyond anything Yong and I could or would do, they *couldn't* go back home. They had bought a one-way ticket down Alice's relativity rabbit hole. There was no "back home" for them to go to. By the time they got back home, 152 years would have passed; it wouldn't be home anymore. It was much as I had told our Pioneers on the ship: Interstellar travel was a time machine of sorts, and it was a one-way street. If they went back to Earth, they wouldn't fit. Not at all. Temporal alienation was real. We had learned that the hard way when we came back from High Noon, and that had been a shift of only twenty-eight years.

My mind segued from the Leavers to my crewmates on the *Dauntless*. Temporal alienation, that disconnection from your world, was an issue for most starfolk too. Charley had joked that we were going to become a new species, *Homo astra*. Gallows humor. Our crew might joke about it now, but the fact of it wouldn't hit them until we returned. Yong and I were different. We had no connections, except to each other. We would take another ship, and then another one after that, and wouldn't care about Earth or anywhere else. I dreamed that we would come on some gorgeous scene, maybe with two suns in the sky, and we would both say that L-word at the same time.

And, yes, someday, somewhere, our luck would run out. Together, I hoped. Everyone's luck ran out eventually. It wasn't such a bad future for two old soldiers who woke up every morning surprised they had survived their last war. But that was us. I hoped the others who traveled the starways would be able to cope.

CHAPTER TEN

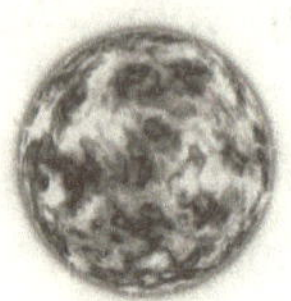

After I got outside, I had to put aside my daydreams of traveling the universe forever with Yong. My first impulse, I will admit candidly, was to go after Jerry and beat him within an inch of setting off the deadman switch, assuming that wasn't a bluff. However, as gratifying as that might have been for me, it wasn't going to help our situation and would probably make it worse.

Our Pioneers were a mess. Sonal got them out of the Dome and loosely grouped them in their cohorts along the inner edge of the Town Circle. These were products of the chip-and-phone civilization, the most advanced one Earth had ever seen, with chips wired to their brains and phone bases that could connect them to the computer on a starship, but they milled around in confusion like a flock of chickens with all their heads cut off.

I grabbed Sonal, who was in a daze of her own. "Sonal! Your kids need food, water, and a place to sleep. It's a short day with Heaven's rotation anyway, and this hemisphere is into late fall. We need them settled by dark or they may really come apart."

That may have been an understatement. If it were me and my old platoon, it would be very different. We'd have been carrying our own water, could have done without food if we had none in our packs, and would sleep on any old patch of ground. In fact, the fantasy crossed my mind that we could have rounded up a bunch of the *Daredevil* colonists, taken over their habs, and given Jerry an ultimatum about meeting our needs. I dismissed the daydream. I was developing the feeling that Jerry would not care what we did to other people as long as he got what he wanted. Anyway, I didn't have my platoon. I had a bunch of scared kids who were on the verge of freaking out, and what I needed to do was take care of them.

Fortunately, Yong reappeared at that moment accompanied by Vanessa, the blonde from the *Daredevil* who had sat next to Jerry at the council table. Three more people from the *Daredevil* crew trailed in their wake.

"I am so sorry about this," Vanessa said. "We did vote, and that was the vote, but Jerry said there would be no issue. You folks would agree and we would go and that would be it. Why anybody believes that man, I don't know, but he has a way of putting things so you go along with it. When there's a problem, though, he gets nasty."

"Apologies are all well and good, but that doesn't take care of my people." I gave her a quick list of what we needed.

Vanessa turned to two of the three behind her, a Black man and a white woman, both about thirty, with the sort of kindly faces that encourage people to talk to them. "This is Cam and Jess," Vanessa said. We call them our Public Safety Squad. They handle any altercations or interventions, thefts, arguments, that sort of business. Well, we haven't needed much, but they've had training to talk people through problems. I think they can help with your Pioneers. I'm sure they're stressed."

I wondered what Cam and Jess's crimes had been. Probably scam artists. I wrote them off.

"Talk is fine and it may help some, but what we need is food, water, and toilets." I turned to the third person, a stocky woman with short, almost black hair, an aquiline nose, and a deep tan. "Can you help with any of this, or are you only here to give me another apology?"

She laughed. "I'm Dr. Francesca Balboni, the town doc. Yes, I can help. That's why Vanessa and your pilot brought me over. If we bring your people to the Medical Unit, it will be crowded, but they will be out of the heat for a bit and they can use the bathrooms. We can give them something to drink as well."

That sounded like a good start. Given a purpose, Sonal rounded up her three cohort leaders and brought them over. I told them to get their people in order and march them over to the Medical Unit. Then I gave instructions on how much water each person should drink, and how to organize lines for the bathroom. I pointed out that the leaders, in particular, had to go last. I shouldn't have had to do any of those things, but it hadn't occurred to them that if there was a limit on available water, it had to be rationed, that certain people would need the bathroom ahead of others, and that if you were a leader, you saw to your people first.

After Francesca headed off with them, I turned back to Vanessa. "I'm a little surprised she's willing to do all of this. I take it she's not afraid of Jerry doing something to her for interfering with his scheme."

Vanessa smiled at me, then tapped the tip of an index finger against her lips. "I'm sure she thinks it's the only way she can get back at him." A pause followed, then, "Jerry's got something on her. She's had to let him bang her ever since we landed—and trust me, it's not 'cause she likes it. I'll bet she wouldn't mind if you did test that deadman switch he claims to have. She just doesn't have the guts to do it herself."

"And how is it you know all this detail?"

"I'm Jerry's partner. We live in the same hab." She had zero expression in those two sentences.

I know at least one of my eyebrows went up.

"Let's just say Jerry knows where the buttons are and how to push them," Vanessa said.

It was pretty clear she didn't want to talk anymore about Jerry's talent for blackmail, so I moved on to other immediate needs. "What can we do about bedding the Pioneers down for the night? I doubt there's enough room in the Medical Unit."

"That I can take care of," she said. "We have more than enough habs. I can open units for your people. Do you know how the units are designed?"

I shook my head. This bit had not been detailed in our mission plan.

"Okay," Vanessa said. "They're all a single standard. The front entry is designed to be coupled to an air lock, so you can use the units even if you don't have a breathable atmosphere. We don't need the air locks, obviously, so those were left out of the build, but the circuitry is still part of the entry. You open the door with palm pressure at the outline. You don't need to be identified." She walked over to a hab and demonstrated it. The door slid open without a sound. "For the same reason, the habs all have air systems that can be turned on and adjusted manually. There's no air lock panel, because there's no air lock, but there is also a panel inside the door on the wall." She showed us the settings. "You can do either air exchange, with filtration if you want, or recirculate and it will cool." She tapped at the panel and I heard a purr from the wall. Cool air ruffled the hair on the back of my neck. "Unfortunately, the rest is standard phone and chip tech. Nothing else will work unless the hab can read your settings."

I got her point, which had been Jerry's as well. These habs were fancy, far better than what we had on the expedition to High Noon, and even nicer than the apartment I'd had all those years ago in Miami. But that was the problem. Back in the day—my day, that is—you could get along perfectly well without a chip. I did for years after I got out of the army. All you needed was your phone. Not anymore, not in our vaunted chip-and-phone civilization. Your chip held all your preferences and settings. All your personal information. If you had your chip directly interfaced with the network—were chipped in—all that information was immediately available to the network, and you could download straight from the network as well. That's why people said you could think with your chip, although that's a gross exaggeration. If you chipped out, your phone acted as the intermediary and would show the settings in your public area to the network. If you didn't have a chip, though, or if you weren't on the network, none of that worked.

The Pioneers weren't on the network, which made the habs not much more than shelter and a place to sleep, about as functional as a hut built from mud bricks. Take the coffeemaker, for example. Each hab had one, but the default setting was Off. Even if you could turn it on manually, the stupid thing would expect you to look at it and then it would pick up the settings in your chip. If you were chipped out, the machine would pick up your settings from your phone base, which was interfaced with your chip. Those settings told it how many ounces to brew, how strong to brew it, and what the temperature should be. All useful functions, but if it can't read your settings, it won't do anything. It's not as though you could shove a pod in and physically press a button. No chip settings, no coffee. Simple as that. Same with everything else in the hab.

I wondered what would happen with the next generation. Humans aren't born with chips—I think folks forget that—and the colony wouldn't be able to manufacture them. Had anyone thought about that? I told myself I should worry more about the colony surviving the here and now and put aside my future-tripping.

The habs would have to be adequate as they were, at least briefly. St. Peterstown had been built for a population of one thousand adults, which meant five hundred identical habs for couples. Nearly all of the Pioneers had paired off, if not before we left the solar system, then by the time we made orbit around Heaven. We would need less than a hundred habs. It would take until after dark to get all of them under shelter, but we could do it.

.   .   .

"What are we going to do now?" Sonal was practically dancing from one foot to the other in the front room of the hab Yong and I had taken, which was next door to the one she and Klaus would occupy. "What the *hell* are we going to do?"

I'd noticed that Sonal avoided using strong language. She was a really nice person. Unfortunately, nice is not a survival trait.

"We've got a problem, Sonal," I said. "We'll figure it out."

"How can you say that so calmly? I mean, how?"

Klaus Koch put his hand on her shoulder, but she shrugged it off. She wasn't interested in being comforted.

"I said we have a problem, but let's have some perspective here," I said. "We're not being bombed. Nobody has died. The corpsman isn't dragging wounded through that door and complaining there's no place left to put them because the place is already full of bleeding men and women."

If her eyes got any wider, they would have swallowed her face. She looked away from me, over to Yong. She found no sympathy there.

"Every one of the girls I liked and graduated with was shot down and killed," Yong said.

"Oh . . . right." Sonal let out a long breath. "The Troubles. I keep forgetting how old the two of you are."

Yes. The Troubles that Yong and I had fought through and been shaped by were history-book material for Sonal. They had been over before she was born. Relativity does weird things to people.

"All right," I said. "I think the situation is basically what Jerry said he rigged." I swept my arm around the common room. It was the same as every hab Vanessa had opened for the Pioneers: We had no power beyond the air system. We had no lights, except for the light from our phone bases. No water, no refrigeration. We had managed some temporary relief for the Pioneers at the Medical Unit, but there would be a limit to how long we could keep running them through there.

"I suppose one approach is to call his bluff," I said.

"You mean we ferry the rest of the supplies down and then leave," Yong said. "We could do that as long as we retain the weapons. You're thinking that when he and the Leavers see they have no choice, they'll cooperate with Sonal and the Pioneers."

"No, no, no," Sonal said. "Please don't do that. What if they don't cooperate? You fly away, but we're here for the rest of our lives. There's not going to be another ship to save us if it goes bad here."

"Sonal, I hate to be blunt, but did you folks realize there's a lot of risk when you go off into the unknown? That people could die? I understand everyone has reasons why they came, but the risk is still here."

"Of course," Sonal said. "We all signed the consent. It was pretty explicit."

"Yeah." I ran my fingers through my hair. "That's not the same as really understanding what you're going to face. Me and the guys who enlisted with me, the ones I was in boot camp with, we all knew people were getting killed. How could we not know? It was all over the newsfeeds every day. But we were all sure, every one of us, that the bullet or bomb would find someone else." I stopped, then decided it was useless to keep talking about risk. "I suppose we could stay in orbit for a while and monitor the situation."

"No good," Yong said. "We have fuel for two trips with the spaceplane, which is twice what we had on High Noon, but we have to use the second flight to bring the rest of the supplies down. More than doubling the population down here without bringing the supplies is going to create a crisis by itself. Once we've done that, we're not going to be able to do anything, even if things fall apart here. All we'll be able to do is watch."

"You would think," I groused, "that the geniuses at Earthbase would have given us fuel for another flight, just in case."

Yong shook her head. "That extra mass means more antimatter fuel at the start for us to get to six percent cee to light the ramjet. If we add that contingency, what about other contingencies? And the extra fuel we would take also has mass that has to be boosted. Starflight is still the rocket principle until we light the fire on the ramjet."

How many times have I said that I hate the rocket principle?

I admitted that calling Jerry's bluff that way was a bad idea and wouldn't work. "We have to get the Pioneers registered in the Demos and on the network. If we don't, we're setting them up for Jerry and the *Daredevil* crew to use the access to the network and to electric power as a way to turn the Pioneers into a servant class. We might end up with a civil war here. We humans are good at that." The air system had cooled off the hab and rid us of Heaven's humidity, but I was generating plenty of heat by myself. "I suppose the other way to call his bluff is to shoot him."

That brought a gasp from Sonal. "And if it's not a bluff? If the reactor shuts down? They haven't done any other work here. We won't survive without that reactor."

"There has to be backup power storage," I said. "The mission plan specifies it."

"Yes," Yong said, "but we don't know whether they have fully charged it, and even if they have, how long it will last under real-world conditions, not the theory in the mission briefing." She turned away from all of us and looked out the window although there was nothing to see outside. Night had fallen. No lights showed through the window, only a dim reflection of our room by our phone base lights. "Have we considered the possibility of letting him win? Sonal, how many people can you spare? He has to be correct that we can spare some, even if it's not all fifty-one Leavers."

Sonal stared at the floor between her feet. She was misery in a uniform. "It's not just a number," she said. "It's who would leave. What if Dr. Balboni left? She told me she's the only actual doc in the *Daredevil* group. She's important and she knows it. We have two with nursing training, but no docs. The Pioneers are too young. There's a limit to what diagnostic AI and surgi-bots can do without a trained doc. What happens if there's a pregnancy complication? What about other critical skill sets? The embryo tanks? The reactor? The entire computer network? Even with bots to do the work, we still need people trained to use the bots. We can't afford to lose many, just by numbers, and we can't afford to lose certain skills at all."

Yong turned back to us, her face hard, her arms folded across her chest. "Suppose we make a secret deal with Whitehead. We sneak him out. Only him. Do you think he would take a deal like that?"

"Maybe," I said. "I doubt fairness is a hill Jerry would die for. And probably if the rest of the Leavers find he's betrayed them, yes, they will cooperate." I didn't like the idea of Jerry winning, but the colony would probably be stronger without him. Addition by subtraction, as it were. "We better make sure it stays very secret, so he doesn't get lynched before we get him out of here. All we need is one hothead."

"It's still the best chance, though," Sonal said.

"Yeah." Why is it that the least palatable idea always has the best chance of success? "We can tell Jerry we're working on the number and will give it to him soon. That will buy us a little time to learn what hasn't been done and what needs to be done fast. Like, how long will it take to set up the photovoltaic panels, and is there a reason they're not already up? What can you actually grow here besides cannabis? I'll bet Penny can answer that one, and I'll bet I can get Malachi to turn on lab instruments for her. I'll ask Malachi about the panels also. Meanwhile, let's get some of our Pioneers back out to the spaceplane so we can get cargo unloaded and transported into town. They can also use the facilities on the spaceplane. Once we do that, they'll have supplies that aren't controlled by the St. Peterstown network. For the ones who stay in town, I may need to introduce them to the concept of a latrine."

It wasn't wonderful, but it was something.

After Sonal and Klaus left and it was only me and Yong in the dark hab, I grumbled something along the lines of thinking we could try a coup. "We still control the M8s and we have our pistols. We could make sure Jerry isn't hurt. We can redo how they run this place, keep Jerry tied up if we have to until the photovoltaics are operating, and then the Leavers can piss and moan all they want."

Yong didn't say anything for so long that I asked her if she had heard me.

"Do you remember the Republic of Sumatra?" she asked.

"Yes, 2061." I had seen the newsfeeds. Part of the Indonesian military had rebelled and set up a breakaway government on most of the island, with Chinese support. We had sent troops and, eventually, snuffed it out.

Nasty fighting, I had heard. "I wasn't there; I was fighting on Mindanao. But I know about it. What does that have to do with here?"

"I was there." Quiet dragged on again, but this time I waited for her. "We flew missions off the *Zhou Enlai* in support of the rebellion. I hit a key target early in the fighting; we were told the government had moved a command center to there. The rebels were exultant about the results of the strike. It was the key to breaking the morale of the government leaders. They had me fly in the next day to tour it with them, along with some of the old elite they had caught." She stopped again. She moved in the dark so that when she spoke again, she was speaking in the direction of the room's desk rather than me. "That 'key target' was a school where the upper class sent their children. Their bodies—and parts of their bodies—had been left there. I saw them. I saw a little girl; she was maybe nine or ten. She could have been me. I could smell the decomposition. The prisoners they had forced to come were crying and vomiting. I did not allow myself to show any reaction. I thought I had put that memory away; I haven't thought about it. Until I saw it all again in my dream coming out of hib this time."

"Oh God." I would never complain about dreams of freezing again. "You didn't know. Before."

"Of course not." Another pause. "I saw the children's bodies again when I looked at the Pioneers in the Demos meeting."

"Yong, it's a flashback. Nothing more. I have them . . . about certain things. You just have to put it out of your mind." Yeah, I was a fine one to be giving advice on this. I moved toward her.

"Please do not touch me." She turned her back to me and spoke to the dark room. "We are the women—and the men—who wielded the weapons. It does not matter who gave the orders. We cannot evade the responsibility for what we did. You know that."

"Yes." I did know it. I had seen the consequences of the fighting I had been in, up close and personal. The old trite line about destroying the village in order to save it came into my head. "It was long ago."

She shook her head. "What we did in the past creates the present. You know I left Earth because I refused to participate in it happening again. It is not for us to step in here with force and make them live the way we think they should and then fly away, ignorant of whatever we leave behind. They must be responsible for themselves."

CHAPTER ELEVEN

It was a tough night for sleeping, but I had a bed and I've slept under far worse conditions. I was up before the light came, courtesy of the approaching winter solstice, and was going to wait for daybreak before going out until I realized I couldn't have coffee. Take away my bed, take away my food, but keep your hands off my coffee. I grumbled and looked over at Yong, who was still asleep. I think the only times I saw her truly relaxed were when she was sleeping. Then I heard a soft groan. I was afraid I knew what was in her dreams. Yong had told me that I would do that, too, would even thrash around and cry out sometimes. That surprised me because I never remember any dreams, except in hib, and Rissi had never mentioned anything when we were together on Earth after the High Noon flight. Well, Rissi had been a short fling, and it's not as though I had a long list of women making observations. I decided it would be better not to wake Yong and headed out in search of Malachi.

It wasn't too hard to find him. There were only seventy-two in the *Daredevil* crew, and with few exceptions, they had taken habs close to the inner ring of the Town Circle. I woke only a few people before I was directed to the hab Malachi lived in.

The person who met me at his door was a woman. Automatically, I tried to check her ident and couldn't because I wasn't on the network. I couldn't get anything through my phone either, because my list of colonists from the *Daredevil* lacked images. That was irritating. She was someone who would leave an impression just by appearance. She was my height, which made her two inches taller than Malachi, with wavy dark brown hair, very prominent eyebrows, a full mouth, and a nose that must have been broken at least once. While she went back inside to get Malachi, I wondered what had led her to colonize Heaven.

"From what you said yesterday at the Demos, I think you want to make this settlement work," I said to Malachi when he appeared. "One of the Pioneers can help, I think, with what we can grow here, if someone can arrange it so she can use the instruments in the Lab Unit. Can you get them turned on?"

Malachi snorted. "About time somebody did some of that. Yeah, I can turn the instruments on, if she tells me which ones she wants. That would be the one who made a fuss yesterday, right?" I nodded and he smiled, just a little. "Yes, and her boyfriend was the one who said he would help. Once the instruments are going with my login, she can use them even if she's still excluded from the network. She won't be able to download with her chip or phone, but there will be screen output. By the way, this is Loretta Sforza." He indicated the woman who had met me. "Give us a minute, will you?"

He and Loretta stepped away from me and had a brief conversation that I could neither hear nor, because of how they stood, see. When they finished talking, we all left their hab, taking the Avenue of Australia close to where it reached the perimeter road, where we had stashed the Pioneers. It had seemed a good idea to keep them as far from the *Daredevil* crew as we could. I led Malachi and Loretta to the hab where we had put Penny and Dustin. By this time, the sun was peeking over the horizon.

They were both up, Dustin holding his head in his hands and Penny rushing around the hab. Penny listened to what I had to say—at least I think she listened—while she tried and retried every panel, switch, and device in the hab as if some magic sequence or combination would turn them on. She was Brownian motion in human form.

"Sure, I can do it," she said when I finished, proving that she had somehow listened even while doing everything except bouncing off the walls. She grabbed that stupid sun hat and was out the door without waiting to see if anyone else was coming.

I looked at Malachi and shrugged, a gesture he returned without changing the neutral expression on his face. I figured we would walk to the Lab Unit together and use the time to talk. I was going to say that to Malachi, but Loretta caught my eye first, as she reached out and put a hand on Dustin's shoulder. Dustin looked at her and the two gazed at each other, a little smile on Loretta's lips. I glanced at Malachi, sure he had seen that little interlude as well. What the hell?

When Malachi saw me look at him, he turned to look out the door after Penny. Then he walked out without looking back. Perforce, I followed, leaving Dustin and Loretta to whatever came next. I had enough to worry about without adding them to my list.

By the time Malachi and I reached the Lab Unit, Penny had already tagged the instruments she wanted and was shuffling her feet in a little dance step as she waited for us. Malachi touched the input screens, looked into the identifier, and logged in without difficulty. The instruments came alive. For a moment, it looked like there would still be a problem. Penny couldn't download any data; she could only read the output on the screens. However, once the lab instruments were on, I could see that they could detect the spaceplane's system. A little jiggering by Penny and Malachi allowed the lab instruments to send to the spaceplane. The data could go from there into Penny's phone base. The communication system had not been designed with security in mind.

We received a quick, over-the-shoulder thank-you from Penny as she pushed a bunch of tubes, reagents, and pipettes into a pack. Then she was out of the Lab Unit on the run, one hand holding the pack and the other holding the sun hat on her head. One person in the colony wasn't bothered by the heat.

That left me with Malachi. A sheen of sweat was already forming on his head. "I do think you and I should have a talk, Leif. Perhaps later in the day, I can get some time with you? I'd like to take you out to the lake and show you some things. You can ask me your questions as well. I'd like to do it late in the day when it's a bit cooler, even if we need to stay out there. Is that okay with you?"

This sounded like more than a casual chat, and I had a lot to do. Still, I was the scout, and maybe I ought to scout both Malachi and the lake. I said I'd let him know once I understood how we were going to handle unloading the spaceplane. With that, I went back to my hab to discuss the arrangements with Yong. She was awake when I arrived and her usual all-business self.

"Bots will do the heavy work unloading the spaceplane," she said. "I'll have Sonal and Klaus bring the cohort leaders and some of the Pioneers. They can organize the cargo once it's unloaded, so we can transport it into town. It will be fine. You can go take a hike."

I don't think she understood the meaning of the American idiom.

.   .   .

Penny came to find me in the afternoon. Yong had wound up leading the rest of the Pioneers back to the spaceplane, as it gave them lunch, water, and bathrooms. Penny hadn't eaten lunch, and I don't think she noticed. Her uniform was soaked in sweat, a band of sweat stained the hat in a ring around her head, and there was dirt on her pants and her hands. We stood in the shade next to the Med Unit.

"I know part of the problem now," she told me. "You know, the aluminum in the soil here is low. The soil is thin to begin with, and the aluminum has been leached. Or somehow it wasn't there to begin with and this is another planet, but it's not there and if it was there and now it's gone, there's part of the problem, although it would be better if I could check somewhere else around here to see if it's there."

"Slow down, Penny. Tell me why this matters. We're not trying to build a car."

"Well, the soil is wicked acid." Her face said that should have been obvious. There followed an avalanche of numbers to do with pH, carbonate this and carbonate that, nitrates, magnesium, and other chemical terms.

I put my hands up in self-defense. "Whoa! Can you give me the dumb-guy capsule version? Is this place going to blow up?"

"No," she scoffed. "That's silly. It means there are a lot of plants that won't grow well here. Not many will. I don't think they should have put the town here. It's even acid for cannabis, which is why I'm sure they're using the hydroponics for that, although they shouldn't waste the hydroponics on that, because we need to grow sugarcane." She put a dirty finger to her lips. "Of course, potato grows in acid soil. That was a staple in Ireland, you know, and the potato blight had nothing to do with the soil conditions, that was a fungus, and in the nineteenth century that actually led to a famine, and the number of people who died because of no potatoes was—"

"Penny! Stop! Please!"

She shut down and looked at the dirt. "I just did it again, didn't I? Went off on a tangent."

"Yeah. Don't worry about it. At least not with me." At least she was working hard and enthusiastic about it. I would put up with stream-of-consciousness science, but not right now. "Listen, this isn't nineteenth-century Ireland. We're on Heaven, seventy-six light-years from Ireland. Are you telling me to plant potatoes here?"

She kicked at the dirt where she had been looking. "Yes, we should plant potatoes. I can put a list together of what will work and check it against the seed bank. I'll figure out what I can grow and how to do it." She kicked more dirt and refused to look at me. "But honestly, we should have better soil. There has to be better soil. I saw a valley on the screens when we flew in."

"You're saying we should explore the valley, maybe move people there?"

"I can't say that!" She did look up then and clasped her hands together because they were starting to shake. "You don't know what it's like. When I say things. And most of the time, it just pops out because I'm thinking of something or excited. But we can't sit here and only grow cannabis. But nobody is going to listen to me. But if it was your idea . . ."

I got the point of the conversation. "My job title says exoplanetary scout. Exploring is what I'm supposed to do." She stared at me with hope in her eyes. "Tell you what," I said. "Come out to the spaceplane with me. Let's see about getting a drone up. And maybe you can have a ReadyMeal while we're doing it."

.　　　.　　　.

Getting to the spaceplane meant retracing our walk into St. Peterstown the day before. The colony rovers were parked where the avenues intersected the perimeter road, but none of them would start for me. I couldn't chip in, my phone couldn't connect to them, and there was no manual override. We walked and sweated. I wondered if Penny would completely melt down and leave only the hat on the ground, the way a certain witch did, but she made it.

When we arrived, the ground near the spaceplane was piled with material pulled from the cargo bay. Bots made a continuous line from the spaceplane with more, and Pioneers buzzed around the piles like insects in a flower bed. Once outside, however, that's where the cargo sat. The spaceplane's bots were adequate to move the cargo outside, but not across the land between the LZ and the town.

Yong met us between two stacks of feedstock for the printers. Sonal came over to join us, her shirt soaked in sweat.

"We have extra rovers in with the cargo," Yong said. "They were intended as a backup for those the *Daredevil* brought. We're getting them out now, but they have to be assembled. Between bots and Pioneers, we can get it done. I'll send the Pioneers back to town with food so they can spend the night in their habs." She turned her face to the sky, which had filled with gray clouds. "Jorge says there's a chance of rain. We're not equipped to set up a campsite for all of them. We need to resolve the issue with Whitehead soon."

"Can you give me until tomorrow?" I asked. "I need to see what Malachi wants to show me, and I'll hope it doesn't rain on us. I can pitch our idea to Jerry after I'm back." I kept it vague because Sonal and Penny were standing there with us, but Yong knew what I meant. She made a noncommittal noise, but the tip of her head meant agreement.

Then I explained Penny's findings about the dirt and her thoughts about the valley. I did the explaining, because for all the squirming Penny did while she stood there, she didn't say anything to Yong.

"Getting a drone up is easy," Yong said. "They launch from a bay at the top of the spaceplane."

The drones we had on this trip were far better than the little ones we had used on High Noon. Each one weighed about thirty pounds, and their electric motors and props could send them 250 miles away, covering that distance at up to 200 miles an hour. In the cockpit, Yong tapped a key and a panel lit up. A few more taps and one of the screens showed us the cover over the drone bay as it split and opened. A platform rose out of the spaceplane with a small unmanned plane perched on it. The drone's wings unfolded and locked in place; its engine started. A catapult launched it into the air, and propellers ablur, it vanished into the sky.

We settled down to watch the screens.

Yong took the little drone up to a few hundred feet, had it circle over St. Peterstown to check the cameras, and then sent it south. From the height of the drone, the high plains we were on looked solid green. It wasn't possible to see how sparse the vegetation was. With the speed of the drone, it didn't take long for it to pass the solitary hill that marked the way to the valley.

"Forty-two miles to where the downslope begins." Yong was focused on the readouts from the drone as she spoke. "You could do it in a single forced march."

"Not with this heat and CO_2," I said. "I'd rather run a rover out there. The question is whether we can take a rover down that slope."

"Doesn't look too bad."

That was always the issue with the flyboys and -girls in the air force. They'd zoom over some route, tell me how short a march it was from my grid location to the target, and have absolutely no clue about the nightmare of jumbled terrain my team would somehow have to traverse. I pulled my mind away from memories of wars past and focused it on Heaven. To me, the slope looked fairly steep and rocky, at least at the upper reaches.

"We could probably pick out a path," I said. Might need some work to clear out a spot or two or make a switchback. We can try it and park the rover if we need to."

"Agreed," Yong said.

She took the drone up higher to give us a wider view. The valley was broad and U-shaped with a river running through it, west to east. Heaven's humidity created a haze in the valley that obscured the finer detail. To the west, I could see that the river came down out of the mountains, its origin lost in cloud. It was a bare, braided river there, brown dirt for banks. The water rushed down over a pretty waterfall, perhaps three hundred feet high, and below that the valley widened and turned green. The river changed, too, from running straight to sinuous curves through bottomland whose bright green was a sharp contrast to the brown above the falls.

"Can you bring it lower?" Penny asked.

Yong obliged and took us to the point where we were skimming the ground.

"Trees," Penny said. "Some kind of trees. Not very tall, nothing like a forest, which fits, I think, but trees. And those have to be shellhounds there, grazing. Lots of them. That means there's plenty to eat."

"Those are the only animals we've seen," I said. "Something has to eat them. There's always an apex predator somewhere." I was uncomfortably familiar with discovering that by surprise. An apex predator might also figure it could eat us.

"It still means vegetation grows much better down in that valley," Penny said. "The river washes tons of dirt into the valley past the waterfall. The soil will be thicker down there. Maybe more nutrients. I can't tell from here, but it's got to be better for growing crops. That river bend"—she jabbed a finger onto one of the screens while Yong grimaced—"would be the place for a farmhouse. Wicked pissah! We have to get down there."

"Long hike," I said, "even with a rover."

"I need the backup haulers," Yong said. "Until the town lets us chip in, I have to keep the Pioneers' rovers with us."

"They're not designed for rough terrain anyway," I said. "The ones for exploration are in the original equipment with the town."

"Whitehead needs to let us take one of the small ones from the town," Penny said. "I'll go talk to him. He's got to agree." She was so caught up in her vision of the valley that she had both hands clasped together and looked ready to jump up and down in front of the screen.

"Uh, Penny." Sonal had been quiet to that point. "Have you forgotten your, ah, performance at the Demos meeting? Do you really think Jerry is going to listen to someone who called him evil and said we should get rid of him?"

"I'll apologize," Penny said. "I'll say I'm sorry, that I was an ass, that I always run my mouth and he can ask anybody. I can do that, and I will, I will."

"Leif, do you think it would be better if you spoke to Jerry?"

I shook my head. "I have to talk to him tomorrow about something else and I can't tell how that will go. Anyway, I'm the one he thinks wants to shoot him. It may be better to let Penny try this. It can't make matters any worse."

CHAPTER TWELVE

We managed to assemble the first of the backup rovers and got it running. Then we loaded it with ReadyMeals and sent Sonal and the Pioneers back to town. I stayed with Yong to recheck the inventory and plan for how to move the rest of the supplies. It also gave us a chance to go over scenarios for the upcoming meeting with Jerry. We didn't really need to do that, but it gave us time together with no one else in the vicinity.

When I returned to St. Peterstown, Malachi was waiting for me by my hab. He had two backpacks, obviously one for him and the other for me. He took a long look at the M8 rifle, now slung over my shoulder, that I had pulled from the stores at the spaceplane. Simply put, when I was in the middle of nowhere—and Heaven certainly qualified as that—I felt more comfortable with a rifle ready to hand. It was an old army reflex, but it had served me well in the past, and thinking about possible predators had triggered it. The pistol at my belt did not do it for me; a rifle allowed me to keep danger at a distance.

I found it interesting that Malachi's face registered approval. I'd become accustomed to my fellow starfolk looking askance at me with an assault rifle. Curious. What had Malachi done that led him to volunteer for a one-way ticket to Heaven?

"You look like we're headed out on a camping trip," I said.

He shrugged. "It's a bit of a walk out, and it's already late in the day. It still surprises me after the months I've been here how little daylight we have now. It's not worth stumbling across the plain in the dark and maybe busting an ankle in a hole."

"Makes sense," I said. "Do you want to leave now, or would you rather wait for morning? I'm told it could rain."

"Can't see any point in hanging around. The worst that will happen is we'll get wet. Your people brought back supplies to take care of them for now, and the crew I came with are only going to sit around and get high." I could not miss the disgust in his voice.

Malachi led me down the Avenue of Australia toward the center of town. After we looped around the circle and started to go out by the Avenue of Europe, I saw a bunch of people clustered around one of the habs, standing and staring. They were listening to a loud argument the hab could not contain. The louder, screaming voice was a woman's. Penny's. I glanced at Malachi.

"That's Jerry's hab," he said.

"She said she was going to go apologize for what she said before and ask if we can borrow a small rover."

"I don't think it's going well," Malachi said.

"Understatement of the year. Do you think we should break it up?"

"No." Malachi shook his head. "If Vanessa is there, she'll put a stop to it. If not, it'll burn itself out. Jerry's probably too high already to listen to reason, but he doesn't get violent. Not his style. He'll also be too high to keep it going for long. I can tell you that nothing we do is going to make Jerry any less pissed about it tomorrow, and I don't need him pissed at me, specifically."

I wasn't sure what Malachi meant by that, but when I asked him, all I got was a shrug and he kept walking. I figured one of the Pioneers would get Dustin before too long, and he would pull Penny out of there. It's not like I was her father.

A little farther up the Avenue of Europe, Malachi said, "Might as well give everyone some live entertainment besides the cannabis."

Yeah, and give the Pioneers one more thing to tease Penny about. Some aspects of human behavior never changed. Not that she was doing much to help the situation. Maybe I should have pounded on Jerry's door and stopped it. Or pulled her out of there myself.

Not much more than a few hundred yards beyond the perimeter road, we came to the little river that ran past the settlement. It wasn't much of a waterway—more a creek than a river, barely two yards across. Steep banks dropped to flats of rock and baked mud that formed a wider channel along the sides of the creek. I suspected there were times when the creek ran a lot higher than we were seeing at the moment. The rocks in the creek were all coated with something resembling moss, but I didn't see anything swimming in the water. No frogs jumped along the banks; nothing croaked or splashed. It was a pretty forlorn creek.

"The *Daredevil* crew dug a well as part of the setup," Malachi said, "so we've got plenty of fresh water. Water table is pretty high. The flow here fluctuates a lot, depending on rain. Nothing to catch, though, so you can't go fishing. We call it Dead Creek."

"Why did the *Daredevil* put the town here?" I asked. "It doesn't seem like there's a whole lot to recommend the site."

"A good LZ was the first priority. This is far enough from the LZ to be safe, but close enough to simplify setting up the reactor and the habs. That let the crew do it quickly, and that's what they were primarily interested in. By the time we were out of hib and briefed, it was a done deal."

I gave him a sharp look, not so much for his critical tone but for the way he had said "LZ." That wasn't a typical civilian abbreviation. I mulled over asking him about it, but before I could, he had a question for me.

"You were a soldier back during the Troubles, weren't you?"

"Correct. US Army Rangers." I'd been out of the service seven years before the first starshot, but I was still proud to say it.

Malachi shook his head. "Never heard of them. Was that a special unit?"

I sighed. "Elite unit. Volunteers of volunteers. Airborne. Our motto was 'Rangers lead the way.' When I got back from the starshot, I found out the regiment had been disbanded in 2077. I'm guessing that's why you don't know us."

"Probably. I've only heard of you, same as everybody else has, because you're famous for killing Miles Richmond. True story, right?"

Crazy Miles, the unofficial patron saint of space travel. "Yes." I paused. "I heard that more than I cared to back on Earth. Even out here, those were about the first words out of Jerry's mouth after we landed. I'm good and goddamn sick of it already."

"Sucks to be you, I guess." Malachi laughed, but it wasn't a sympathetic laugh.

We walked along the bank of Dead Creek in a general southwest direction without speaking for a while.

That's when I decided I wasn't interested in being careful with my conversation anymore. "So, Malachi, what did you do back on Earth?"

"I started out as a chemist."

A chemist? Of all the jobs I could have pictured Malachi having, being a scientist in a lab wasn't among them. "And what deep, dark, and erased criminal secret led you to come here?"

"I fell into bad habits." Malachi pointed ahead of us over ground now marked by troughs and rises. "The lake is up there. That's where we're going."

That was about the most abrupt change of topic possible. I decided to let it pass. For the moment.

"You'll see more and more of the shellhounds as we get close to the lake," Malachi said. "If you want to grill a steak for dinner, they're pretty easy to catch, even without a gun. Taste like chicken. We've taken one apart. There's actually no brain in that head, like some people I know." He laughed briefly at his own joke. "Each leg has something Francesca thinks is a kind of brain, but no central controller. Only real problem with grilling dinner is it's hard to find firewood around here. There's low trees all along the slopes past the lake, but the wood's pretty wet. I put ReadyMeals in the packs."

We passed a pair of the shellhounds as we talked about dinner. They squatted low to the ground, looking like a pair of rocks, but chomped continuously on the grass around them. The rear legs did resemble a dog's, even close up.

"What eats them? Other than us?" I asked. Same question as at the spaceplane. "I can't believe that's the top of the animal food chain."

"It's not," Malachi said. "I've seen some small animals with teeth around the lake and creek, and something does prey on the shellhounds. I've found one partly eaten. Nothing big, though. I can't imagine there are too many predators. I don't think these shellhounds would survive if there were."

We walked up the next rise in the ground, and that gave me a better view ahead. The lake was before us, cupped in a low depression. Scraggly reedlike plants grew along the shore, with the ubiquitous thistles interspersed among them. The lake itself lay flat and empty in the middle of the reeds. Low trees—call them that—grew on the gentle slopes around the lake. Flickers in the air suggested small insects, but nothing like a bird flew over and nothing broke the surface of the water. With the star now at the horizon and the thick air darkening, it was a desolate place.

"That's Dead Lake," Malachi said. "Nothing in it except the moss we saw in the creek. Nothing wrong with the water that we can find—and I've drunk it—but nothing lives in it. Nothing like fish, not even microscopic stuff. That's part of what has Jerry and the Leavers spooked. They've convinced themselves that life here is teetering on a knife edge and could all go away. So they smoke leaf and want to escape."

I could hear disgust in his voice again as we climbed the higher ground that surrounded the lake. From where I stood, it could have been a lake on Earth except that it reflected the three moons now visible in the darkening sky. The clouds had mostly cleared. We wouldn't get wet after all. I thought about what Malachi had said, that there was nothing in the lake. I didn't even see a ripple on its surface. Malachi picked a spot, set down his pack, and pulled out eight campsite fence bases, disks the size and depth of his palm. While he was doing that, I pulled up a clump of the reeds and grass. The roots gave way easily. Around the stalks and in the dirt, I could see, even in the fading light, many tiny wriggling and crawling creatures.

"Plenty of life in this dirt," I said.

Malachi stopped what he was doing and looked over. "Yeah. Similar to worms and insects, I suppose, although nobody has taken them apart to see how they're put together. You could probably roast them to get protein, if you had to."

"I'll pass." I'd eaten insects on Earth because I had to; I didn't plan to eat them on Heaven.

Malachi gave more of a snort than a laugh and finished setting up the bases in a generous octagon around us. A tap on his phone base started antennas extending up from the bases to a height of seven feet. He waited until a green light turned on at the tip of each one, then came back and sat down next to his pack.

"That will discourage anything that mistakes us for shellhounds," he said.

"This is what we took a hike for?" I sat down next to him. "To look at a dead lake?"

"To talk," he said. "Far enough away that I'm not chipped into the network and without it being obvious that I'm chipped out."

"People chip out all the time," I said. "That was true on Earth, and it has to be true here. You don't have to be chipped in for your vid screen in the hab or anything else to pick up your settings. Devices pick up your public profile and settings through your phone. Even an old-time guy like me knows that." Malachi didn't comment, either about my chip knowledge or my old-fashioned status. I watched him watch me for a second. "So that would make you a very cautious and suspicious man, and it makes me even more curious why you came here, if that's one of the bad habits you picked up."

Malachi leaned forward with his arms on his knees. "I would say that I was neither cautious enough nor suspicious enough. At least on one occasion I wasn't, and that was all it took. I'm a free company man. The Grand Company." He stopped and waited for my reaction.

"I've heard about free companies. Supposedly independent mercenaries left over from the Troubles, although I have a hard time believing that. The Troubles were too long ago. How does a chemist like you get mixed up with them?" I glanced over at him.

He smiled grimly. "I like to blow things up, and we were well paid to do it."

So, Malachi had made a career out of blowing up various "things." One thought led to another.

"Should I assume you blew up people too?"

"Of course." Malachi found a convenient rock and threw it at the water. It sparked when it passed between the antennas, then made a splash and we watched the ripples. "The Troubles never really ended, Leif. The treaties may have ended the open fighting among the Powers and demilitarized the world, but the Troubles just went underground. That's the best way to say it. Everybody proclaims this New Golden Age as the best period in human history, the time everything is for the best. Meanwhile, this Power hires a free company to hit a target of that Power, or a free company working for another Power, and on and on. It was a good business to be in. Of course, before we left, the Powers were starting to talk about rebuilding their strength openly. They will. They'll rebuild their armies and when they do, they won't need the free companies anymore. There'll be no place left for us."

It was close enough to what I had heard on Earth that I believed him. "That's not a future you want to go back to, is it? Even after another century and a half?" He nodded. "The woman who was with you, Loretta Sforza, was she with your company too?" He nodded again. "And the rest of the Remainers? That's why you all want to stay?"

"No. Only six of us are from free companies, and Loretta and I are the only ones from Grand Company. The others, well, each one has their own story."

I threw a stone at the lake, but I was too far away to make it skip. It sank. "I'm surprised you got here at all. Jerry said no one here had any violent crime in their background, and I don't see how people from free companies could meet that criterion. Were backgrounds . . . adjusted?"

Malachi laughed. "They were short on volunteers with useful skills. People who will give up a golden age aren't necessarily the type of people you want for something like this. And don't trust what you hear from Jerry. He's known for playing fast and loose with the truth. That British accent of his, that's fake. He's from Wichita, Kansas. His name isn't Whitehead. It's Whitley. The truth about him is that he orchestrated the biggest financial fraud of the twenty-first century. Ruined families, businesses, actually made one country insolvent. Sent most of his own family into hiding."

"That tells me why he came here and was glad to have been erased," I said, "but I don't see how he would be put in charge."

"Jerry can talk his way into all sorts of things. That's part of how he pulled off his fraud. He had everybody happy until, suddenly, they weren't."

I thought of the argument we had heard as we were leaving town. Penny had thought she was going to talk him into letting her use the small rover if he didn't agree right away.

I mentioned that to Malachi and he said, "Hah. You don't win arguments with Jerry. Certainly, that girl won't."

So, Jerry was a fraudster. What else had he faked? "Is that deadman switch he claims he's got real, or is that another fake?"

"I would bet it's real," Malachi said. "Jerry's a manipulator. He's gotten favors from lots of people, and I'm sure he got favors on Earth even while he was waiting to be shipped here. He had something on all sorts of people, ones who could do favors. God only knows how he got his information. That'll be true here too. Something people don't want known, even here. Lots of folks, Leavers and Remainers, hate him. Don't bet on the deadman switch being fake. Now, the power system does have backup storage and that's supposedly good for a month or two, but who wants to bet we can fix whatever his switch does?"

We threw more stones at the lake. Malachi managed to get one to skip.

"Did you ever think about staying, Leif?" Malachi was throwing a stone as he said it.

That wasn't a question I had seen coming. Not with the state of the colony and of the whole damn planet. The fact that he even asked made me cautious about my answer. "Why would I stay?"

Malachi laughed. "It's more a question of why wouldn't you? What are you going to do, go back and be the man from the history books who killed St. Miles? And I told you the Troubles never really went away. Do you want to go back to whatever that produces?"

I was silent.

"Here?" he went on. "Yeah, it'll be hard, but we can do it. Not with Jerry running it, but we can do it. You know the saying 'Life's a bitch and then you die'? Well, this idea for the colony, our constitution and Demos—a true democracy, everyone equal with no classes—that's crap and it won't last. Never does. Some always rise to the top. Here, you could be one of the men on top before you die. That's not the worst thing in the world. This one or any other."

I had an idea of the offer Malachi was edging his way toward, and I didn't want him to go any further with it. I was only going back to Earth long enough to catch another ship with Yong. I didn't really care what developed there, or how I was remembered. Not that I was going to talk to Malachi about Yong.

"If you think you can make it work here, I'm surprised you Remainers haven't put more effort into setting up the town." I kept my voice level. "If you're going to make it work, where are the photovoltaic panels, the plantings, any animals?"

"Because none of the twenty-one of us Remainers care to be busting our asses so Jerry and his Leavers can live off what we do while they sit around, smoke dope, and wait for a ride out. If you and Yang had said you would take us all off, anything we did would have been wasted effort. We can't stay by ourselves. Not twenty-one of us. Since we're all going to stay, everyone can share the work."

There was a certain logic to what he said, although it also said a lot about the social structure of the *Daredevil*'s settlers and how Malachi saw the future. Down below us, a shellhound had appeared and was chewing on a thistle.

"Shellhound on a bed of thistle for dinner?" I said.

"Don't touch the thistle," Malachi said. "At least, don't eat it. We tried mice on it when we arrived and that didn't go well. Not at all."

"Some kind of poison?" I asked. "It doesn't bother the shellhound."

"Biology is different enough, I guess," Malachi said. "We haven't taken the time to look into it. At least I haven't, and I don't think anyone else could."

In the end, we pulled out ReadyMeals from the backpacks and munched through them. I said I would be more comfortable if we kept a watch, and Malachi didn't argue. We agreed to split the night and start back as soon as it was light.

I had the watch when the eastern sky began to turn red. An alarm hit my phone and projection field and made me jump. I could see Malachi wake suddenly as well. My call was from Yong at the spaceplane.

"Leif," she said, "you better get back to St. Peterstown as quick as you can. Jerry Whitehead is dead."

CHAPTER THIRTEEN

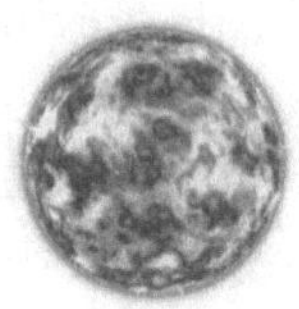

If we could have run back to St. Peterstown we would have, but that wasn't happening on Heaven. The air was as stale as a conference room full of lawyers who'd spent the day arguing. And even with the star barely up in the sky, I would bet the temperature was pushing a hundred degrees. We set the best pace we could and tried to maintain it. While we did, my field lit up with notices that led to a babble on my phone. I wasn't on St. Peterstown's network, but Yong had set up a channel so people in town could pick up the spaceplane and route calls to me that way.

Beyond the obvious fact that Jerry was dead, everyone and everything sounded confused. Vanessa had found him when she went to the hab around dawn. Why would she be doing that, even if dawn came fairly late at this season? Well, she lived with him, I was told, so, of course she would be going there. That also meant she had spent the night with someone else, but that didn't matter right then. The predominant conclusion I heard on the phone was that Jerry had had a heart attack. That was mostly because Vanessa said his shirt was wet, and everyone knew that men who had heart attacks sweated heavily. Of course, his bladder had released, so maybe that was why his clothes were wet. St. Peterstown did have a doctor—Francesca Balboni. Had anyone asked her? Apparently not yet. Jerry, like everyone else in the modern era, had a chip that would have a record of all his physiological parameters. Had they taken him to the Medical Unit and interrogated his chip? No. Would somebody please find Francesca and get Jerry's body over to the Medical Unit? They would see what they could do. Speaking of Jerry's chip, one other fact was clear in all the chaos of the phone calls. The reactor had shut down. The deadman switch was real. St. Peterstown was running on battery backup. For how long? No one seemed to know that either.

It wasn't until we reached the Town Circle that we saw anyone. There, the street was full of people, milling around randomly, both *Daredevil* crew and Pioneers. They were all talking on their phones and not doing anything useful. They clustered around Malachi and me but didn't stop their conversations or do anything except get in the way. Malachi shoved his way through them and crossed Town Circle to the Dome. I stuck with him, and people trailed behind us. I sent a message to Sonal, asking her to round up the rest of the Pioneers and bring them to the Dome also.

Once inside the Dome, Malachi jumped up onto the platform and went to the table. People streamed in, although most of them stayed standing. They had spotted someone acting with purpose, and their first instinct was to follow. Malachi did not bother with the ritual opening that Jerry had used.

"Okay, the most important thing is the power." Even without the microphones in the table, Malachi's voice boomed out over the people who had gathered. I've addressed troops in the field, and from the way he stood and sounded, I'd bet he had too. "You three." He picked out three people with his index finger, one by one. "Get over to the reactor and check all the circuit boards. With your eyes on them, you check those boards. Jones!" He spotted a man standing in an aisle and pointed at him. "You're IT. Get on the computer and see if the problem is in the software. See if you can fix it through the network."

"We need an alternative in case it's not an easy fix," I said. "The photovoltaic panels will do it, that's what they're for, but none of them have been set up."

"Right," Malachi said. "Davis!" Sonal had come into the back of the Dome. "I'll send you the names of people from the *Daredevil* who were trained on the panels. Get some of yours to add to them so we have a work crew, and start setting up panels. I need to know how long it takes to set them up so I can figure how long it will be until we can run the town off the panels."

"While you're at it," I said, "get someone to add us to the network. That'll help in a lot of ways."

Malachi nodded. "Jones, with Jerry gone, the computer will default to Ibiana and Vanessa for approvals. I doubt he booby-trapped that because he never boasted about it. I'll message them for approval, and you add the people from the *Dauntless*."

Malachi Oates was acting like the man in charge, and the settlers at the Community Dome, both the *Daredevil* crew and ours, responded to it. This was the tonic they needed to snap out of their funk and begin to function. Since no one was sure when the stored power would be exhausted, this activity might save their hides. What made me uneasy, however, was the memory of Malachi's comments when he'd asked me about staying behind when the *Dauntless* left. He sure had sounded like someone who relished the idea of being in command. Was it simply falling in his lap now and he was taking advantage of the situation? I couldn't tell, but he was doing what the colony needed, so maybe it didn't matter.

While this was happening, a woman pushed through the people crowded at the front of the platform and reached up to grab my arm. I recognized her even without the ident. Francesca Balboni, the doc.

"I need to speak to you, and also Ibiana and Vanessa." Her words came in gasps, as though she was short of breath.

I didn't see either of those women, but one look at Francesca's strained face told me this wasn't something that should wait. I helped her up to the platform and pulled on Malachi's arm to turn him away from the table.

"Why don't you start with me and Malachi," I said to Francesca. "We'll sort it out with the others later."

"It's about Jerry."

That got Malachi's attention even more than my grab had. "What about Jerry?" he asked.

She looked from one of us to the other and licked her lips. "Jerry didn't have a heart attack," she said. "After they called me, I went over and we brought him to the Medical Unit. I was able to download from his chip before it went dormant. He stopped breathing."

"Wait a minute," I said. "People don't stop breathing without a reason. What else did the chip have?"

"Not much." Now she was looking everywhere except at the two of us. "His breathing slowed down; it's not like he choked on something. The way I read the data, it looked like wheezing, like asthma, but Jerry didn't have asthma. His blood oxygen went down. There was some sort of muscle activity I don't recognize. Then he had a seizure and stopped breathing completely. That's when he had a cardiac arrest."

"He stopped breathing," I repeated. "Are you trying to tell us someone stopped him from breathing?"

"No!" She shook her head violently. "I mean, I don't know for sure, but I don't think so. Vanessa found him. She said he was lying on his back on the floor, like he had fallen out of his chair. His face was up."

"A pillow over the face is an old trick," I said.

"Couldn't be," Francesca said. "His nose had been running. There was still mucus on his face. If somebody did anything like that, the mucus would have been smeared or wiped away. I told you, I saw him before we took him to the Medical Unit. And nobody choked him. I mean, I'm not a pathologist, or forensics or anything like that, but there're no marks on his neck."

Our conversation was starting to attract an uncomfortable amount of attention. Malachi pulled me close, his mouth next to my ear.

"Why don't you go over to Medical with Francesca," he said. "Talk there. See for yourself. I've got to get everybody working so they can calm down and not drive themselves crazy thinking the power will die in two hours."

"And if the power does die in two hours?" I asked.

"All the more reason for them to bust their asses on the photovoltaic panels." Malachi grinned. "Let's hope it doesn't die."

Given that I used to be a paramedic and had transported more people with heart attacks and seizures than I cared to count, I probably was the best person to go with Francesca. Certainly, I didn't have the skills to work on the reactor or the computer network, and Malachi was in his element organizing work crews. A notification popped up on my field. The St. Peterstown network was now available to me. I chipped in and walked partway around the Town Circle with Francesca to the Medical Unit.

The inside of the unit was pretty standard for a small field unit. Immediately past the entrance was a triage station with half a dozen diagnostic beds. Jerry's body lay on one of them, and the area stank. Both his bowels and bladder had let go, and no one had cleaned him up very well. Leads dangled from the diagnostic array over the bed but were not connected to him. No need at this point, I supposed.

I turned to Francesca. "You said you're not a pathologist or specialized in forensics. What kind of doc are you?"

"I used to be an obstetrician," she whispered.

"Used to be?" Obstetrician made sense for a colony that would need to have plenty of children, but I didn't understand the past tense.

"I used to get high." She looked at the floor. "All the pressure for school and grades. Then it was pressure at work. I botched a delivery. More than one." She stopped and took a breath. "I don't do it when I work anymore. Everybody else here gets high as much as they can, but I don't."

"Are you one of Jerry's Leavers, then? Are you figuring by the time you get back, you can be a doc again?"

"No. One of those deliveries was a cousin. A court's sentence is finite; a family's sentence is forever. I'm here. Whatever happens. Give me a minute." She walked away from me to the back of the unit.

My eyes followed her and I checked the rest of the unit. They had a pedi-diagnostic unit for kids, three baby isolettes, and a dozen inpatient beds. Two surgi-bots were in wall cradles. Beyond the patient area I could see lab benches. The unit could serve a small community.

I used my chip and newly granted access to go through the readouts from Jerry's chip while Francesca was collecting herself. It was as she had said. He had stopped breathing. That's not how otherwise healthy men die. A man with severe asthma might die that way, but Jerry didn't have asthma at all.

"What did the AI give us?" I asked when she returned.

"Not much."

She hit the Interpretation and Intervention tab on the diagnostic unit where Jerry's body lay. The output displayed in my field was: THE PATIENT IS ALREADY DECEASED. FURTHER INTERVENTION NOT WARRANTED.

Artificial stupidity, if you ask me.

"No toxicology section?" I asked. "There has to be a lab section for possible poisons on a brand-new world."

"We've got a full medical-grade molecular analyzer in the Lab Unit," Francesca said, "but I have no idea what I would even look for. It's not like

I can take a sample from his body, put it in the machine, and have it tell me there's a strange molecule there. If I don't know what I'm looking for, how am I going to find it?"

I suppose, but it's what you don't know about or plan for that kills you.

"Could he have inhaled something?" I asked. "Could he have reacted to something he ate?"

"We only eat the ReadyMeals," she said. "Some people have tried shellhound steak, and that's okay, but basically, we don't eat anything that grows here. We haven't tried growing anything from the seed bank, because we voted to leave as soon as you got here. As for inhaling, Jerry was a leafer, a real heavy one. The air system in his hab was on with full filtration. There's no way he inhaled anything he didn't usually inhale. You don't die like that from pot."

"I know that." Jerry's death made me uneasy. I had seen—and caused—more deaths than I cared to count, but the reasons for those deaths had been clear or easily determined. There was no apparent reason for Jerry to have died, and the artificially unintelligent diagnostic unit was no help. I couldn't avoid the possibility that someone had killed him, even though I couldn't tell how it had happened. A murderer in a small, isolated colony under stress was not a good thing.

"You said Vanessa found him?" I asked Francesca.

"Yes. Vanessa Huggins. She's his partner. Sort of."

"I need to talk to her." Apparently, I had become the first interstellar private eye.

CHAPTER FOURTEEN

Vanessa Huggins wasn't at the hab she officially shared with Jerry. In response to my message, she said she was at Ibiana's hab, and the two of them were there when I walked in.

"I wasn't with Jerry last night," she said, even before I asked. "I was here. With Ibiana."

Ibiana reached out and took Vanessa's hand. "Vanessa is here most nights."

"Wait a minute," I said. "You two are together? I thought . . ."

Vanessa favored me with a wan smile. "Sure. Volunteers are supposed to be cis-het. Babies, after all. I'll have sex with men. So will Ibiana. But I like to avoid Jerry. His idea of sex . . . Well, never mind."

"You like to avoid Jerry? You were his partner."

"Yeah." The same sad smile came back. "That's how I'm on the Council. And remember, I told you about Jerry knowing secrets. That's how I kept mine."

"Are you telling me that Jerry found out whatever you were hiding, and he blackmailed you into being his partner by threatening to blab it around the colony? I thought everybody here was running away from stuff that was out on the Community in the first place."

She laughed. It was a laugh with no humor in it. "Everyone has secrets, you know. Me, Francesca, everyone. Even ones that weren't all over the Community. Jerry knew them all. I don't know how, but he did. I think he knew people who knew how to find things on the Community that you thought were buried so deep . . . Never mind. He knew them. He would boast about it in bed." She laughed again, this time a real laugh. "That was the only thing he did in bed he could boast about."

I didn't want the details of Jerry's bedroom antics. "Francesca says you're the one who found him."

"Yes. I leave Ibiana early in the morning, before people get up, and go over to Jerry's hab, our hab. I always turn on the air system, put it on as high as possible, because Jerry smokes so damn much. Shit, you can barely breathe in there overnight. Everybody smokes leaf on Heaven, but Jerry is, was, extreme."

"Everybody?" I asked. "Francesca says she doesn't."

"Francesca is a liar. Like everybody else on Heaven."

I recalled the old, old puzzle about the liar who tells you they're lying. "Can we go back to Jerry? Why did you make a point of saying you put on the air system?"

"Because I didn't," she said. "That was the first thing that was strange. The scrubber was already on—it must have been on all night—but Jerry never puts it on. He wants to keep all that smoke inside. He keeps the system on Recirculate with the filters off so he can get, as he says, 'the full effect.' But there wasn't even a scent of pot in the air. The only smell was, well, he'd shit himself. I know that happens after people die."

"And where was Jerry?"

"On the floor next to his desk in the front room. On his back. In his clothes. His mouth was open and he was sort of purple. I did try to shake him, but he was already cold."

"Cold and stiff?"

She looked a little sick. "Yes. And wet. Well, damp. And I pushed at his shoulder. I guessed he pissed himself also when he died. Not sure how that would get his whole shirt wet, but it must have, and it hadn't all dried. The cleaner bot gets anything on the floor, so, like, even his roach was gone, but it didn't clean up him. I came back here and washed my hands for a long time. I'm not sure who called Francesca. I don't remember if I did."

"Except for you going over there in the morning, you and Ibiana were together the whole night?"

Vanessa nodded. "I stay chipped in, I guess because I've always been compulsive about input to my records on what I eat and when I exercise and so forth. I mean, there're no cameras or anything like that here, but if you're chipped in, the door will keep a record if you go in or out."

I thought of what Malachi had said out by the lake. "So, does that mean that if you went into the hab with Jerry—say, in the middle of the night—there would be a record? And if someone else went in there, there would be a record of that person?"

"Well, no, not necessarily. If it was me, yes, because I stay chipped in. It's more convenient. Not if it's someone else. If you're chipped out, the hab won't record you. The door will show an entry or exit, but not who. Some people do chip out, you know."

"So, you could have chipped out and gone back there," I said. "And it sounds like you had a reason to want Jerry dead." Was this the way a detective would slip that question in?

Vanessa's expression was more of a smirk. "Lots of us would have loved to see Jerry dead. But I wouldn't have risked that switch of his any more than Francesca would. So, no, I didn't chip out and I didn't go back and kill him. And, you know, those Pioneers from your ship weren't in the system at all until today. Like that girl who had the screaming match with Jerry. She won't show on any record."

"Do you think she was the last one to see Jerry?"

Vanessa shrugged. "I don't know. What I do know is that she had that screaming hissy where she was saying she ought to kill him. Among other things. Everybody in the street heard that."

·   ·   ·

I messaged both Penny and Dustin and arranged to meet them outside the Community Dome. They were already there when I arrived, but it wasn't the scene I'd expected. Usually Penny was glued to Dustin, but now she was standing away from him with her arms wrapped around her chest, hugging herself. Dustin was with Loretta. The awkward conversation I expected was going to be even more awkward.

"Ah, Penny," I started, "when you left Jerry yesterday after that argument you had—"

"Yes! He was still alive!" The words shot out of her mouth with explosive force. "Don't you think every human on this planet has already asked me that, including Pilot Yang, who messaged me because even she had heard about when I went to see him and she's at the spaceplane, I mean, you're about the last one. I mean, yes, I know I lost my temper and I know I said I wished he was dead, and I know I said I wanted to choke the shit out of him, but . . ."

She peeled her arms away from her torso, held her hands in front of her face, and looked at them as though she did not believe those hands could choke a man. To be honest, I didn't think they could either, even if she'd wanted to. I tried to think of a question to ask. This sort of shit never happened in a Ranger platoon.

"What was he doing?" I asked. "When you were there?"

"Smoking!" She was still looking at her hands. "One joint after another. He went through two while I was there. He had this little metal case with his joints in it. Must have been half empty. I thought I'd get high and pass out from the air in that hab. He had it sealed up, no air movement, never mind the heat. I thought I would barf."

"And what finally happened? You wanted him to let us use the small explorer rover. I assume he said no."

"Not . . . exactly." Penny was now quite red in the face.

I had a feeling I knew what came next, but I had to ask.

"He said . . . he said, if I wanted to use the rover, I had to get down right then and . . . and suck his dick. And he was going to make a vid. And then he'd think about it."

Loretta giggled. Dustin was grinning. Penny's eyes darted all over, a trapped animal looking for an escape.

"So did you do it so well you gave him a heart attack?" Loretta asked. "I wouldn't think you were good."

"What!?" That came out in a scream. "I left! I ran out! I thought I was choking!"

Even if Penny was the killer, I liked her a lot more than I liked Jerry. If Jerry wasn't already dead, I'd consider killing him myself.

"When you left Jerry's hab," I asked, "did you go back to yours?" She nodded. "You didn't go back to Jerry's later, did you?" She shook her head hard. "And Dustin was with you the rest of the night. Correct?"

"No." It was a whisper. "I was alone last night."

"I was with Loretta last night," Dustin said.

Loretta corroborated that.

Penny was crying.

Shit.

.   .   .

"Are you sure somebody killed him?" Yong had come back from the space-plane and stood with me outside the Community Dome, not far from where my calamitous interview with Penny had taken place.

We could, of course, have spoken just as well by phone or field message, but there was something comforting about being face-to-face and within arm's length of someone . . . who is very important to you. I'm sure she felt the same way, and that had more to do with her presence than her stated desire for "direct visual inspection" of the town.

"Yeah." I got two syllables out of that word. "Adults don't just stop breathing and die. Babies do, but not adults. Something stopped his breathing."

"Do you think Penny did it?"

"I don't know." I kicked a clod of dirt away that didn't have enough grass on it to hold it together. "I can't see Penny being able to kill anyone, just physically, never mind having the will."

"People can surprise you," Yong said. "And you said there were no marks on him, so physical violence doesn't fit. Poison, somehow? A bio vector, somehow? She's smart, that one is."

"I can't discount it." I wanted to discount it completely. Penny could be a real pain in the ass who didn't know when to shut up, but there was something endearing about the way she did it, like the kid sister who always has to tag along. Okay, I never had a kid sister. I just didn't want her to be a killer.

"Plenty of people wanted to see Jerry dead," I said. "Vanessa and Francesca, to start with. And I bet if I talk to Ibiana, she'll come up with a reason too." I was pretty sure that screaming in front of a crowd about killing someone didn't make you a more likely suspect. Yeah. "I wish I could say this isn't our problem."

"But you know it is," Yong said. "Forget Whitehead's comments the other day. Our mission is to leave a colony with the parameters in place that are specified by the mission plan. If there is a murderer loose, who has knocked out the reactor, and the colony lacks a secure power source, what is our situation?"

"That's not mission accomplished." I sighed. "And we can't leave it to the Public Safety Squad of Cam and Jess. What do you want to do?"

"Have a look at Whitehead's hab."

Jerry's hab looked like any other hab in St. Peterstown. It was hot and stifling when we entered, because the systems had been shut down after they removed his body. The odors of death and excrement permeated the interior.

"This is going to need a cleanup crew," I said.

"Some air movement would help." Yong studied the control panel by the entry, then tapped a series of commands. A soft whir sounded above me and I felt cool air blow.

"None of this is locked down," she said. "I'm sure there are some private and protected domains on the computers, but the basic hab controls will work as long as your settings are available. The air system is available on an emergency basis even if you're not on the network, because this circuitry was designed to work with an air lock. You can use it manually without any settings."

I stopped where I was, a little past the entryway. "So here's something interesting. Penny said this place was choked with smoke when she was in here. Vanessa said the air system was on full, and the air was clear and cold. That's about as different as it can get."

"One of them is lying."

"Or," I said, "someone else was in here in between and turned the air systems on. Vanessa said she didn't, but maybe she lied. Or Penny came back. But why turn the systems on?"

"This we can check." Yong walked over to the hab's work desk and tapped at the pad there. She glanced at the screen and tapped again. "The records for the hab functions are available. They're not protected. Why would they be? The door opened and someone exited at 16:39. This clock is set for local time, which is a twenty-one-hour day, but that doesn't matter for this. There is no ident in the system, but it was probably Penny. She couldn't have been chipped in anyway. Then the door opens again for an entry at 20:53 and another exit at 20:56. Again, no ident. We can ask if any of the people who heard Penny arguing saw someone go in, but they were probably gone by then. Then, nothing until Vanessa at 6:02, and she is identified because she is chipped in."

"Are you saying Penny came back at night and did something in just a few minutes?"

"No. I didn't say that. It could be anyone who wasn't chipped in. Anybody from the Pioneers, or even from the *Daredevil*, if they chipped out."

"And, of course, no camera," I said. "Why would you have a camera in a hab seventy-six light-years from Earth with only a few dozen people on the planet? Can you tell me when the air system went on?"

Yong tapped the screen once. "20:55."

"So, what we're down to is somebody came in hours after Penny was here, killed Jerry in a few minutes, and left."

"Or they found him dead and left in a hurry." She studied me. "You don't want it to be Penny. She could have turned on the air system when she came back, you know."

"You're right." I looked around the front room of the hab, hoping to find I-don't-know-what. A bloody knife, maybe. A pistol with one shot fired. Never mind that Jerry had no wounds. Dammit, adults do not stop breathing without a reason. Poison could be an obvious reason, but what—and how? I saw nothing out of place. Jerry's work desk was clear.

"Wait," I said. "They found Jerry on the floor next to this chair. The stains and smell on the chair cushions fit with that. Penny said he was at his desk. She also said a metal case holding his joints was on his desk. Where's the case?"

"I don't know. I don't see it."

We made a quick survey of his hab and didn't find it.

"All right," I said, "granted, we didn't tear the place apart like they do in the vids, but I don't see the case, and Penny said it was out on the desk. Where did it go?"

Yong shrugged. "With the number of leafers in this place, maybe somebody came by afterward and took it to get the joints. We don't have whatever he was smoking right before he died either. Why is it important?"

"I don't know. Vanessa said the cleaner bot would have taken something like a roach on the floor, but those bots wouldn't take a metal case. I was never trained on how a detective works. I don't know how to figure out something like this."

Yong gave me one of her tight little smiles. "I thought that's what you infantry 'boots on the ground' types do. Figure out the situation on the ground."

"Yeah. And what is it you air force flygirls do?"

Her smile broadened. "We come and save the day after you've gotten up to your neck in the situation on the ground."

CHAPTER FIFTEEN

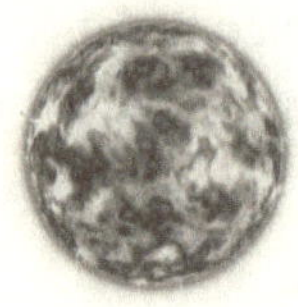

Yong and I were standing in front of Jerry's hab, muttering about whom we should talk to next, when a notification flashed at the periphery of my field. I looked that way and it opened to reveal: DEMOS MEETING. COMMUNITY DOME. FIFTEEN MINUTES.

We walked over to the Dome and could see clusters of people ahead of us going in to take seats. Even without counting, I was sure every human on Heaven was going to be under that dome by the time the meeting started.

Vanessa and Ibiana were seated at the table facing the assembling Demos. In between them, Jerry's seat was empty. Yong and I went up the steps to the platform and stood, as before, to the side of the table. We weren't part of the Demos, but neither one of us was going to miss this meeting. Besides, having us standing by the Council might lend support.

Vanessa waited until everyone was seated. Then she spoke. "This meeting of the Demos of St. Peterstown is now open. Vanessa Huggins, vice-mayor and *Daredevil* crew, is presiding in the absence of a mayor. Before any other business is discussed, I would like to ask Malachi Oates to be recognized and report to us about the power situation."

Malachi stood up from where he sat in the front row and gave his name. "The reactor is offline," he said. "Jerry did have a deadman switch on his chip. We're not sure yet exactly what it did, but it looks like there is physical damage to chips on one of the boards. We are running on stored backup power now."

"For how long? I mean, how long can we?" Vanessa's voice was little above a whisper, but the microphones picked it up and amplified it across the Dome.

"Don't know for sure," Malachi said. "It's obviously a function of how heavily we draw on it, as well as how much is stored. The system connects with the reporting from the reactor, and that's damaged, which is why we can't be sure. Best guess right now is a couple of Earth months. I can tell you we won't be out of power tomorrow, but I could be off by fifty percent either way."

"My God," came from several places among the audience, and a variety of expletives as well.

"I'll bring down one of our nuclear engineers from the *Dauntless* when I bring the rest of the supplies," Yong said. Her voice carried by itself. "If you can send up all the information you have on your system, we may be able to replace the damaged area or do a work-around."

"Thank you," said Malachi. "In the meantime, I've got crews organized to start putting up the photovoltaic panels as fast as we can. Once we have enough of them up, we can run without the reactor. We just need to get them up and online first."

"That's goddamn slave labor in the heat!" A man in the second row jumped up without giving his name. His ident said Oscar Gradison of the *Daredevil*. "There aren't enough bots to go as fast as you're telling us to. We're having to lift and carry ourselves. It's brutal in this fucking heat!"

Malachi was unfazed. "I know it's hard work," he said. "We don't have a choice, though. We have to be generating enough power to keep us going before the backup is exhausted, and like I said, I can't be certain when that happens."

"Wouldn't need to do it at all if that fuckin' newcomer bitch hadn't killed Jerry." Gradison turned around, his eyes roving across the seated people. "That one, there!" He pointed at Penny. "What do we do about her? It better be more than having Public Safety talk to her."

I saw Penny's mouth drop open.

"Yeah." A woman stood up. "I've got nothing good to say about Jerry, but if she killed him and now we're all in deep shit, she should pay for it. We should put her on trial and make her pay."

I heard someone shout, "Second!" and then there were more shouts and more people standing.

"You're not going to do a goddamn thing!" I was even louder than Yong had been. I hadn't needed a microphone with my platoon in the field, and I didn't need one here. "We're not even sure how he died yet. If he was killed, as far as I'm concerned, it could be any of you who did it."

"We all heard her threaten him, and you could hear her screaming in his hab halfway across Heaven!" Oscar was shouting again. "Anyway, it had to be a newcomer. Any of us who were on the *Daredevil* would know enough about him not to risk it."

"Oh, I think you would, Oscar," said another man who stood up. "Jerry had that vid of you giving him a blow job behind the hydroponics facility."

"What!?" All the color drained out of Oscar's face.

"Yeah. He showed some of us. Jerry wasn't really into secrets for other people. I'll bet you thought you could make the ship take us by killing him."

"The pilot already said she won't take us!" I didn't see where that shout had come from.

"We'll make her take us!" That came from more than one person.

"You're fucking idiots! They're going to leave us here to die!"

Shouts and screams came from people around the Dome. Even more so than at the first meeting, I saw people climbing over seat backs to get at one another. This was ridiculous. And I had another person with a good reason to want Jerry dead.

I drew my pistol and fired two shots into the ground. The loud clap of the bullets exploding out of the muzzle cut off the budding fracas. The people on their feet stopped where they stood, and stared at me. We had silence.

"That's enough," I said. "All of you, sit down and shut up. Next person who wants to fight gets to fight me."

I saw plenty of hard faces and hard eyes, but all of them sat down. No more talk came from the crowd.

"Thank you, Leif," said Vanessa. Her voice shook, and I couldn't blame her. We had been closer to a riot that I wanted to think. "Malachi," she went on, "please continue doing what you need to do to get the panels online. Pilot Yang, we accept your offer to bring down an engineer. Neither action requires a vote." She paused. "We need to fill the position of mayor of St. Peterstown. I do not want that office. Neither does Ibiana."

Ibiana nodded in agreement.

Loretta stood up and identified herself. "I nominate Malachi Oates."

I heard an immediate second.

Malachi walked in front of the platform and turned to face the Demos. He had a smile on his face. When no one spoke for a few minutes, Vanessa asked if there were other nominations. None were offered.

"In the absence of a contested election," Vanessa said, "I will only ask for a show of acclamation. The Pioneers from the *Dauntless* have been added to the Demos and may join the vote."

A roar in favor echoed through the Dome. I guessed that while some might object to hard work in broiling weather, most of the Demos appreciated having someone who could organize the work and get it done. Malachi said a quick thank-you, then jumped up on the platform and took the center seat at the table.

"We should move on to other business," he said.

"Before we do," said Vanessa, "I have to say that I'm stepping down. I can't do this job. Not anymore. Please find someone else."

Malachi nodded. "I would like to nominate Loretta to be vice mayor." It was smooth enough and quick enough that he must have expected the opportunity.

After a second from one of the *Daredevil* crew, one of the Pioneers stood up and nominated Sonal. A glance at Malachi told me that he had anticipated that. I saw him exchange looks with the man who had seconded Loretta. That man twisted around and caught Bjorn's eye. Bjorn nodded. Reality was watching Bjorn, and she gave an okay sign with her hand as soon as Bjorn nodded. It was only after enough moments went by for all the looks, nods, and signs, that Malachi spoke.

"Are there other nominations?" he asked. No one made any. "Okay. This is contested, so we can't do it by acclamation. You must be chipped in to vote, and you can do so as soon as I open the ballot in your projection field."

There were 128 Pioneers to 71 of the original crew, and this was a secret ballot. Sonal ought to win. Somehow, I had the feeling Malachi had a different plan.

Bjorn was on his feet and started to bellow a chant. "LOR-ET-TA! LOR-ET-TA!"

He pointed at Pioneers from his team as he shouted, and they rose and shouted too. Reality was up only seconds behind Bjorn and added her voice to the chant, pointing at members of her team and raising her hands in the air and clapping them. Men and women from the *Daredevil* crew got up and chanted also. As will happen in crowds, more people stood on their own to chant with them. It sounded like a gym at a high school basketball game. The shouted chant continued until Malachi announced that the ballot field had closed. Loretta won, 150–49.

While Loretta walked up to exchange places with Vanessa, I looked for Sonal among the Pioneers. I won't say she was crying, but she did look like she'd been hit between the eyes with a two-by-four. As democratic coups go, this one had been clean and tidy. I supposed that if Malachi was going to try to keep this colony alive, he wanted to do it his way. Under the circumstances, it was hard to argue with him.

"Okay," Malachi said. "We need to get down to business, that business being surviving. We're going to divide everybody, *Daredevil* and *Dauntless* together, into work teams. These people will be team leaders." He started with Loretta, who would supervise the other leaders along with him. Then he named three men, David Gruenig, José Velasquez, Vo Hiep, and a woman, Angela Kirsch, from the *Daredevil*. He finished with Bjorn, Reality, and Miroslav from the Pioneers. Each of them stood as he called their names. "We have a lot of work to do and the weather is hot, but I grew up in southern Alabama, so I can tell you it can be done and it must be done. If you're going to draw resources from the colony, you're going to work for the colony. I believe I have Town Council approval for this."

Since Loretta gave an immediate approval, it didn't matter what Ibiana said. I didn't even see her vote. It did not go without a challenge, however.

A man stood up and gave his name as Ajit Mistry. "You can't do it that way. You're making new organizations, and it sounds like you're going to impose punishments if people don't do what you want. The Demos has to vote on these things. The Council can't simply do them."

Malachi proved ready for it. "Thank you, Ajit, for correcting me. I suppose I'm in a hurry with all the problems we have, but you're right. Our constitution is clear; matters like these require a vote of the Demos. Before I open the ballot field, though, let me say one thing. If the Demos votes against me, I will resign. If I'm to do the job you gave me, I need to be able to do it the best way I can. If you're not willing for me to do that, I'll step aside and you can figure it out."

I heard murmurs run through the assembly and saw plenty of worried faces. Malachi had made a stroke of genius, an offer there was virtually no chance of being accepted. In fact, the vote was 181–18 in support of Malachi.

"The final item for now," Malachi said, "is almost where we started. Jerry Whitehead. Whatever secrets of yours Jerry was holding, well, we'll wipe his storage areas on the network. Two people can watch the process so you can be sure nothing is transferred. Whatever Jerry had will be gone." There was close to a collective sigh of relief from the *Daredevil* colonists. "The other thing is," Malachi continued, "we don't know what happened to Jerry, as Leif said. Someone may have killed him, and that means we may have a murderer among us. Not saying who, 'cause I don't know, but someone. I'm sure that makes you as uneasy as it makes me. The *Dauntless* brought us some rifles. I'll take delivery from Leif personally, and I'll lock them up. There's a space in the reactor area that has double locks. Then we'll plan for a guard that can be called if there's trouble. Obviously, the guard will be people who know how to use a rifle. Just in case, like I said. The rifles will be locked up otherwise. Cam, Jess, you've been our Public Safety Squad, but this isn't what you do. I'd like you to keep your roles in case we have, well, social issues, but we need different people for this. We have a few with the right training, and since our ammunition is limited to what the ship brought, we can only afford to train a couple more. We can put this to a vote, if you want, with the same condition as before."

No one asked for a vote.

A message from Yong flashed on my field. YOU CAN SEE WHERE THIS IS GOING, it read.

YEAH, I sent back. But was that my problem, and Yong's? I remembered what Yong said a few nights ago. If they elected Malachi and he kept the colony alive, did it matter if he called himself king, or dictator, or whatever funny name he chose? It wasn't for me and Flygirl to impose someone or some system we chose. Not when we were going to fly away forever.

"Good," Malachi said. He gave the names of the people he would appoint to the guard. They were the same as his team leaders, minus the Pioneers, who obviously did not know how to use firearms. Malachi did promise that he would pick two of the Pioneer team leaders to be trained on the rifles. That was going to set up quite the competition in loyalty, and I knew it would be Bjorn and Reality who would be jostling each other for first place.

The meeting of the Demos should have been finished. Malachi had everything he could have wanted from it. However, before anyone could move to adjourn, one person stood up to be recognized. Penny. I could hear a groan run through the Pioneers as she gave her name.

"You haven't said anything about planting crops or about growing farm animals from the embryos," she said. "That's dumb. We can't eat ReadyMeals forever. We probably can't have big animals because of the climate, but there are plenty of small ones we can raise. And this is a lousy spot for the town because of the soil. That starts with the acid and the minerals, and there's more than that, but we have to try to grow some crops. Maybe we have to move the town."

"Pennywise, give it a rest!" That was Bjorn.

"Give us a break!" came from multiple mouths.

"Shut up," Penny said. "You don't know what you're talking about." She wrapped her arms around herself in a hug, in a futile effort to keep from shaking. Her face was a study in fright, but she did not sit down and she did not stop. "I don't see any of you growing anything except cannabis. Electric power won't do you any good if there's nothing to eat, and if we're going to eat, it looks like I'm going to have to grow the food. That river valley to the south looks like better land by drone, but we have to explore it, check the water, check the soil. I tried to tell Whitehead that we needed to take the small rover there, but all he could think about was being high. That and his dick. And I didn't touch him. And I mean not anywhere!" She screamed that as laughter ran through the crowd. Her hands dropped to her sides, fists clenched. "What about you, Mr. Oates? Maybe I can set up a farming station there, if it's good and you give me some panels. Can I take the small rover to the valley or do you just want to stay here and starve?"

There was probably a more diplomatic way for her to phrase that, but Malachi was grinning as he turned to me.

"Leif and I have already discussed taking a look elsewhere. Leif, why don't you take the rover and see what's there?"

"He doesn't know what he's doing!" Penny shouted.

Did I ever say she could be endearing? Her fists were so tight, I could see white knuckles from where I stood.

"When was the last time you self-drove a car, off-road, down a slope?" I asked. She stared at me. "Heading into the unknown is my business."

"But you don't know carbonates from borax!"

Well, she had me there. "Then bring your chemistry set and come with me," I said. "But if I tell you to stay away from something, or back off, you follow my orders. Otherwise, this colony is going to be short one farmer."

"I agree she should go," Malachi said. "If nothing else, it will be good if she is out of town for a little while." He turned back to the Demos. "Vo Hiep, you go with them also. That will improve the odds that the group comes back. We can't afford to lose a rover." He gave a soft laugh. "David will cover your team while you're away."

At Malachi's words, a young man stood up from the second row. His ident showed VO HIEP, AGE 23, NO SPECIALTY in my field. Malachi had called his name as both a team leader and a guard. He had his shirt off and I wasn't sure if that was a concession to the heat or to show off a washboard abdomen and a lean upper body with every muscle clearly etched under skin burned to obsidian by the sun. Black hair that fell to the base of his neck and thick eyebrows defined a square face devoid of expression. What also caught my eye was a scar on his upper left arm that had to be the entry wound from a bullet.

"Glad to do it, Malachi," Hiep said. "I'll take one of the rifles."

"Yes. Leif, you take one as well. And now," Malachi said, "I would like to adjourn this meeting of the Demos."

They all filed out of the Dome, headed for a ReadyMeal dinner and some sleep. Instead of spending my time trying to figure out what had happened to Jerry Whitehead, I was going to scout for farmland. On balance, I wasn't going to complain. This was more my line of work.

I guess Jerry was a dead issue.

CHAPTER SIXTEEN

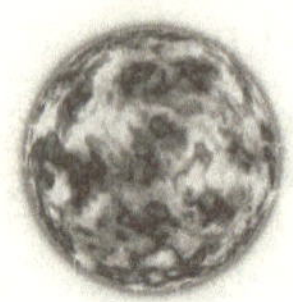

The next morning, I was up early in the dark to check out the explorer rover. This was the smallest of the colony's rovers. With its six big puncture-proof tires and ability to allocate power independently to each wheel, it could handle almost any grade or terrain. Based on the specs, it could probably climb a boulder. Like all the rovers, the vehicle had a layer of photovoltaic cells as skin over the metal and plastic to keep the battery charged, although the short daylight hours in this season limited its utility. That skin also made scrapes and kicked-up dirt a concern, which was a problem for a vehicle that was supposed to explore the unknown, but I would take those problems over a battery that ran out of juice. What the rover couldn't do was swim, but it came with an inflatable boat in a backpack that we could use if we decided to venture onto the river that ran through the valley.

While I was checking the rover's systems, Penny showed up, sun hat included. She had a pack on her back and was dragging two more behind her by their straps. She stopped to catch her breath, sweat dripping off the tip of her nose. Then she pulled the pack from her back and dumped it into the rear bay of the rover, where it made a loud *thunk* as it hit the flooring. I went to hoist one of the others into the rover, and the weight was a load even for me. I was surprised that she had managed to drag it from the Lab Unit to where the rover was parked. She tried to lift the remaining one over the rear gate of the rover, but couldn't raise it high enough. I grabbed it and swung it up and into the compartment.

"Thanks." She had her hands on her knees and dripped sweat into the dirt.

I would have liked something more along the lines of, *Sorry for some of what I said yesterday*, but that wasn't happening.

"What did you do?" I asked. "Haul out every analytical instrument in the Lab Unit? We can bring back samples, you know."

"I don't have the molecular analyzer unit; that takes up a whole lab bench. But I took what I could because bringing back samples isn't the way to do this. I need information in order to decide on other tests or what I should check next. We have to do this right, you know."

"Yeah, I get the concept." I paused. "Do you have any filter at all?"

She gave me a quizzical look. "You mean, like, for crystals or precipitates?"

"For your mouth."

I wasn't sure if all the wetness on her face was sweat. Shit. I hadn't expected to make her cry.

"I only get one chance to do this," she said very softly. "I have to do it right."

Vo Hiep picked that moment to amble up, rifle slung over one bare shoulder. He tossed his pack into the back and pulled himself into the rover, a walking display of muscle definition glistening in the sun that had now cleared the horizon. I saw Penny's eyes follow him. He could have been an ad for body oil or on the cover of a steamy e-book romance. I'm not flabby by any stretch of the imagination, but this was ludicrous. Maybe I'm a little vain.

"You don't need to make this trip," I said to Hiep. "I'm comfortable scouting and I can watch out for Penny." I chopped the name off short. I had almost said Pennywise, and I didn't want to do that. She looked so damned earnest.

"We elected Malachi as mayor," Hiep said. "He said to go. So, I go."

I noticed the easy, familiar way he handled the M8. I walked over to be next to where he sat in the rover and leaned close to him so our conversation was only between us. "You're going only because he could give you an order as mayor. You were in a different free company... before."

"Correct," Hiep said. "However, I do know Grand Company's... reputation."

The pause before his last word was obvious. That had to mean something, but if he was going to be cryptic, I could wait for the answer. I filed it for future reference.

"I appreciate the chance to go with you," Hiep said suddenly. "Whether Malachi said to or not."

I gave him a sharp look. "Why?"

"You're a pivotal figure in history," Hiep said. "If you hadn't killed Miles Richmond, maybe the New Golden Age never happens. The same way, perhaps, if Pontius Pilate hadn't ordered the Crucifixion of Jesus, maybe Christianity would never have taken off and history would be totally different. That's how important you are, and it's remarkable to have the chance to work with you."

I went to the driver's seat and busied myself with starting the rover. I was the Pontius Pilate of the New Golden Age. Great.

       .   .   .

No matter how flat a plain looks, it's not like driving on a paved road. As long as I kept our speed to about twenty miles per hour, though, the combination of the rover's tires and suspension smoothed out the ride well enough. The other nice feature of the rover was that the cabin could be enclosed. It had air-conditioning! After all the dreams of freezing as I came out of hib, I thought I would never want to be cold again, but the climate of Heaven—if you can call a sauna a climate—had cured that. Unfortunately, Penny kept her window open, which let the outside steam bath in.

She poked her head out the window from time to time to look at the grass, or the tire tracks in the dirt behind us, or the clouds in the sky. She chattered nonstop about what the tracks told us about the dirt, or what the root system of the grass must be like, or whether the gray bank of clouds ahead of us was the same as something called nimbostratus on Earth, or all sorts of other details that I couldn't see in this flat, boring plain. I decided that the talk was her way of covering up shaky nerves—and, hell, I'd seen worse ways of doing it. I tuned her out and concentrated on keeping the rover on a straight track for the valley. That was simple to do with no obstacles in the way and a map generated by the drone's flyover on-screen in the rover's dash, but at least I had something I could focus on. I thought the talk would drive Hiep crazy. But when I glanced back, he seemed to be listening closely. Whatever serves to pass the time, I thought.

A little over two hours of driving took us to the rim of the valley. The ground dropped away steeply at that point, so I stopped the rover and we got out for a look. The clouds had cleared during the drive and the distant sky across the valley had that ground-glass appearance I associated with hot August afternoons on ballfields in the US. A breeze blew across the rim where we stood, but offered no relief from the heat. The valley below, its image softened by haze, was so verdant as to make the plains we were on bleak by contrast. The broad river meandered through the middle of the valley, its banks bright green.

"This U-shape makes me think a glacier carved it," Penny said, "but that only makes sense if it wasn't always this hot. I'll bet it's fertile down there, especially by the river. I was afraid to go into the countryside at home because of that Super Lyme we have, but I'm sure it will be fine here. Can we name it Happy Valley?"

I shrugged. "First person to see it gets to name it, so Happy Valley it is. However, if you want to see if it's really happy and fertile, we have to get into it." I eyed the slope in front of us. "I make that to be about forty degrees."

"I agree with you," Hiep said.

"I've driven US military vehicles that can handle that grade," I said. A quick recheck of the rover's specs projected on my field showed that the rover ought to be able to do it also. "I'll drive it. As long as we go slow, it ought to be okay."

"I'll walk in front," Hiep said, "and check the ground."

"No mines here, Hiep."

His eyes locked on mine, unblinking. "None buried in the ground." His voice stayed soft and quiet. "I will check anyway. This will be close to the operational limits of the rover, and you will not want to drop a front wheel in a rut or hole you cannot see."

"Of course not," I said.

I don't think Penny understood that exchange, but for the moment, that was okay.

I inched the rover forward and we crawled sideways across the slope to a point Hiep indicated would allow us to make a switchback. We repeated that maneuver once more and then drove farther along the slope, angled slightly down. We hadn't descended very far before Penny started shrieking about some kind of rock. She was out of the rover and scrambling along the cliff before I could bring the thing to a halt and yell for her to stop. The rover wasn't the only thing that could tumble into the valley if it tipped over, and frankly, the rover had better balance.

The rock that had excited her was brownish and layered. She started chipping pieces into vials, which meant it couldn't be all that hard. She hustled back to the rover huffing and puffing, her prizes secured at her belt.

"Want to tell me what's so special about that rock?" I asked.

"It's sandstone!" she said. "I'm sure of it."

"What's special about that?"

"Sandstone. It's silica. There's a whole cliff of it and you can see it's washed down to the bottom. We can make glass out of it. And concrete."

"You're sure of that?" Hiep asked. "Just by looking at it?"

"Well, I have to test it, but I can do that when we stop for the day," Penny said. "That's why I brought all the equipment. I'll show you how it works."

The slope became gentler about halfway down as it gradually curved into the broad bottom of Happy Valley. That made the rest of the descent with the rover much easier. I could drive straight down the grade, but we still proceeded with Hiep walking in front because the grass grew taller on the lower slopes and holes remained a risk.

By the time we reached the bottom, Heaven's short day was near its end. I parked the rover where the land was flat, got out, and stretched. To our left was a stand of something between low trees and large bushes. None was more than ten feet high. Otherwise, the land around us was open.

"I'd like to check the trees," I said. "Just to be sure there's nothing hiding in them."

Hiep nodded. He went with me while Penny broke out her chemistry set. Watching him as he headed toward the trees reinforced my earlier impressions. He advanced with his rifle at the ready, scanning the ground from side to side, prepared for an enemy hidden in the trees. In a way, he was no different from me—but that was the point. The trees, when we reached them, were less interesting than our advance. Shellhounds were underneath, same as everywhere. They reached up, or climbed clumsily, to chew leaves on the lowest branches. We saw no other animals, on the ground or in the trees, nothing that could be called a threat.

Back by the rover, I pulled out ReadyMeals and water and we sat down to eat as twilight descended on Happy Valley. Penny was eager to talk about proving that the rock she had taken was sand—specifically, the kind of sand that went into glass and concrete. She was eager to continue talking about what minerals we should look for in order to make interesting types of glass, ones with colors or for cookware. I interrupted. There was something I wanted to clarify. Fast.

"Hiep," I said, "you're too young by several decades to have fought in the Troubles. I did, though, and I can see from how you move, especially with the rifle, you've seen action. No national militaries have done any fighting since the Treaties of '62, so you've been in combat with a free company. Right?"

The valley was quiet while Hiep studied his ReadyMeal, and Penny's eyes grew wide.

Then he said, "Yes," and was quiet again.

"You weren't with Malachi, though, you said. Not with the Grand Company."

"Also correct. I was Dragon Company, initially. I learned my soldiering skills from them. After a few years, I was exchanged to Sicarii."

"That sounds like a prisoner swap or property being sold," I said.

"More like a football player being traded," was his response.

"What made you come here?" I asked.

Hiep gave me a wry grin. "We had a contract for an assassination. Who or where doesn't matter. It was a setup, and we were taken. I wasn't the leader. No governments were after me. So they gave me the option of being released. But the Sicarii would have assumed I had turned informant to buy my freedom. They would have killed me. This was the other option."

"But you have seen combat."

"Of course," Hiep said. "I said so already. There is always one government willing to pay for a job here or there, and usually there is a fight. Sicarii trained me as an assassin. They taught me computer skills, network skills. They saw to it that I learned English, not simply learned it, but learned to speak it like I was born in America. How do I sound to you?"

I thought for a moment. If I hadn't known who he was, I would have guessed he came from somewhere in Ohio. I told him that.

He nodded. "They taught me how to learn, if you will, and I work hard at that. I can fight by myself, silent and dark, or in the field with a company. The world isn't as peaceful as people in wealthy countries like to think."

Malachi had said much the same thing. I wondered how many of these free companies were running around.

"But . . . but . . . free companies." Penny was practically spluttering. "You're . . ."

"Evil?" Hiep suggested. "All fangs and claws?" He bared his teeth and raised his hands.

"I'm sorry," she said. "That's what I see on the newsfeeds. Or did. That's how they show free companies. And Sicarius. The assassin company." She shuddered. "I read the book by Nathalie de Jong. *The Way of the Knife*. It was number one in current affairs on the Community for weeks!"

"Stupid title," Hiep said. "She didn't know what she was doing. All she could think of was sales. I will tell you there was debate over whether we should kill her."

"What side of the debate were you on?" I asked.

"I wasn't asked," Hiep said. "That was among commanders. I was a soldier."

"But if you had been asked?" Penny leaned forward.

"I would have killed her." Hiep leaned toward Penny when he spoke. "There was no need for all that detail to be published, not by someone who only wanted a sensation. I have even read that most people who downloaded it thought she made up all of it."

Penny's eyes grew even wider. I couldn't tell if it was rock star awe or pre-puke. "How can you say something like that?"

"You asked me a question," Hiep said. "I told you the truth. I always will."

After a time when we were all silent, but did nothing more than look at our food, Hiep spoke again. "Listen. We do fight and we do kill people. I make no excuses. Leif did the same in the Troubles. One thing I learned in the Dragons was about the US Rangers, that was Leif's unit, and Leif is famous anyway." He leaned closer to Penny. "Leif fought for his country in the Troubles. I fought for my company. For money. It's not so different. And here? And now? Even high explosives are safe without a detonator."

"I am sorry again," Penny said. "All I know about free companies is the vids and the newsfeeds. I never even traveled away from home, except to the school co-op farm or on school trips with a group. I was scared; my parents said I couldn't handle it. If I hadn't met Dustin and hadn't failed my exams and interviews, I'd probably still be at home. I don't know the world outside of books, and I didn't know anything about your people."

"Don't make me out to be a saint, now," Hiep said. "Ask Leif what fighting is like."

She looked at me. I was reluctant to talk, because Hiep was right. Combat was ugly. Killing, seeing your friends die, bleeding out in the dirt. So many scenes were in my mind despite all the years that had passed. Penny didn't need that visual detail. She also didn't need to hear how combat could make me feel truly alive, even if I could be dead in the next minute, and how I had looked for that feeling after I left the service. I suspected Hiep knew exactly what that feeling was.

"Hiep is right," I said finally. "I killed Russians and Chinese and their allies, because that's what the US Army sent me to do. Hiep killed because a government paid his company to do it. I decided I'm done with it and left. So did Pilot Yang. She and I are basically the same; we just fought on opposite sides."

It was an uncomfortable conversation. I had conflicting feelings about mercenaries. As a Ranger, I had been proud to be a member of a storied unit and I had been proud to serve in the US Army. Still, I hadn't enlisted in '55 out of patriotism or for honor. After my mom died, my father turned into a drunk and then a broke drunk. The army had been a reliable paycheck for a kid who couldn't afford the kind of college he wanted to attend. Given that, how different was I from Hiep? You could even argue that he was more honest about it. He said right up front that he fought for pay. Also, let's face it, when the shooting and dying start, you're fighting for the men and women who are there with you. Abstractions like honor and country don't exist in foxholes when you're taking fire.

I wondered if Yong might feel differently. She had been an academy girl, whatever the academy in China was called in those days, and had told me how patriotic she and her friends had been, although she had ultimately rejected the "us versus them" mentality that went with national pride. Would Yong think of mercenaries more the way Penny did? Penny seemed, on one hand, aghast at the idea that she was sitting next to a person who would kill on a contract yet ashamed of viewing him as less than her.

I had no answers to any of those questions and I wasn't going to ask them out loud. I set out the campsite wards and sat awake while the two of them slept. Meanwhile, the sky darkened. Stars twinkled in the high haze above us. I was struck again, as I had been at Dead Lake, by the absence of sounds in the night. Go camping on Earth, and the night is full of chirps and croaks. Not here. Not on Heaven. At least it should be more comfortable sleeping, now that we were down in the valley. If I had to sleep on the ground, I always preferred bottomlands to high, stony plains. The ground was softer, and as long as it didn't squish, I was fine.

That was when I became aware of eyes watching me, watching the three of us.

Those eyes were luminous, green like a cat's. I eased the phone base out of my equipment harness without making any noise or sudden moves. I switched the light on. Caught in the beam was an odd creature. If an iguana mated with a kangaroo, it would produce something like this. It had the size and general configuration of a baby roo, including the ridiculously oversized rear legs. Its skin was scaly green, however, and the tiny forelimbs ended in claws. A mouth that should have been too wide for the small muzzle gaped open, revealing a double row of sharp teeth.

The sawtooth roo stuck its head forward at me and into the field between two antennas of the ward. There was a snap and the head jerked back. I thought the animal would turn and run, but it didn't. Instead, it reared back on those huge hind legs and leaped. If that thing could play basketball, it would be a star. The height of the field was limited by the length of the antenna above the base. Seven feet. The damned roo cleared it with no trouble and landed inside our campsite with us.

Thank God I had my pistol on my belt! The one place a pistol is superior to a rifle is in tight quarters like this. I drew and fired two shots as the roo was aiming its teeth in my direction. Flesh and blood flew from the exit wounds, and the shot's impact knocked the roo down. It should have been dead, but it rose up again on its legs. One of the forelimbs was useless now, but the teeth were still there and its disposition had not improved. I fired again. Four shots, and all of them hit. It still didn't die, but the force of the bullets knocked it back into the ward field. A loud pop came from the field, the roo screamed, and lurched back toward me. Then it turned, bounded back over the ward and vanished into the dark.

I turned from searching the dark for the roo and saw both Hiep and Penny on their feet. I gave them a brief description of what had happened. "Those things are distressingly hard to kill," I concluded.

"We need to see the anatomy," Hiep said. "Anything living can be killed. We need to know the right places. Either that, or perhaps the M8 would be better. Those rounds are more damaging. In any case, I think we now know something that eats the shellhounds."

"Yeah." In a way, I found that reassuring. Something had to prey on those shellhounds, and finding it was like finding balance amid strangeness. However, it left us with a more immediate problem.

"We can eat shellhound meat," I said. "That means those roos may be able to eat us." I had faced that problem before.

"Makes sense," Penny said, more calmly than I expected her to. "If it judges the jump by the green lighting along the antenna, maybe we need to figure out how to extend the antennas by a couple of feet."

"We can work on that when it's light," I said. "I think we should sleep in the rover for tonight."

That was good from the safety angle, but not from a comfort perspective. The rover seats reclined and were padded, but they were not as close to a bed as a nice patch of soft ground. Also, we decided that having the windows wide open would not be much of an improvement on being on the ground. At the same time, I didn't want to run the air-conditioning all night. The storage batteries of the rover were limited. If I drained them keeping us cool, we would be stuck in the morning until the photovoltaics could recharge them. We settled for opening the windows a little because we needed some breeze but not to the extent we thought a roo could get its head through. I wound up dreaming of snakes slithering up the sides of the rover and into the opening we left in the window. I can't say any of us slept very well.

CHAPTER SEVENTEEN

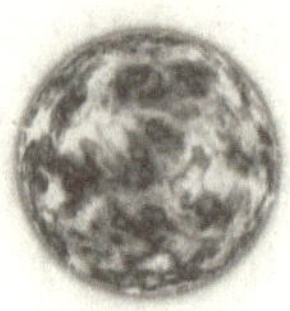

Fortunately, coffee will cure most of the problems of a bad night and we had plenty of coffee packets with our ReadyMeals. I won't say it was good coffee, mind you, but it was brown and rich in caffeine, which were the characteristics that counted. I didn't bother to heat mine. I had stim pills, too, in the medikit, but I wanted to save those in case we needed to go without any sleep.

We spent the day working in the area near where the rover was parked. One stretch of valley looked a lot like any other stretch of valley, if you excluded the river. Penny delayed her start barely long enough to bolt down some coffee and a protein bar. She did not stop for lunch. She kept herself busy digging up dirt and small plants and feeding all of it into the machines she had dragged along. We found that the shellhounds shed their shells as they grew, so Penny took samples of those as well.

There wasn't much for me and Hiep to do. Unless we went under the trees, which Penny did for a while, the valley floor was wide open. Nothing was going to sneak up on us, unless it could hide in three inches of grass or burrow under the ground.

Hiep slung his rifle and spent most of his time watching what Penny was doing. He would ask about the dirt, and the plants, and even the shellhound shit. That gave Penny license to talk a blue streak about all of it, along with whatever tangents flew into her head. She was a Community page given life, one of the ones stocked with vids of a personality answering this question or that and set so that when one vid finished, another would pop up, possibly chosen at random. Hiep shook his head a lot, but he listened. I wondered if Penny would have talked as much even if only the shellhounds were there to listen.

Hiep did take time for lunch. Afterward, I noticed that the display of musculature went under cover. "Why'd you put a shirt on?" I asked him.

"Penny nagged me," was his answer. "I never figured I would live long enough to worry about cancer, but the girl is less annoying this way."

That was good for a chuckle. I patrolled around our work area in ever-widening circles. The heat made me think of afternoon naps, and I suspected that if I didn't keep moving, I'd take one. I took time to pull some wire out of a parts box in the rover and jury-rig an extra two feet on the campsite ward antennas. It didn't look elegant, but it put the rods with their green lights higher. After a zap from the field if a roo tried to come between the wards, I hoped the extra height would dissuade one from trying to jump over it. I kept trying to warn myself that Heaven was deliberately lulling me into complacency and would strike the moment my mind wandered. For a guy who used to relish the brief moments of peace among crises, it was an odd sensation.

We moved closer to the river in the afternoon, which brought waist-high reeds and more need for attention, but other than flushing out shellhounds, nothing happened. The river and its banks we would leave for the next day.

My excitement for the afternoon was a call from Yong. The *Dauntless* was overhead to patch it through, which we needed since the valley wall blocked any direct transmission to St. Peterstown or the spaceplane. Yong kept emotion out of her voice when she was on duty, but I knew her well enough to pick up her exasperation.

"I've spoken with Dev," she said. He was one of our two nuclear engineers on the *Dauntless*. "He's reviewed the reactor circuitry and the outputs we can get. He thinks he'll need to bring down some boards and chips and play around, but we should be able to get the reactor back online."

That sounded promising, so why was I hearing an edge in her voice?

"I am having some difficulty with the spaceplane launch," she said when I was direct about it.

Yong "having some difficulty" was on a level with having your one-man outpost stormed by a thousand crazed zombies.

"Mechanical or spaceplane systems?" I asked. This was more than mild curiosity. Our only way back to the *Dauntless* was on that spaceplane.

"Neither. The spaceplane is fine. The problem is that, while I had it open to reload the bots we used for moving the cargo of the first load out, six Leavers got into the passenger cabin. They're refusing to leave and demanding that I take them up to the *Dauntless* so they can return to Earth."

An interstellar sit-in. Lovely. "That would set a bad precedent, never mind our conversation with Sonal about the risk of losing people."

"I agree," she said. "Apparently, Malachi is making people work. Unfortunately, when I called him, his first thought was to send one of his so-called guards with a rifle."

"I'm starting to worry that our new mayor of St. Peterstown is developing a taste for dictatorship."

"It's not our concern how they run this place. However, I have no intention of having one of his pets waving a rifle around the spaceplane and possibly shooting. If I wanted to do that, I have a pistol, but I do not want to risk putting a bullet into the spaceplane. I told Malachi I would shoot any armed individual I see around the LZ. I think he believes me."

Believing Yong was a good idea. "We don't need a war here."

"No."

"How are you going to get them out of the spaceplane?"

"I think I will tell them that I am going to take off and will vent the cabin when I make orbit. That should do it. We will have to be careful about the spaceplane when I return."

When I was finished with Yong, I found Penny waiting for me at the rover with Hiep behind her. She held a small vial of white powder. She shook it back and forth and watched the powder flow around the vial. For some reason, that made her giggle. Then she looked at the screen of an instrument she had set up on one of the rear seats. Something displayed there made her giggle also. She shook the vial again and giggled some more.

"Care to let me in on the joke?" I asked.

"I was just thinking."

Penny thinking could be dangerous. "About what?"

"Know what this is?" She tapped the vial.

"That's from the piece of back shell from the shellhound you had me grind up," Hiep said. "That's what's left after I added the liquid you gave me."

"Right," Penny said. "Cleaned it up, got rid of the organic gunk. These are the minerals from that piece. It's a mixture, of course. I thought it would be, like, seashells, calcium carbonate, but some of it is zinc oxide. How funny is that?"

She opened the vial and stuck a forefinger in. The fingertip came out white. She stepped over to me and drew a line down the bridge of my nose.

"It's sunscreen!" She giggled again, blushed, and looked down at the ground like a shy teenager. "You should use it, Leif, with your skin under this sun. We could build a sunscreen factory here!"

"Why is zinc oxide in a shellhound?" Hiep asked.

"I don't know." Penny grew serious again. "The soil samples show more zinc than on Earth. Some plant, maybe more than one, must take it up, and the shellhounds eat lots of plants. Those hounds must have an enzyme that makes zinc oxide, although I can't think why. Maybe it protects them from the sun. First thing to do is find the plant."

Penny leaned into the back bay of the rover and fished in her pack. She came out with a pair of leather gloves, which she put on. Then she reached back into the pack and came out with a sheathed knife with a red handle.

"Why the gloves?" I asked.

"Cut-proof," she said. "Leather over cut-proof polymer. I got this knife at a specialty store in Portland. It will cut anything. I wanted to use it when I did my farmwork for my degree, but I didn't take it out for a year, because I was so scared I would cut myself. I couldn't use it until I got these gloves. With these on, I won't cut myself. Now let's go get some big plants and branches!"

She whipped the blade out of the sheath. It was eleven inches of thin and menacing steel. Knife in carefully gloved hand, she marched off to do battle with the plant kingdom.

It didn't take too long for her to find what she wanted. The little berries on the thistle plant turned out to be loaded with a protein that bound zinc. The shellhounds ate the berries and absorbed the zinc, turning themselves into a walking display of lifeguard sunscreen. That started Penny tracking what the shellhounds did, from cataloging what they ate to taking a shit. I thought she took an excessive interest in shellhound shit. She looked at it, charted where they dumped it, and scooped chunks of it into sample tubes destined for her instruments. I had no idea what she was looking for. The one thing I could tell from a close encounter was that shellhound shit smelled like any dogshit.

Heaven's star was dipping toward the horizon, casting long shadows in our valley. The wind from the west picked up, as it usually did around dusk, but neither that nor the fading light brought much change in the temperature. Gray clouds were building up overhead. I wanted to set our camp for the night and eat, but Penny was still away from us. She stood, arms akimbo, staring down at a patch of ground. She hadn't moved in several minutes, so I walked over to see what had her transfixed. Aside from its white to gray color with little brown flecks, it looked like a pile of dogshit. Shellhound shit, in this case.

"Penny? What's up?"

"This."

"It's shit."

"Ayuh."

I think that meant yes.

She didn't turn. "It's shellhound poop. But see this?" She pointed with one finger to where a small purple thistle had sprouted from the edge of the shit pile. "This fits so perfectly."

At that moment, I wanted to eat and settle down for the night. I have eaten all sorts of things out of necessity and I've done it under conditions I don't want to describe or remember, but digging through shit before dinner was not what I wanted to do.

"Will you come join us? I'll put your ReadyMeal on a rock so it warms up."

"It's not that hot here." She had a shy grin, which she kept aimed mostly at the ground, but walked back to the rover with me.

When the three of us had our ReadyMeals open, I asked, "What is so fascinating about that shit?"

"The poop, you mean? It's the thistle and the poop."

I knew where this was going to lead, but I had to ask. "Why?"

"Well, those thistles are angiosperms. They have fruits around their seeds. I wouldn't expect them because of where the animal evolution is, but they are here. The shellhounds eat all sorts of vegetation and plants—anything, really. They'll even eat leaves from the lower tree limbs if they can get to them, which is interesting because they're not adapted to eat tree leaves, but we don't see any animals that are, so they've filled that niche, but what's interesting is when you or an animal eats protein and breaks it down, that makes ammonia, which is toxic, so your body converts it to less toxic compounds you excrete, and that poop is full of guanine, which means there are enzymes for the urea cycle here like on Earth and that's why the thistle there in the poop is so interesting, and—"

"Penny!"

She blinked. "Sorry. It's exciting. The shellhounds eat those thistles. The seeds go through the shellhound and come out in the poop, which is loaded with guanine. That's like guano on Earth. It's wicked good fertilizer. So the thistles can spread and grow even on ground where the soil isn't that good. That means we can do it too! I can make a farm with plants that grow in hot weather and—"

"Penny, okay, I get it now."

"There's more. Because of the shellhounds, I think I'm almost putting it together."

She sounded happy. Her face was as happy as I had ever seen it. Her mind had gone rocketing down a dozen tangents at the same time and there was a conclusion in there, somewhere. That made her happy in spite of the heat, the dirt, and the sensation the colony was on the edge of disaster. It was a good thing we had her. I glanced over at Hiep, figuring he would be focused on his food, but his eyes were riveted on Penny. His food hadn't been touched.

"How do you know so much about so many different things?" Hiep asked.

Even in the twilight, I could see Penny blush. She kept her eyes on the ground, where she was digging a small trench with the heel of one boot. "I just read. Anything and everything. That's all I do, really. If it wasn't for school, I'd hide in my room and chip in and be reading something. My parents thought there was something wrong with me."

"I can't believe that's all you did," Hiep said. "A pretty girl and so smart, you must have had boys chasing you."

"I am not pretty, Vo Hiep," Penny said. "Don't try to tell me otherwise. And boys don't like smart. No one ever paid attention until Dustin." She stopped to sniffle. "I'm sure it worked the same way where you went to school."

"I stopped going to school when I was fourteen," Hiep said.

That brought Penny's head up so that she faced him. "Why? Why did you stop? I can tell you're not stupid." She shook her head quickly. "I'm sorry. I didn't mean to say it that way. I can tell, when you talk, the questions you ask, you're smart."

"I've been smart enough to stay alive," Hiep said. "When I was fourteen, Dragon Company came to my village. I told you I was in Dragon Company; that's when I joined them. That's why I didn't go to school anymore."

"Why did you go with them?" Penny asked.

"The alternative was to be killed and have my family killed too." Hiep tossed a pebble into the dark. "That's the way it is in our New Golden Age. For some of us, anyway."

Penny hugged her knees to her chest. "I'm sorry."

"Don't be," Hiep told her. "You had nothing to do with it."

I thought again of what Malachi had said to me. The New Golden Age was nothing more than the Troubles by a fancy name.

"Hiep, do you want first or second watch tonight?" I asked.

"I'll take first," he said. "You and Penny get some sleep."

The clouds overhead chose that moment to unleash a torrent of rain, along with thunder and lightning. We beat a hasty retreat into the rover and couldn't test my extended antennas that night.

CHAPTER EIGHTTEEN

The next day started with us moving the rover toward the riverbanks so we could investigate that area and maybe play in the Happy River, as Penny dubbed it. Otherwise, we divided up the labor much as we had before. I patrolled around, looking for anything new and interesting and stood guard as a fresh air inspector. Penny went after samples of dirt and mud from the banks of the river and, armed with her impenetrable gloves and sharp knife, cut reeds, thistle, and bush branches. Hiep again turned himself into her assistant, digging up this and that and running everything back to the rover for later analysis. Penny gave him a quick tutorial on some of her instruments, and he picked it up fast enough that she had him doing some of the analysis.

"If you can keep those going," I heard her say, "I want to get some water samples and some stuff from the river bottom where it's shallow."

She pulled off boots and socks and sank into the muddy riverside. Long, rodlike stalks grew there and different ones poked up from the water. Based on the colors of the flowers, several varieties of the basic thistle grew there, while some of the reeds in the water were almost as stiff as wood. Penny sawed through a few with her knife and stuffed the stalks in a sack that hung from her belt. Shellhounds walked through the reeds, ignoring Penny, and munched on everything within their reach.

They would crane their heads up to reach the thistle flowers and swallow the clusters of berries that grew from the branching points of the leaves. Penny stopped what she was doing to watch one of them as it flicked a tongue out to the underside of a leaf cluster, then chomped down on leaf and berries together.

I watched the two of them. Kids on a field trip. I was useless.

Hiep studied the thistles, too, probably because Penny was focused on them. He pulled off some of the leaves near the crown of one, and some flower petals, and rolled them in his fingers.

"There's some kind of oil on or in the leaves," he called out.

"Yes!" Penny shouted back from the edge of the river. "I've seen little beads of it. I wonder if that's what attracts the shellhounds."

The air was suffocating and we were all sweating. Standard operating procedure for Heaven. Hiep straightened up from the thistle he had plucked and wiped his hand across his face to clear the sweat.

A minute later, he called out. "Leif, something's wrong. My eyes hurt. I don't think I'm seeing right, like the light's dim. Something in those leaves?"

I rushed over as fast as I could. He turned toward me as I came close. My eyes riveted on his, and those eyes were all I could see. His pupils had constricted down to tiny little pinpoints. The whites and rims were bloodshot. I felt as though I had been hit in the gut with a sucker punch.

"Nerve gas!" The words tore out of me in a scream.

In that instant, I was back in Central Asia. The Russians had hit one of our units with a nerve gas attack. We were moving up as fast as we could in full chemwar suits to block the Russian advance and keep them from exploiting the hole they had torn through our defense lines. I came on one of our soldiers—a boy, really, younger than I was, and I had just turned nineteen. His eyes were classic pinpoints, the whites injected red. Snot was running out of his nose and across his lips mixing with drool; he had crapped and pissed himself; his breath was coming in labored wheezes. Of all the miserable ways to die on a battlefield, nerve gas is one of the worst.

I had my chemwar kit. My fingers were clumsy, made so both by the horror in front of me and by the impenetrable gloves of my suit. I slammed the injectors for the antidotes, atropine and 2-PAM, against him and hoped they would do some good. Then I moved forward toward the sound of gunfire and never saw if he lived or died.

I pulled myself away from the nightmare that lived in my head. There was no gunfire on Heaven.

"What? What are you saying?" Hiep was asking, staring at me with the same eyes as that dying soldier.

"Fuck!" I yelled, then turned and ran for the rover. I leaned my rifle against the side of the vehicle and reached for the PCAD, the personal chemical agent detection monitor—and no, I was on Heaven, not under attack in Central Asia. No PCAD! I jerked my hand back, tried to think, and knocked the rifle onto the ground. The medikit! I reached for that and yanked it out of the vehicle, my breath coming in heaving gasps. The medikit banged against the holstered pistol on my belt. I put the pistol on the seat and clipped the medikit to my belt so it wouldn't swing around, leaving both hands free. I spun back around and started toward Hiep, then stopped halfway. Why would this kit have atropine and 2-PAM? What could I do if those drugs weren't there?

While I stood, frozen, and racked my brain, I saw, past Hiep, something rise out of the reeds at the river behind Penny. She was focused on us, trying to figure out what the hell was going on with Hiep, his hands on his face, and me, acting like a crazy man. The creature behind her looked like a small gator, its hide a lumpy, mottled green and brown. The snout was long and narrow and ended in a curved beak as sharp as an eagle's. The jaws opened wide and were full of needle-tipped teeth. All of this was on a doglike undercarriage, four legs and a tail.

Penny looked over her shoulder and saw it. She shrieked and tried to run away but stumbled as she pulled her feet free of the muck of the riverbank. She flailed at the gator with her knife; she had no idea how to use it for defense.

The gator lunged. Its jaws snapped closed on Penny's lower leg. Her screams filled the entire valley.

I yanked the medikit off my belt and dropped it. Thoughts can fly through your head in no time in a crisis. My weapons were at the rover. Hiep had his rifle, but what about his vision? He might be as likely to hit Penny as the gator. Or the other side of the valley. If I went back to the rover or to Hiep for one of the weapons, that gator would roll Penny into the water and keep rolling her under the surface. That's what a gator on Earth would do to drown its prey. I'd have no target, not unless I got right on top of them, and the extra time to get a firearm would cost her life. I spotted the red handle of Penny's knife on the bank, where she had dropped it when the gator bit. I sprinted for the river.

I scooped up Penny's knife and launched myself into a dive, landing on the gator's rigid back. Those bumps on its skin were as hard as a tortoise shell. I ignored them. My weight squashed it down. Its legs couldn't bear up under the weight of a human—and I'm six-three and 220 pounds. The gator opened its jaws and let out a screech of its own. Penny wriggled up the bank, pulling at the ground with both hands and pushing with her uninjured foot. I slammed the knife, all eleven inches of titanium-hardened steel, into the top of the creature's head.

The knife in its head served only to annoy the gator. It lashed its tail and tried to twist its neck around to get its teeth on me. What was the deal with this thing? No brain in the head?

Its jaws snapped closed but, thankfully, bit only air. I got my left arm around its snout and squeezed the jaws together. As powerful as those jaws might be in biting down, they weren't designed to force themselves open against pressure. It was a precarious position, but between my weight on top of it and squeezing its jaws together, I had bought myself a few moments.

I yanked the knife up and free of the skull. Then I reached under and cut deep into the neck. I sliced the goddamn head right off the body. The legs and tail kept thrashing, but I was able to throw myself free. The headless gator continued to splash around in the shallow water until it finally collapsed.

I scooped up Penny, who was crying and retching all at the same time. I carried her away from the river and laid her down on dry grass. Her knife was still in my hand, and it was an effort to loosen the vise of my fingers and put that down next to her. Hiep ran over to us. His pupils were still pinpoint and his eyes were red, but otherwise he seemed okay.

"We need to take care of her. And why were you yelling about nerve gas?" he demanded.

I picked up the knife, cut off part of a sleeve and used that to put pressure on the wound where most of the bleeding came from. While I was doing that, I told him about his eyes. "I've been on a chemwar battlefield. That's what it looks like. One of the things anyway. How about the rest of you? Your nose isn't running; I don't see drool. Any stomach cramps? Any breathing trouble?"

"No. Nothing."

"Maybe whatever is in those leaves isn't absorbed so easy. You got it on your hands and wiped your eyes. It got into your eyes but nowhere else. Penny was cutting the plants, but she had gloves on." I could spare only a moment's thought just then. Hiep wasn't dying and Penny needed help urgently. "Go wash your hands," I ordered Hiep. "Pull some wipes out of the medikit, scrub 'em and dry 'em off on the ground. Don't touch the thistles. Then come back here with the medikit. I'll bet your eyes will normalize, but it may take a day or two. I don't think we have atropine in the medikit."

He went to follow my instructions and I lifted the bloody cloth to see what the bleeding was doing and to examine Penny's leg. The back of her left leg was a bloody mess. It had been filleted from just below the knee through the calf muscles. Blood welled up from the wound and spilled out onto the ground. It wasn't spurting up into the air, so at least no artery had been cut. I could stop the bleeding with pressure. The baggy pants of her Pioneer outfit had saved her leg, and maybe her life. The pant leg was much wider than the skinny leg under it, but the gator hadn't known that. It must have thought the pants were part of its target. That, and Penny must have moved just enough that the gator got a mouthful of Pioneer pants instead of chomping down across her lower leg. That beak at the tip, though, had caught her leg and ripped it open.

Once the bleeding had mostly subsided, I had her lie facedown. I cut the pant leg away to get a good look. It was a deep and ugly laceration, almost the full length of her calf. It was going to take two layers of sutures for sure. The saving grace was that it was rather straight and clean. I didn't see other punctures. I could treat this. Rangers often operated in the middle of nowhere, far from any help. We were trained to take care of each other, and I had worked on worse wounds on battlefields. My paramedic training afterward also helped. As I finished my assessment, Hiep came back with the medikit.

"Penny, I need to talk to you," I said.

The reply I got was a sniffle and a sob.

"Penny! I need to tell you what's going to happen and what I'm going to do. I need you to understand."

"I can hear you!" she screamed. Even with her face in the grass, it damn near deafened me.

I told her about the leg, what I saw when I examined it. "I think I can put a nerve block in. I'll put a needle in behind your knee to numb the back of your leg and most of your foot. It won't get everything on the inside part near your shin, and maybe not at the very top of this cut, but I can shoot some numbing med in there if it hurts. Then I'm going to clean it out with antiseptic. Really clean it. I'll get rid of any tissue that looks dead. Once I've got it clean, I'm going to suture it—that is, I'm going to sew it closed. I'm no surgeon and we don't have a surgi-bot out here, but I can do it. I'll load you up with antibiotics in case you got Earth bacteria in there from your skin or pants. If there are Heaven bugs that can infect you, well, I don't know that our antibiotics will do much. That's why I'm going to clean the hell out of it before I close it. It's going to hurt after the block wears off. I can give you pain meds to help. Once I get it all ban-daged, we'll load you into the rover and get you back to St. Peterstown."

I was prepared for screaming but not for *what* she started screaming.

"No! No! No! You won't do that! You're not doing that!"

"Penny, I have to take care of your leg. That's not really a choice."

"Yes, yes! I know that. Don't be so stupid! But you're not taking me back! You're not!" She pulled her gloves off and ripped up chunks of grass and dirt in clenched fists.

"Penny, listen to me. If your leg does get infected, especially with something from here, you'll need the Medical Unit at St. Peterstown. Even then, worst case, you could lose the lower leg. But out here, if it goes bad, you could die. Do you get that?"

"Yes, I get it!" Even prone on the ground with her face in a tuft of grass, she got a lot of volume out. "And if it's an infection from something here, I could die anyway and don't you try to tell me otherwise. Right?"

"Odds are better with the Medical Unit and the doc."

"You're the one who doesn't get it!" She twisted her shoulders and neck, to scream that to my face. Her cheeks were soaked with tears. "I heard what you said, Leif Grettison. I heard you say I could die. And I am scared of dying. And I'm scared of being hurt. And I'm scared of being alone. I'm nothing but a scared little girl from outside Portland who's never really gone anywhere. I'm scared of almost everything!" She paused for a sob and a breath. "But you listen to me, Leif Grettison and you, too, Vo Hiep. This is the first time anything depends on me, and you better believe me, everything does. We can't live up where the town is now, we're not going to make it the way we're set up. We need to know if we can make it here. I know how to do this. You don't. Nobody else up there does. Bots won't do it by magic. So I better put my big-girl pants on and do my job. And if I get so scared I shit my pants, I'll just have to clean it up and keep going. And if you don't like it, fuck the both of you."

Until that moment, I didn't think Penny's vocabulary included the word *fuck*. "Look, it's one thing to say you can take the pain. It's different to actually deal with it, step by step, all day and to put it out of your mind when you have to work."

"I don't care." Penny's tone was firm, even if her face belied her words. Tears ran down her cheeks and snot dripped from her nose. "I don't care. This is the first actually important thing I've done in my entire life and I'm not going back, and I'm not quitting because I got a chunk of my leg bitten out. You need me to do this!"

Before I could come up with a response, I felt Hiep touch my arm.

"Leif," Hiep said, "in the companies, I learned about you and the unit you were part of during the Troubles. If you had a mission, a vital one, you would complete it even if it could cost your life. Even if you *knew* it would cost your life. I would as well."

What he said was true, even if I wasn't fond of being reminded of it.

"We should allow Penny to do what we would do," Hiep said.

There wasn't anything I could say to that. I knew Yong would say the same, and I knew, for certain, what she would do herself in such a situation. I opened up the medikit and prepared to play surgeon.

Penny wouldn't take a lot of pain med. As scared as she said she was about being hurt, maybe she was more afraid that if I gave her enough to make her loopy or put her out, I'd pack her up in the rover and head back to town. I sighed, then pulled up the reference I wanted from the ship's library and studied the diagram for this nerve block. Then I studied the landmarks made by Penny's tendons and muscles at the back of her knee. Skinny as she was, they were easy to find. I loaded a syringe, stuck the needle in where it needed to go, and injected while she grabbed on to Hiep's arm and hand with a ferocity that dug in her chipped and bitten-off nails to the point where I wondered if I'd need to treat him for lacerations. He held her hand all the way through the ordeal.

In the end, I got the wound clean and closed. Time would tell if I had done it well enough. It was going to leave a nasty scar. No question about that. My training was practical, not cosmetic. When I was done, Penny rolled over and we helped her up. She put her arms over both our shoulders and walked, one legged, between us back to the rover. She found the energy to ask for her sun hat. I had glimpsed it in the water while we were getting her up the bank and fetching it had not been high on my priority list. When she asked, I looked back at the river but it had either sunk or been swept out of sight. She couldn't manage a protest.

None of us felt like eating. Hiep and I put Penny in the rover. We wrapped her leg in whatever we could find that was soft and protective and told her not to move around until feeling returned. I told Hiep to get in as well. I wasn't ready to trust the extension to the antennas without someone keeping watch. I wasn't going to do that all night by myself, and I wasn't going to trust Hiep's eyes in the dark, so I climbed in also. Even though the sun was still up, and without the ability to 'paque the windows, the two of them fell asleep.

While I listened to both of them snore, I thought about what had happened. To Hiep more than to Penny. Most nerve gases were compounds that blocked the breakdown of a specific chemical transmitter in the nervous system, acetylcholine. The symptoms were stereotyped. Once I started thinking about it, a memory from a few days ago bothered me and wouldn't go away. With the *Dauntless* overhead, thanks to its geosynchronous orbit, I chipped in to the rover's system and used the link through the *Dauntless* to access the records at the Medical Unit I had seen before. Yes, Jerry had had mucus running out of his nose before he died. Francesca had made a point of it because to her, that meant no one had smothered him with a pillow. She'd also noted that he emptied his bowels and bladder and attributed that to his sphincters relaxing after death. Which is what happens. However, Jerry's chip had a record of when his heart stopped. It also had a time stamp for his bowels and bladder activity. That was something I'd always hated about chipping in when I was in boot camp. The drill sergeant knew what you had done and when you did it. The chips we had gotten after we returned from the first starshot were even fancier—that is, more intrusive—than the ones that were around when I joined the army.

Examining Jerry's records told me that he'd gone in his pants *before* he died, not after. That was another thing nerve gases could make you do, just like the poor soldier I saw in my flashback. There was nothing in the record about Jerry's eyes. Of course, he hadn't been found for several hours after his death. All muscles relax after death, including the iris. How long did it take for the iris to relax after nerve gas killed you? I didn't know that, and I couldn't find it with a quick search.

Had Jerry been killed with an irreversible acetylcholinesterase inhibitor—a form of nerve gas? The findings fit, mostly. But how could it have gotten into him? If that's what was in the thistle leaves, the only effect on Hiep was to his eyes. The thistles were all over. Could Francesca have figured this out also? As a doc she might know, and she had reason to hate Jerry. Well, everyone seemed to have a reason to hate Jerry. Even Penny. Who was really smart.

Did she know about the thistle leaves? Was she really wearing gloves because of the knife? I didn't want to think about that. And anyway, how could it have gotten into Jerry? It's not as though he was gassed in his hab. Vanessa would have keeled over the next morning when she went in. Except the air system had been on. How long would that take to clear the air? I fell asleep wondering about all of it.

CHAPTER NINETEEN

The next morning, Hiep's pupils were still pinpoint, but the pain behind his eyes was almost gone. Penny gasped and grabbed at her leg the moment she moved it. I took the dressing down and looked at the wound. It was clean. Blood had seeped into the dressing, of course, but I saw no sign of infection. She had a hand over her mouth when she saw the dressing, and there was another gasp when she twisted around and saw the wound. I put a new dressing on it and told her to stay out of the water. Otherwise, she could do her work.

I expected that she would take one step out of the rover and decide that going back to St. Peterstown was a really good idea. That didn't happen. Oh, she cried out the instant she tried to walk. In fact, she nearly fell over the first time she put any weight on her leg, but she managed to steady herself with most of her weight on her right. I heard a loud "Fuck!" and then she took her knife and hobbled around the rover so that it was between her and us. She emerged a few minutes later, having hacked off the other pant leg to convert her pants into a pair of shorts.

"Hiep, can you bring my equipment?" she called back over her shoulder. "I don't think I can carry much."

With that, our all-guts, no-glory girl was off. The morning went by with Penny limping around, giving Hiep directions on what to do, along with rambling explanations of what it was about, and leaning on him for all the actual work. Sometimes, she was leaning on him physically as well. When we broke for lunch, she had dirt on her knees and tears on her cheeks but no quit in her voice.

While we were opening ReadyMeals, I asked her about the thistle leaves.

"I don't know what happened," she said. "I think something in the thistle, the flower or the leaves, attracts the shellhounds so that they eat the berries and that's how the plant spreads."

I explained about the chemical transmitter, how it works in nerves, and what happens when the enzyme that breaks it down is blocked, the way nerve gas does.

"There are insecticides that used to do that," Penny said. "I know about them; anybody who knows about farming does, or should. They were banned fifty years ago because people can get poisoned and die. I don't have the right instruments here to tell me if some compound in the thistle has that kind of chemical structure. We need the molecular analyzer in the Lab Unit. Maybe what the shellhounds use for nerves uses a different chemical transmitter. Or they have a different enzyme. No reason the chemistry can't be different. I'll work it out."

I put up a hand to stop her. "Penny, it may be better if you're not the one who does this work."

"Why? I know how to use the instrument. I'm good." She looked indignant.

"It has nothing to do with your ability," I hastened to say. "With all the talk about you and Jerry, it's just better if someone else does this analysis. We'll talk to Francesca when we get back. Let the doc do it."

She frowned. "Okay, I get it." Both her face and her tone said she didn't like it. Then she brightened. "But for some things, like soil, chemistry is chemistry, and that's what we have here."

I could see we were headed down a classic Penny tangent. She did not disappoint.

"There's a limestone layer low in the valley wall," she said. "I'm sure of it, even if I can't get into the rock."

"Why? And what difference does it make?"

I was the straight man setting up the comedian for a zinger, but I couldn't help it. Hiep munched a bar out of his ReadyMeal, but I could see him intent on what she said, as always.

"It neutralizes the acid," she said. "The soil isn't as acid down here, and we've checked a lot of sites now. It's in the water coming down, but the soil isn't bad. Between that and all the dirt washed down, that's why Happy Valley is so green. We can grow Earth crops here; I can. We need to take the rover downstream. I want to get to the bay we saw on the drone camera."

If limestone made her happy, I was all for it, but moving farther away from St. Peterstown would add to the risk we were already taking. "Are you sure your leg can take it?" I asked. "If you've got what you need, why push your luck?"

Penny shook her head. "I think I'm getting what's happened here. We need to get down to the bay. I promise, I won't go swimming." She tried to laugh, but it didn't work. I could still see the pain in her face.

"I vote we go forward also," Hiep said.

"Who the hell said we were voting?" I grinned at both of them. "Or gave the two of you votes?"

When I started the rover, I headed it downstream toward the bay.

·   ·   ·

We could have made it to the shoreline that day, but I was driving slowly. The farther we went from St. Peterstown, the chancier getting back would be if anything happened to the rover. Hiep and I could make it, but Penny probably couldn't. I wasn't sure she could make a hike like that even if her leg were sound. As the light of Heaven's short day began to fail, I called a halt and ignored Penny's protests that we were almost there. Driving in poor light simply increased the risk that I would drop a wheel in an unseen hole.

After our usual dinner of ReadyMeals, I left Penny to work with her samples and instruments and Hiep to listen to her lecture about all of it. I strapped on my pistol, picked up my rifle, and took a walk. Widely spaced ranks of ten-foot-high trees, like the ones we had seen farther up the valley, grew on all sides. To the left of the rover, the crown of a low hill projected above their leafy tops. I climbed to the top, where I could hear the sounds of surf and see the ocean at the horizon, even if the shoreline below was hidden from view. Heaven's three moons were all in the sky, casting a pearly light across the landscape. It was enough light, and the hilltop offered enough open ground, that I did not think a sawtooth roo, or any other marauder, would be able to sneak up on me.

It says something about me, I suppose, that I thought about clear fire zones first and only noticed how pretty the quiet scene was afterward. That was my training, though, and my training was the reason I'd stayed alive to be on that hill. A breeze coming down the valley picked up and made my shirt flap. I wished for a truly cool breeze, but at least it wasn't as hot as the one that blew during the day. I pulled myself away from the scene and back to the purpose of my evening ramble. Despite there being only three people on this planet within multiple days' drive, I'd climbed up here to make a private call.

As it had when I searched the records before, the rover's transmitter and antenna boosted my phone signal to the *Dauntless* and the ship connected me to Yong. As it turned out, she was on board, having brought the spaceplane up while we were driving through the valley.

"No further trouble with your sit-in group?" I asked.

"No. They took my threat seriously."

That was wise, I thought. I told her what I had learned about the thistle plant and what that might mean for the mystery of Jerry's death, which was why I wanted a private conversation.

"I'm sure you're right about what killed him," she said. "The Russians used chemwar agents along the Ussuri and in Mongolia. I didn't see the actual casualties, but our command made sure we all saw vid and photos. Every night for a while. We responded in kind, of course."

"Of course." In her own way, Yong was as trapped in memories of the Troubles as I was. That wasn't something I wanted either of us to dwell on. "Penny thinks we can use the molecular analyzer at the Lab Unit to see if there is a cholinesterase inhibitor in the leaves."

"Maybe." Her one-word comment was hard and doubting at the same time. "Song Jing had some training in biochemistry and cell biology before she became a doctor. I'll ask her to come down on the second run, along with Dev. I don't want to leave the analysis to someone who's not trained to do it and who could be the killer. You are too unwilling to consider that possibility."

I wasn't unwilling to consider the possibility. I simply didn't think it was true. "I already told her to leave the analysis to Balboni. And Penny's not the only possibility," I added. "You're too sure it's her."

"I am not," Yong said. "And we don't know how good Francesca Balboni is with this sort of specialized equipment. I would be more comfortable with Jing. For that matter, you haven't mentioned Malachi as a possible culprit. He told you, I gather, that he's a chemist, and he is a Remainer. He also told you what happened when they fed the thistle to mice."

"Malachi is a blow-'em-up kind of chemist. Anyway, he was with me out at Dead Lake that night. And Malachi wouldn't be the only one who knew about the mice."

I had the feeling the conversation was turning into a cataloging of what I had overlooked or failed to consider, so I changed the topic. I told Yong about what we were doing in the valley and what we were finding. I was complimentary about how Hiep and Penny were working together, especially about how Penny was carrying on despite her leg. All right, maybe I babbled and gushed a bit about how Penny was soldiering on. I *was* impressed. I hadn't thought she could do it.

As I went on about how Penny was doing, Yong grew quiet and when she did speak, she was curt. We finished the call soon after, because she didn't have anything more she wanted to say.

I mulled the conversation over before I left the privacy of the hill. I hadn't talked *that* much about Penny before Yong cut me short. Well, maybe I had, but why should that bother her? Was that Flygirl being jealous? Who would have thought it possible? I hadn't said anything wrong, and God knows, I hadn't done anything wrong. I hadn't done anything. I wasn't interested in Penny. Not in that way. Watching Penny and Hiep in the valley was like keeping a benevolent eye on grandchildren. Okay, I never even had kids that I know of, but that was the kind of feeling I had. Of course, if you only counted the years I'd lived awake, I wasn't that much older than Penny biologically, about eleven years, but that didn't account for the year she was born: 2075. I was born in 2038. That made her a kid to me, almost a grandkid. Temporal alienation. That was what we called the effect of relativistic time-slowing on how people perceived their place in social networks and society. It made me feel *old* relative to Penny and Hiep. It made no sense that Yong couldn't see that. I didn't think jealousy made sense.

I do not understand Chinese women.

Given my history, maybe I simply do not understand women. Period.

CHAPTER TWENTY

The next morning, I joined Heaven's navy. Maybe I founded it.

The Happy River broadened out as it reached its mouth and flowed into the bay. The river was shallow there, with sandbars glistening wet under the sun. On either side of the waterway, where the valley met the bay, a wide sandy beach stretched out in a long crescent. From a distance, that beach was pure white and smooth. Sunlight shone off it. Gentle waves rolled in from the turquoise bowl of the bay and slapped against the sand. It would have made a terrific vacation photo. The wind off the water, however, was every bit as hot as it was inland.

I didn't want to drive the rover onto the beach. The visual in my mind of our rover being stuck in the sand and then washed out to sea when the tide rolled in was not one I liked. Instead, I stopped the vehicle on a low rise overlooking the beach.

Our inflatable boat fit into a large backpack, with four folding oars clipped to the side of the pack. I pulled that out of the rover and swung it onto my back. Hiep's eyes had come back to normal by this time. He carried a pack filled with tubes and probes that Penny had selected, along with something resembling a long fishing rod that would lower those tubes and probes into the water. Penny was still limping and gritting her teeth with every step. The wound was clean, though. It had stopped bleeding into the dressing and I saw no sign of pus. She would do.

We hiked from the rover to the beach. Our footprints in the sand were the only marks marring that perfect arc. I stooped to scoop up some sand and let the fine grains run through my fingers. It was hot to the touch.

"No shells," Penny said. "No shells at all. Nothing like shells."

That was true. The beach was pure sand. I saw no shells, no seaweed washed up on the shore.

Penny asked Hiep for a filter from the pack he carried. She poured a double handful of sand through that. Nothing was left on the filter after the sand ran through.

"We'll take some samples back in case there are microscopic ones," Penny said, "but I doubt it. This fits." She didn't elaborate on that, only struggled the rest of the way across the soft sand to where the water came up and stared out at the bay.

I set down the pack with the boat at the water's edge. It took a few minutes to extract the boat and a few minutes more to inflate it with the compressed air canister from the pack. Penny could not get her leg over the side. It took Hiep and me together to get her into the boat, and even then, she mostly fell into it.

"I'm sorry," Hiep said.

Penny only shook her head. Then she pushed herself to the bow of our vessel without ever lifting her butt from the bottom. Once installed there, she clutched the sides with a death grip that turned her knuckles white.

I looked at Hiep and shrugged. Getting Penny back out of the boat was probably going to be as difficult as getting her in had been, and the likelihood of her agreeing to get out before we made this little voyage into the bay was less than zero. I pushed us off the beach and jumped in myself. Hiep and I took two of the oars and rowed us out into the bay. We did not try to give Penny an oar.

It was even prettier out on the water. Past the crescent ends of the beach, high cliffs marked the terminus of the valley walls on both sides. The haze in the air blurred the sides of the cliffs, making them seem even farther away than they were. The water was bright blue and crystal clear. I could see straight down to the bare dirt and rock at the bottom even as we pulled farther away from the coast. Low waves rocked the boat gently.

The idyllic setting was spoiled by the sounds of Penny vomiting over the side. It wasn't only one retch. It was heave after heave until nothing remained to come up, and even then she dry heaved. She pulled herself forward and hung over the side to scoop water over her mouth and chin. Then she let her hands trail in the water.

The thought popped into my head that if Yong could see this, she would probably make some cutting remark about the wretched picture Penny presented. I chased it away. I was being unfair. To both of them.

"If you get that seasick," I said, "you could have given us directions and stayed on the beach." I was a Ranger, not a SEAL, but I manage fine on the water. Hiep nodded his agreement with vigor.

"I've never been in a boat before," she said. "I didn't know." She heaved again.

"Okay," I said. "Let's get done as quick as we can so we can get you back to land. And maybe don't leave your hands in the water, in case this bay has swimming things with teeth."

"There won't be," Penny said. "I'm already sure. You can put your hand in, too, Leif. Unless you're a scaredy cat." It took two heaves for her to get all those words out.

I've been known to be impulsive on occasion. Daring me to do something isn't a good idea. For me. I stuck my left hand in the water. It was scalding! That bay was a goddamn hot tub. I jerked the hand back out.

Penny laughed around a little retch and a burp. Then she pulled her hands out. They were pink up to where the waterline had been, above her wrist. She turned over and flopped into the bottom of the boat. From there, she gave Hiep directions about tubes of water to collect and how to fasten a fancy probe to the end of the thing that looked like a fishing pole. She wanted that probe checked at various depths, and she spouted numbers and settings while she looked up at the sky.

Eventually, in true Penny fashion, she rolled on her side and pointed to the cliffs at the end of the valley wall, past the river. "See that whitish rock? That's limestone. I wish I could get up there."

I squinted through the haze and thought I saw what she was talking about. I would have needed equipment to get near it. "Don't even think about going there."

"I'm not. I'm sure anyway." She had a longing look on her face.

"About limestone? What about it?"

"That's my point."

I gave up. Penny said she didn't need anything else, so Hiep and I packed up and rowed back quickly, since the alternative was watching a young woman try to die of seasickness. Once we beached the boat, Penny stumbled out of it and fell, face-first, onto the sand. Hiep pulled the equipment out of the boat, while I deflated it and packed it up.

"If you take that back to the rover," Hiep said to me, "and bring back some ReadyMeals, I can scavenge enough wood from above the beach to make a campfire. That will be nice, I think."

I agreed. God knows we didn't need the heat from a fire, but a campfire on a beach made a nice picture and it couldn't make it feel any hotter. By the time I returned from the rover, Penny was sitting up, apparently revived. Hiep had the fire going. We took selfies and managed a group shot with the bay behind us.

Penny reached for a ReadyMeal as soon as we had the photos. "Thanks," she said. "Now I'm really starved."

"How come you've never been in a boat?" Hiep asked. "I thought Portland was near the shore."

"I was always scared to go out in a boat," Penny said. "I don't know how to swim."

"But you got into an inflatable plastic boat in the middle of nowhere on another planet," I said.

She sighed. "I had to make myself do it. I had to. And it all fits."

"What fits?" I knew this was another setup for a Penny stream of consciousness, but I was actually curious.

"It's all because of those volcanoes we saw from space when we made orbit around the planet," she said. "It's not like one big volcano spouting ash into the air. This is an area more than half the size of America that blew up and all the dirt and rocks for miles under it, all melted, and cooked, and burned up with lava. That makes CO_2. Oh my God, I can't even guess how many gigatons of CO_2 went into the air. That's why the level is so high and why it's so hot. It made a greenhouse. It would have sent acid into the sky too. That's why the soil is so poor. Acid rain. For God knows how long. There's no oxygen in the water in this bay. None. That's part of it. That's why nothing lives in the bay—that, and the water's too hot. That's why there are no shells on the beach. Those volcanoes caused a huge extinction. Most of the animals and plants here died. With the heat and carbon dioxide, the surviving ones are small. The shellhounds are all over because either they got lucky when everything else died, or, more likely, all the zinc oxide in their shell protects from UVB—because the volcanoes also got rid of most of the ozone. And it did happen. All of it. The limestone, it's made up from things that had shells, so they used to be here. But not anymore."

"Are you saying everything here is going to die?" Hiep asked.

Penny shook her head. "No. It's getting better. Slowly. The limestone helps neutralize the acid. The soil in this valley is better, much better, than the highlands. That shellhound poop is wicked good fertilizer." She leaned back and looked at the sky.

"How long will it take?" Hiep asked.

"Not too long. A couple of hundred thousand, maybe a million years."

"That's a bit long for us," I said. I thought about the scale of years. If Yong and I flew far enough, pushed the ramjet close enough to cee, we could come back and see it after Heaven recovered. Thank you, relativity. The concept gave me chills.

"But I could have a farm in Happy Valley now," Penny said while I contemplated being a real Flying Dutchman. "I can grow food here. I could have mangoes and probably bananas. I can grow bamboo and we can build with that and I can even grow sugarcane, I think, for the cell foundries. I mean, those are grasses, if you think about it, and bamboo grows fast. Some plants won't work, because they need a cool time of the year, but we have enough in the seed bank that will grow. The food may be bland because jalapeños don't do well when it's this hot, but maybe I can still get small ones and that will work. I can have chickens. I don't need lots of power. Photovoltaics will give me enough. I could have a little farmhouse. Although I don't know about plumbing. I might have to have an outhouse. Maybe I could get used to that."

"Penny!"

"Sorry."

She stopped, but from the little grin on her face, she wasn't sorry at all. That was when Hiep asked the obvious question. The one that should have been obvious for a long time.

"I don't understand," Hiep said. "You know so much. You're so smart. Why are you here instead of being somebody important back on Earth?"

"I'm not that smart," she said. "This all happened before, long ago, on Earth. Similar, anyway. I read about it, that's how I know. I didn't figure out all of it."

"Excuse me," I said. "You read about it. Then you put it all together out here. With no help. Sorry, that's smart."

Penny scratched in the sand with a forefinger. "I told Leif before. I failed my entrance exams to the doctoral programs. I'm like everybody in the Pioneers. What we wanted to do didn't work out, because we weren't good enough at it. That's all."

"How could you possibly fail your exams?" Hiep was persistent.

She gave him the same reason she had given me. She got nervous, went off on tangents.

"I don't believe you," he said. "That's bullshit. I've seen you hurt; I've seen you scared. Your mind works fine. I've seen plenty of people when shooting starts. Some people can keep their head straight no matter what. That's you."

I had to agree with Hiep. I'd seen more combat than I wanted to re-member, and what he said was true.

Penny turned around in the sand so that she was facing out to sea. "Well, ain't that a pissah," she said to the bay. "You want my big secret." She took a deep breath and blew it out. "It was deliberate."

"What?" That came from me and Hiep at the same time.

"Ayuh." She was silent for a minute, staring out into infinity. Then she said, "I knew all the answers—well, almost all of them. I could figure how many to get wrong so I would just miss the cutoff. They publish that score every year."

"Why would you want to do that?" Hiep asked.

"Dustin." When neither of us said anything, she went on. "I knew I would lose him if I had my career and he had lost his. He's the only one who ever loved me. I would rather have given up everything else to keep him. And now I'm here. Ironic, isn't it?"

"I think I should rearrange his face. For starters," I said. From Hiep's expression I think he had more drastic ideas in mind.

"Don't do anything," Penny said. "I made my own choice. I mean, I knew what he would do if . . ." She shook her head. "It was still my choice. I'll live with it and be fine."

It occurred to me that Penny had invented a story about how she came to Heaven, and until we sat by the bay, she'd told it very convincingly. Could she have known about the thistle leaves? She was the closest to a true polymath I had ever known. Could she have figured out the thistle leaves and found a way to poison Jerry? And lied about it? Until that moment, I hadn't thought her capable of lying. It bothered me, and I almost missed when she started speaking again because her voice was very soft.

"I can still have my little farm," she said. "I could have an Australian cattle dog on my farm. They're good in hot weather and do farmwork. They're on the embryo manifest. I'd like a dog. I was never allowed to have one, because no one thought I'd take care of it. I mean, I'm not good with chores like dishes, and my bed was never made. But I would take care of my dog.

"I can still have my farm. Everything can still be for the best and this can still be the best world for me."

A couple of teardrops fell onto the white sand. I looked over at Hiep. That was the first time I had seen him look concerned. I didn't know what to think.

PART II

Better to reign in Hell, than serve in Heaven.

John Milton, *Paradise Lost*

CHAPTER TWENTY ONE

It was obvious as the rover rolled back into St. Peterstown that Malachi had done something to get the colony off its collective ass. I won't use the cliché about a stirred anthill, but people were out and working, which I had never seen around St. Peterstown before. As we came in from the south, headed toward the Avenue of the Americas, I could see that a field off to the west of town had sprouted photovoltaic panels. Frameworks to hold more of them were in various stages of construction. To the east, as we reached the perimeter road, there was activity near the cannabis patch. Yes, they were building an extension to the hydroponics facility. I hoped that meant they were going to grow some food instead of smokables, although Penny muttered about sugarcane and polymers for photocells. Maybe the hydroponics would keep her occupied if she couldn't go to Happy Valley and be a farmer, unless she started a sunscreen factory instead.

I needed to see Malachi, but I wanted to take care of Penny first. Her wound was still healing cleanly—no swelling, redness, or drainage—but I wanted a real doc to look at it. Even an obstetrician. I messaged Francesca and asked her to meet us at the Medical Unit.

Hiep bounded off the rover and went to find the work team he hadn't led yet. Then I drove to the Med Unit and watched Francesca put Penny facedown on one of the diagnostic tables and examine her calf.

"No sign of infection," Francesca said after she looked at the readouts from Penny's chip and poked around the leg with her fingers. "So that's good." She turned to me. "You got it cleaned out well enough. The suturing, though . . ." She let out a long sigh. "I don't mean to criticize," she said, and then did it anyway, "but the edges aren't quite aligned or completely opposed in a couple of spots. You're going to have a really bad-looking scar, Penny. On Earth, you could have a plastics guy clean that up, but I can't do it with the surgi-bots we have here and I wouldn't want to try. You may always have a limp. I can't get a prediction on that from the AI, so it's just a guess, but don't be surprised if this leg is never quite right. I'm going to give you some exercises to do, and we'll see if we can stretch this out so the limp won't be so bad." She flexed the foot with Penny's leg straight and stretched out the calf. That provoked an "Ow! That hurts!" from Penny.

"It shouldn't hurt too much now," Francesca told her.

"Yeah, you try getting sliced open," Penny shot back.

Francesca ignored the comment. "You come see me every day after work so I can check."

"I'm sorry," I said. "I did the best I could in the field."

"That's okay," Penny said into the cushion on the diagnostic bed. "I'm the one who said we weren't coming right back, and my legs aren't much to look at anyway." She rolled over, sat up, and looked at Francesca. "We need something checked on the molecular analyzer. How good are you with that instrument array? Do you know how to use it? I can tell you the type of compound we're looking for, but Leif doesn't want me to do it."

"I've trained on all the instruments in the lab." Francesca furrowed her brow and put a finger to her lips. "I can use them as a doc, but I'm no expert. If what you want is medically related, I can probably do it."

"We're trying to find a cholinesterase inhibitor in some leaves," I said.

Francesca's head whipped around and her eyes locked on mine. "There's a reason behind this, I assume."

I told her my thoughts about what had killed Jerry.

Francesca had a gleam in her eyes; I was sure of it. "I can do this," she said.

. . . .

I messaged Malachi as soon as I walked out of the Med Unit. He told me to meet him out by the field of photovoltaic panels. I found a small hab unit there, which he had set up as an office. It wasn't much more than a glorified tent, with only a desk and chair for furniture, but it kept the sun off and, sealed up with the air system on, mitigated the blistering heat outside. I was a little disconcerted to see Loretta by the door with an M8 slung over her shoulder, but if that sort of display was what Malachi's ego needed, who was I to complain?

The scene inside when I arrived was a good, old-fashioned ass-chewing. Malachi was seated at his desk with another M8 propped against it and Miroslav standing on the other side. Malachi gave no sign that he had noticed me come in. Miroslav's Pioneer uniform looked like it had been crumpled into a ball without time for the sweat to dry before he had put it back on. The top of his red armband hung loose from his sleeve. The kid looked miserable as Malachi lit into him.

"Your team isn't pulling its weight. I can understand not keeping up with the ones my people are leading, because they have more experience and know what they have to do, but your team isn't close to Bjorn's, or Reality's either. That's on you. I don't want to penalize the team because you're not doing your job. Understand me, son?"

Miroslav nodded.

"Look, Miro, I need to finish this up." Malachi made a show of looking over to me. "Okay. The *Dauntless* is going to send down an engineer and parts so we'll get the reactor back online, but that doesn't mean we can take it easy. Our lives depend on everybody getting their work done. We have to push twice as hard to make up for all the slacking under Jerry. Vo Hiep is back. I'm going to have him check on you for the next few days. He'll see whether your team can meet its targets or not. If not, you know I've got a squad of number twos and threes, and each one of them would like to be a team lead. You understand where this is going, son?"

"Yes, sir," Miroslav said.

"Good. Get out of here."

Malachi waited until Miroslav had left. Then he stood up, walked around his desk, and extended a hand to me. I shook it.

"Good to have you back, Leif," he said. "Welcome to Command Central."

"What was that all about?" I asked.

"Work not done. I don't have enough people who understand how to lead a team. I'd boot that kid already, but I suspect the twos and threes are just as pathetic. I'm trying to build a leadership team here. Another job I have." He shook his head. "That's something you'd know about, isn't it?"

I knew a lot about teams. I didn't say anything, though, only tipped my head.

"Listen," Malachi said, "you come out here tomorrow morning. See them go through their paces. I'd like to show you where we are so far."

Sweat stood out on Malachi's forehead. The air system in the hab was keeping up with the heat, but it wasn't really cool inside.

"I'll come and watch," I said. "This is all about the power situation?"

"In part." Malachi grunted. "People do not understand how much power this little town of ours needs. I had a physical scorecard put up in the Dome so they can see where we are against where we need to be. I could send them all a notification every morning, but most of them wouldn't open it. This way, they can't miss it." He grunted again. "We need power. It's maintaining the frozen embryos and seed lines. It's the hydroponics, which we need to expand. It's running the computer and the networks. It's the AC that keeps us all from dissolving into puddles of sweat, and we're going into winter, for God's sake. It's every goddamn toilet flush that draws power from the hab. It's all the bots that do not have their own photovoltaic chargers, and we have to run them all the time because when people here say they're trained to do something, what they mean is that they're trained to click on a bot's panel or their phone base to make the bot do the work. Don't even get me started on any real lift and carry. Between the kids you brought and the crooks we started with, I have to be the bad guy."

"I take it this means no luck with the reactor."

"No." Malachi's face was grim. "We have people who trained to run it, but like I said before, that boils down to knowing what to click or tap and when. They can't fix whatever happened. We need your engineer."

"The spaceplane will be down. One of the engineers will come and he'll bring parts as well. That should do it."

"Your lips to God's ears," Malachi said. "I'm counting on it. There's a lot more work than just that. I need people to do what they're told. You could help with that."

The implication of that statement was clear. I chose to ignore it. I wasn't going to be Malachi's police. "You mentioned expanding the hydroponics facility. That may be a short-term fix, but I've got really good news on that front. The valley we checked out can be farmed with Earth crops. Penny thinks so, and I'd bet on her being right. We're not limited to the hydroponics, and that's a whole lot less power consumption right there."

"Wonderful." His tone meant anything but. "In the middle of all of this, you want me to divide my forces and go colonize an area you've been in exactly once." He shook his head. "Maybe we should give this Penny one of these"—he waved at the little hab—"and a few seeds and see what she can do. If nothing else, that would get her out of here so we don't have people wasting time and energy trying to guess if she killed Jerry." He shook his head again. "Forget that. Let me tell you something else, Leif. Relying on the hydroponics and our stores, and maybe a few fields outside town—if they'll actually grow anything—isn't all bad. Control of the food supply is one way to keep teams motivated. People raising gardens all over doesn't help with that, and they can't do that so easy up here. Something to consider."

I considered it and didn't really like what percolated through my mind. "Sounding a bit dictatorial, now, don't you think?"

Malachi turned from cordial to brusque in an instant. "Look, Leif, I asked you to think about staying with us and you said no. That's fine. But you're going to climb back into your spaceplane and go up to the starship, and you're going to leave. ISC claimed they'd send a ship every three to five years, but that's forever, as far as I'm concerned. I live here. I need to do what is necessary to make sure we keep living here. If that's tough on some people, so be it. And I'll tell you something else. If I make myself comfortable in the process, that's my due. You saw what this place was like. Don't tell me you don't know exactly what would have happened without me doing what I'm doing."

There was a certain logic in what he was saying, although I could still remember my mom telling me that you caught more flies with honey than with vinegar. Of course, the army didn't operate according to my mom's saying, and neither had I when I was a noncom. This colony wasn't a military unit, but if that was the only way Malachi knew how to get things done, it wasn't for me to tell him to do it differently. As he'd said, he was going to live here, while I was going back to Earth as soon as Yong could land the next load of supplies and have it distributed. There was, however, one more bit of information I had for him that I figured would matter to someone who was going to live here. I told him what we had learned about how Jerry had died. That caught his interest. He was a chemist, after all.

"A naturally occurring form of nerve gas, you think," he said slowly. "That's not something anyone would have expected. I'm sure that explains what happened to our mice, and it means we'll have to check carefully before we eat any native plant. Makes the hydroponics even more important. I'll make sure to have the instruments in the Lab Unit set up to test for this on plants we bring in. I hadn't really planned on eating native growth, but better safe than sorry. Thank you."

"Francesca is already going to look into the thistle leaves with Penny," I said.

Malachi's eyes searched my face. "Penny. Do you think she's searching—if we can use that word—for something she's already found?"

"I think that's jumping to a conclusion. Somebody killed Jerry. I don't think there's any question about that anymore, and I'll bet that whatever is in the thistle is what they used. But I don't know who it was or how they got it into him."

Malachi put his hands on his hips. "I think that's more my problem than yours. For the same reasons we just talked about. I'm not even sure it should be one of my major problems." He sighed. "Look, Jerry's dead, and trust me, nobody misses him. Truth is, I don't even care that much if Penny or somebody else killed him. With what you just told me, for all I know, he did something really stupid and wound up dead. Maybe that's all there is to it."

"Maybe." I agreed with him that far. "But if somebody did kill him, then you've got a killer here who has figured out how to poison people with the product of a plant that grows all over the place. I would think that's concerning. And, no, I don't think it's Penny."

"Yeah." He said the word slowly enough to make a whole sentence of it. "What do you suggest I do with everyone working as hard as they can to keep us surviving when you leave? Should I torture people at random until someone confesses?"

"No. Of course not."

"Right." He thumped his fist against the desktop. "And do you, Leif Grettison, have a plan, brilliant or not, to catch the killer loose among us?"

I had to admit that I did not have a plan. Yet. "I think we should see what Francesca finds. I do think it would be a good idea to come up with a plan."

"Fine." Malachi sounded tetchy. "You come up with a plan. When you do, you let me know. If you want, I can call the Demos and everyone can vote on it. Or maybe you'd rather I do it as a secret op. When you have a plan, we can decide. In the meantime, what I will do is assign my people who have the status of guards to patrol our community, especially after dark. I'm not going to have Cam and Jess do it. Do you think they should go in pairs?"

"That's probably a good idea."

Malachi threw his hands in the air. "Good. For the Pioneers, it will be a chance to strut around and look important. See what I mean when you come out tomorrow. But when these people want to know why they're losing sleep when there is still work to do the next day, I'm going to send them to you for the explanation."

After my less-than-satisfactory conversation with Malachi, I called Yong up on the *Dauntless* to see if I was overreacting.

"Have you considered the possibility that he's right?" she asked. "Maybe what happened to Jerry isn't the most important thing for this colony right now." I thought her tone was a bit frosty, almost accusatory.

"What? Jerry was a schmuck, certainly, but someone killed him." I tried to tell myself I was overthinking her tone.

"Schmuck?"

I sighed. I had spent part of my childhood around New York. Yong had grown up in Wuxi and I doubted she had ever thought about New York except as a possible target.

"It means he was a fool, but never mind that," I said. "We can't have people going around killing other people." As soon as I said it, I realized that Yong and I had spent a chunk of our adult lives doing exactly that.

"Leif, it's possible that someone took the opportunity to take revenge; it was personal. We know plenty of the *Daredevil* colonists would have had a reason. You have to view that in light of all the problems the colony is facing. Malachi knows now that the thistle leaves can be dangerous.

He's telling you where his priorities are, and the Demos elected him to this office."

"True, and he is starting to sound more and more dictatorial about doing it."

"That is definitely not our business." Her tone was sharp. "This colony has a constitution and a government. It's up to them how they manage and not for us to play savior if we think they are doing it wrong."

"I thought you were the one who said our mission was to make sure the colony was set up to function on its own."

"You know exactly what I meant," Yong said.

If a microwave transmission could freeze solid, the ice in her voice would have done it. I wished I had talked about something else, even complained about the weather. The silence that followed felt like it went on for an hour.

I did not want it to go cold between us. I kicked myself every time one of us stepped on one of the emotional land mines we each had. Somehow, I had made it worse by talking about Penny when I was in the valley. Depending on how far we flew, I was going to spend the next several thousand years with Yong. Okay, those were EFOR years and didn't count, but it was true that after one more flight, she might be the only living person in the universe that I knew. I needed to thaw the atmosphere between us, regardless of how I had screwed it up.

"When will you bring the spaceplane down?" A brilliant line.

"Probably four days to finish the loads and all the checks." I told myself her tone was normal, even though four days was a lot longer than I'd expected. Was she delaying coming down because of me? "Jorge has asked to go down on the flight," she said.

Did she not want to come down at all? "Is he recovered enough that Charley will clear him to fly the spaceplane down?" That would mean I wouldn't even see Yong until we were finished on Heaven and I went back up. Maybe I had misread her voice.

"That's not what I meant," Yong said. "He's afraid to go back to Earth—afraid of what may happen to his gut in hib."

"He wants to stay here?" What I really meant was that I was really, really happy that Yong would be coming down. I owed Jorge an apology for not being concerned about his gut.

"He said he wants to think about it," Yong said. "I told him that I thought it was a mistake, but I would not deny him the chance. Matters are, shall we say, unsettled on the planet. If something were to happen, there should be a pilot on the *Dauntless* to take the ship home. I would prefer not to trust the flight to the AI."

The only sort of event happening the way Yong was hinting would be catastrophic. Maybe that was her way of telling me I hadn't been overreacting at the beginning of the call. Maybe that accounted for everything I was hearing in her voice, and I was worrying needlessly about how she felt. Maybe I had overreacted to all of that as well. I doubted it.

CHAPTER TWENTY TWO

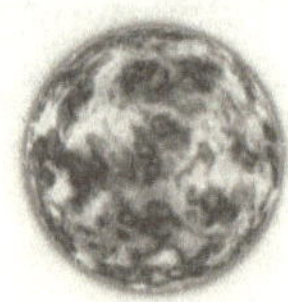

I was up before dawn to see Malachi run his embryonic leadership team through their paces. I did consider ghosting his little demonstration, then decided against it. There was no point antagonizing him without a reason. The timing wasn't a problem for me. I was accustomed to early-morning hours from my years in the service. In fact, I was used to much earlier hours. Most of my deployments had been in Central Asia or on Mindanao, and dawn broke early in those places. With the approach to winter at the circumpolar latitudes of Heaven, I could be a slugabed and still beat the sunrise.

Predawn or not, Heaven smoldered as I walked out to the practice field, past where the Avenue of Europe met the perimeter road. I had adapted to heat before. It had been broiling hot on Mindanao as well, and there it wasn't just the heat that was trying to kill me. The local insurgents and their Chinese advisers had been shooting at me too. I had survived that; I could survive this.

The air was a different story. I had forced myself to stay in shape after I left the service in 2062, and would think nothing of rolling out of bed and taking a five-mile run. That was part of how I kept my repaired knee from going stiff and cranky. Heaven was different. Some subconscious carbon dioxide sensor in my brain kept signaling that I needed to yawn and made me feel that if I tried to run, I would fall on my face in less than a quarter mile. Charley and Jing up on the ship told me that it was all in my head—hah!—and that if I needed to run, I could run. What really mattered was the oxygen, and there was plenty of it. I told them it was easy to say that from the comfort of a starship in geosynchronous orbit and they should come down and try it. I don't recall getting much sympathy.

Regardless of the medical opinion—and second opinion—I walked out to the practice field.

"Good morning, Leif!" Malachi, a black figure against the red eastern horizon, waved to me as I strolled up. "Come see my leadership team in action."

I looked around the field in the still-dim light. Five figures I recognized as the other free company members who had come on the *Daredevil*. They stood near Malachi but in no particular order. Of them, Hiep and Loretta held M8s. Out on the field were a group of Pioneers. Bjorn, Reality, and Miroslav were at the front of this group, red armbands marking them out. Behind them were three ranks of six Pioneers each, all in a ragged formation that would have been unacceptable anytime after the first day at boot camp.

The poor light could not disguise how much worse for wear the ragged crew's Pioneer uniforms were. To say they were rumpled would be kind. There wasn't a crease anywhere. Pant bottoms had frayed; some patch pockets had torn off. Most of the kerchiefs had been converted to headbands. Those uniforms would have been as unacceptable as the formation.

"Hiep, would you run the program?" That was Loretta.

Hiep tipped his head barely enough for me to see the acknowledgment and stepped in front of the Pioneers. At a command from him, Reality took two steps forward to explain the structure to me. The Team Leads were the highest status position for the Pioneers. The assistants, or firsts, were behind them, then the seconds, and then the thirds, although any of them ranked above a regular worker. All the ranks were temporary. If anyone slipped up, or didn't do their job well, the best-performing person at the rank below would replace them. Rank translated into food selection, vid time, and private time. I could guess what *private time* meant. When she was done, Reality moved back to her position.

This was followed by what Malachi called the criticism period. Each of the Pioneers was called on and had to offer a criticism, first of themselves and then of another member of the group, based on the previous day's work. This could involve anything from handling a circuit to hygiene. It got personal; it got nasty. I could see some of them being picked out and ganged up on. This was, clearly, one way to reshuffle the rankings. At the end, Malachi put two seconds back to thirds and promoted two of the thirds. My skin crawled.

Hiep barked an order, and the physical training part of the program began. They ran laps around poles that marked the perimeter of their training field. By eye, I estimated the distance around the field at about a mile. Their time wasn't impressive, even allowing for the air. Fairly basic calisthenics—squats, push-ups, sit-ups, et cetera—came next. Again, they were not impressive. There is a proper way to do push-ups and sit-ups. I don't think I saw any of them do a full set of either correctly. Any drill instructor I could remember would have been all over them. Hiep kept his face impassive as he shouted the commands. Once I saw him look over at me, and I read disgust on his face. I would bet he knew how to do all of this and could do it perfectly himself. He knew they were only going through the motions. He wasn't trying to fix their performance.

Between each set of exercises, Bjorn or Reality led chants. "Pioneers have no peers!" and "Pioneers have no fears!" rang out across the field. I struggled not to laugh. In my mind's eye, I could see this group doing the summer camp chant of *Two, four, six, eight, who do we appreciate!* for Malachi.

"We need to build a sense of team here." While I was watching the show, Malachi had come up next to me.

"Don't take this the wrong way, Malachi," I said, "but you've got a long way to go."

"I know that, Leif. You have to work with the material you have, though. You have to mold it, shape it, toughen it." He emphasized those last two words. "They already see themselves as different from the rest of the people in St. Peterstown. They compete with each other. They understand loyalty. You know, building a team is a slow process."

Yes, I thought, and you have to know how to do it. I was a Ranger, a member of an elite unit of the US Army, one of the most elite units in military history. I knew what it was to be part of a team, to lead a team. This was pathetic. I wondered what Malachi thought he was building here. I mumbled my thanks for the opportunity to see the morning training. Then I said that I had work of my own that needed attention.

Penny messaged me and then came to meet me at the Dome at the end of the day that had started with Malachi's leadership team demonstration. The neutral meeting ground was my idea. This was my first visit to the Dome since we'd come back from Happy Valley, and I figured it would give me a chance to look at Malachi's scorecard. A flapping sound caught my attention as I walked under the roof. The noise came from three huge printed banners secured to the top of the open framework behind the Council table. They read:

WORK IS FUN.

WE VOLUNTEER BECAUSE WE MUST.

OUR PLAN IS PLANNED.

The first two contradictions reminded me of something I had once read but couldn't place. The third? Our plan is planned? Seriously?

Below the banners, a scorecard showed the number of photovoltaic panels needed for full power and the number operational. A second line showed the area of hydroponics needed and the percent available. We had a long way to go for both.

While I was scrutinizing the banners and scorecard, Penny arrived. She glanced up at them, shook her head, and stepped directly in front of me. She had given up on trying to pull her hair into a ponytail, and sweat-soaked curls fell on both sides of her face. She was her usual hyper self, with her arms swinging at all angles as she talked.

"Nobody is listening to me," she said for the fourth time in a very short conversation. "I can't get them to listen. All they do is tell me to work on the hydroponics, like that will fix everything. I mean, I do work on the hydroponics and they need me to do it, so I would anyway, but that's not the point. They don't listen to me."

The first words in my mind were, *So what else is new?* I managed not to say them, however. Penny was obviously upset, and she wouldn't take it well. *Truth is, Leif,* I told myself, *those words would only be another cheap one-liner at her expense, so shut it down.* "What won't they listen to?" was what I did say.

"The valley. Farming. Crops. *Food.* It's not even in one ear and out the other. They *ignore* it. Like I didn't say anything."

"Have you ever considered that maybe it's the way you say it?"

That stopped her, stopped the shifting weight from foot to foot and the swinging arms. It all stopped. "You may be right." She locked eyes with me, which was not something she would usually do, and stared at me long enough for me to worry that I had triggered something that would be worse than being ignored.

"What are you thinking now?" I asked.

"This colony has a constitution," she said. "I've read it. This place is a democracy, a true democracy. We're supposed to vote on any major decision. Any member of the Demos, that's anyone who lives in St. Peterstown, can call for a meeting of the Demos, and that's just an old Greek word for 'the people.' If it's an important topic, the Demos has to meet at the Community Dome and vote. You've seen it. That's what I can do. I can call the Demos."

"They don't have to come," I said.

"Yes, they do," she insisted. "If it's an important matter, the Demos has to meet. I know how to put it so they won't have a choice."

Now I was certain that this could end up worse than being ignored by people you were trying to talk to. "Penny, it may be a democracy, and that sounds fine, but that doesn't mean people are going to sit there and make a careful assessment of what's said. That's not how it usually works. You saw what happened the last time."

She made a quick jerk of her head forward, which I think was an acknowledgment of the history. "I saw. I'm going to have the shakes about this the moment I leave here. But I have to do it. Will you be there?"

"I will. But I'm not part of St. Peterstown, not part of the Demos. I don't get to speak and I can't vote."

"I know that. Just be there."

She turned and ran out of the Dome.

·   ·   ·

The notification hit my field around midday on the following day. PE-NELOPE PANAGIOTIDIS CALLS THE DEMOS TO DISCUSS AND VOTE ON A MATTER CRITICAL TO OUR SURVIVAL, it read. I had to admit that Penny had found a way to phrase it that would be hard to ignore. Survival would qualify as important in anyone's consideration of the word.

That proved to be correct. The next notification on my field was a call for the Demos to meet at the Community Dome immediately after work. Of course, that put the Demos meeting in between work and dinner. With the meeting standing between people and their food, I thought, it might be short.

The lights were on under the Community Dome and dusk had fallen outside as people began to take their seats. Malachi, Loretta, and Ibiana were already seated at their table on the raised platform, the banners and scorecard bellying out in the wind that blew through the framework. They waited, without speaking among themselves, as the Dome filled. After several minutes had gone by without more people entering, Ibiana opened the meeting.

"Penelope Panagiotidis has called for a Demos meeting on a matter of survival. The Council judges that is important under our constitution to have a meeting and has further decided that the meeting should be held immediately. Penelope, the floor is yours."

Public speaking terrifies most people, and Penny was scared of her own shadow to begin with. This wasn't like the time before, when she had gotten mad and jumped up without thinking to yell at Malachi about ex-ploring the valley. She had had plenty of time to think this over, and that's the way fear builds. Her hands were fluttering when she stood, but she was able to keep the shakes out of her voice.

"Penelope Panagiotidis," she said. "I need to talk to you about food, about what we're going to eat when we run out of ReadyMeals. Right now, all we're doing is expanding the hydroponics. That's not going to work." I could see her take a deep breath and blow it out. She plunged ahead. "The hydroponic farm was only ever supposed to be a bridge to planting fields and growing crops. At most, the hydroponics can support two hundred people, which is what we have now. That means we can never grow past that, but it's even worse. Two hundred people will need everything we can grow in the hydroponics. It means we can't grow feed for animals and we need animals and there's only so much feed in the supplies. It means we can't grow sugarcane for the cell foundries and we need them to synthesize medicines, plastic, and polymers for more photovoltaic panels. We can't even support all two hundred of us unless we rip out the cannabis, and that's only the two hundred of us now. It won't work the way we've got it."

I saw Bjorn on his feet and waving to his team. A chant began. "Pennywise, telling lies! Pennywise, telling lies! Pennywise, telling lies!"

Not to be outdone, Reality was up, too, waving her team to their feet, to join in the chant. "Pennywise, telling lies! Pennywise, telling lies!"

Other people were up now as well, all of them chanting. "Pennywise, telling lies!"

The Town Council sat and did nothing.

Penny was shaking. I could see it from where I stood by the platform. She did not sit down, however, and she did not back down. She found the presence of mind to connect to the Dome speaker system with her phone, because her scream, "Listen to me!" drowned out everyone else. The squeal of feedback that followed left people wincing, and a brief hush descended on the Dome.

"Listen to me!" Penny's amplified voice rolled through the Dome. "We are going to die if we don't fix this! We can't grow enough food to live on with only the hydroponics even when we expand the facility, and we can't expand it beyond the material we brought with us and there's no way to get more. We have to farm the land, but the soil here by the town is wicked poor. Really, really poor. It won't work. We can grow sugarcane in the valley and food in the hydroponics, or food in the valley and sugarcane in the hydroponics, but either way, we have to have farms in the valley." With that, she launched into a barrage of numbers about acreage and projected yields, the number of bots needed, and the estimated kilowatts to run everything. I don't know when she had done those calculations, but I couldn't believe she was making them up on the spot.

Unfortunately, if Penny could tap into the speaker system, so could others. Another chant started up, Bjorn and Reality giving it all they had to lead it. "Pennywise, not so wise! Pennywise, not so wise! Pennywise, not so wise!" The din was overwhelming.

I jumped onto the platform and walked up behind Malachi. He startled when I touched him on the shoulder. It was so loud in the Dome, he hadn't noticed me.

"I would like to think you have some control over these morons," I said. I can roar when I want to and his ear wasn't much more than a foot from my mouth, but I sent it as a message, too, to be sure.

He nodded. He must have had a master control for the speaker system because, suddenly, the amplification stopped. The chanting was still loud, but when Malachi spoke, his was the only amplified voice. He overrode the rest of the crowd.

"All right, all right," he said. "I think we have all heard enough and the Demos must attend to its business."

The chanting cut off as abruptly as if the blade of a guillotine had dropped on its neck.

"Thank you," Malachi said. "Ms. Panagiotidis, if you have had your say, you may sit down."

Penny looked around her. She folded up and sat quickly.

"Thank you," Malachi said again. "Penelope, well, Penny, let me make sure I have the question correct that the Demos must vote on. You are asking the Demos to vote to abandon our plan, pack up this town, with all the work and risk that involves, and move it down into the valley and set it up again? Right?"

"No! I didn't say we had to move everything. That's dumb," Penny said. "But we do need to set up farms in the valley. That's the only way we can have enough food and sugarcane. And I'll do it. I'll do it for you."

"Okay. We can put a second question to the Demos," Malachi said. "Does the Demos vote to do extra work so that Penny can have a farm in the valley? We still have to do all our work up here for our plan, so this will be extra on top of that."

I didn't need to see the vote tally to know how it came out with the questions put that way.

Penny wasn't giving up, though. She was back on her feet and I could see from the way she screwed up her face that she was losing her tenuous grip on self-control. "Those questions weren't put fairly! That was as biased as it can get. If you're going to do it that way, there's no point in asking these questions. We need to have leaders who are fair and understand what has to be done. We need to have leaders who understand I'm right and I'm telling the truth about how much sugarcane the foundries need and how much food we need in the future and what it takes to grow it. If you think all we have to do is make the numbers match on that stupid thing up there"—she pointed to the hanging scorecard—"you're even dumber than I thought." She was red in the face by this point, fists clenched at her sides. "We don't need you idiots sitting at a table who can't figure the yield from the hydroponics. Let's vote on that! Let's vote on replacing you with new leaders, with people who are fair!"

Malachi's face told me, without words, how unwise that outburst had been. Penny should have left it alone, taken the defeat, and let it go. I hadn't known what she was going to do and I'd bet she hadn't known what she was going to do before she did it either. Even if I had seen it coming and sent a message, she wouldn't have seen it before she spoke. It wasn't as though I could have run over there and clamped a hand over her mouth.

"You are out of order," Malachi said slowly. "The Demos was called for a specific purpose and that business has been completed. This matter is finished and over."

I doubted that.

CHAPTER TWENTY THREE

From the moves Malachi was making—starting from the way he gave orders to his leadership team—he had every intention of becoming the boss of this little corner of hell in the cosmos. After a public challenge, even one as easily brushed away as Penny's, I figured it was only a matter of time before Malachi found a way to demonstrate his bosshood. He didn't disappoint in this and he didn't wait too long to do it.

In fact, it took only until the next afternoon for the notification to show up. THE DEMOS IS CALLED TO A MEETING AFTER WORK ENDS TO CONSIDER A CHARGE OF SABOTAGE AGAINST MIROSLAV PETROVIC. Sabotage sounded both ominous and over the top. I had no doubt Miroslav was incompetent as a leader and no doubt that Malachi was going to replace him. That was why he had Hiep watching what Miroslav did. But there hadn't been much time for Hiep to see anything. And sabotage? Really?

As before, the Community Dome was lit up against the early darkness, and it filled quickly. It may have been my imagination, but I didn't see as much chitchat among people coming in as I had seen before. Everyone had read the message the same way I had, and they were in a "hold your breath until you see what happens" mode. The usual number of seats was not filled when Ibiana called the Demos to order. Some people had obviously decided they did not want to see what happened or did not want to be forced to vote on it. I wasn't sure that was wise, because attendance and voting were recorded. If Malachi was going to flex his muscles tonight, he might well do it again.

Penny was one of those who did not show up. No surprise there. I considered sending her a message telling her to get to the Dome no matter what she thought, then decided against it. Coming in late, all eyes on her, might be worse than not coming at all, especially since God only knows what might come out of her mouth if someone called her on it and she took umbrage.

Miroslav was brought in by Bjorn and Reality after the call to order. A small end table with a folding chair had been set for him in front of the Town Council's platform. He would sit facing them with his back to the Demos. He didn't look good. He had a large reddish and swollen blotch over one cheek. That would blossom into a gorgeous shiner in a day or two. His lower lip was swollen and split. He was walking okay, however, and on his own. His hands were free. Whoever roughed him up had been going for cosmetic effect rather than serious damage.

Malachi opened the meeting by stating its purpose in the same words the notification had used. Then he peered down at Miroslav. "Young man, do you understand the charge against you?"

"Yes, sir."

"And what happened to your face?" His tone was kindly, a voice of concern.

"The work team became very upset with my performance. It's my fault, really." The words came out in a mumble that I had to strain to hear.

I was quite sure that particular question and answer had been coached.

"Well." Malachi paused. "This is the first time we have needed to hold a trial on Heaven. I think we need to hear from your work team and find out what made them so upset. Bjorn, if you would, please."

Bjorn shot up from his seat as though he had been waiting for that cue. He walked to the back of the Dome behind the Town Council table and returned with another folding table and chair. He set that up a few feet away from where Miroslav sat.

Malachi proceeded to call up the members of Miroslav's work team. He didn't know their names; I could see his eyes go to the side for what had to be the team list and idents on his field. One by one, they came up and sat at what I thought of as the witness stand and told their stories in response to Malachi's questions.

A depressing sameness ran through all their testimony: Miroslav had not properly supervised the team. He had not pushed them to work harder; that was why they missed their targets. He had let them goof off; that was why they didn't meet their work goals. He had overlooked mistakes they made; that was why work had to be redone. He had given incorrect instructions to people, and they damaged two of the photovoltaic panels as a result. And on and on, one after another. Each member of the work team was essentially confessing to being a lousy worker, and lazy to boot, while Miroslav was portrayed as the screwup-in-chief with the hint that he might have had malign intent. It was quite a performance.

When the last of them was done, Malachi let out a big sigh and leaned back in his chair, as though he were exhausted from listening to all of it. "I think that is a lot to process," he said. "Miroslav, do you have anything to say? Is all of this false?"

Miroslav shook his head. His "No, sir. I have nothing to say" was barely audible.

"Right," Malachi said. "One person, or even two people, could be telling a story to get you in trouble for some bad reason of their own. When it's like this, however, one after another, it's very hard to argue with. I think you are wise not to contest it."

Malachi brought his head up to address the Demos. "By our constitution, guilt or innocence is not decided by the Town Council or by me as the mayor. It is the decision of the Demos in assembly, as is proper for a democracy. The charge here is sabotage because Miroslav's repeated mistakes, time after time, and his persistent failure to correct his errors go far beyond simple incompetence or even negligence. It is at a level where it is no different from intentionally destroying our work, which is what sabotage is, and that puts our very survival at risk because we need the power from these panels his team was working on. That will be true even after the reactor is repaired. What say you? Guilty or innocent? I am opening the voting box now."

After that buildup, Miroslav never had a chance.

"Very well," Malachi said after the vote was announced and displayed. "The Demos finds you guilty as charged. The penalty is for me to propose and the Town Council to vote on. I propose that you be stripped of all rank and privilege. You are no longer a member of the leadership team. You are the lowest-ranking worker. That and half rations for a week. Also, the work team will have half rations for three days for their self-confessed negligence, but that does not need a Council vote, because it is only an administrative matter."

The Council immediately approved Malachi's punishment.

I was puzzled. All this show for a simple demotion and less food for a week? Granted, it had been humiliating, but this had been a big production to achieve only that. What did Malachi get from this?

That was when Bjorn started the chant. "Not enough! Not enough! There must be more! There must be more!"

Bjorn was on his feet, his fist pumping, urging the others on. Reality shot up after him, the way she had before. "Come on, leadership team!" she shouted and joined Bjorn in the chant, trying to outshout him. The leadership team stood up and chanted. Then work teams joined in. The chant filled the Dome.

"We want more! We want more!"

"Okay, okay." Malachi held up his hands. "I hear the Demos." The speaker system amplified his voice, and the chanting stopped immediately. "I am sorry for having been too lenient. We will add ten lashes with a cane. I will not go further than that," he said, as though admonishing the Demos. "Not this time."

I noticed there was no vote on the lashes.

Again, Bjorn ran to the back of the Dome behind the council table. This time, he returned with a thin, flexible rod about six feet long. I couldn't tell if it was metal or plastic. I did find it interesting that such an object had been conveniently positioned there.

Reality got to Miroslav first. She and Bjorn walked him to the edge of the Dome, where they pulled his shirt off. Miroslav moved like a man in a trance. I don't know if he couldn't believe what was happening or had given up on the idea of resisting. He did what he was told. Someone produced a length of plastic fiber cord. Again, I found it interesting that such an item was conveniently available. They tied Miroslav's hands together, then tossed the cord over one of the exposed girders of the Dome's structure so they could haul him up on his toes. The cord was just long enough to be tied off at the base of one of the Dome's supporting struts. As though it had been measured in advance. About half the Demos stayed, gathered in a cluster to watch.

"Ten," Malachi said. "No more, no less."

Bjorn handed the rod to David Gruenig, who flexed it with both his hands. He stepped away from Miroslav, measuring the distance between them by eye.

That was when Malachi raised his hand and said, "No."

During the pause that followed, all eyes fixed on Malachi. "You take the rod back," Malachi said to Bjorn after the tension in the Dome had grown. "You led the call; you do it."

Bjorn hesitated.

"If you won't do it, you'll take his place and I'll have Reality do it." Malachi's voice was curt, his posture impatient.

At those words, Bjorn snatched the rod back. It was clear he had no desire to find out what Reality would do if given the chance. He licked his lips, moved next to Miroslav, and made a flat-footed strike against Miroslav's back. Miroslav yelped. A red line appeared on his back where the rod had hit.

"Pitiful," Malachi said. "I wonder if a woman's arm is stronger."

Bjorn took the hint. He took a step back and hefted the rod. Then he took a big step forward and whipped it overhand. The rod slashed into Miroslav's back with a loud crack. Miroslav screamed. Blood ran from the cut that appeared across his back and droplets fell to the ground from the rod. Bjorn looked at the result and nodded. He backed off farther, took two quick strides to cross the distance, and swung hard enough that he grunted. He repeated that performance seven more times. When he was finished, Miroslav hung limply, held upright only by the cord. His back was a bloody mess.

"Take him down to the Medical Unit," Malachi said. "Make sure those wounds are taken care of. He has to be back at work tomorrow."

Malachi didn't wait to see what happened after that. He stood up from the table and left. Interestingly, as soon as he did, it was Reality who went over to take Miroslav down from where he had been hauled up against the framework. She said something to him I couldn't hear; then he leaned against her back and she helped him away from the Dome.

Most of the people who had been watching looked sick. I heard someone retch. Bjorn, though, had an eager light in his eyes.

By the time I made my way to the Medical Unit, they had Miroslav slabbed out on one of the treatment tables, and Francesca was working on his back, making clucking sounds. His back was awful. I've seen that kind of slicing in an underdone roast. Blood was leaking from all the cuts, rolling down onto the table and then dripping onto the floor.

Francesca was busy lining up the edges of each cut. Once she had them approximated, she would apply a line of SkinGlue and seal them together. I've used that stuff in the field, and it's handy. As long as the muscle underneath isn't pulling the wound open, which is why you can't use it for a scalp wound, and as long as the wound isn't too deep, SkinGlue will zipper a cut closed and hardly leave a scar. Once you're down into muscle, though, the way Penny's wound was, for example, SkinGlue isn't enough. The wound can pull apart, or you can get pockets forming down in the muscle. From a quick look at Miroslav's back, I thought there were several spots where she could have used the surgi-bot to close it up with suture, neat and tidy. But, hey, at most, I was a paramedic.

"So, what do you think?" Francesca said. "Almost closed. Good as new in three days. Not bad for an obstetrician."

Miroslav groaned, but just a little. They must have given him some happy juice. I craned my neck as though I were getting a better view of his back, and made approving noises for Francesca.

"Fuck Malachi," Miroslav said. "And Bjorn. And Reality."

I edged closer to the table. "Want to tell me about it?"

"No. Malachi said the more I tried to defend myself, the worse it would be. I can only imagine. I know I'm not good at this team shit, but you can't just quit. That's not allowed. And Bjorn and Reality, each trying to upstage the other. Bjorn started all that crap with the chants. Malachi loves that, so now everybody does it as soon as Bjorn starts. So Reality is always looking for a way to be even nastier. Then, after it's over, she's going to help me. Lucky I didn't get killed. I guess."

"Why are they doing this? Bjorn and Reality, I mean."

"Why do you think?" Miroslav's head was hanging over the end of the table, and his eyes were focused on the floor. "It's the same shit we had on the *Dauntless*, but it's not just points on a scorecard anymore. They each want to be his favorite of the Pioneers. They want to be the same as the free company men and women. It's like Minor Powers think they can be Major Powers. Fat chance of that. They want to get the guns. Fat chance of that."

The M8s? "The only people I've seen with the rifles, other than Malachi, are Loretta and Hiep."

"Yeah." A bit of drool ran out of his mouth and splattered on the floor. "Loretta was with Malachi in Grand Company. I guess he trusts her. Some. I don't know the story with Hiep except the man is a killer. Everybody seems to know that. Malachi's killer, I guess. And Hiep and Loretta hate each other, so I guess that works for Malachi. Malachi doesn't trust any of the others. Bjorn and Reality, each of them wants to be the next best thing. Not likely, but I think Malachi gets a kick out of watching them go at each other and having the free company people wondering if either of them might get a gun. Should have known I was screwed. Especially when he had Hiep watching me. That man scares the shit out of everyone."

All in all, it sounded like a delightful group dynamic developing on Heaven.

I heard someone come into the Medical Unit but I didn't turn around to look. Footsteps squeaked on the floor and came up to where I stood.

"Well, if it isn't Malachi's little messenger boy," Miroslav said. "Loretta done using you for the moment?"

I turned around to find Dustin standing behind me. His face flushed pink at Miroslav's words. He was still wearing those fancy team shoes.

"I wouldn't be the one making smart-ass remarks if I was lying there like you are," Dustin said. "Everybody saw what you're good for."

"With whatever the doc gave me, I don't care right now," Miroslav said. "I just say what comes into my head, and what I see is the asswipe who gets out of working by running errands and being Loretta's boy toy. You spend most of the day sitting on your ass doing nothing. You think we don't know?"

"Listen, idiot," Dustin said. "I don't care what you think or what you say. I take care of myself, which is more than you know how to do. I'm here because Malachi wants you to report to Hiep for your work assignments starting tomorrow, and I'm here in person so we know you heard it, not like a notification you can say you didn't read."

"So we know," Miroslav mimicked back. "Who's 'we'? You and Reality? I bet this is her idea."

"I don't care what you think," Dustin said. "Good luck with Hiep, little man."

"Yeah." Miroslav let his head sag down to look at the floor again.

Dustin spun on his heels to leave, but Francesca said, "Wait." Dustin stopped and looked back over his shoulder.

"As long as you're running errands, do one for me." Francesca drew herself up. I could have sworn she was preening. "I want you to tell Malachi something, and I want you to tell him because I know he doesn't look at half his notifications, but he'll want to hear this. You tell him I want to talk to him about Jerry Whitehead's death, because I've got it figured out. Almost. I'll have it all together soon."

"What?" Dustin turned back around quickly to face her.

I was completely surprised myself. "You mean you did the work with Penny on this?"

"I did the work myself, thank you very much. I didn't need Penny. I can use the molecular analyzer and I don't need or want her playing with it." She was gloating. "Tell Malachi, errand boy. I worked it out on my own. We'll see who's important here now." She pointed at me.

Dustin flushed again. I guess when everyone in town has your number, it's hard to maintain your pride. "I don't even think he cares anymore," he said dismissively. "We've got more important things to do." I could see the muscles around his jaws bunch, but he didn't say anything else. He just turned around, yet again, and left. Miroslav was giggling at the floor. Francesca had a big smile on her face as she turned toward me.

"You see, Leif," she said, "I know how to get the work done. I don't need you to play detective, and I don't need your little pet Pioneer."

CHAPTER TWENTY FOUR

I didn't want to go to sleep when I went back to my hab. I was too gloomy, mostly about the way Malachi was running the place and also about the way his ostensible leaders were behaving. I knew that Yong would tell me it was none of my business, but Yong wouldn't be down with the space-plane for another day.

I had seen Reality help Miroslav, even though she waited for Malachi to leave first and had been an active participant in getting him caned in the first place. I wondered what she was thinking. I found her by herself, out by the hydroponics facility, working under a floodlight on a bot. Apparently it wasn't going so well. She gave it a kick as I walked up.

"Working late?" I asked.

She turned with a start, saw it was me, and relaxed. "Always. Something's wrong with the control interface, and of course, nobody on the team told me during the day or knows how to fix it, so if I don't do it, we'll be behind tomorrow. I don't suppose I can give this to you. Did they even have bots when you were growing up?"

I probably could have fixed the bot, but if I was going to get that attitude, I wasn't interested. "Nope," I said. "We had just invented fire. Got a minute?"

She sat down on the ground next to the bot, arms locked around her knees. A drop of sweat rolled off the tip of her nose. Her Pioneer shirt was soaked. She looked exhausted. Or stressed. Maybe both. "What do you want?"

"What's going on in the circus that I'm seeing? You and Bjorn in particular. He starts something, even something stupid like those chants, and you pop right up and sing along."

She leaned her head between her knees for a second, then looked back up at me. "Bjorn is an asshole. He plays up to Malachi, though, and if I don't keep up . . . I have to show Malachi I'm good as a leader. I can't let Bjorn hog it."

"What about earlier with Miroslav? You helped him at the end, but you were part of making it happen with Bjorn."

"I didn't think they were really going to whip him. Not like that."

"When Bjorn hesitated, it looked like Malachi was going to give you the cane. Would you have done it?"

Reality looked at the ground. "I . . . I don't think so." She ran her fingers through her hair. "Look, I have to get this thing working, okay? It's late, it's still hot, and I'm tired." She stood up.

"Penny's on your team, isn't she?" I asked. "She's willing to work, from what I can see. Have you asked her to help?"

"Pennywise?" I heard disbelief in Reality's voice. "That's like opening the database and clicking Random Selection."

"You don't like her, do you?"

"No."

"Why not? She seems to know a lot about what the colony needs, but all any of you do is pick on her." I felt I was going off on a tangent, like Penny. This was not why I had come to see Reality, but now I wanted an answer.

Reality sighed. "She started all that Almost Good Enough crap back on the ship. I don't need that in my face. I can be the best; I am going to be the best leader. Look, I'm not denying she's smart, in her own way, and I'm sorry for how Dustin behaved. Shit, he's said things about women; anyone who's ever dated should have known what he was about, although maybe not her. That's not the point. Malachi has a plan, and that's what is going to work, and I'm going to be the best at making it work. She's stupid to talk the way she does in front of Malachi. And I don't buy that scared and helpless act. That girl wants to do something, she does it. I'll bet she did kill Whitehead." Reality paused and gave me a searching look. "Why are you so interested in Penny?"

"Just trying to understand what's going on here."

Reality gave me a sidelong glance as she turned back to the bot. "Sure. Let me give you some girl advice. If you're planning to have a go at her, I'd think about your pilot first. She's not somebody I'd want to piss off."

Thanks, Reality.

Reality's parting shot brought me back to Yong, and not in a way I wanted. Yong would be down in one more day, and there was something I needed to do, something that had been set off when Yong talked about her experience in Sumatra. The *Dauntless*, of course, had all the launch and flight parameters, so I checked them through the computer system without calling Yong. No reason, really, to be checking the launch and landing times to the minute. Certainly no reason to bother her with that. Of course not.

I needed to conduct a test of my own. One I definitely did not want to discuss. Yong had told me about her flashback. I had not forgotten mine of the dying soldier that had hit me in the valley. I'd had others too. I had told myself I was over this. Maybe not. It made me think how often my mind floated back to the Troubles when I thought of Yong, back to us in the Troubles. I needed to know something. About myself. About my triggers. So I headed out to the LZ the next day, ahead of the planned landing.

It was quiet and windy by the landing strip. I shared the LZ with only a couple of shellhounds rooting around in the sparse grass. Otherwise, it was a typical sweltering day on Heaven.

A boom from high in the sky heralded the arrival of the spaceplane. I couldn't see it at first; only the sound reached down to me. Then I saw a dot against the white-blue sky, far out over the ocean.

Quickly, the dot grew larger and dropped lower. I saw its wings. I watched it. I checked for my rifle. Where was it? Where were my men? I seemed to be alone on the defense line outside Camp Schwarzkopf on Mindanao. Low over the water, the dot became a thin black line that grew into what could only be the shadow of a J-45 superstealth. Nothing on instruments, no warning in my ear from the base. Of course. Shaking and sweating, I screamed to my platoon to fire on visual because the damned plane didn't register on our instruments. I realized I didn't even have a rifle. My hand went to the holster for my pistol, a futile move against an attack plane if there ever was one. I could feel my heart pound, and my jaw clenched tight. I was going to die as soon as that damned pilot fired their missiles. Then the roar of the incoming spaceplane washed over me and penetrated my waking nightmare. You never heard a J-45 until it was right over you. I cursed and fought to free my mind of the images, to slow my heart, to shut off my adrenaline. I had failed my test.

I had convinced myself that I was past all of that. Past having that happen when I saw a plane, or sometimes even a bird, flying in low over the water. It had been Yong's plane. It was always Yong's plane. I wished I had left well enough alone. Maybe it would never go away, not if I stood on a thousand different planets under a thousand different suns. I cursed again.

My mind cleared. I stood on the windswept plain of a godforsaken planet under the baleful glare of its star and was grateful to be there. I told myself that the sweat under my arms was only from Heaven's heat. I tried to believe that.

A spaceplane landing isn't much different from an airliner landing, except spaceplanes are bigger. This one was huge, designed to ferry in two trips the supplies that a colony of two hundred people on another planet would need. That size became clear as it neared the LZ, a giant delta-wing shadow that blocked the sun. The ground vibrated from the roar of its engines. Yong turned it in a graceful arc—as much as anything so big could be said to have grace—and lined it up with the marks for the landing strip. Slowly, the spaceplane settled the last few feet to the ground. The landing skids touched. With a gunshot bang, the final parachutes deployed. The friction sections of the skids bit into the earth, and the engines blasted to help with the braking. Smoothly, the huge spaceplane came to a halt. Yong could make even the impossible look routine.

Even before the hatches to the passenger cabin and cockpit opened, the belly of the spaceplane split open and extended a ramp. As soon as the ramp touched the ground, a line of bots began to roll down it laden with crates and pallets. The cargo would unload without the need of human intervention. People wouldn't be needed until the cargo had to be arranged for transport to St. Peterstown, as it was impossible for the bots to be programmed to anticipate what transport would be available.

While I watched the start of the unloading, Yong and Jorge came down from the cockpit while Dr. Song Jing and Dev Likhar came from the passenger cabin. Charley would be up in orbit with only the second nuclear engineer and the two ship systems engineers for company. I tried not to look only at Yong as the four of them walked over to the rover—or at least not to be obvious about where my eyes were focused.

Jing wrinkled her nose as a gust hit her face when she reached the rover. "Worse than Shanghai in monsoon season," she said.

"I won't bother saying you get used to it," I said. "Maybe it won't take us that long to get finished."

Dev patted a small pack he had slung across his body. "The reactor shouldn't take that long at all," he said. "We have the failure spot pinpointed, so, if nothing else, power will not be a problem."

"Then let's get to it," Yong said. "The bots here will be busy enough with the unloading. Once the power situation is fixed, they can spare people to work on getting this stuff into town. Jing, you should meet with the doctor here. See what you can do with the equipment once we get you chipped in. She's broadcasting to everyone that she's got the poison figured out, that she knows all about it, but I haven't actually seen any specific information. Jorge, we'll have you chipped in also. You're good with IT systems."

When she finished with those dispositions, Yong took a careful look at me. Close inspection, really. It made me think of a drill instructor checking for deficiencies in my uniform or gear. She didn't say anything, though, and I didn't see anything in her face that told me what was in her mind.

I probably should have asked.

. . .

We messaged Francesca to meet us at the Medical Unit, and she was there when we arrived.

"Welcome to St. Peterstown, Dr. Song," Francesca said. "I'm sorry you felt you had to make the trip down, but I'll be glad to show you our facilities and tell you what I've been able to do on my own. Maybe that will make the trip worthwhile for you."

Francesca's voice held a wariness that belied her friendly greeting. It was present in her eyes and the way she held herself. She was anything but happy to see Jing. Why? If the work was done, it wasn't as though Jing would try to take the credit. Jing didn't notice Francesca's attitude, or if she did, she didn't let on. I figured the two of them would work it out, so the other three of us piled back into the rover and drove to what I thought of as Malachi's command tent.

Malachi was there to meet us, freshly shaved and all cordiality, as though nothing had happened the previous day.

"You know how to get to the reactor?" he asked.

"It's out there somewhere." I gestured to the door of the little hab with one hand. "I assume I can bring up the directions on my phone base."

Malachi grinned. "That you can. However, the entrance to the reactor shaft, which is where you access all the circuitry, is restricted. One of the very few doors in St. Peterstown that actually locks. I'll have Hiep go with you to get you in."

His eyes shifted to his right as he brought up Hiep's contact in his field. "Hiep, will you meet Leif and his party by my field base and get them into the reactor shaft?" He waited for an instant, obviously listening to the response, then focused back on me. "If you wait outside, Hiep will meet you here. Just give him a minute or two."

It wasn't much longer than that before I saw Hiep headed toward us at as close to a trot as anyone would do on Heaven. He arrived, breathing heavily, with the M8 over his shoulder. He was wearing a shirt. He pulled himself into the rover without a word. The three of us exchanged glances and shrugs, then piled in after him. I started the rover bouncing over the plain, following the directions to the reactor that showed on my phone base.

"I thought you were supposed to be giving directions to Miroslav and what used to be his team," I said after Hiep did not say anything.

"Malachi told me to do this," Hiep said.

"And then you'll go back to that team?"

"Whatever Malachi wants," Hiep said. "He's the boss."

It didn't seem likely I was going to get any more conversation out of him. When I looked over at Yong, her face was every bit as closed off. The ride was silent except for the occasional jounce over the uneven ground.

The reactor site was marked aboveground by a silvery metal shield and a set of antennas. The reactor itself had been buried in a shaft excavated by the crew and bots of the *Daredevil*. This was not a nuclear plant in the sense of a fission reactor, the type of reactor that supplied power to wide swaths of Earth. Those plants were huge facilities and required extensive water flow for cooling. Setting one up on a planet around another star was far beyond the ability of any starship crew, even if we had a starship big enough to transport the material it would need. The reactor chosen to power the human colony on Heaven for a couple of centuries was a simple radioisotope decay model. The actual reactor was underground and away from town because, well, who wants a radioactive generator in their house? Reactors like it had powered the initial Mars settlements. They were easy to manage, durable, and nearly foolproof. Apparently, however, they were not proof against sabotage via a deadman switch.

A small hab unit, similar to the one Malachi was using, was set up next to the ground-level reactor shield. Hiep's chip interfaced with the door controls and we were admitted. A trapdoor inside that also had a lock, which opened to reveal a short flight of plastic stairs down to where the circuitry for the reactor and the electrical grid could be accessed. Another rover showed up while we were looking at the descent, bringing one of the *Daredevil* colonists who had been trained on the reactor operation.

"This shouldn't take long," Dev said. "It's just a matter of matching the physical layout to the circuit diagram, popping in the replacement, and we're done."

There was only room for two at the bottom of the stairs, so he went down with the woman from St. Peterstown.

Their time down the shaft was not, however, brief. While we waited, Yong matched Hiep, lack of word or expression for lack of word or expression. That left me with the choice of talking to myself or copying them. I copied. When Dev came back up, he did not look pleased.

"We have a problem," he said. "The reactor itself is fine. You would damn near need a bomb to do anything to one of these. Whatever malware the dead guy here let loose wound up frying a chip in the transmission circuits. I've got the chip we need. I can even replace the entire board." He stopped and looked disgusted.

"There is a 'but' here," I said. "What's the problem?"

"The connector slot the board goes into is damaged. I can't tell you if whatever fried the chip caused it or whether the connector was damaged when the guys here examined the system. Maybe they tried to jigger it. I don't know and it doesn't matter. I've replaced the board and it doesn't work. I've got two replacement boards and I've tried both. I could replace the chip directly on the board, but I didn't bother, because the problem is at the connector."

"Is the connector something that can be replaced?" I asked.

"Oh, sure," Dev said. "Any part store would have it. Order it and drone delivery the next day. But not here. I could probably find the right one in a noncritical system on the ship and take that apart to get one I could use."

"However," Yong said, "the spaceplane cannot make a third round trip, nor can we drop a free fall capsule."

"Correct," Dev said. "The reactor is useless."

"The stored power," I said. "How long?"

Dev shrugged. "Another week at full power, I guess, from the readings here on the power draw. Maybe another week at reduced power. If you scale back the draw, it can be extended, but it will go down sooner or later. I hope they have the photovoltaic array to the point where that can take over."

"I need to call Malachi," Hiep said. He turned and went outside.

CHAPTER TWENTY FIVE

The four of us rode back to St. Peterstown together. It was a glum ride. Dev felt like he had wasted his time. I wasn't so sure of that, because without him I don't think we would have known the problem went beyond the chip, but Dev could only focus on the idea that the colonists should have found the connector problem themselves. Then he would have been able to come down with what was needed and would have fixed it. As it was, all he wanted to do was get off this, as he put it, steam bath of a planet. It wasn't too polite of him to carry on that way with Hiep in the rover, but Hiep either paid no attention or pretended not to. Of course, Dev couldn't go back to the ship until we were all ready to go, and that did not improve his mood in the least.

While I was driving, a message notification flashed on my field. It was from Jing. She needed to see me and Yong as soon as we returned.

Song Jing was standing outside the hab Yong and I had been using when we rolled up in the rover. She had her arms crossed over her chest and was pacing back and forth in the roadway. Yong and I were barely out of the rover before she was directly in front of us.

"We have a problem," she said.

I really, really hate that phrase.

"Did you run a sample from the thistle leaves through the instruments and come up with something really odd?" I asked. "I'm surprised you had enough time."

"I did not come up with anything, and that is part of the problem," she said. "Francesca will not let me on the molecular analyzer. She said she does not need help and she showed me her results. The leaves do contain a cholinesterase inhibitor. It will not, probably, be absorbed through your skin. If you swallow enough of it, or inhale it, yes, that will be trouble. If you rub a little of it in your eyes, you will get a local reaction only."

"That is what I did," Hiep said.

I had not realized that he had joined us, but he was there, listening closely. I remembered that he had been trained as an assassin.

"Ah," Jing said, "Leif told me about what happened in the valley, but I didn't realize it was you. Did you have any other symptoms? Any runny nose, drooling, anything like that?"

"No," Hiep said. "I know what happens with these chemwar agents. I had nothing else."

"That fits," Jing said. "This is a poison, a dangerous one, but it's not weaponized. Francesca would not, however, let me access the analyzer to check for myself."

"Do you think you need to? Do you think she got it wrong?" I asked.

Jing shook her head, albeit reluctantly. "Probably not. She's had some research training. But that is part of the bigger problem. When I challenged her and we spoke, one thing led to another. The real issue is about her as a doctor."

"So she told you about the deliveries she botched," I said. "She told me about them."

"Yes, she spoke about that," Jing said, "and, as I said, one question led to another and answers led to other questions. The problem is that she is not a physician."

"Excuse me?" I said.

"Wait." That came from Yong, her voice hard and cold. "How is it possible that the physician for the settlement is not a physician? What is she?"

Yong advanced so that she was practically on top of Jing, which led Jing to back up two steps. Hiep was right behind Yong, staring at Jing past Yong's shoulder.

"I can't tell you how it happened," Jing said, "although we all know that electronic systems can be hacked. Sometimes records can simply be altered, if you know the right people, ones who already have access. What I can tell you is that she went to medical school but never finished, so, of course, she never had any specialty training. But she got a job somehow—she won't say how—and then there were problems. Those didn't happen because she was high. She didn't know what to do when complications came up. She managed to keep it hidden coming here, but Jerry found out. He was blackmailing her for sex."

"A doctor who can deliver babies, both from a woman and an artificial womb, that is one of the most important jobs we have," Hiep said. "This doctor also must train the next generation here."

"No shit," I said. "I think you're going to be giving Malachi another call he's not going to like." I paused for a second. "How is it possible the ISC could screw up this badly? How can they send out a crew to start a colony around another star and come up with people who are so ill suited to the task?"

"You know the answer, Leif," Hiep said.

I jumped a little at the words. My question had been mostly rhetorical; I had seen plenty of ISC screwups before. But I really hadn't expected Hiep to answer it, of all people. Nor did I expect the anger in his voice.

"You all know why." More heat, more emotion, colored that one sentence than I had heard in everything he had said before put together. "In my country, in Vietnam, there are villages where people live much as they did in the twentieth century. They would come here to live, if they could. They would use less than one percent of the power this settlement does, power this town cannot live without, and still be successful. They would grow their food, raise their animals, have their children. Here, they would be able to do it without fear of free companies or Major Powers. But they do not get the chance. Because the Americans, and the Chinese, and the Russians, and the Europeans reserve the stars for their people. Even if they send criminals, and incompetents, and hopeless ones who are little more than children." He spat on the ground at his feet. "I will call Malachi about this, and I will walk back to his post myself to see what duties he has for me next."

Hiep was gone before I could think of anything to say.

·   ·   ·

After Hiep left, Yong, Dev, Jing, and I repaired to the interior of the hab, where we could benefit from air-conditioning while we kicked around the information we had. Dev flopped on a soft chair that reclined under him and interlaced his fingers behind his head. It was a pose that suggested polite attention, but his mind was elsewhere. Jing was the opposite. She paced back and forth in front of the chairs Yong and I had taken with enough shakes of her head that the bun containing her hair threatened to come loose.

"He either ate it or he inhaled it," she said for the third time. "It won't cross the skin. Could someone have put it in his food?"

"He didn't eat it," I said. Jing stopped and stared at me. "These agents all work the same way," I continued. "If he ate it, he would have had trouble with his gut first. I have the data from his chip. He had breathing problems first."

Yong nodded.

"Okay. Then he inhaled it," Jing said. "But how? If somebody walked in and sprayed him with it, they would die too."

"Right," I said. "There are no chemwar suits on the planet. I'm not even sure the Medical Unit has atropine and 2-PAM. Anyway, it would be really ballsy to expose yourself while gassing him and bet on giving yourself the antidotes in time."

"What about the air intake?" Jing asked. "Maybe it was put in that way?"

"That would not work," Yong said. "These habs are a basic design; they all use the same standard. The entry is designed to fit an air lock. They don't need them here, so the air locks aren't included, but the build has the electronics and also has multiple filters in the air systems to take care of unexpected allergens or even unexpected gases in the air. Granted, they're not set up for chemwar with nerve agents, but I think elements of the filters will react with those agents and take them out."

An idea clicked in my head. "Jerry was a leafer. The people here say he smoked a lot. Could someone have doped his joints?"

"But if he was smoking it, then why didn't Vanessa die when she came in?" Jing asked. "It would still be in the air."

"Vanessa said the air system was on when she came in," I said. "If the filters cleared it, that would explain why she was okay."

"Penny said his hab was full of smoke," Yong said. "If she put it on his joints, or gave him laced ones, she could have left and turned the system on when she went out."

I found I didn't want it to be Penny. Did Yong feel the other way? "Could Penny have turned on the air system if she wasn't on the network?" I asked.

"You know the answer to that," Yong said. "The air system has manual control for emergencies. It's part of the air lock circuitry, and we used that the first night we were here. You should not look past the obvious, even if it leads to an answer you don't want."

I didn't want to hear that. "Penny said Jerry had a little case he kept his joints in. If we could check that for the agent, it would help. Vanessa didn't mention seeing it when she came in."

"Penny could have taken it with her," Yong said.

"This all assumes she knew what was in the thistle leaves before we went to the valley," I said. "I don't think she did." I was afraid defending Penny this way made it look as though I had an ulterior motive. I tried to remind myself how surprised I had been on the beach at the lies she had kept hidden. "What about Francesca, our doc who's not a doc? Even if she didn't finish, she would know about these agents and how to handle them."

"She didn't know until you came back from your trip," Yong said.

"No!" Jing was practically dancing on the floor. "That isn't true. Not possible. Look, she knows about these agents, yes, and she knows how to run the molecular analyzer, yes, but there is *no way* she had enough time to do all the work between when you came back and when I got here and she showed it to me. That analysis had to have been done before, which means it could have been done at any time. That's why she didn't want me in the instruments! Time stamps. You have to get me access to the records from the instruments."

"Sure," I said. "I can ask Malachi."

"Malachi is a chemist," Yong said.

"Malachi was at the lake with me that night."

"But, as Jing has said, this could have been done in advance." Her retort came back fast and without any inflection.

I thought about our outing to the lake, how it had not felt like it served any purpose. It hadn't felt like an attempt to become buddy-buddy. What had been the point? His question about me staying did not need to be asked in the middle of nowhere.

"I was his alibi," I said. "Maybe he didn't need to be here. Hiep takes his orders. He says that's because Malachi was elected mayor, but did he take them before? And Hiep is a trained assassin." Now, that was a profoundly disturbing thought. Then I decided I was following a false path.

"Can't be," I said. "Malachi was convinced the deadman switch was real. He wouldn't take that chance. And if we are ignoring the deadman switch, don't forget Vanessa and Oscar and practically everyone else here who hated Jerry. Maybe we should try to identify the one person on the planet who didn't have a reason to want him dead, and that will turn out to be the real murderer."

"Was that supposed to be a joke, Leif?" Yong asked.

I wished I could tell if she was angry at what I'd said. I thought I could hear an edge in her voice, but her face told me nothing.

"Dumb joke or not," Jing said, "none of these other people would have had a clue about the molecule. We need to see the records from the molecular analyzer, and we need to find Jerry's joint case. I think we also need to have another conversation with Francesca. All of us together, so she can understand we're serious and she can't duck it."

Sonal slumped into the hab at that point, ending the conversation. If a person could ever be said to be a poem, she was "The Wreck of the Hesperus." She dropped into a chair with a sigh and, as a ship, looked ready to sink. She tilted her head back and looked at the ceiling.

"Are you okay?" Jing asked, which was a silly doctor-type of question because Sonal was obviously *not* okay.

"My poor kids," Sonal said. "My Pioneers, I mean. You can't work all day with only short breaks, not in this heat and sun. We're going to have heatstroke cases, and some of the sunburns are pretty bad. We have to split the day up, shorten the outside working hours, but all I hear is 'faster, faster, faster.' That Loretta is the worst of them, and my Pioneers who were appointed Team Leads are copying her. When I went to her, she told me if I kept making trouble, she'd have me do double work with no breaks while everyone watched. I mean, what is this? A labor camp out of the history books?"

Yong and I looked at each other. We were out of the history books.

"Sometimes history repeats itself," I said. "The reactor cannot be salvaged." I pointed to Dev, who gave a nod with a sour face. "Stored power will be gone in maybe two weeks."

"It's also getting to be winter," Yong said. "The axial tilt is only ten degrees, but we are so far south the daylight hours are short already, and that will affect what we get from photovoltaics. I'm not trying to excuse the working conditions. The colony needs to survive, and killing people with work is as bad as not doing the work."

"Why didn't they put photovoltaics in the roofing of the habs?" Sonal asked. "That would have helped a lot. The rovers are designed that way."

"The rovers go away from the town," I said. "They need their own power source. As for the habs, you can drive yourself crazy wondering why people on Earth miss stuff that's needed out here. It happened on the first starshot. Either they didn't think, or they thought it wasn't an issue, because you have a reactor and a large field of photovoltaic panels that are more efficient than rooftops."

Sonal shuddered. "If this is winter, I'm not sure I want to see summer." She put her face in her hands. "It's too much physical work, not just bot work, and they're forcing us to make up for what the *Daredevil* crew didn't do when they had plenty of time for it. And I'll tell you, that one, Hiep from the *Daredevil*, there are rumors about him. This isn't what we came for. It's not right. It's not."

"You mean it's not that line from *Candide* Penny said they taught in school? You know, the one about everything being for the best and this is the best of all possible worlds?"

Sonal grimaced. Yong glared—at least, I think she did.

I was trying to lighten the mood, but I could see it was a flop. Too much cute line, too little empathy. I've been told I don't win awards for empathy.

"We used to laugh when people used that line," Sonal said, "but right now, I'd give almost anything to be back there groaning about it." She rubbed at her eyes.

Jing walked into the kitchen area and filled a cup with cold water. She brought that back to Sonal, who gulped it down.

"Thanks," Sonal said. "I didn't mean to cry on your shoulders. I . . . well, we'll get through this. I'm going to find Klaus and get some sleep."

"We'll talk to Malachi," Yong said. "He needs to understand that he will not succeed this way."

"I'm afraid the people he has appointed don't know any other way," I said. "He needs to have them change, but I'm not sure he's going to do it."

"Thanks for whatever you can do," Sonal said.

After Sonal left, we split up with Jing and Jorge taking the next-door hab, and Dev one by himself. Yong didn't offer any conversation once we were alone. Her face reminded me of the way it looked when we first met, when we had seen each other as enemies.

"What are you thinking?" I asked.

"There is trouble here." Tension was obvious in her voice.

"I thought our job wasn't to tell the colony how to run themselves. Or is the trouble between us?"

"The colony is obviously the issue. If you are thinking about making bad jokes when someone is ready to cry, you should think again. Your Malachi does not govern gently."

When did he become my Malachi? She ignored my raised eyebrow.

"From what Sonal said, I would like to hear more about this person you traveled with," Yong said. "This Hiep."

I managed to keep my sigh to myself. I knew why she was only interested in talking about Hiep. My mouth has gotten me in trouble more than once. I did not want to have screwed it up with the only woman I've ever . . . well, been simpatico with, really gotten along with.

"Look, Yong, I'm sorry if I said something wrong. Especially from the valley."

Her face was still, although her eyes narrowed. "There was nothing you said, and nothing is wrong."

I think that meant something was.

CHAPTER TWENTY SIX

An alert from my phone woke me in the darkness. I checked the time in my field. It was early morning, a little before five on Heaven's adapted clock. It would not be light for hours. I groaned, sat up, and focused on the blinking notification. It was Sonal. I looked at it to connect the call.

"Leif." Her voice shook just saying my name. "Can you come over to the Medical Unit? We have a problem."

That phrase again. "Should I bring our doc?"

"Too late for that." Sonal clicked off.

Yong was already sitting up beside me. I repeated what Sonal had said. She nodded without a word and got out of bed to pull clothes on. We might not have resolved our issue—spat, if you will—from before, but if there was a problem, Yong would have my back and I can't think of any-one I would rather have doing that. I went over to the next hab and woke Jing. If there was some problem in the Med Unit, I wanted our doc with me regardless of what Sonal said. Doctors are accustomed to being wak-ened at all hours. She was ready as fast as Yong and I were.

The lights were on in the Medical Unit when we arrived. Inside was quite a scene. Sonal and Yuki Watanabe, one of our two young nurses, were standing over a body that lay on the floor in a substantial puddle of blood. Yuki had stepped in the blood, tracked it around, and was now scraping the sole of her shoe against the floor, trying to get it off. As I went over to them, I could see she also had blood on her knees, lower pant legs, and hands. That figured, I supposed. If she had found the body, she would have kneeled down to check for life. Which was clearly not there. I walked over, along with Yong and Jing. The corpse was Francesca.

"How did this happen?" I asked. "Wait. We obviously don't know. So what do we know?"

Sonal shook her head. "Yuki found her and called me. This is . . . I don't know . . ." She wrung her hands and looked ready to cry. "I called you. That seemed to be the right thing. Yuki, tell Leif what you told me."

Yuki was small and nervous. Being the focus of all four sets of eyes was not where she wanted to be. Her voice trembled. "One of the girls in the Pioneers, she told me she was out walking here, out late, and she heard screams. She went and got me because she couldn't sleep afterward and because I help Francesca at the Medical Unit. She was upset. She was sorry she didn't call anyone when she heard it, so she wanted me to check it out. She was scared. So I came down here and found . . . this." She spread her hands wide, taking in the scene in front of her. "She was dead when I got here. I swear there was nothing I could do. I mean, I thought I should try something, and I looked around for something to use, but she was really dead and nothing I did was going to matter."

I followed her eyes as she looked around the unit. Of course, she had checked Francesca first and gotten the blood all over her hands. Then she had gone around the unit and smeared that blood across exam beds, benches, drawers, and instruments.

"That was why I called Sonal," she said. "I couldn't think of anything else to do."

"Which brings us to now," Sonal said. "What do we do now?"

I looked at the people with me, one of them dead. I looked at the bloody mess that was the body and that Yuki had left in the Medical Unit. I was now the first interstellar crime scene investigator. Great title, but how was I going to do this? Lord knows, I had killed enough people in combat. But under those circumstances, all I'd cared about was that I was alive and they were dead.

"Can we put her on one of the exam tables?" Jing asked. "I want to see what killed her and I'd like to download her chip."

With Yong and me helping Jing, we were able to get Francesca's body onto an exam table without getting too much blood onto ourselves. The body was still warm but it was stiffening.

"It's been several hours," Jing said. "Hang on. I don't remember the exact timing. I specialized in rural medicine, so I can do some of almost everything, but not forensics."

I saw her look to the side as she pulled up a reference.

"As little as three, as many as eight hours," she said. "That's not very helpful. Wait until we download her chip."

Before she went for the hookup, though, Jing started peeling the clothes off the body. Stab and slash wounds were everywhere on the upper body, all in the front. Yuki let out a gasp. I hoped we didn't have a nurse with a weak stomach.

"This was done with a knife," Jing said. "Thin blade, not serrated. I spent enough Saturday nights in the emergency room to know. Anybody see a knife?"

We looked around but did not see one on the floor or any of the surfaces.

"Our killer took it with them," Yong said. "When we leave, we should check the ground around the unit."

"Forty-seven discrete wounds," Jing said when she finished her inventory. "I saw enough messes in the ER to know what I'm looking at here. Defensive wounds here and here." She pointed at cuts and stabs on the outside of both arms. "And see this." She spread one of Francesca's hands open to show cuts across the fingers and palm. "She grabbed the blade. This is what happens."

"She didn't know how to fight," Yong said.

I agreed. "All she did was try to shield her face and grab the knife away by the blade, like Jing said. Then I think she gave up."

"This is what finally did it." Jing pointed to a stab wound between two ribs and over the heart.

"Whoever did this had no idea what they were doing either." I peered at the wounds. "They were in front of her, and obviously close. With someone who doesn't know how to defend themselves, it takes a fraction of a second and one thrust. At most, two to be sure."

"Unless they wanted it to look this way," Yong added.

While we were talking, Jing had turned on the chip connector and pulled its cord out of the instrument panel at the head of the exam table. An implanted chip has a neural interface and it is powered On as long as there is brain activity—as long as the brain is "on." On Earth, folks have their chips set to send alerts or other information to their doctors; if you have high blood pressure, it will send your blood pressure however many times a day the doc asks you to set it for. When you go for your doctor visits, the doc fastens the diagnostic reader over where the chip is—closer to the chip is best—and pulls out all sorts of information about what your body has been doing. At death, the chip goes into sleep mode. Normally, if information is needed after someone dies, as in been murdered, the hospital would remove the chip, insert it into a socket, and download its memory. We couldn't do that in the Medical Unit on another planet, but, just as Francesca did with Jerry, we could use the diagnostic interface to make the chip wake up and give us some information. Jing fussed with the settings, then tapped a button on the screen, and we watched a line on the screen draw a circle for a while. Then it flashed DOWNLOAD SUCCESSFUL.

Jing scanned through the readouts she brought up on the screen. "I have the time she died from the chip. It's Earth time, I'm afraid, but I've got current Earth time on my own field. Give me a sec to convert the difference to Heaven hours and minutes." After a pause while she did the arithmetic, Jing said, "She died at 21:03, Heaven time. I wonder why she was here so late."

"She always was," Yuki said.

I spun around at her voice. I had forgotten that she had stayed with us. "Why?" I asked. "There can't have been that many people who needed the doc or the Medical Unit."

"It wasn't work," Yuki said. "Francesca made a big deal of telling all of us that she didn't smoke leaf anymore, but she came back here after dinner to get high. She'd close the place up and have the air system maxed, but we all knew. She knew we knew but she kept pretending."

"Okay." I really didn't care anymore about people's fiction or pretense. Out of two hundred ill-assorted people sent to colonize a strange planet, two had already been murdered. "So the entire population knows she'll be here late, alone, and high. Why does one of them kill her?"

I received blank looks for answers.

"Whatever kind of criminal history the *Daredevil* group had, they wouldn't be given to sudden, irrational homicide," I said.

"Well, the Pioneers were carefully screened. I *know* that," Jing said.

However, psych screens could be adjusted. *I* knew that. Hiep was an assassin, and the other free company men and women were certainly killers in the past. Still, this didn't make sense as a spontaneous, irrational event.

"I can think of possibilities," Yong said, as though picking up on my thought. "Either she had something someone wanted, or she was threatening someone and they decided to kill her to shut her up. I suppose . . . I suppose it could have been a refused demand for sex."

Yong and I had grown up in a very prudish time in history, a reaction to the early part of the twenty-first century. I think Yong would rather have flown solo into the entire North American air defense than talk about sex in public. I wasn't that bad, but maybe that depends on whom you ask.

That was when I had an instant of what people like to call blinding clarity, although it really wasn't any more brilliant than realizing two plus two equals four. "Wait a minute. When Vanessa found Jerry's body, who went over and examined him? Francesca. And remember, Penny said she saw Jerry's little case with joints in it on his table, but no one ever found it in his hab afterward. Vanessa didn't mention it, but she was a little shocked. Maybe she didn't notice. Could Francesca have taken it, or known who did? Remember, she said she had worked out the poisoning. Could someone have gotten nervous?"

"That's a lot of ifs." Yong was dubious.

"Yeah," I said, "but we should look to see if the case is around."

Yong and Jing searched through cabinets and drawers without success. They found nothing. As a last check, Jing went through Francesca's clothes. No case.

"No phone base either," Jing said. "Where's her phone base? Could she have been able to record who came in and attacked her?"

The phone base was not something Francesca would have hidden, but we checked the unit again anyway. No phone base. The attacker must have taken it. The electronics were probably ground up and buried by now.

"Even if we had it," Yong said, "how many people would be able to start recording when someone surprises them and attacks with a knife?"

"Probably no one," I said. "Is there anything in the download from the chip?"

Jing laughed. "That's only in vids where your chip has a record of what your eyes saw. That's not the way they work."

"I knew the old chips didn't work that way. I just wasn't sure if in the last few years, the new ones might have had more capabilities." I hadn't lived through those years. Sometimes the gaps in my knowledge were embarrassing.

It did make me think to check the information collected by the entry door. It took only a few minutes to locate those records. "The Medical Unit door opened just before she died and then again right after she died." The next set of lines on the screen brought me to a stop. "Two people came in and out, with the same times for the door opening. Does that make sense?" Then I saw the ident line. "One of them was chipped out. The other was Penny." I said that slowly. "That doesn't make sense at all. Penny doesn't hang around or go anywhere with anyone else."

"There was only one weapon, and from the wounds, I'm sure she wasn't being held." Jing was emphatic.

"If two people come to commit murder, I have trouble with the idea that one does it and the other only watches."

"Things like that happen," Jing said.

"Yuki," Yong said, ignoring the expression on my face, "you told us one of the Pioneers was near here and heard screams. Someone, maybe Penny plus someone else, went in and out of that door. Did she see anybody?"

"She didn't say."

"We need to talk to her," Yong said. "What's her name?"

"I don't want to get her in trouble. She didn't do anything wrong." I could see Yuki shaking under Yong's interrogation.

"I didn't say she did." Yong's tone became sharper. "I'm not expecting any of you to bare-handed take on someone with a knife, but it would be useful if she saw someone. Now, who is she and where do we find her?"

"Athena Markopoulos," Yuki said in a whisper. "She'll still be asleep."

"Then she needs to wake up," Yong said. "Now, before we go see her, is there anything else we can get from here?"

I scanned the unit, trying to think of what I should look for. "Whoever killed her would have gotten blood on their shoes or boots, same as Yuki did. Anybody see a different footprint?"

Jing walked around the unit, head down, checking the floor. "Most of these look like Yuki's," she said. "But here and there"—she pointed—"looks like a different one. Yuki's feet are very small. These are larger."

"They're smeared," I said. "Could someone have seen their own tracks and wiped them?"

Yong shrugged. "It's possible. I can't tell if it would be a man's or a woman's. Everyone gets ISC-issued gear, even if they have their own personal stuff."

"I'll record it anyway," said Jing. "There's also a smear on this bench back by the window. Could someone have climbed up here and opened the window to get out?"

"They may have checked the window," Yong said, "but it's not consistent with two people going through the door. We can look for footprints in the dirt back there when it's light. It will be obvious if someone went out that way."

It was frustrating. Here we were, not counting Yuki, three highly trained individuals, entrusted by humanity with the fate of missions to the stars, and we had no idea how to handle a crime scene. It wasn't just the crime scene. It was ironic that for all the advanced technology we used to fly across interstellar space and plant a town on a new world, we didn't know how to take samples for DNA or check for fingerprints. True, we could have looked up how to do it and, maybe, found the materials we would need, but would that do any good? This was the Medical Unit for everyone in St. Peterstown. Would it even matter if we found that someone had been in here? Hadn't everyone in St. Peterstown been in here at one time or another?

Now I was the one who had to call Malachi.

CHAPTER TWENTY SEVEN

"You have a point, Leif," Malachi said after I told him what we had found and what must have happened. At least I hadn't woken him with the call. He was also up early. "I said I would have a patrol at night even though I believed what happened with Whitehead was only about Jerry Whitehead and was not an immediate need.

"You may have noticed that I have a few things on my mind. The reactor cannot be fixed; the photovoltaics have to supply all the power for the town but they don't yet; the daylight hours get shorter, and people can't work faster. I haven't set a night watch. I guess that was a mistake." It was impossible to miss the sarcasm in his voice. "Do me a favor and help me find this killer before you leave. That would be the best thing you could do to put this colony on a sound footing."

I guess that was Malachi's version of a guilt trip.

It was still dark when we left the Medical Unit to call on Athena Markopoulos. We checked the ground around the unit for the murder weapon before we left, but without any luck. I figured one of us would need to come back when the sun was up. It was too easy to miss a knife on the ground searching by phone base light.

I sent a message with an alarm to this Athena Markopoulos so that she would be awake, if not happy, to see us. The hab she had taken was in the middle of a large group of the Pioneers along the Avenue of Australia, about halfway out to the perimeter road. It didn't take us too long to walk there.

She met us outside the door to her hab, arms folded across her chest and a face showing a mixture of pissed off and being too scared to show how pissed off she was.

"Why did you need to wake me up?" she asked before I was even close enough to make out her features in the predawn light.

"Francesca was killed last night, murdered," I said. "You told Yuki you were down there and heard screams. Want to tell us about it?"

"I had to tell them," Yuki said quickly. "It's awful."

"Yes, stabbed forty-seven times qualifies as awful." I wasn't being gentle. "You were down there. What did you see?"

"N-nothing." Her voice quavered and tears started from the corners of her eyes. "I had a . . . a fight with my partner. Nothing physical, nothing like that, just some yelling, and I was upset, so I took a walk. Seemed like the smart thing to do. I was right outside the Medical Unit when I heard the screams. I could hear them in the Town Circle."

"What did you do?" I asked.

"Nothing," she said, and broke down with her face in her hands. "I just stood there. I froze. I didn't do anything. I should have gone in."

"No," Yong said. "All that would have done was get you hurt too."

Yong actually sounded gentle, and she was probably right.

"Did you hear anything but the screams?" I tried to make my tone match Yong's. "Was anyone yelling anything you could understand?"

Athena bit her lip and shook her head vigorously.

"Okay," I said. "How long were you outside the Med Unit?"

"I don't know. A couple of minutes, maybe, I don't know. Maybe it wasn't even that long. It felt like forever. Then I was afraid someone would come out and see *me* and I ran."

"You were afraid someone would come out," I repeated. "Did you see anyone? Did anyone come out?"

"No." She shook her head three times for emphasis. "It's not like I was right in front of the door. I was coming down the Avenue of Australia on the side. Look, can I go back and lie down a little more? I've hardly slept and I have to work on the hydroponic expansion, and that's hard enough in this heat even without listening to that damn Pennywise going on and on about what we should be doing with the hydroponics, or what to farm, or making sunscreen out of shellhound shells. And those guards of Malachi's get nasty if they think you're not keeping up, and . . . I'm sorry."

"Don't be sorry," I said. "You didn't do anything wrong."

We stood outside the hab after Athena vanished through the door. *That didn't accomplish much.*

I turned back to the others. "Jing, why don't you take Yuki and get the Medical Unit cleaned up in case someone needs it. Also see if there's a body bag or something we can put Francesca in. When it's light, go look behind the unit and see if there are footprints below that window. When you have a chance, check the unit again and check Francesca's hab for Jerry's joint case."

"I have to be back at the spaceplane," Yong said, "but if you need me, message me."

"I'll do that," I said.

As soon as it was properly morning, there was someone else I needed to see. Hiep.

· · ·

Hiep replied to my message saying that he would be with the work team at the photovoltaic panel array. The field of panels was growing, slower than I had thought it would with bots to do much of the heavy work, but fast enough, I hoped, to provide adequate power for St. Peterstown even with the lessening daylight. It was easy to spot Hiep. He stood away from any shadows offered by the panels, as if disdainful of the sun's glare. Ominously, it seemed, he had an M8 slung over his shoulder.

As a way to start the conversation, I went up to him and said, "I see you're still wearing the shirt."

"The girl knows what she is talking about," he said. "Do you?" His voice still held the harsh edge it had when we found out Francesca was a fake doc and he spoke of who monopolized the chances to go to the stars.

Hiep was not my friend.

"Francesca was killed last night," I said.

"And you want to know if I killed her." That was a statement, not a question.

"Did you?"

"No." His face betrayed no emotion. "Of course, why should you believe me, and why should you expect that I would tell the truth?"

Those were both good questions. "Where were you last night? Say around 21:00."

"In my hab. I was reading."

Hiep did not strike me as a bookworm. "Anyone there with you I could ask?"

Hiep shrugged. "I live by myself and I sleep by myself. No one shares the hab."

Okay. Hiep did not have *any* friends.

"How about the data feed from your hab? Can I check that, like your door? Were you chipped in?"

"You can check anything you like," Hiep said. "I don't care. You do know that any digital record can be altered."

Yes, I did know that even if I, like most people, tended to assume that whatever was in our databases was a faithful record of what had actually happened. How much of what we thought was our history had been tinkered with at some point? Why should it be any different on Heaven, even if no armies of hackers were around? More to the point, this was not going to be like a vid, where I would make some dumb statement about the evidence and he would correct me to show how smart he was and, thereby, show his guilt. That only worked in vids.

"How about I send you a file and you tell me what you think?"

"That's fine with me," Hiep said.

I pulled up the information we had put together in the Med Unit, checked the attachment on my field, and sent it to him. Then I waited while he reviewed it.

"I would have been more careful," he said at last and again without emotion. "Even if I wanted you to think that the killer was an amateur, I would have placed more wounds on the right side and you would not automatically conclude the killer was right-handed."

Sure, a right-handed attacker from the front tends to leave wounds on the left side. I had not picked that up and I should have.

"The information feed has been altered," he said while I was thinking about his previous point.

"What?"

"That is certain. Your record shows two people entering and exiting at the same time. That is not possible; there is always a difference in timing, no matter how slight. Further, you have a time stamp from her chip for the time of death. The lethal wound is through the heart; she did not die slowly. It was immediate. Now look at the time stamp for when the door opened. Even if your killer fled as soon as she died, the door would not have opened that close to the death time stamp. Changing a chip record is difficult—not impossible but difficult—especially when the person is dead. A door record is easy."

I looked at the times he had highlighted. "The door time stamp is in Heaven time. Her chip is Earth time."

"The conversion is arithmetic," he said.

Yes, and when I plugged the numbers into the equation, I could see his point. "Could you hack the system for the times?"

"Of course," Hiep said. "I was trained to alter and falsify data in home systems on Earth, where systems are hardened. Here, it would be easy. I would not make this mistake. Also, I would not use Penny's ident as cover." He stopped immediately after saying that.

I guess that was Hiep's way of giving me evidence that he hadn't done the killing. Did that also mean that Malachi wasn't involved? Or would Malachi have done his own dirty work, or would he have used one of the other free company people? Maybe it had nothing to do with them or with Jerry. Maybe it was about sex. I had a headache and the growing heat of the day was doing nothing to improve it.

I turned away from Hiep and watched the work on the panels. Even with the bots, the team in front of us was struggling with the setup of bases for new panels. One of the assemblies tipped sideways and fell. There was a shout as one of the Pioneers jumped out of the way in the nick of time. A cluster of workers gathered in front of the fallen framework. It was too far away to hear what was said, but I could see them pointing. A bot rolled over and they fussed with the controls, apparently trying to have the bot lift the framework off the ground. Intermittently, heads turned to look over at Hiep. He did not move a muscle.

"There are enough of them there that it would be simpler and much faster for them to pick it up themselves and reset it," he said. "They will not think of it. They need bots for mechanical work, even if they are strong enough to do it themselves. It is the same with everything. The criminals are even worse. At least the Pioneers try."

"Do they need better team leaders?"

Hiep shrugged. "I do not make the decisions. Malachi does. But it will make no difference."

"You're saying they're all like that? Hopeless workers?"

"Not all. Penny is different. She knows what she is doing; she is not afraid to work. She answered every question I asked in the valley. She does not smile much, but when she does, there is a light in her eyes and her face. It shows her intelligence." He said the last sentence quickly.

I gave him a sharp look. "Hiep, you have to realize that you are probably the only person in forever who listens to everything she says."

"What is wrong with that? I was taught to ask questions and listen to the answers until I understood, and I always try to learn everything."

"Well, Penny hasn't made herself too popular with the crews working on the hydroponic expansion, from what I hear."

"Then the others are fools," Hiep said. "Eventually, Malachi will become frustrated. He will not simply replace, he will make an example. Grand Company has a reputation. It may achieve what Malachi wants."

That was not the first time Hiep had said something about the reputation of the free company Malachi had belonged to, but again he did not elaborate. "Is that why you're carrying the rifle?" I asked him. I wasn't sure I wanted to hear the answer.

"No," Hiep said. "It makes me more comfortable." He turned so that he was facing the group still trying to reset the panel.

CHAPTER TWENTY EIGHT

I left Hiep to whatever he was actually doing and went back to the Medical Unit, where I searched the grounds around it carefully, along with Jing and Yuki. We did it twice. We found nothing. No footprints under the window. No knife. Our killer had taken the knife with them. It had probably been ground up in St. Peterstown's recycling unit, along with Francesca's phone base. I thought for a moment about checking the door monitor for that unit but discarded the thought as soon as I had it. A chipped-out entry and exit, even if it occurred shortly after the murder, wasn't going to tell me anything.

Lacking any other inspiration, I went out to the LZ with the idea that I could help Yong organize the unloading and transport of our cargo. All else aside, this work needed to be finished before we could leave. It was obvious, as soon as I came in sight of the spaceplane, that the process was going slowly, and this was being exacerbated by the short and decreasing span of daylight. Oh, we could light the immediate area around the spaceplane well enough and the bots could *unload* cargo even in the dark, but darkness made loading the cargo onto transport rovers difficult, and driving back to St. Peterstown by moonlight and headlights was a good way to lose cargo and, possibly, a rover. A big part of the problem was exactly what Hiep had told me. The Pioneers assigned to the job were earnest, willing to work, and as incompetent as any crew I had ever seen. I would have had more confidence taking a platoon straight from boot camp into combat. Okay, that's an exaggeration. Still, these kids couldn't seem to do anything physical beyond pushing a button. They needed a bot ready to do the actual work and we didn't have enough bots. This hadn't been obvious when we had preflight training at Earth and were working with simulators, but it was abundantly clear in the field. They hadn't even cleared all the cargo from the first load. The next generation on Heaven was going to need to learn how to work from scratch, and not by example. If there was a next generation.

It made me think that it was good the settlement hadn't been planted farther south toward the pole. Yes, going closer to the pole would have moderated the climate some, but I doubted that would compensate for the increasing darkness in the winter, especially not this first winter. The reactor was dead, so the only power was going to come from the photovoltaics. With the sun above the horizon for less than five Earth hours a day by my chip, those panels were not going to produce that much electricity. If St. Peterstown were at eighty degrees or farther south, Heaven's equivalent of the Antarctic Circle, there would be no sunlight at all for some period of days. I wasn't sure the town would make it through a sunless stretch, even if they had their full array working when the sun was in the sky. Sure, the wind across the high plain could power wind turbines and the falls on the river leading to Happy Valley could be used for hydroelectric, but St. Peterstown lacked the ability to build either one. Yet. I wondered if Heaven had accessible fossil fuels. With the amount of carbon dioxide already so high in this greenhouse of an atmosphere, I didn't see how a little more could hurt. Of course, St. Peterstown wasn't equipped to drill for that either.

The problems with the cargo had Yong wound even tighter than normal. She didn't say it; she wouldn't say it, but I could tell by the set of her jaw and the tightness around her mouth. Probably the tension between us didn't help. I could tell that was still present because I didn't get any of the "Soldier Boy this" and "Soldier Boy that" that would usually pepper her conversation with me, particularly when she was giving instructions, or needed something to be done, or was simply happy I was around.

It probably didn't help that I had to tell her about my conversation with Hiep, which meant I had to mention his comments about Penny and what I thought about it. Probably, I should have left Penny out of the conversation entirely. The look I got after I brought it up suggested that Yong's only interest in Penny would have been to stake her out on Heaven's equivalent of an anthill, if we could find one. I did not understand where all of this was coming from. Where Penny was concerned, it wasn't as though I had *done* anything. I hadn't even been *thinking* about doing anything.

I do not understand women. I believe this wasn't the first time I had figured that out.

When darkness shut down our work in the late afternoon, I went back to St. Peterstown to see how Jing was doing. Yong said she still had work to do at the spaceplane and would be along later. Maybe. It's not as though the cargo that was still sitting there needed a guard, but my opinion was not asked.

Jing and Yuki had mostly cleaned up the mess in the Medical Unit. I took over mopping the floor to remove the last traces of blood. I figured that if someone was hurt and coming to the Medical Unit for treatment, the last thing they would want to see would be bloodstains on the floor. I'm not sure if a proper detective would have kept all the stains as they were—and I couldn't find a reference in the computer to tell me—but we had the murder scene all recorded, and we did need to be able to use the Medical Unit to treat people.

Cleaning up the unit and thinking about the recordings we had made me realize I needed to talk to people whose habs were near the Medical Unit. With the onset of nightfall, they would be back from their work assignments.

First, Jing and I checked to see if anyone in the nearby habs could have heard the screams that Athena did. The large public units that fronted on Town Circle and the Community Dome all had high privacy walls behind them that formed a sound barrier between the busy areas and the habs. I dialed up my sergeant's bellow as a test, but between the insulation of the unit itself and the privacy walls, I could stand in the unit and scream my lungs out without being heard in the habs behind. To hear Francesca, someone would have had to be about where Athena had said she was, out in the street past the privacy screen.

Of course, whoever had killed her must have come out the door. Hiep convinced me that the time stamp had been changed, and that told me why Athena hadn't seen anyone. She must have missed the person going in and had fled by the time they came out. I decided, based on Hiep's assessment of fakery, that there had been only one person. I also decided that Penny's ident was the fake. This was a completely unbiased assessment on my part. Still, at some point, that person had come out and would have had to go past the habs on one street or another.

I went up and down those streets, checking at each occupied hab. "What were you doing last night? Did you see anybody in the street? Did you hear anybody in the street, maybe running?"

The answers were all variations on exhausted from work and sleeping, watching vids, having sex, or getting high, the last often in combination with the previous two. What they all distilled down to was: no. No one claimed to have been reading a book, other than Hiep, which I found curious, but that didn't alter the results of my questioning. No one had heard anything. No one had seen anything.

I had another brilliant idea. St. Peterstown wasn't a surveillance state, far from it. It had no cameras to track residents by face. It had no means of identifying any individual's location unless they were chipped into the network. However, those stupid hab doors did record whenever they opened, even if the person who went through them was chipped out. The town now had only 198 inhabitants, and most of the habs were empty. I talked to Jorge and he downloaded the data for all the hab doors, and we started working through the list of all the doors that had opened in the time period around Francesca's death. Discovery: about half the population of St. Peterstown had gone out, chipped out, in the late evening. So much for what everyone had told me about their activities. I sent messages to people asking where they had been. "Visiting" was the predominant answer, and who they had been visiting was not disclosed. If not who, I could guess what they had been doing, and suspected I would need drugs or sharp instruments to get more specific answers. Plenty of people had been out and about. None had seen someone run up the street with a bloody knife, or slink up the street as if hiding something, and no one had seen someone with blood on their clothes. Four people claimed to have had a late-evening urge to get food from the dining hall. When I checked the dining hall, that door showed a matching number of openings. Penny's hab door had opened as well. Since Dustin was no longer with her, she must have gone out.

Penny's response to my message was that I could find her at the hydroponics facility. She wasn't with any of the other crew working on the expansion, which didn't surprise me, and no one, including Reality, the team leader, could—or would—tell me where she was. After walking around for a good fifteen minutes, I came upon her at the most recently completed expansion section. This portion of the facility needed only final fill and planting to go into operation.

Penny was seated cross-legged in the dirt. She had disengaged an input and readout panel from the framing, and it rested in her lap while she hunched over it mumbling what sounded like an incantation made up of random words I remembered from chemistry and biology in college.

"Penny?"

"Yeah? I'm kinda busy. People have no idea how root systems are affected by cations in the nutrient solution." She did not look up.

"Penny, did you go out of your hab last night?"

"Ayuh." She still did not look at me.

"Where did you go?"

"Here. The way they want to use this facility isn't going to give us what we need, but I need to get the work done or we're not even going to get what it can produce. Eventually, they will want it done right. I hope." She tapped at the panel in her lap without looking up.

"Did you go down to the Med Unit?"

"No. I told you, I was here."

I took a deep breath and let it out slowly. "Look, Penny, Francesca was murdered last night. The door entry record has your ident with entry and exit around when she was killed. I need you to tell me where you were and who else might know you were there."

That broke her focus on the panel. She dropped it in the dirt and stood up to face me. Her eyes were wide, her mouth open.

"Francesca was killed last night? Nobody told me. Of course, the star could go supernova and nobody would tell me, although that wouldn't matter because—" She stopped abruptly. "You think I did it? Just like the people think I killed Mr. Whitehead, and I didn't do that either. You can't be so stupid as to believe that."

I ignored Penny's gift for subtlety. "I don't believe it, but some facts would help. Particularly when other people get involved. Your ident is in the door records."

"Well, I went there in the afternoon. I do every day so Dr. Balboni can check my leg and make sure I'm doing my exercises. She doesn't believe I'll do them right if she doesn't check, so, yes, I was there, but that's the only time I go because she won't work with me on the molecular analyzer no matter how much I ask, and I didn't go there at night and I didn't hurt her. I'm only chipped in when I go for the leg check because the diagnostic needs it. Otherwise, I don't chip in. Not unless I have to, like if I'm on an instrument that needs it. I'm never chipped in otherwise."

That could describe my relationship with the chip, but my reasons had to do with the army. "Why not?"

To my surprise, she got red in the face and looked down as she scuffed one boot at the ground. "My parents always had my SafeChildAlert-Tracker, the SCAT, enabled so they always knew where I was and, mostly, what I was doing, not that I ever did all that much, but if I ever did, they'd message me so that I stayed safe. You know, like if you're out with a guy, the SCAT can tell from your pulse and blood pressure and breathing and blood chemistry if you're, well, you know, and your parents can get an alert and, I mean, not that it even came close to that before Dustin . . ."

"Why didn't you just disable the damn thing? Or delete it?" I asked.

"I was afraid of what my parents would do. I mean, I suppose they couldn't have done anything once I was eighteen, but I didn't think that way then. It was only after I met Dustin that we had a big fight—my parents, I mean—and then, after I failed, they quit checking. That's why I hate chipping in and I won't do it. I didn't go in that door that night."

"I believe you," I said. "I feel the same way about chipping in but for different reasons."

She was still looking at the ground. "Well, you can see where always being safe got me. Could you please leave me alone?"

I left the hydroponics facility certain that Penny was not the culprit and that the door's entry record was bogus. I needed to talk to Yong, but I was afraid that if I called Yong to talk about Penny, even about how it wasn't possible for her to have killed Francesca, Yong was going to freeze harder than the Greenland icecap before global warming.

Eventually, it occurred to me that instead of trying to check the entire population of St. Peterstown to see who might have gone to the Medical Unit, or been near the Medical Unit, it might be more profitable to see where Francesca had gone and whom she might have seen. I suppose this qualified as an astonishing flash of insight, as my sergeant on my first deployment called my grasp of battlefield tactics. He had also said that I, for sure, wouldn't last very long, and I've lasted a lot longer than he did. There is some justice in the universe.

Searching through the door records, I found that Francesca had gone to see Vanessa the day before she was killed. Vanessa had been fairly high on my list of possible Jerry-killers. I thought this murder got her off the list, but maybe not.

As soon as it was dark the next day and everyone was back from work, I headed to Vanessa's hab. This was the hab that she'd shared with Jerry, at least some of the time. It was not where Ibiana lived. Her strawberry-blond hair a loose mass behind her head and a frown on her face, Vanessa didn't seem surprised to see me.

"You've been through Francesca's records, I guess," were her first words.

"Yes." That seemed like the best answer under the circumstances.

"Then you know what she had about the poisoning that was so important."

Now I was stuck. I had to shake my head and confess that I did not.

Vanessa sighed and gave me a sad smile. "I should have played dumb, shouldn't I? When Jerry wanted to be petty, he always used to say I would always *be* dumb except when I ought to *play* dumb."

"Want to tell me what Francesca found that was so important and why finding it would bring me to see you now? I'm here because the stupid network sensor in your door says Francesca was here the day before she was killed."

"I don't know what it was." Vanessa dropped into one of her chairs.

"Then how do you know it was that important?" I asked. "What did Francesca tell you?"

Vanessa's face molded itself into a cunning look. "Why should I tell you anything more? It's not like you can call the police or have me dragged into court."

To me, this was a way of saying, *Make it worth my while*. I didn't want to try to come up with a suitable bribe. I didn't want to play games. "What I can do is go from here to Malachi and tell him you're hiding something. I'm getting the impression that Malachi doesn't follow the police or court procedures you're used to, but we can try that if you want."

Vanessa's face lost its color. "You're a prick."

I've been called worse. I waited.

She sighed again. "You're a prick," she repeated. "Just like Jerry. Well, maybe he was worse, but all of you men are the same."

"If we are done discussing my anatomy, what was Francesca doing and how did it involve you?"

"Francesca wanted to talk to Malachi. She said that she had worked everything out. She thought that would show Malachi how important she was, that she could have a seat on the Town Council as a reward."

"And what had she worked out?"

"She didn't say. Only that she could get a big reward for it, and the reward she wanted was to be on the Council. She always had a thing about being important."

Personally, I thought this was idiotic. I could barely get Malachi to pay attention to Jerry's death. I couldn't see him giving Francesca a reward for solving how it had been done. And if, somehow, Malachi was involved, going to him would be even more idiotic.

"So why didn't she just do it?" I asked. "Go to Malachi, I mean. Why come to you?"

"She wanted me to talk to Ibiana, convince her to resign, like I did, and then have Ibiana support her—Francesca, I mean—for the seat. She thought it would look better that way in front of the Demos."

I thought it was stupid, but possibly Francesca thought that the Demos was still a popular democracy and its votes mattered. I'm sure there were Roman senators who had similar thoughts even after their time had passed. "Did you talk to Ibiana?"

"Yes. She said that if Malachi talked to her about it, she wasn't going to be stupid. That's all I know. Malachi hasn't talked to Ibiana, not that I know anyway, and Francesca is dead and I don't know anything about that."

"Thank you for what you told me," I said. "I do have one more question, though. Do you know what happened to the little case Jerry kept his joints in? Do you have it?"

"I don't have it," Vanessa said, "and I don't know anything about it. It's not like it was important to me. Why is it important to you?"

"I'm not sure," I said. "However, no one has seen it since the time you entered his hab and found him dead." I wasn't sure if she was surprised or upset or concerned. Her face was pretty blank.

Now I needed to talk to Ibiana, although I doubted I would get to do it before Vanessa told her about my visit. After that, I was sure I was going to have to have a delicate conversation with Malachi about who had said what to whom. I wasn't looking forward to that.

CHAPTER TWENTY NINE

Ibiana was waiting for me with a cup of coffee sitting on the table when I entered her hab. I accepted it with gratitude. Coffee was always welcome.

"Vanessa obviously let you know I went to see her," I said.

"Of course." Ibiana smiled and patted her curly hair. "She told me this is about Francesca."

"Yes," I said. "Did Malachi or Francesca talk to you? Before Francesca was killed, I mean."

"No, and I don't know whatever it was about Jerry that Francesca figured out. I can tell you that if she did talk to Malachi, it was a stupid thing to do. That man does not like being pressured to do anything. But Francesca could never think of much beyond what she wanted at the moment. I suppose that's true of most of us who came out on the *Daredevil.*" She forced a little laugh. "That's what led most of us here."

I drank some coffee as a means of creating a pause. "You said Malachi hates being pressured. You're on the Council with him. Do you think he killed Francesca?"

The first answer was another smile. "He would have told Hiep to do it. Maybe Loretta, but probably Hiep. It's always the quiet ones you have to be careful of."

"Francesca was stabbed forty-seven times." Ibiana winced. "Does that sound like either of them?" She shook her head.

"What about Vanessa?" I went on. "We think Jerry was poisoned. You and Vanessa were together a lot. Was poison in her background on Earth?" I'd never gotten around to asking people about Jerry—which is probably what a good detective should have done—because Malachi had packed me off to Happy Valley so fast I didn't have a chance. But if there was a tie-in, I wanted to know it now.

Ibiana shook her head again. "Nothing like that. Vanessa, well, ran an escort service, you could say. There were drugs involved, yes. Celebrities also. Some very embarrassing stuff. No poison. Vanessa's not the type."

I finished the cup. "People think Penny did it, and she's hardly the type either."

Ibiana leaned back in her chair, hesitated. "That girl can get angry. Vanessa doesn't lose control."

"Okay, let that be. What about you? Why did Jerry have you on the Council, and why does Malachi keep you there?" Maybe I could catch her off guard. Twenty questions had never been my favorite game, though.

This time Ibiana laughed. "I was a swindler on Earth. Like Jerry, but nowhere near his scale. Inheritances, savings, things I was supposed to take care of, they disappeared. Not really big-time, and my family would have been content with me in jail, but some people were angry enough to want me killed. That made this a good place to come. I'm on the Council because I'm pretty good at persuading our *Daredevil* people to do what needs to be done. I'm good at persuading. That's why Malachi drives the Pioneer teams so hard; they respond to that. He doesn't waste time with the *Daredevil* crew. He leaves that to me. I will help where I can. I'm sorry I can't help you any more with this."

I thanked her and left.

Before I spoke to Malachi, there was one more person I needed to speak with: Dustin. I would have preferred to message him or, at most, talk to him on the phone. In any group of people, you can always find one who has worked out that the way to get through life is to find someone in a privileged position and fervently kiss their butt. People like that make me feel I need to wash my hands after I've been in their company. One of the advantages of belonging to an elite volunteers-of-volunteers combat unit is that those kinds of maggots don't crawl in there, but I've dealt with plenty of them since I got out. I had that feeling about Dustin.

I found him the next day during the daylight work hours at the hab Loretta used. From the odor inside, he had been smoking and the air system needed to go up a notch. Or two.

"I was here that night with Loretta," he said almost as soon as I got inside.

"That wasn't actually my first question," I said. "What I'd like to know is what you told Malachi after Francesca made that big deal about figuring out what happened to Jerry. What did you tell him, and what did he say?"

Dustin shrugged. "I didn't actually talk to Malachi. Reality said he was busy, and I wasn't going to try to interrupt him. So I told her about what Francesca said. I don't know what went on after that."

I translated that to: *I don't know anything, and no matter what you say, I still don't know anything.*

He was lounging, pretty slack, in one of the chairs in the front room of the hab. I felt an urge to kick the chair out from under him and repressed it with some difficulty. Yes, Dustin was the type of guy who, if he learned someone was going to be attacked, would do absolutely nothing.

"I might have thought you were doing some real work today," I said, "but I guess not."

"I am working," Dustin said. "My job is to be available if Loretta needs something done. That's what I'm doing."

"Oh. And you're going to be doing it in those." I pointed at his feet. He was wearing bathroom sandals rather than his customary Specials or the regular work boots. "What's with those team shoes of yours? I thought they were glued to your feet."

"I can't find my Specials or even my boots. Somebody must have taken them," he said. "Some people try to get back at me because I'm with Loretta. One in particular, and I'm going to find out if she did this. Count on it." His voice developed a nasty edge. "If you're going to be our resident detective, why don't you go ask Penny about my Specials?"

"Why don't you ask her yourself? And I'm going to bet there are plenty of people here who would enjoy watching you look like a fool. You might as well start asking everybody about those damned shoes."

I sent Malachi a message so I could get that conversation about Francesca over with, but he was busy. So said his reply. I hung around my hab most of the day waiting for him to get unbusy, but that didn't happen. The call I did get late in the day surprised me. It was from Sonal. "Leif, I need you quickly. There's going to be a fight."

It's nice to be needed, but maybe not so nice when you're needed only when people are ready to start swinging at each other.

"Where?" I sent back.

"Penny's hab," was the answer.

Uh-oh. Visions of a chanting mob carrying torches popped into my head. That may have been a little melodramatic, but I hustled to get there.

The scene, when I arrived, was ridiculous. Yes, there was the typical circle, in this case semicircle, of onlookers who gather round to watch two guys pummel each other bloody, usually for no good reason. Three people were in the cleared area at the center of the semicircle. One was Penny, no surprise there, her face screwed up with streaks on her cheeks indicating previous tears. She was shrieking something I could not decipher as I pushed through people to reach the center. The target of her cries was Dustin, who stood there in the bathroom sandals I had seen before, holding a pair of boots in his hands. Sonal was in between, her arms outstretched while the two of them circled around her like moons orbiting a small planet.

"What the hell is going on here?" I asked.

"He broke into my hab!" Penny thrust her arm and forefinger as far as they would go in Dustin's direction.

"I did not break into anything!" Dustin shouted back. "I walked in through the door like any normal person does. You're making it up or getting it wrong, like you usually do."

"I was working on the hydroponics. I wasn't here. And you weren't in the common room. You were in my room! And I wasn't here!"

"Yeah, well, you stole my boots and I came to get them back." Dustin pointed at the boots he was holding, which explained why he was holding them.

"I didn't take your boots! I don't want any part of you anymore. You go back to the one who's keeping you like a pet."

"Oh, please. If you didn't take them, why were they under your bed? And where are my Specials? They're gone too. Where did you hide them?"

"I didn't touch your stuff. Why were you in my room?"

"You didn't touch them? You always used to put them on and dance around in them, and you were the one who wanted to keep them under the bed."

Penny's shriek turned into more of a squeak. I could hear laughter from the people who were enjoying the show. That's when it turned nasty.

"I was only screwing you because you begged me to!" Dustin was red in the face and jabbing his index finger in Penny's direction as he tried to circle around Sonal, who managed to stay in between them.

"You begged me!" Dustin shouted again, and drew more laughs. "You said you never had sex and you were afraid you never would."

"Dustin!" Penny screamed.

This was way over the line, over any line. I stepped in front of Dustin and pushed him back. "Shut it down, Dustin," I said. "That's enough."

He tried to get past me then, and tried to circle around when I blocked him. The laughter surrounding us had become continuous.

"You're the only girl who lies there and talks about farming during sex." The laughter escalated, and that provided Dustin more encouragement to keep going. "Shit, fucking you is like fucking a mannequin. You just lie there like a board. Not that you have any hips to move, even if you knew how to move them."

I got in Dustin's face, shoved him backward, and told him again to shut up. Behind me, I could hear Sonal grab Penny and keep her from rushing at Dustin. Penny was screaming that she was going to kill Dustin, which may have been a poor choice of words given the situation we had in St. Peterstown.

"Oh, you're going to leave my body lying around like the others?" Dustin yelled that out and got applause.

I stepped forward and hit him with an uppercut to his solar plexus. It was hard enough to bend him over and make him gasp for breath. He dropped the boots.

"Dustin," I said, "this ends now. I don't care what started it. If you don't stop, I am going to fix you so it stops. Understand me?"

He was still sucking for air, so I think he knew exactly what I meant. I looked around at the crowd, nearly all Pioneers, maybe half of them still in their uniforms, now shabby with hard use and sweat. The rest wore a mixture of their own clothes with parts of the uniform, all equally ragtag. "Show's over," I announced.

I didn't think they were going to mob me to support Dustin, but, if anything, they were shuffling closer. I put my hand on my pistol. At that, they started to back away. That was when the loud crack of an M8 rifle discharge split the air. Shoulders hunched and heads ducked involuntarily.

Vo Hiep pushed through the ring of people and they gave way with an eagerness to put space between them and a man who'd just fired a weapon. A little wisp of smoke trailed from the barrel. One man didn't move fast enough and Hiep swatted him with the stock of the rifle.

Hiep planted himself in front of Dustin. "These yours?" He gestured at the boots with one foot. Dustin nodded. "Take them and crawl back into your hole," Hiep said. "If I do the killing, no one will ever find your body."

Dustin fumbled the boots, dropping them twice. Then he clutched them to his chest and scuttled away through the onlookers.

"The rest of you, find something else to do," Hiep said. "Now."

The crowd scattered, leaving Sonal, Penny, and me with Hiep in front of Penny's hab. Hiep reslung his rifle.

"You know how to make an entrance," I said to him.

"That was bullshit," he said. "I ended it."

"For now." I turned to face Penny. "What was this business with his boots and his Specials?"

"I don't know." She jammed her hands in her pockets and looked down at the ground. "I really don't. Somebody set me up. That's all I can think."

"To give everybody a good laugh?" I asked rhetorically. I thought the answer was obvious.

Sonal nodded sadly. "As much as I hate the work and the pace, it does keep everybody busy during the day. The problem is that it gets dark so early and there's not much to do then. If we had kids, and dogs, and cats, it would be different."

"We can't have children here," Hiep said. "Not until we know we will have enough power and food."

Hiep was right, of course, even if I hadn't expected him to say something like that. If St. Peterstown couldn't generate enough power or grow enough food to replace the ReadyMeals they were consuming, having children would only mean more to die.

"I can't say about the power," Penny said, "but I can tell you about the food. I don't care what the stupid scorecard shows. We're not going to make it. We're going to run out of ReadyMeals and we're not going to have enough from the hydroponics and we don't have any animals growing and they don't just pop out as adults and I know what to do but nobody wants to hear it. This sucks."

"You said that at the Demos," Hiep said. "Don't keep saying it. Please. As for him"—Hiep looked in the direction Dustin had gone—"Loretta likes to gossip. I've heard about some things he's said. Stay away from him." He turned back to Penny. "And don't let these assholes turn you into a spectacle. Malachi won't like it if I kill someone."

Penny looked up at him and smiled. "Thank you," she said.

CHAPTER THIRTY

I didn't receive a reply from Malachi until the next day. When I opened it, I was surprised to see: COME SEE ME. ABOUT JERRY. I hadn't mentioned anything about Jerry in the message I had sent him.

I found Malachi at midday out at the farthest extent of the photovoltaic panel array. The sky was white with haze and heat, the sun visible only as a brighter section of sky. The panels were angled to take best advantage of its position, which was not that high in the sky. Malachi stood there, hands on hips, staring at the panels as though he was calculating the angle to the sun for each of them. For all I knew, he might have had an app projecting exactly that on his field. The depths of winter might be coming, but the nearly triple-digit temperature and high humidity had sweat running down my spine as I walked over to him. He turned around at my approach.

"We're going to make it, Leif," he said.

"Well, that's good news."

"Yes." He smiled. "Even at winter solstice, we're going to have enough power to keep our essential functions going. The embryo storage and incubators. The computer network. Basic hab functions. Although I think we're going to have to get used to the climate, because we won't be able to run the air systems full out. We can run the hydroponics. That facility has to become our priority now. When the ReadyMeals run out, we have to be able to grow enough to feed ourselves."

I was glad to hear about the power, although I wasn't sure what that had to do with Jerry. The issue about the capacity of the hydroponic farm had been played out before. Very publicly.

"Maybe if the power is going to be okay," I said, "you should look into a dirt farm. I know Penny has zero tact, but if you forget about the source, that could be your solution. If you have adequate power and food, St. Peterstown will be self-sustaining."

Would that mean that Yong and I could check off our "mission accomplished" box and fly out? Even if we left two unsolved murders behind us? What did Malachi want to talk about regarding Jerry?

"Penny." Malachi said the one word and stopped. His eyes searched my face as if he were looking for a clue. "I messaged you that we needed to talk about Jerry again," he said. "I told you before that whatever happened to him was irrelevant now, that it was a waste of our time and effort to keep digging into it. However, Francesca came to me about this before she was killed. She claimed she had proof Penny had worked out the nerve agent before Jerry's death and that she could show that Penny killed Jerry."

This was not what I expected to hear from Malachi. Yes, it was confirmation that Francesca had gone to see Malachi, but not what I imagined she had told him. "Care to tell me what she showed you?"

A document popped into my field. Malachi waited while I opened it and read. What I saw was a record from the molecular analyzer with Malachi's login and Penny's ident from the day Jerry died. It showed a chemical structure with the interpretation that it was a cholinesterase inhibitor.

"And why did Francesca go to you with this? To be a good citizen?"

"Hah!" Malachi's laugh was nasty. "Yes, I am the mayor, and Cam and Jess wouldn't know what to do with something like this if she brought it to them, so you could say that of course she'd bring it to me. Fact is, though, nobody does anything for nothing. Certainly not the people who came here. Francesca wanted to be a big shot; she wanted to be important. She always did. In this case, she wanted a seat on the Town Council. But she was scared."

"Scared of what?"

"Penny."

It was my turn to laugh. "I don't think Penny could scare a grasshopper. Seriously, I'm supposed to believe that?"

"Leif, Francesca said she went through the records in the molecular analyzer. That's where she got the file I just showed you. She also said that Penny was on that instrument a lot. Was in there all the time. She said Penny would see that Francesca could have found her work, and, well, your little girlfriend Penny, who's as scrawny as a scarecrow and the butt of everyone's jokes, still managed to gas Jerry. If she could gas Jerry, she could gas Francesca. That's what Francesca figured. She wanted me to protect her when this all came out.

"Now, personally, I didn't care all that much about Jerry or Penny at that time. He wasn't important anymore and she never was. I told Francesca this wasn't worth a Council seat and she could keep quiet, for all I cared." Malachi let out a sigh. "Well, I didn't figure on a knife attack. We talked about that, and it's beyond me setting up a night watch. I'm hearing that people are upset. Very upset. I'm going to have to do something about this."

"You think Penny killed Francesca? With a knife?"

"It looks that way," Malachi said. "We know she worked out the nerve agent and she was with Jerry right before he died. We know she could have seen that Francesca was in the analyzer records and would have the information that Penny had worked out the nerve agent, and now Francesca is dead. I'm not going to be arbitrary, Leif. I will find the proof and put it all in front of the Demos for their decision. I will only execute what they decide. That's why I wanted to talk to you now. Once this is done, that will solve these murders. Everything is now under control. And then, once we have all the supplies in town, I think your job here will be complete. Correct?"

CHAPTER THIRTY ONE

I went back to see Yong and the others about as low in spirit as I've ever been. I sent them copies of the file Malachi had given me and dropped into a chair. Heaven's atmosphere felt like it was pressing me down and sapping my energy, but I knew it wasn't the planet's fault. Yong actually sounded gentle when she said she was surprised too. Obviously, I didn't repeat Malachi's crack about Penny being my "little girlfriend."

I went out for a walk to clear my head and found myself at the Dome. In fact, as Malachi had told me, the scorecard showed that the number of photovoltaic panels that were operational matched the number we needed. Except, something was wrong. I don't have a photographic memory—that's why we have chips and phones, after all—but I am observant. The number needed was smaller than it had been. Not by much, but it had changed. I suppose that's one way of hitting your target, but why change it when anyone could have a pic of the previous one? Another question for Malachi, so I called him from the Dome.

"We're getting to be quite the chat-friends, aren't we, Leif," he said when he came on.

I asked him about the changed number.

Malachi didn't miss a beat. "Of course. The original number was wrong. I told you we're not going to run the air systems on full. I told this to the Team Leads."

"And what did they say?"

"They didn't say anything." Malachi's tone turned brusque. "A team needs to believe whatever you tell them, follow whatever orders you give them, and not one of them will ever defy you, because they can't trust the others to join them. That's when you have a team. You're a military man, Leif. You know this."

I was a military man. That wasn't any kind of team I ever had or would want.

.   .   .

I had a headache the next morning that could have been a hangover, except that I don't drink and St. Peterstown lacked alcoholic beverages. The notification from Malachi hit my field before I had even finished my coffee, which I was hoping would fix both the headache and the lassitude.

A WORK CREW FOUND SOMETHING YOU SHOULD SEE AT THE HYDROPONICS FACILITY, the message read when I opened it. I HAVEN'T EVEN SEEN IT YET. MEET YOU THERE.

The first thought through my head was that we were going to be dealing with another dead body. I sent the message to Yong, and one look at her face told me that she had the same thought. Without a word, we both left our coffees on the table, slipped pistols into holsters to complete our outfits, and headed out the door.

The hydroponics facility was outside the perimeter road. Away from the buildings of St. Peterstown, the high plains of Heaven stretched off into the distance, flat and featureless in the gray light of the morning. Cloud cover diffused the light of the winter sun, now just above the horizon. Between the clouds and the sun that would not climb too high, I had hopes that the day wouldn't be too hot, which at this point I took as mid-nineties.

Ahead of us, I could see a cluster of dark figures, backlit by the sky. They were standing around the end of the facility's framing where it was being extended. A bot was there as well, and looked like it had run into the framework. One figure separated itself from the group and walked in our direction. Malachi.

"Good morning, Leif, Pilot Yang," he said. "Reality's crew found this, so I'm going to let her tell you about it."

Reality didn't move from the edge of the framework, so we walked the rest of the way to her and I positioned myself so the light wasn't in my eyes. The bot did appear to have run into the open frame of graphene. The framing had taken no damage, but the impact had lifted the footing off the ground. I didn't see a body, however, and I took that as good news.

"My crew was out early," Reality said. "It wasn't fully light but all of us want to beat our targets."

Spare me the propaganda, I thought. "What happened?" I asked.

"It was probably an honest mistake," she said, "because we were out so early. We've been having trouble with this bot. Possibly the bot's sensors were fooled because it wasn't fully light with such an early start."

"I get that you and your crew were so gung-ho to get to work you were out in the dawn's early light. It looks like the bot ran into the framework extension. Is that what this is all about?"

"Yes. I mean, not entirely. The bot did run into the framework. That's what I meant by a mistake, by the controller or its sensors. I told Malachi how early we started."

I'm sure you did, I thought. *I'm sure you also told him you started before Bjorn's team.* I hoped Malachi would tell her to get to the point, but he let her ramble on.

"Anyway," Reality said, "I had them shut down the bot immediately and I came over to inspect. I did that myself. The impact lifted this last footing off the ground. We'll probably have to replace it, but to be thorough, I checked to see if the base was intact. See what's there? I haven't touched it, haven't moved it." She flicked her flashlight on and directed the beam at the ground beneath the raised footing.

Given my mood at that moment, I was expecting to see a body part, maybe a hand reaching up. I didn't. What I saw looked like the end of a red handgrip.

"Go ahead and pull it out," Malachi said. "We're all here and I'm recording."

Reality squatted down, reached out, and gripped the object. It was not jammed into the earth. All she had to do was lift it out. It was a knife. In appearance, it was identical to the one I had seen Penny use in the valley.

The daylight was already brighter than when we had started out. I didn't need the beams from phone bases that played across the blade to see dark material stuck on the metal and on the hilt.

"Is that blood?" Reality asked.

"Maybe," Yong said from my side. "That we can check at the Med Unit."

"Whose knife is it?" Malachi asked. "It doesn't look like the standard model the printers will produce."

"Penny Panagiotidis has one like it, I think," Reality said.

"Does anyone else?" Malachi asked.

No one said anything.

We found a cloth to wrap the blade in and stuck it in a gear pouch. With any luck, the tip wouldn't poke through the wrap and the pouch before we got to the Medical Unit. I'm sure there is a careful and very specific protocol that police investigators follow when they are collecting evidence—and that's what this was—but neither I nor anybody else there had any idea what that protocol was. My primary concern, in fact, was to have the knife in something, so we weren't walking down the street with a naked blade that looked like it had dried blood on it. I messaged Jing with a quick summary and told her to meet us at the Medical Unit.

"It's blood," Jing said after some time spent with reagents and instruments. Not only is it blood, it's Francesca's blood. I compared it with a sample from her body. I'm not really skilled with this kind of analysis, but I had enough to repeat it multiple times. The DNA matches. Not only that, the blade of the knife is a good match for some of the puncture wounds. This is the knife that killed her."

"Can we tell who did it?" Jorge asked.

"No." Jing frowned. "Even if we had DNA samples on file from everyone in town, and we don't, I couldn't tell you. I mean, yes, even with the knife in the dirt under that footing, it would be possible. A really good tech could do it with maybe a dozen cells. But I'm not an expert at this kind of work. Even if I were, how many people handled it when you picked it up?"

My face pled guilty. "Several of us, for sure."

"So there is that answer," Jing said.

"We can still tell whom the knife belongs to," Yong said. "Reality said Penny had one like this." With no concern any longer about handling the knife, she picked up an ultra-fiber cloth from the lab bench and wiped the dirt off the hilt. Engraved in the grip were the words MAINELY HUNTING AND TRAIL SUPPLIES, PORTLAND.

"Penny is from outside Portland in Maine," I said slowly.

"I think we need to talk to Penny," Yong said.

I messaged Malachi. He asked us to wait until the end of the workday. Then he would meet us at Penny's hab.

. . .

When we showed her the knife, Penny's eyebrows went up, her eyes widened, and her mouth fell open into a small *o*.

"That's my knife," she said after a period of staring at it. "Where did you find it?"

"It was under a footing for the framing for the new hydroponics extension," Malachi said. "Would you like to tell me how it got there?"

"That makes no sense." Penny spun around and dashed into her hab, leaving us standing in the street.

She reappeared a couple of minutes later holding an empty sheath identical to the one I had seen her with in the valley. Her expression was every bit as baffled as it had been before. By this time, we had attracted a ring of onlookers.

"I don't understand," Penny said. "My knife is gone. I mean, it's not gone, you have it, but it's not where I keep it. Somebody must have taken it. Somebody's going through my things. Dustin was in my hab before. Ask him about it."

"As I recall," Malachi said, "it was his boots that somehow got into *your* hab."

"What's on the knife?" Penny asked.

"Blood," Malachi said. "Francesca's blood."

"Oh, no . . ." Penny's voice was little more than a whisper.

Among the group watching us, I could hear a soft chant start. "Pennywise, full of lies. Pennywise, not so wise."

Penny whirled around, trying to see who was saying it, but wherever she looked, the words came from somewhere else.

"This is wasting time," Malachi said, "and it's not getting us anywhere." He wiped the sweat off the top of his shaved head. Then he pointed, first at Bjorn, then at Reality, who had come with him. "You two, you stay here with Penny. I want you to go through everything in her personal hab space. Make sure everything in there belongs to her. If there is something there that's not hers, I want to know about it. If you find anything else with blood on it, I want to know about that."

"Wait," Jing said. "If you think there's blood, bring it to me. I want to test it."

"Fine," Malachi said. "That makes sense. And Bjorn and Reality, you do all of it in front of her so she agrees that everything you find in there came from her hab. And the two of you watch each other, so nothing is taken." Malachi's eyes went to the side as he made a connection. "Hiep," he said into the air, followed by a short summary of the situation. "I want you down here also. Watch all three of them."

I think he wanted the phone conversation so that we could hear it. I guess this was Heaven's version of a search warrant.

CHAPTER THIRTY TWO

We reconvened at the Medical Unit. The mood inside was glum. Well, my mood was glum. But no one else was chattering or jumping for joy either.

"It looks like Penny's knife killed Francesca," I said in a half-hearted way.

"Maybe she is our interstellar killer after all," Jorge said.

"The fact that it was her knife doesn't mean the knife was in her hand," Yong said.

"You don't think she did it?" I was a little surprised Yong would take that position.

"I didn't say that either, Leif. But there are some things I find curious about all of this."

"Such as?" Jing beat me to the question.

Yong started to tick off points on her fingers as she spoke. "How did the knife end up under the footing now and how did Penny put it there? Francesca was killed days ago, but that footing is the last piece so far in the addition to the hydroponics. It was just put down yesterday. While you have been talking to people, Leif, I have spent time checking the work Malachi's teams have been doing, so I am certain of when that part of the hydroponics facility was set up."

"Maybe she had it somewhere else," Jing said. "Then she moved it because under the footing was a better hiding place. Penny is out at the hydroponics late. We know that."

"But not with a shovel," I said. She doesn't do that kind of work. You can't just slide something under one of those footings and you can't scoop the dirt out with your hand. That won't work."

"She could have gotten a shovel or some kind of scoop." Jing wasn't going to give up her position. "She's out there alone sometimes. You've said no one works with her. No one would see her."

"True," Yong said. "But then Reality's crew is so eager to get to work that they start before it's light and a construction bot, which is programmed to avoid installed structures, is accidently driven into the framing, and it hits at the very end of the structure where there is no framing beyond that point so the footing lifts up easily. Then someone looks under the footing instead of simply having the bot reset it, which they could have done because the framing was only pulled up. Graphene structural supports are too tough to be damaged by a bot like that."

"Are you saying that Reality did it and manipulated the whole situation to frame Penny?" Jorge sounded dubious.

"That certainly doesn't make sense," Jing said. "If Reality killed Francesca, that knife would be gone for good. She's not going to arrange for it to be found by herself so someone could question if she had it. Anyway, why would Reality kill Francesca in the first place?"

I had to laugh at that. "If Malachi told her to do it, or if she thought Malachi wanted someone to do it, she would. She competes with Bjorn to see which one of them can look tougher or meaner to impress Malachi. I can believe that's all the reason she'd need."

That was when a notification showed up on my field. From Malachi. THEY FOUND JERRY'S JOINT CASE IN PENNY'S BEDDING. THEY'RE BRINGING IT OVER FOR TESTING.

I could see the others all look at me. Even without checking the copy list, I knew we had all received that message.

A threesome arrived scant minutes later: Bjorn, Reality, and Hiep. Bjorn had a small silvery case clutched in the palm of one hand. It was probably just as well we couldn't check for fingerprints or do a forensic exam for DNA anyway. Bjorn raised that hand high in the air, brandishing the case like a trophy from a competition.

"It was between the mattress cover and the mattress, at the foot of the bed," he said. "I'm the one who found it."

"Tell that to Malachi, not me," I said.

"I did," Bjorn said.

From his face, I was sure he had. Reality looked sullen. Hiep was his usual impassive self.

"Drop it in here." Jing held out an open plastic bag. "Then go wash your hands thoroughly and don't touch your eyes or lick your fingers until you do."

That startled Bjorn out of his cheeriness and sent him to the nearest sink.

"Well, aren't you going to test it?" Reality asked.

"Not with an audience," Jing snapped. "All of you, out of here."

Reality and Bjorn looked like they wanted to protest, but Hiep gave a quick jerk of his head in the direction of the door. Crestfallen, Bjorn headed out, his hands still dripping. Reality followed him. Hiep waited until both were outside.

"Malachi wants you to message him with the results as soon as you have them. Don't worry about the time. Copy me also." After a moment, he added, "Please."

After Hiep had left, Jing told us she wanted to use the molecular analyzer in the Lab Unit, so we all followed her over there. Jing's objective was a cluster of instruments that took up an entire bench top. Magnetic field warnings in yellow and black marked a perimeter around this bench. From my years working as a lab tech in Miami, I recognized the instrument array. It was a gas chromatograph coupled to a mass spectrometer and a miniature nuclear magnetic resonance spectrometer. I'm not saying I knew how to use that instrument—I worked in the hibernation lab—but I knew what it was. Inject a substance through the port at one end, and the screen readouts would show you the possible chemical structures and properties ranked by likelihood.

Jing pulled on a pair of lab gloves and took the case out of the bag. The inside of the upper lid was engraved: TO MY DEAREST FRIEND, JERRY WHITLEY, WILMA. Whitley, yes, that was Jerry's real name when he was working his swindle. I found a couple of seconds to wonder who Wilma was and if she had been one of his financial victims on Earth. I discarded the thought quickly. It didn't matter. What did matter was that this was

Jerry's joint case. Resting in the bottom half were a few tiny fragments of leaf, little more than dust. Cannabis or thistle?

"Give me a minute to look at that file Malachi gave you, Leif. It will make this easier." Jing sat at the bench for a couple of minutes, eyes fixed on a projected page only she could see. Then she muttered, "Okay," selected some reagents, and got to work with the material in the case. She ended with a yellowish solution in the bottom of a tiny tube. After watching a timer countdown, Jing sucked the liquid up again with a syringe and injected it into the molecular analyzer.

While we were waiting for the machine to spit out the results, Jorge poked at the screens and looked at the system settings.

"You know this has an RGDP rating?" he asked.

"Which means what?" I asked.

"Really Good Data Protection," Jing said. "This equipment is certified for medical use, so it would have to."

"And Really Good Data Protection means what?" I was sure I sounded like a dunce, but I was equally sure I needed to know this.

"It has multiple levels of protection and the ability to verify data for inspectors," Jing said. "Any equipment that's used with patient data has to have that certification because of all the hacking and data fakes."

"Does it matter to the results we get?" Yong asked. "Or does it slow down the system the way multiple security levels usually do?"

"No, no," Jorge said. "That's not the point. It will have redundant logs in locked, hidden directories. Isn't that right, Jing?"

"Yes," she said. "That's been a requirement for a few years now. Or, I mean, it was a requirement for a few years before we left. We had to learn about it in my postgrad training for rural medicine because we would need to run these machines. We had to know what government inspectors would look for."

"Do you know how to get into those files?" I asked.

"No. I'm no computer jockey," Jing said. "I only know they're there."

"Well, I'm an amateur computer jockey," Jorge said. "If you want to get in, let me know. I can use the ship's computer to help."

We had no time to go exploring then, however. The readout screen flashed, and a list of the compounds the machine had found began to appear. The screen kept scrolling. It was a long list. When it finally finished,

Jing sat down and checked through the output. Chemical structures flashed on the screen as she did.

"A mixture of compounds, as you would expect. He had joints in the case. Plenty of THC. That nerve agent from the thistle was in here too. I can't tell, obviously, whether thistle leaves were chopped up and mixed with the cannabis or a solution of it was dripped on joints, but I don't think it matters. Jerry smoked it and inhaled the stuff."

"At that point, it would be like inhaling nerve gas," I said. I saw that dying young soldier again in my mind and shuddered.

"Are you saying," Yong asked, "that Penny had a huge argument with Jerry and then either laced his joints with the nerve agent or snuck a joint with thistle leaf into his case?"

"I didn't say any of that," Jing said. "All I'm saying is that there was nerve agent in his joint box."

"And why would she swipe the box and hide it in her bed?" Jorge asked. "If she was going to bury the knife under a footing, why not put the box someplace like that too?"

Something else was bothering me while Jorge was talking. It took a moment to realize what it was. None of these folks had been on a chem-war battlefield. "It's more than that," I said. "She can't have been there while he smoked it. Even if she turned on the air system, if she was there while he smoked it, she would have inhaled it too. Doesn't make sense."

"Could she have done whatever and then left before he smoked it?" Jing asked.

"It's possible," Yong said, "but consider something. You have a big argument with someone and they accept a poisoned joint from you right afterward, you flee, and then they smoke it? That's an odd sequence."

It was an odd sequence. Odd enough to be impossible. However, we had to let Malachi know what we had found in the analysis, and I was sure he was going to take the quick and easy route to a conclusion. Why was it that every time our reasoning made it difficult for Penny to have killed these people, something else showed up that made it look like she had? There was, naturally, one obvious answer to that. I needed to speak with her, but I doubted she was back in her hab.

We sent Malachi the results of the analysis. Then I called him. What I got from him first was a grunt, then a pause.

"I had her arrested," he said after a while. "We don't have a procedure for doing that, but that's all right. The Demos will want action. They will expect me to take some action, and I am doing it."

"I'd like to talk to her."

"You think she's going to spill her guts to you?" Malachi laughed. "It would make my life simpler if she would, but I doubt it."

"I don't know what she's going to say," I replied.

"Yeah. If you did, why would you need to talk?" Malachi laughed again. "We don't have a jail either, so I had them put her in the school building. It's the only place on the planet that can actually be locked up from the outside and the inside. So little kids can't run out into the wild." He finished with another laugh.

"I'm not sure I'd worry about locking her up. I mean, where's she going to go?"

"Nowhere, I suppose." Malachi's voice was terse. "But she murdered two people, and folks are nervous. You haven't seen the messages I'm getting. I want to keep her alive, at least until we have a trial. It's safer for everybody to keep her locked up. I'll have one of my people at the door. I'll let him know you're coming."

I noticed Malachi had not said she may have murdered two people. He just said that she had done it. I did not like the way this was developing.

·　　·　　·

The school was on the other side of the Community Dome, a short walk around the Town Circle. At three stories, the school was the tallest building in St. Peterstown. It had been designed on the assumption that the settlers would have a lot of kids, both from stored embryos and naturally grown. At this point, however, there were no children and the building stood empty. Well, not quite empty on this night. A light in the windows at one corner of the third floor told me where Penny was.

As Malachi said, there was a man standing by the front door looking, in equal measures, bored and in need of a chair. Maximum security, this was not. The guard was Miroslav.

"I see you drew the short straw," I said.

"Never any question about that," Miroslav answered. "You heard what they said when I was set up. I'm hearing talk she'll get fifty lashes. I still wake up if I roll on my back at night. But I guess I'm hoping it's just fifty and not something worse."

"Do you think she did it?"

He shook his head. "To you, I'll say no. I could see Vanessa taking out Jerry. Francesca, who knows? Maybe Hiep or Loretta, although I can't see why, and people are careful now what they say and to whom. Nobody wants to cross those two. Or Malachi." Miroslav shrugged. "Malachi's got a plan that's going to work. She called him stupid in public, and if anyone knows what happens when Malachi feels challenged, it's me. It's not like she's got any friends. Sad."

I clapped him on his shoulder and went in.

I took the stairs to the third floor. The stairway continued up from there, presumably to the roof, but I followed the light streaming from under a door. I pushed the door open and saw that Penny had taken, or been put in, a classroom intended for young children. It contained a stack of mats that would serve for rest hour when the room had a class. She was sitting cross-legged on one of them. Her face was a map of misery, and I couldn't blame her for that.

"I didn't kill anybody," she blurted as soon as she saw me. "I say things sometimes when I get excited, but I never do anything. I don't."

"Any idea how someone could have gotten your knife, or put Jerry's case in your bed?"

She shook her head, then said, "It would be easy. Nothing is locked. There aren't that many people around. Usually, it's just bullshit. With me, that is. I mean, people pick on me—nothing new about that; they have since grade school. I'm used to it. Even Dustin, well, he had his moments. But it's always stuff like Dustin's boots. Somebody set it up, he got good and pissed, and they made fun of me." She shrugged. "I get mad; I get over it. I mean, what can I do about it?" She spread her arms out wide. "Never mind. That's just me pissing and moaning. I try not to think about it. But this . . . They said they're going to put me on trial. Do I even get a lawyer or anything like that?"

"I don't know." The settlers who came out on the *Daredevil* were all criminals, so I would bet one or two of them were lawyers, but I didn't think she would find that funny and it probably wouldn't help anyway. "I think Malachi and his Council will run it however they want. I don't think a lawyer will matter. What would help would be if you can think of a good reason why you couldn't have done it. An alibi."

She nodded. "I'll try. I'm usually by myself, though. I mean, Dustin was the only person I ever really spent time with. When I work, I usually work by myself. In the valley, Hiep was probably the first person who ever worked with me on anything."

"Think it over carefully," I said. "If you made any computer entries, anything timed, if you were chipped in when Francesca was killed. Anything like that. Think about it."

"I will."

CHAPTER THIRTY THREE

When I stepped outside the next morning, the air was soggy on my face and thickened to soup as I breathed it in. Above I could see low haze in the sky with a mass of gray clouds accumulating higher up. The air cooled through the morning—although *cool* is a relative term—and the sky darkened ominously. By midday, big, fat droplets began to fall. Thunder rolled across the high plains and lightning flashed overhead in the clouds. Then, all at once, a cascade of staccato blasts sounded that would have done justice to an artillery battery. On the heels of the thunder, a series of jagged white bolts lanced sky to ground, with more peals of thunder almost simultaneously. The heavens above Heaven opened up in a downpour worthy of a Noah. I couldn't see the hab next to us through the sheets of falling water. I wondered if the small creek that ran out of Dead Lake would overflow its banks and send water cascading through the streets of St. Peterstown. A crash followed a bolt of lightning, and a flash lit up the entire sky. That bolt had hit something in the town. I hoped that whatever it hit was grounded or, at least, not vital. An alarm sounded from my phone and blinked repetitively on my field.

CEASE ALL OUTSIDE WORK. GET UNDER COVER.

The warning was a tad late. Anyone still outdoors had issues that went well beyond getting wet.

About an hour later, another notification came through. THE TRIAL OF THE DEMOS VS. PENELOPE PANAGIOTIDIS WILL TAKE PLACE AT 15:00 HEAVEN TIME. ALL MEMBERS OF THE DEMOS ARE EXPECTED TO ATTEND.

I couldn't decide whether Malachi had decided not to risk Penny coming up with an alibi or defense, or just wanted to take advantage of the fact that no work could be done outside. Then a grimmer but probably more realistic thought sank in. Malachi had in place what he needed; he simply wanted to finish this.

The downpour showed no sign of letting up. It was going to be a very wet Demos that sat in judgment in the Community Dome.

We were not members of the Demos, of course, but I intended to see how this played out. Not well for Penny, I was quite certain. I tried to find a solid reason why I could be sure she hadn't killed either Jerry or Francesca, and I couldn't. It didn't feel right, but maybe that was because I liked her.

Yong said that she was going to attend as well. She kept coming up with questions about the chain of events but refused to give a yes or no answer on Penny. It's possible that her main reason for going was to keep an eye on me. Dev was going with us, too, but his reason was simple. He was bored. Jing and Jorge both said no. They wanted to keep playing with the programming on the molecular analyzer and see if they could access the hidden folders and find out if there was anything interesting in them. I suspected that what they really wanted was some time to themselves. One way or another, our stay on Heaven was drawing to an end, and Jorge would need to make a decision.

The Demos trooped into the Community Dome with water dripping off their rain gear. The Pioneers all had camouflage-style gear with a hood, while the original crew from the *Daredevil* sported ISC logos on long gray jackets. It was another reminder that these were two separate groups of people.

Someone, their face obscured by the Pioneer hood, brought Penny in and sat her at the chair in front of the council's platform, the same chair Miroslav had occupied during his trial. No one had bothered to get her rain gear. Penny's Pioneer uniform was soaked and her usually out-of-control curls were plastered flat against the side of her head. That little but intentional indignity did not sit well with me. I suppose my irritation showed, because Yong touched my arm and a private message flashed on my field. NOT THE TIME FOR HEROICS, it read. Yes, she had come to keep an eye on me.

With Loretta and Ibiana flanking him and the slogans and score-card hanging from the framework behind, Malachi opened the meeting by calling the Demos to order as he had done before. "We are here today to consider very serious charges," he said. "I know all of you have been alarmed by what happened to our doctor, Francesca Balboni. If someone could do something like that to her, I know you have been saying, is any one of us safe? There has never been a situation like this in the short history of our town, and we need to take steps to make sure we are all safe in the future. I will explain carefully what we must do.

"One member of our Demos, Penelope Panagiotidis"—he pointed to the bedraggled Penny as though some of the Demos might not know who she was—"is charged with the murders of both Jerry Whitehead and Francesca Balboni. Both of these killings were premeditated. There is no question here of self-defense. Our procedures will be very simple. There will be no complicated maneuvering, no theatrics like you would see on Earth—like some of you have been part of on Earth. We will present the evidence we have and hear from witnesses. Ms. Panagiotidis will then have the opportunity to defend herself. Evidence can be challenged when it is presented, and witnesses can be challenged when they speak. This is fair and open. Then it is for you, the Demos, to vote on guilt or innocence. All of this must be done within this meeting of the Demos. We will not drag it out." He leaned over the table to stare down at Penny. "Do you understand what you are charged with and how serious this is?"

The rain was a drumroll on the roof that echoed through the Dome as Penny nodded without saying anything.

"Are there questions from the Demos?" Malachi asked.

One man from the *Daredevil* stood up and identified himself. "What happens if we find her guilty? What is the punishment? We don't have a jail in St. Peterstown. What do we do with her?"

"Those are good questions," Malachi said. "Our constitution does not prescribe specific punishments for crimes. The laws in the different countries we came from on Earth are different, and don't apply to our situation here. What our constitution does say is that if the Demos judges someone guilty in the case of a serious crime, the Council is responsible for deciding on the punishment, and that decision is not subject to a vote of the Demos. The Council will make its decision within a day, if we need to. That is my commitment to you."

I did not like the way this was sounding. Not at all.

"Loretta, would you present the evidence?" Malachi asked.

With that, Loretta proceeded to read off a list. Penny had publicly threatened Jerry; she had been in Jerry's hab the night he was killed and had been shouting at him loud enough to be heard from the street. Jerry had died from inhaling a nerve agent while he was smoking his joints. Loretta supported this with statements I had made and the analysis of the thistle agent that we had done. Then she said Penny had known about the nerve agent before Jerry died and showed the screens Malachi had shown me.

"That's not right!" Penny burst out. "I didn't do that analysis and I couldn't have done it."

"Are you saying there's something wrong with the results?" Malachi asked.

"They're fake. That's what I'm saying," Penny said.

"Why?"

"Because Jerry had blocked the Pioneers from the network. I couldn't make the coffee machine in the hab work. How would I log in to the molecular analyzer?"

"You were able to use the lab instruments that day," Malachi said. "You did all the soil analysis. The Demos heard all of that. What's more, I logged you in, so I know you were on the instruments."

Penny didn't give in. "Those were different instruments," she said. "I didn't do complex organic chemicals, and you didn't log me in to the molecular analyzer."

Why hadn't I thought of that when I spoke to Malachi? Once again, for all of Penny's fears and jitters, her mind worked under pressure.

Malachi had a response, however. "Well, I don't know about that," he said. "I got you logged in, but I wasn't paying attention to specific instruments. I didn't know what you would need. You probably did have access to the molecular analyzer, and it's hard to disregard the computer output."

"I wasn't even in the lab then," Penny said. "Look at the time stamp. That's not when I did the other work."

"Okay," Malachi said. "Were you chipped in somewhere else that would have a time stamp so we can be sure where you were? Anywhere. Even your coffee machine." He got a laugh from some people with that one.

"How could I be chipped in anywhere when Jerry had us blocked from the network?"

Malachi rubbed the top of his head. "If you can't prove you were somewhere else, then how do we ignore the computer output? You need to give us some proof that you weren't on the molecular analyzer."

That was a bit too much for me. I'd never been a defendant in a trial on Earth, but I'd endured a rigged inquest after the incident with Miles Richmond, and this wasn't right.

I took a step toward the council table. "Wait a minute," I said. "Aren't you supposed to prove she did do it, not make her prove she didn't?"

I was off to the side of the platform, so Malachi had to turn around to look at me. He glared. "Leif, you're not a member of the Demos and you have no right to speak. I won't tolerate it again. As I said, we need a reason to disregard the computer output, and in fact, this is only one of many points Loretta will bring up. Now, either be quiet or leave."

I felt Yong touch my arm very lightly. "Starting a fight we can't win won't help, Leif. Listen to the rest of it and then we'll see."

She was right, but that didn't make me feel any better. I was in a mood to start a fight, even though I knew it was stupid. I looked around and found Hiep at the very end of the first row. He was slouched in his chair, but his eyes were on me and nowhere else. Was he waiting for me to do something dumb? He didn't move, not even his eyes. Malachi took my lack of action as a sign he had won that point. He signaled Loretta to start again.

Loretta cleared her throat and continued her recitation, now with Francesca's murder. She had been killed with Penny's knife. Loretta was careful to enumerate the wounds and where they had been inflicted. The knife had been hidden under a footing in the hydroponics facility expansion where Penny worked, usually by herself. There was no evidence anyone else had taken Penny's knife. Someone had gone in and out of the Medical Unit around the time Francesca was killed. Penny's ident was in the door records. There was no evidence that Penny had not been in the Med Unit.

My hand itched. It wanted to draw my pistol. How well would that work out? I ground my teeth together because I knew the answer.

Malachi called for witnesses. Bjorn signaled to a young woman in Pioneer uniform. She stood up and identified herself.

"I saw Penny before she went to Jerry's hab that day," she said. "She was rolling a couple of joints. I thought she was just going to get high; I thought it was just cannabis. But she didn't smoke them. She still had them in her hand when she went to Jerry's hab because I saw her going there. She didn't have them when she came back."

Penny's mouth dropped open and her eyes grew very wide.

Reality was not to be outdone. She snapped her fingers and pointed. A man, also in Pioneer uniform, stood up and identified himself.

"I saw her the night Dr. Balboni was killed. It was late, after the doctor was killed. She was headed past the habs out to the hydroponics area. She had something in her hand. I'm sure it was a knife. I didn't think anything of it then because she's always out there by herself. But I did watch for her to come back. Her hands were empty then. I never saw the knife after that, not until Reality found it under the footing."

"Thank you for your candor and for coming forward to speak," Malachi said. "I know these things are difficult." He looked down again to focus on Penny. "What would you like to say in your defense?"

"I didn't do any of these things," Penny said. "I didn't kill anyone. I didn't roll any joints that night, not for myself and not to bring to Jerry. I don't know who took my knife. I wasn't carrying it out to the hydroponics area. I don't walk around with a knife."

"I see," Malachi said. "That means you're saying that what these two other Pioneers said isn't true. That they're lying. That's what it means, doesn't it?"

Penny nodded but did not say anything else.

"Okay. Well, that's two different people. Is there anyone you can point to who can say that what *you* are saying is true? I'm not even asking for *proof* that they're lying. I'm just asking you to give me anything that would even *suggest* that they're not telling the truth."

Penny turned around in her chair to scan the audience. I figured she was looking for Dustin. I spotted him in the last row of seats that was occupied. He seemed to be shrinking in his chair, angled so he was partly hidden behind the person next to him. No one stood up for Penny.

"Why do I have to prove I didn't do any of this?" she asked.

Malachi looked past her, out to the audience. "The Demos will decide which side of the case they accept. You give yourself a stronger position if you can offer something more than your word, but that's really up to you."

That's when Bjorn's stupid chorus started up. "Pennywise, full of lies; Pennywise, no surprise; Pennywise, full of lies."

By the third time through their chant, Penny had shriveled up into a ball at her table. Malachi raised his hand and the chant stopped. The thought of shooting Bjorn did flash through my mind.

As if by telepathy, Yong called me on our private connection. "Don't do what you're thinking."

After that, the only sound was the rain drumming on the roof of the Dome. Malachi waited, but Penny didn't say anything else. I think she recognized it was useless. I glanced back at Yong. Her face held no expression. Dev was tense. His eyes flicked to me in a wordless *What do we do?* I had no good answer.

Malachi asked the Demos to vote: guilty or innocent. The only thing I will say about the guilty verdict is that it wasn't unanimous.

CHAPTER THIRTY FOUR

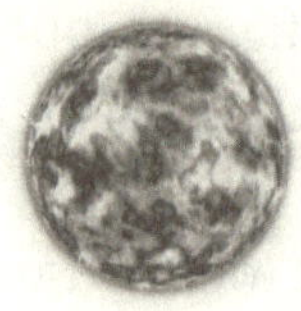

"That was a farce," I said after we got back to the Lab Unit, stripped off our rain gear, and filled in Jing and Jorge on what had happened.

"I wouldn't call it a farce," Yong said. "It was a show trial. Malachi got what he wanted. He has someone blamed for the murders, and the Demos here owns the verdict. They voted on it; they all have responsibility."

"It's still Malachi's doing," Jing said. "He's like a puppet master."

"He has effective control here," Yong said. "I think that's clear."

"What do we do about it?" Jing asked. "There are no people anywhere else on this planet and no place else to go, and I'm sure if the people in the town try to go against Malachi, he'll just bring out the guns. That we brought."

"I don't think Malachi wants to do things at gunpoint," I said. "He can't afford to shoot people; there's no one to replace them. It's almost the same issue with Jerry's original demand about taking people back. Also, I don't think he dares hand the rifles out. I don't think he trusts the free company people that far. Not unless there's an emergency like an actual riot or rebellion."

Yong frowned. "You're probably right about the lack of trust. I think that's why he is concentrating on the Pioneers. He wants a cadre that he has created and that he can trust. It's not a new pattern. It's all happened before." She looked at Jing as if scrutinizing the doc. "I think this is somewhat beside the point. Our mission here is not about regime change, even if we don't like the one that's here."

Jing bridled at that, but as much as I didn't like it, I could see Yong's point. I remembered her agony over what had happened—what she had done—in Sumatra. "We can't start a war here," I said. "Even if we were going to, against the eight rifles Malachi controls we have two automatic pistols. And we're going to leave anyway."

"Fairly soon," Yong said right after I finished. "We have unloaded, the colony is as stable as it is going to be, and the murders are solved to their satisfaction. We should be planning departure."

Jing brushed her hair back with her hands and came to stand right in front of me and Yong. "So you two are saying we stand by and watch whatever Malachi decides to do to that poor girl? What if he decides to execute her? Or do you think you can talk him out of making an example of her? Because there is still a murderer here, and it isn't her."

That got my attention. "Can you be sure of that?"

It had Yong's attention too. "Did you find whatever information Francesca had?"

"In a way," Jing said. "Even if I didn't, it may be good enough."

I didn't understand what she meant by that, and I could see Yong didn't either. Jing smiled a thin smile that didn't show any of her teeth.

"I can't see anything in Francesca's folders." Jing tapped at the computer to bring up a list of directories on the screen. She highlighted one with Francesca's name. "This is locked up tight," she said.

"Really tight," Jorge said. "I had a go and couldn't get into it either, which tells you something. It's protected by more than voice and eye."

People have wanted to keep secret what they write probably since writing was invented. Half a millennium ago on Earth, they came up with letterlocking, ways of folding a letter and looping a piece of paper through it that made it impossible for a third party to read the letter without it being obvious the letter had been tampered with. Your secret correspondence might have been read, but you would know it. The twin desires to keep secrets and to spy them out only developed more intricate means with the invention of computers. Passwords were a first try at keeping secrets. They became useless in a short time. When we left Earth on the *Dauntless*, the standard lock was a person's voiceprint sent through their chip and phone simultaneously, with an image of their retina taken from their field. People marked emails, documents, and folders LOCKED BY VOICE AND EYE and believed they were secret.

"I was able to access Francesca's medical files," Jorge said. "That allowed me to create fake digital files for her voice and eye. Well, they weren't fake—they were her real voice and eye—but it was my file. Didn't work. When I tried, all that happened was I was sent to an authorization program that generated a random ten-digit code that changed every thirty seconds. That code was synchronized with Francesca's chip, so it was easy for her to unlock, but a brutal hacking job for anyone else. I won't say it can't be done. Anything can be hacked, and we've all seen plenty of examples, but I can't do it. We don't have that kind of software on the ship. Why would we take that kind of hacker tools on a starflight?"

"I can't pull it from her chip now either," Jing said. "I can take her chip out physically, of course, and Jorge can try to hack it. A forensics person with the government could do that, or a really good hacker."

"But that's not me," Jorge said. "I play with this stuff because I like fooling with systems, but I don't have the tools or the training for this. There is also a block in the town system that prevents data being sent from her files to the network. I don't think she put it there."

"I don't understand," Yong said. "You are showing us that you can't get any information from Francesca's files. How is this useful?"

"Why would anybody go to such lengths to lock up a computer file here?" Jing asked. Then she pushed her chair away from the console and let the silence build.

"Habit left over from Earth?" I suggested. "Or," I added slowly, "she's got something really significant about somebody here."

"Good enough for blackmail," Jing said. "Maybe good enough to be killed over. Why would someone else block data transmission from the folder?"

"Your conclusion makes sense," Yong said, "but we still don't have the information. We're still guessing."

"Maybe we do have it." Jing stood up. "Francesca was smart, but not as smart as she thought she was."

"We need to show you something." Jorge ran his fingers through hair as disordered as I had ever seen on him.

Jing walked over to the lab bench with the molecular analyzer. "What's interesting," she said, "is that when you use this instrument array, the machine's little computer, which is an isolated local system, creates a folder where you can save your work. Only one person, however, has any work saved here, and that's Penny. She's got a lot, uses this often."

"Are there more records with the cholinesterase inhibitor than the one Malachi showed me?" I asked.

"Have a look at this." Jing tapped at the panel. She brought up Penny's work folder and opened it. Then she tapped one of the files. "What do you see?"

I saw Malachi's login and Penny's ident. The date was the day Jerry died. The molecular structure was the same as the cholinesterase inhibitor Jing had extracted from Jerry's joint case. On the screen was the same file Malachi had shown me.

"Pretty damning," Dev said.

"Wait. Wait." I crowded close to the screen, as if that would change any of the pixels. "If this is sitting here and all you need to do is click the folder and the file, then why does Francesca have a folder locked up tighter than a national security briefing, and what is in her folder?"

"Good questions, Leif," Yong said. "But if we can't get into it, we can't know. For all we know, she set it up in case she found something. It might be nothing more than an empty folder."

Jing shook her head. "We can infer it. Let me show you all the work files by login date." Several more taps changed the screen to rows of dates and logins. She slid them up with her fingers until she reached Malachi's login, the day Jerry was killed. I looked for a file with Francesca's login. Didn't see one.

"Wait again. I'm a little slow." I felt that way. "Penny is the only one with anything saved. Nothing from Francesca?"

Jing was giggling at my discomfort. "I told you Francesca wasn't as smart as she thought. Neither was someone else. Now we're going to look at the RGDP files the machine saves for an inspector. In case someone played with patient data." Jing brought up a menu on the instrument's screen and tapped around on it.

Jorge picked up the story from there. "While you were off watching the kangaroo court, we figured out how to access the hidden inspector folders on the molecular analyzer. Well, Charley on the ship helped a lot.

Since we are all the way out here on our own, there has to be some way for us to access these files if we need to. No government inspector is going to stop by. So, according to the mission plan, the pilot-in-command can give access rights to a file with the instructions on how to get into the hidden folders. With Yong flying the spaceplane, I'm pilot-in-command in the system; I gave Charley the rights. This instrument down here is no different from the ones on the *Dauntless*, not in this respect, and the procedures that work on the ship's instruments work on this one. This readout shows you every person who logged in to this machine since it was set up, with the date and time of login."

Another list of times, dates, and idents filled the screen. Again almost all of them were Penny. But not all. The last login was Malachi's, the day after Francesca was killed. Francesca's ident was also in the list. Once.

"Francesca's is the day before she was killed," I said. "Before she talked to Vanessa, in fact. What did she do on the instrument?"

"Nothing," Jing said. "She actually didn't know how to use the molecular analyzer. That's why she doesn't have a work folder. But she did log in and looked around at the files she could see. She would be able to see the work folders. But not the hidden ones."

"What did she find?" Yong's question was curt. Jing was enjoying the tale of her detective work, but Yong wanted the answer.

Jing scrolled the list of logins upward with her fingers. Past a long string of Penny logins was another one with Malachi's ident.

"That's a month and a half ago, never mind the correction for Heaven time." I drummed my fingers on the workbench. Something was out of place. "Wait. The record Malachi showed me, with his login and Penny's ident, was the day Jerry was killed. We saw it here when you showed us the work files. But I don't see a Malachi login at that date in this file. This one, a month and a half ago, is the only Malachi login in this list before the day Francesca died."

"Right," Jing said. "You have to go to here. Six weeks ago. Penny wasn't on the planet."

"I don't see a work folder for Malachi."

"I think Malachi deleted it, but too late. You'll see. Francesca must have copied it, and that's what is locked up in her folder. That would fit. There's that block on anything being sent from her folder, and that would also fit with Malachi trying to clean up after the fact. Now, let me show you the final piece. It's not just the logins. An instrument that is certified for medical lab use also duplicates the top-line output separately in another hidden file, with a time stamp. You can match up the login time stamp with the output time stamp. That's what I did, and this is what the top-line output was when Malachi was logged in six weeks ago."

Jing tapped on the screen again, and it displayed a chemical structure. Below the structure was a brief interpretation: PROBABLE CHOLINESTERASE INHIBITOR. It was the same structure as the compound in the file with Penny's ident and the one Jing had analyzed.

"Shit." I let out a long, slow breath. "You're telling me that Malachi knew, over a month before we got here, that those thistles had a nerve agent in their leaves. Why would he leave all his work in the machine for somebody to find later? It doesn't make sense."

"Yes, it does. Malachi may have forgotten his work folder was here; he may have thought no one else would look through this machine. That was his mistake. Now, let's assume Francesca saw his work file and copied it when she was in the system, and before she spoke to Malachi. Then Malachi went in the day after she was killed, changed the work file, and put it in Penny's folder. He deleted his work folder from six weeks ago. Or thought he did," Jing said. "I can't tell you if Malachi didn't know about these hidden files. I doubt Francesca knew about them. It doesn't matter. Go ahead. Delete Malachi's login and this result."

"We might need them later," I said.

"I wouldn't worry about it. Delete them."

I hit delete. The screen blanked. I went to the login records and deleted Malachi's entry. Again the screen blanked.

"Now, exit the file, go back in, and scroll to that time point."

I followed Jing's directions, and there was Malachi's login, staring at me as though I had never hit Delete. The output with the compound structure was in the output file as well.

"You *can't* delete these records," Jing said. "This is the way RGDP works. You know all the chaos we've had over the last five or so years with people hacking databases and changing history or other records?" She eyed me and Yong. "Maybe you don't. You two were on a starshot. Anyway, as a safeguard now, to be certified for medical use, a lab instrument has to store this information separately and permanently. I trained in rural medicine. We have to be able to use a lot of these machines ourselves, so we got drilled on this stuff. Francesca never finished med school, much less postgrad training. She wouldn't have known. Unless Malachi worked in a medical lab, there's no reason he would know either."

I had my hands on my hips and I stared at the screen. "Malachi knew about the nerve agent in the thistle long before we ever got here," I said. "He is a chemist and a free company man. He knew exactly what that compound would do. When he told me that night out at the lake that the mice died when they ate the thistle leaves but no one knew why, he was lying. I'll bet that's what made him do the analysis. He just waited for the right moment."

"That's why he took you on that hike out to the lake," Yong said.

"Sure. I made a great alibi when Jerry died. Nobody could accuse him because he was with me, and no one else knew why Jerry died anyway." I squeezed my head between my hands as I thought through the tangle. I had Jing show me the logins again, stared at Malachi's login the day after Francesca's death. "Malachi logged in after Francesca was killed, saw the file he had left in the system. So, yes, he must have rigged the files in the work folders to make it look like Penny got the results from the thistle, and he fixed that date also. Cleaned it up and covered his tracks, or tried to. But, you're saying, even if he did get to the hidden files, he would have thought that Delete meant Delete. Which also means," I added, "that he had someone kill Jerry for him."

"Who?" Jorge asked.

"Hiep," was the quick reply from Jing.

"Or Loretta," said Yong.

"Or one of the others from the *Daredevil* who hated Jerry," I said. "We don't know, and they're not going to tell us if we ask."

"We need that connection," Jorge said. "Otherwise, all we have is a long, twisty argument that sounds good, but no proof. I mean, we get it, but try explaining this to someone else. It's not as bad as what they did to Penny, but we need more to accuse Malachi of murder."

"No," I said. "This is a lot stronger. The motivation is obvious. Get rid of Jerry and manipulate the situation to take over."

"What about the deadman switch?" Dev asked. "You said Malachi knew about it and thought it was real. Doesn't that say he would *not* have done this?"

The question startled me. Dev had been so quiet, kept so much to himself, I sometimes forgot he was with us. The next instant, though, the answer clicked into place.

"That's why he waited," I said. "He knew how to get rid of Jerry, but he was afraid of the deadman switch. However, he knew we were coming and he waited for us. He figured we could repair the damage to the reactor. That way, the deadman switch wouldn't matter. Jerry's gone; he takes over. Everything is fine."

"Good plan," Dev said. "He would have been right, too, except for what happened to the socket. So, that's Jerry. What about the doctor?"

"That's pretty simple too," I said. "After we figured out about the thistle leaves in the valley, Francesca was pretty loud about working out Jerry's death herself. She didn't want Jing involved, wanted to do it herself. She just wanted to be a big shot. But when she found the info in the instrument, it was too good an opportunity. She didn't go to Malachi asking for a reward for finding that Penny was the murderer. She tried to blackmail him. Malachi can't afford to have this come out. He must have arranged the block on her files so that, even if she set up a transmission to go in case she died, the information never went out. Even if he could get away with killing Jerry, rifles can be aimed in more than one direction. It would only take one person from a free company nervous about what Malachi might do with nerve gas. Again, I doubt he did it himself."

"It all makes a sad kind of sense," Jorge said. "Penny is just a convenient person to frame because she has no friends."

We were all silent a moment. I was thinking about how Penny had looked so defeated at the end in the Community Dome. Beaten and alone.

"What do we do about this?" Jorge said. "What do we do now?"

"Are you suggesting that I just walk down the street and shoot Malachi?" I said.

"No," Yong said. "We were not given the power of summary judgment. Even if we were, I would not agree. I do not think we can even arrest him and try to put him on trial. We know Malachi is not the actual killer, and I am not certain we can prove he gave the order without finding the person he gave it to. Think about the situation here. Removing him still leaves the killer loose, and it still leaves eight M8 rifles that we would have to secure, or risk having them used against us. Again, think about where we are. Unleashing a small war here is the same as giving everyone a death sentence."

"So we do nothing?" Jing said.

"I did not say that either." Yong closed her eyes for a moment, and I suspected she was reliving a scene from her past. I knew which scene that was. She opened them again but did not look at any of us. "I am a pilot and a soldier. I have followed orders and left death and destruction in my wake, including the deaths of innocents. I have done it more times than I like to think. I do not want to allow it here. What Malachi is doing now is a crime. We need to prevent it."

I wanted to hug Flygirl. Maybe I should have actually done it.

"How?" Jorge asked. "Put all the information in a file and broadcast it? Obviously, Malachi or one of his people like Hiep had no trouble stopping Francesca from sending it out, but they can't stop us. However, I'll bet that will start a war."

"I don't see why we are agonizing over this," Dev said. "We can do whatever we want. I can't see that anyone at ISC or any of the governments are going to care what we do. It's going to be more than a hundred and fifty years from when we left by the time we get back. If we want to shoot Malachi, we do it. We tell them whatever we want when we get home, and that's the end of it. No one will ever know differently."

"I can't agree to that." Yong's voice rang with command. "I will not play God. There is truth and there are lies, and I will not tell lies because it is convenient, even if no one else knows the truth. I am done with that and with people who do that."

"I'm with Yong," I said. "We know the difference between right and wrong even if no one else will ever know."

"That's a fine sentiment," Dev said, "but what is right here, and what is the truth? Do we side with the wannabe dictator who we think has blood on his hands, but who has this colony organized so it may survive, or with the annoying young woman who probably didn't do it and whom Leif has become fond of?"

"Wait a minute!" I had some heat in my voice. "That's not a fair characterization."

"You mean you're not fond of her?" Jorge laughed.

I hate it when I blush. Especially with Yong looking at me.

"It doesn't matter," Yong said. I wasn't sure, at first, whether she meant it didn't matter if I was fond of Penny or it didn't matter which side we took. Fortunately, she had more to say. "What I think does matter is that Malachi is likely to execute this woman. Since I now believe it is unlikely that she is guilty, I don't think we should allow it. I have a way we can do this without starting a war. If we can bring her on the spaceplane, we can have a discussion with Malachi about what will happen. If he won't talk, or we don't like the outcome of the discussion, we can take off. That will save her and it does not put us in the position of unilaterally imposing a government that we will leave behind us."

One by one, we agreed that Yong's plan was the best one we had.

"I doubt Malachi is going to hand Penny over to us," I said. "We're going to need to get her, and I'm the one best suited to do it."

"Agreed," Yong said.

After that one word, she didn't move. Neither did I. This spur-of-the-moment mission could easily go sour, and we both knew it. I could live with that, but not without trying to fix the situation first. With a hand gesture, I signaled for Yong to join me in a far corner of the building.

"Look, Yong," I started, then stopped. I could feel my face going red and was looking for a place to put my hands. This was not my usual pre-mission self. "Look, I'm sorry for what I said that I'm sure made it sound like I was feeling something different than what I really feel, and, I mean, Penny's like a kid, or my kid, or I think what my kid would be like and that's all, I haven't thought anything else and, God knows, I haven't done anything, and you're the one I want to be with and fly through the universe with and I don't know how to say it much clearer than this, but if I haven't said it enough, I want to say it now, so you know how I really feel, because I need you to know that, in case what could happen happens and I don't get to say it later. I'm sorry."

I think she smiled. A little.

"When we got back together at Earthbase," she said, "I asked you to come with me on this flight. There was a reason."

"And there was a reason I said yes."

"I know that. Even if we both talk around it." She really did smile. "Now, go get the girl, Soldier Boy."

The moment I heard the "Soldier Boy," I knew life was worth living, for however long I got to live it. I gave her a smile broad enough to split my face and we walked back to where the others were waiting.

"The rest of you need to go with Yong to the spaceplane now," I said. "None of you are trained for this, so I'm going to go solo. I don't know how this is going to turn out, and I don't want to take any risk of any of you turning into hostages."

Jorge looked from one of us to the other and sighed. "I guess I knew it would come to something like this. I'll go with Yong."

"Good," Yong said. "We're not going back to the habs. Let's go to the LZ now. Good luck, Soldier Boy."

"Good luck to you, Flygirl."

Interstellar extraction specialist. My new title.

CHAPTER THIRTY FIVE

I felt better once I was outside and on my own. The interminable discussions about "whodunit" and what to do about it were not my idea of passing the time. If that's what I enjoyed doing, I would have become a lawyer and never left Earth, and my life would have ended years ago. We were never going to reach certainty. It was better to go *do* something. Granted, the pistol on my belt was not much for armament, but I would be surprised if I needed more than that. I was not assaulting a heavily guarded fortification.

I suspected Yong was a little miffed when I included her with the others as not being trained for this, but it was true. She could be the most daring and capable attack pilot in the history of the world—and that might well be true—but she had no experience with ground actions or exfiltration. Even more important, aside from my own personal feelings, we couldn't afford the risk of her being killed or captured. I didn't know if Jorge's gut would survive another stretch in hib, but the chance had to be considerable if he was considering staying on Heaven, as dubious a place as this was. No, we could not risk Yong. Further, with her shepherding the others, I was confident they would make it to the spaceplane.

The rain was not as heavy as it had been, but was still falling steadily when I stepped out of the Lab Unit. I was thoroughly wet within a minute or two. Of course, my rain gear was good: completely waterproof, breathable, weighed next to nothing. It was as comfortable as clothing could be in the sauna that was Heaven. However, the ISC had designed it for explorers whose greatest risk was being lost. The rain gear was impregnated with reflectors and iridescent stripes. I needed to rescue a captive and sneak her to safety in the dark. Being easy to see was the last thing I wanted. I did without the rain gear.

No one was outside in the downpour as I strolled around Town Circle to the school building. Most of the exterior lights were off to save power, and there were no cameras to monitor the streets. I ducked behind the dining hall, then worked my way around the back of that structure until I reached the side of it that faced the school across the Avenue of the Americas.

The light in the third-floor corner in Penny's cell was on, but the exterior lights on the school building were off. That was a piece of good luck. In the dim light from the third floor and from exterior lights on the dining hall, I could make out a single guard at the front door. I couldn't tell if it was Miroslav again, because this guard was scrunched up tightly into the entry, trying to stay out of the rain. Reflective patches on his Pioneer rain gear helped me locate him. Was there another guard not so easy to see?

My field had a night vision setting I could trigger with my chip, but—let's be honest—it wasn't very good. The old-style glasses we used to wear before I went on the first starshot were much better in that respect. Even they weren't nearly as good as the combat visor on my old service helmet, but the physical lens was better, for this purpose, than the fancy, modern, lensless projection field I had now. I waited patiently for a few minutes and saw no sign of another guard.

The situation presented two options. I could kill or disable the guard, shoot out the lock on the door, try to rush Penny outside, and evade the hue and cry on the way to the LZ. The beginning was easy and fast, but whether I killed the guard or not, if he was chipped in, there would be an alarm when I took him down, and the run to the LZ would be problematic. If I could find another way in, however, and slip out with Penny unnoticed, the odds of getting to the LZ would improve. That made up my mind, even though Penny wasn't the most agile person around. It was also a good thing for the guard.

So, how to get in? Ideally, on a mission like this, we would review the details of the target in advance, sometimes even practice with a mock-up. There had been plenty of occasions, however, where our orders amounted to, "Go there, do that, and make it up as you go along." This would be one of those times. I spent some time studying the structure. It had no windows on the ground floor. Despite being three stories high, it had to be similar to the framework-and-panel self-assembly habs that made up almost all of St. Peterstown. Construction bots would lay out the base and place components at the site. Then internal mini-bots in the framing would self-erect the framework, and other bots would attach panels to create the enclosure. Co-bots, with their human partners, would install the interior fixtures and additional structure.

We didn't have this when I flew before. We'd had to set up our little base with muscle and some bot help, but we weren't trying to build a town this size either. This sort of self-assembly was the only way a permanent town could be built with the little time and few humans available to the *Daredevil.* That meant all the construction was stereotyped. All of that meant the building had protruding framework and grippable points all the way up. It wasn't smooth. I could climb it, much like climbing a rock wall where the hand- and footholds were in a pattern that never varied. Piece of cake. I sprinted across the Avenue of the Americas and got into the darkness on the other side. Then I skirted around to the back of the school, where the privacy wall screened away the residence habs on the radiating streets.

I saw a handhold on a horizontal piece of framing about eight feet off the ground. I jumped, grabbed it with both hands, and pulled myself up until I could get my feet on a little ridge of framing. Then it was only a matter of extending an arm to reach another grip point and working the rest of my body up while staying as flat against the structure as I could. I tried to be a bug on the wall.

I was shielded from the rain because the roof, like the roofs of the other large public units, overhung the sides of the building. While this kept the grip points dry and reduced the chance I would slip, it did mean that I had little to no chance of being able to grab the edge of the roof and pull myself up to it. The roof would be too slick in the rain to risk that. So after considering gaining access through the roof, which must have a door leading to the stairway near Penny's classroom, I decided against it. Entry was going to have to be through a window.

The privacy wall that screened the school from the residential habs and streets behind it rose only as high as the top of the second story. This made another decision for me. While I doubted anyone would be looking out on a rainy night to see a man climbing the school's wall, there was no advantage in going higher.

I worked my way sideways across the second floor until I found a window set into a wall panel. Closed, of course. The panel had tracks, however, which meant the window could be opened. Only one problem: All parts of these structures, except the doors, expected you to interact with the network to make them function. What was the risk that someone would be watching the network and observe me open the window? Why was I thinking about that only now, when I was splayed across the building halfway up? This is what comes of no advance planning.

I chipped in. My field displayed the control panel for windows and a green checkmark indicated that I was old enough to be allowed to open them. Well, it was a school building. I tried to avoid laughing. The window slid open and I climbed in. It closed behind me and I chipped out. So far, so good. If I could find some rope, which would probably be in a gym area, I could lower Penny down that way.

Would Malachi have stationed a guard inside with Penny this time? That would be a reasonable step for him to take. If he had, I would need to take care of the guard. That would likely set off an alarm and we would then be on the run for the front door, so the rope went to the back of my mind. I moved silently through the darkened corridors and checked every corner before I went around it. I found no one.

I halted before the lighted corner classroom. The door was shut, with light leaking out under it. I did not see a guard in the corridor, but what if one was in the room with Penny? If the guard was armed, the weapon would be one of the M8 assault rifles we had brought. What were the odds a guard was sitting there with the rifle pointed directly at the door, hour after boring hour? Damn small. I decided that the surprise of me bursting through the door would freeze the guard for the instant I needed to get off a shot. In the confines of a small room, my pistol would be as deadly as the guard's rifle. If the guard was unarmed, I didn't think there was anyone, other than maybe Hiep, who could take me hand to hand, but I wasn't going to take the chance. I would shoot first and worry about whether the guard was armed later. Pistol in hand, I inched up to the door.

I brought my knee up to my chest and smashed the bottom of my foot into the door. It burst open with a crash. I leaped into the room, out of line with the doorway, weapon leveled and ready to fire. The room was empty.

No guard. No Penny. Shit.

The mat Penny had sat on before was still on the floor. I twisted around, looking for what I had missed in those first frantic split seconds. I hadn't missed anything. No one was there. There were no wet marks on the floor or the mats. Penny had been soaked from the rain, and the water probably would not have completely dried without visible spots. No one had been here since the end of the trial.

A call notification flashed on my field. Malachi. I sighed and opened the connection.

"Evening, Leif," he said in his Alabama drawl. "I had a suspicion you would come, either for her, so she's not there, or for me, in which case, you'd have found a reception even you couldn't shoot your way out of."

"I should have gone for you," I said. "You're the murderer, aren't you?"

Malachi laughed. "No, no, no. I'm not. I trust you have that on the recording you're making and that your pilot is also hearing."

Of course it was set to record, but I suppose it's only in the vids that the real criminal slips and gloats on a call. At least he was wrong about Yong. She would be busy leading the others to the spaceplane, and he didn't realize that.

"Well, I hope you don't think that stupid circus you put on convinced people that Penny is a double murderer. Especially since I know she didn't do the analysis of the nerve agent. You did."

"Leif, Leif, the Demos voted on her guilt, even if you are not convinced."

"Look," I said, "I don't know what the issue is with her, but you're right. I'm not convinced she did anything beyond being a pain in the ass. If you want to be rid of her that badly, we'll take her out. Let that be the end of it."

"No, Leif. If I let her go back with you, I'll have a riot from the old Leavers. I can't have that. And I will have her answer for these crimes. That will set the governance here, and that is important if this community is to function and survive. You are getting this on your recording, I hope? Oh, and by the way, Leif, you are trying to challenge the rule of the Demos. I can't permit that either."

Sure. While we were talking, Malachi had undoubtedly sent some of his people to get me. I needed to get away from the school fast, or he would have two people to makes examples of.

"Good luck trying to catch me," I said as I scooted back toward the window. "I'll be back here in a thousand years and I'll dance on your grave."

Occasionally, I indulge in bravado.

"I'm not going to lose sleep over it." Malachi laughed again.

I had come to really hate that laugh.

CHAPTER THIRTY SIX

If I didn't get out of that school building and away from it fast, I was going to have major problems. Penny was nothing more than a convenient tool for Malachi to put the murders to rest, consolidate his power in the colony, and get us to leave. I told myself I didn't have time to think about it anymore. Shooting my way out the front door was probably a bad idea. I had to assume Malachi had sent some of the free company people with M8s. He might not trust them a lot, but I had to figure he would arm them to go after me. Going back out the window and climbing down was no good for the same reason. The privacy wall would force me around the building to the Town Circle at the front, which is where people would be showing up with rifles. Automatic fire can make up for deficiencies in marksmanship.

That privacy wall gave me an idea, though. I went back to the window I had come in through. It slid open and left me staring at the top of the privacy wall. A little while ago, I had worried I would be visible to people if I climbed above it. Now I didn't care. What I did care about was that the top of that wall was not too far from the window opening. I needed only to climb into the opening of the window with my feet under me, while contorting myself to keep a grip on the top of the frame. From that twisted, half-bent-over position, all I had to do was leap across the gap to the top of the wall where I could see rain spattering. In the dark.

Sometimes it's best not to overthink things. I jumped.

My chest and stomach hit the top of the wall with a thump that threatened to knock the wind out of me. The wall was narrow—only about six inches wide—and slippery, made of the usual graphene panels stiffened with carbon nanotube struts and beams. I felt myself skid when I hit and grabbed frantically for the sides to keep from falling off. The surface was smooth. My legs swung over the edge but my arms held on. I managed to pull one leg up and over and perched atop the wall while I got my breath back.

From where I sat, I could look away from the center of town and up the dark expanse of ground between the privacy screens of the habs along each street. That darkness was my avenue out.

I looked down, but the ground below was hidden in the dark. I was going to bet that it was dirt, with or without some of the sparse grass cover that grew on the high plains. It wouldn't be concrete. Would it? I lowered myself as far as I could along the wall to shorten the fall, then let go and dropped. I landed on my feet with my knees bent to absorb the shock and curled up into a forward roll. It was like landing from a low-altitude jump—not too bad. I got up and tested my various body parts. My right knee wasn't happy but the surgeon's work held together, and happy or not, it functioned. I figured it would take a few minutes—hopefully longer—for my pursuers to figure out where I'd gone. I needed that time to put some distance between me and them.

I took stock of the situation as I started moving toward the periphery, and I didn't like how it added up. I had failed in rescuing Penny. Worse, I didn't even know where she was. To this point, Malachi had outfoxed me. I needed to get his posse off my tail before I could stop to work out where Penny was, and I didn't have forever. Would Malachi hold off on Penny's punishment while his people chased me around? Even if he did, there would be a limit to how long he would wait. At the same time, since I was now persona non grata, there was a real risk he would go after Yong and the others. I hoped they were well on their way to the LZ, but I would be happier when I had a call that they were on the spaceplane. All of this suggested a plan to get out of town and head toward Dead Creek. That would take me in the opposite direction from the LZ. If they chased me, that would improve Yong's chances.

I figured I could lose them along the creek and then double back and try to find Penny. Same concept if they didn't go after me. Unfortunately, there were lots of empty habs. I would not have time to check them one by one, even if no one was looking for me. I wondered if Ibiana might have an idea of where Penny was. That seemed like a good first stop, once I was clear of the pursuit. She had sounded as though she would help me out when I had spoken with her.

The rain was beginning to taper off by this time, but that provided scant solace. I was already soaked, and the roll after my jump off the privacy wall left me coated with a layer of mud. I recognize that mud is good for concealment in the dark, but that doesn't mean I enjoyed wearing it.

On my way to the perimeter road, the privacy walls screened me from anyone in the habs who might be looking. However, my brilliant plan evaporated as soon as I reached the perimeter road. A rover was parked there with a set of lights shining on the roadway in both directions. I stopped and knelt down in the slop. A glance behind me showed a brief flash, far back toward the wall I had jumped from. Then another. Light off the reflective surfaces of the rain gear. The Pioneer rain gear had the same type of built-in reflectors as the ISC standard ones. Someone or more likely a few someones were coming up the same route I had taken. Malachi's likely plan for corralling me came into focus. He knew I had been in the school building, and by now they had probably searched it and found me gone. So he had sent a group of Pioneers up the route between the habs. Similar groups were probably moving up the radiating avenues, checking habs as they went. If they didn't come upon me, they would flush me out of the inhabited part of St. Peterstown. One or more of the five free company people, the ones I bet carried the rifles, would be at the perimeter road waiting for me. If I wasn't forced out into their net, I would be found and they would move to where my position was. Not a good situation. What was I going to do about it?

Well, Malachi had only eight rifles. The odds were that the Pioneers behind me were unarmed. I doubted Malachi would care if I killed a few of them. The problem was that I could kill all of them, but the likelihood that I could do it without giving away my position was about zero. They would be chipped in, and all it would take was one notification, or even one of them going down, and the folks with the weapons would know where to go. I had to not only get out of St. Peterstown but go far enough out that anyone pursuing couldn't be chipped in. Then, if I couldn't lose them, I could kill them in the dark and no one would be the wiser. Maybe I would get lucky and I could ambush one of the free company people and take an M8. Malachi would not like seeing what I could do with one of those.

Task number one: get out of their net. I crept over to the privacy wall of the closest structure and edged forward to the roadway as far as I could without coming into the open. I wished St. Peterstown had trees or bushes or hedges, but they probably wouldn't grow well and hadn't been planted. Cover was limited to whatever the fabricated structures provided.

The rover and the lights were still more than half an American football field away. Let's face it, a pistol is not a distance weapon, and this was in the dark and drizzle. Still, I'm a good shot and I had no choice. I took aim and fired. A loud pop, and one of the floodlights went out. Oaths followed. That was the best start I was going to get. I broke into a sprint for the darkness beyond the road. I was illuminated for an instant by the remaining flood as I crossed the perimeter road.

There was another oath, and the crackle and flash of an M8 firing split the night. I dived into a roll, came up in a crouch, and fired two shots of my own back at the rover. I had no idea if I hit anything and I didn't really expect to. What I wanted to do was discourage anyone at the rover from taking careful aim at me. I turned and ran into the night, zigging and zagging as I went. Behind me, I heard the M8 fire again and I dropped flat. I could see the bright yellow flashes at the muzzle and the red of the tracer rounds as they streaked out across the plains. It was a wild show, a spray of bullets not aimed at anything in particular, but a random shot can kill you as dead as a carefully aimed one if you happen to be in the bullet's path. When the shooting stopped, I got up and ran again.

I wanted to go at full speed, but I couldn't. The poor dirt with its thin ground cover didn't absorb the rainfall very well. Puddles were everywhere, and if I splashed through them, I would give myself away. There was another wild spray of bullets, and again, I dropped face-first into the mud until the shooting stopped. Another run from there brought me to a low rise. I dropped to the ground on the far side of it and peered back at St. Peterstown.

I wished for the true night vision of a combat visor. I wished for magnification. I might as well have wished for Santa Claus. The projection field of my New Golden Age civilian chip offered neither. I hugged the mud and tried to make out what was happening behind me.

The rover that had been on the perimeter road was still sitting there. I strained to see if anyone had set out on foot. By this time, the rain had stopped and breaks in the cloud layer allowed some moonlight through. That was a double-edged sword, of course, but at that moment, I did not see anyone on foot slogging toward me. Were they going to give up on me?

Another rover drove up to the one parked on the perimeter road. Some conversation must have taken place, because the new vehicle turned its lights off and moved off the road and in my direction.

Crap. I had a feeling I knew who was in that rover. How good was he at this type of game? I wasn't sure I wanted to find out. I thought about entrenching myself, basically burying myself in the mud and waiting, hoping he would come within a sure pistol shot. Unfortunately, the mud was superficial; the ground below it was hard and I had no tools. If he had true night vision glasses or infrared, he'd kill me with that rifle of his long before I had a chance. I watched the rover for a few minutes. It rolled and paused, then rolled again. Yes, he was tracking me.

Without being able to dig in, my low rise wasn't a great ambush location. I retreated in the direction of Dead Creek, sacrificing speed in order to cover my tracks. I thought I would be able to use the bank of the creek as a natural trench and set an ambush there. Unfortunately, when I approached it, I found that the runoff from the rain had the creek in full flood. It had overflowed its banks. It meant I could wade through the spreading water and leave no track, but the moonlight was strengthening as the clouds broke up and the third moon rose. I was becoming easier to spot from a distance, track or no track. I needed cover, real cover.

Only one place I knew on the high plains could give me the cover I wanted. If I could get to Dead Lake, the trees on the slopes around the lake and even the rushes by the shore would do it. There, we could play hide-and-seek in an environment that would even up some of his advantage in weaponry. Of course, going there put me even farther away from Penny. But if Hiep killed me, I would be no use to anyone. I made for the lake.

I never thought I'd be so happy to see a bunch of scraggly, dwarfed trees. I ducked into them and breathed a sigh of relief. I was a little surprised that I hadn't presented enough of a target along the way for Hiep to take a shot, but I wasn't going to complain. I picked a tree with a reasonably thick trunk and stationed myself behind it, where I had a good view of the approach to the lake. Indeed, after a short wait, I saw moonlight glint off the rover as it came toward my position. Then it rolled down into a fold in the land. It did not come up. I strained my eyes looking for a man. I did not see one approach.

Fuck. Hiep had figured I was in the trees. He'd dismounted and taken another route, using the fold in terrain to conceal his direction. He had to be headed to my right, to come up behind me and flush me out. Time to change position.

I moved deeper into the trees and toward my left. I wondered if there would be a chance to make a try for the rover. Could I take it and leave him behind? I discarded the idea almost as soon as I had it. It was an obvious trap. If I wanted to survive this game, I needed to assume he was as good as I was. I shifted position again, upslope now and away from the lake. I wanted to get behind him without giving my own position away. He had made no move, done nothing, to tip where he was. Yes, he was good at this. Very good. Again, I wondered if he had night vision or infrared.

"Drop the weapon, Leif." Hiep's voice came from behind me.

CHAPTER THIRTY SEVEN

Damn! He had gotten behind *me*. And now I was dead. Except... he hadn't shot me and I wasn't dead. Yet. If he was going to do it, why wait?

This is where, in the vids, the hero pivots with blinding speed so that the bad guy, who has the hero in his sights with his finger on the trigger, still misses and fires only one shot despite having an automatic weapon, and the hero returns a single, unerring kill shot. Yeah, right. It doesn't work that way. He didn't intend to shoot me, because he hadn't done it, but if I tried some crazy move, I was sure he would. I dropped the pistol.

"What happens now?" I asked.

"You were trying to rescue Penny."

"Yes." I couldn't see that letting him record a confession was going to change my situation very much.

He surprised me by saying, "Good." Then he said, "I need you to do something for me. I want your word that you will do it."

"You do have me at gunpoint," I said.

"True." A soft chuckle followed. "We need to do this differently. Take three steps away from the pistol," he ordered.

I complied.

"Now," he said, "I am going to step into that small clearing to your right where you can see me. Turn around." I turned toward his voice, and he said, "I will throw my gear bag and rifle to the side, where you can see them, and I will put my hands on my head."

Huh? "Why would you do that?"

"I said that I want your word that you will do something for me. It is worth my life. I need you to work with me, and this is not something I can compel you to do. Your agreement obtained at gunpoint is worthless. I cannot trust it. This is the only way for me to be sure."

"Okay. Go ahead." Some things are easy to agree to.

I turned in the direction he had said and found a shadow amid the darkness that moved. He walked into the small opening among the trees and tossed his rifle aside, as he'd said he would. Then he pulled a small bag from his belt and dumped the contents on the ground. He put his hands on his head, sank to his knees, and waited.

This was crazy. I retrieved my pistol, trained it on him, and walked over. I stopped a couple of paces away, although why would he try to attack me after what he had done? I found that I did want to hear what he had to say.

"You do understand," I said, "that once you tell me what you want, I can simply put a bullet in your head."

"Of course." It was a matter-of-fact statement. "I bought my ticket to death a long time ago. As long as you do what I want, it doesn't matter, although I think you will agree the odds will be better if we work together."

"Okay, Hiep. I'm curious as hell and it's time to talk."

"Yes. First, please understand something. I like you, Leif, and I respect you. However, if Sicarius had a contract on you, I would kill you without hesitation."

"I appreciate your honesty."

"Always. Malachi is not Sicarius. Even if he was, I will not allow Penny to be hurt. Malachi promised me that she would not be hurt. I should know better than to believe promises, especially when it costs a person nothing to make them, but sometimes it is too easy to believe what you want to believe. What you need to believe. I know I am . . . useful to him. I believed him." Hiep's voice sharpened. "He told me things have changed, that I needed to see the larger picture." He spat. "I will break any oath I have given; I will give up my life, as I am doing. I will accept anything you choose to inflict. I want you to take Penny away from here. I want you to take her back to Earth. This cannot happen without you, without your active participation; your pilot might not agree. I cannot be sure of making this happen without you. This is what I want from you."

Pieces fell into place. Sometimes craziness makes sense.

"Hiep, you've fallen in love with her."

"I do not use that word."

Well, I didn't either. "You're acting like it."

"Penny is special. I've known it since we worked together in the valley, since she held my hand when you sewed up her leg. I will not let anything happen to her."

"Your Demos voted that she is guilty of murder."

"Penny did not kill Dr. Balboni," Hiep said. "Look at what I had in the bag."

I backed over to where the bag and its contents had been dropped on the ground. I made certain to keep Hiep covered with the pistol, although that may have been nothing more than force of habit. When I was next to the bag, I shined the light from my phone base onto the ground. What I saw was a pair of gloves. Penny's cut-proof work gloves.

"Dr. Balboni was killed with Penny's knife," Hiep said. "We agree on that. However, Penny was so scared of cutting herself with that knife that she wouldn't draw it without those gloves on. The gloves were in her room in the hab when we searched it, so she had them and could have worn them. Look at the gloves." I squatted and picked up one of them. "The exterior is a soft, rough leather," Hiep said, "and there is no blood on them. None at all. I know how to test for blood, and I have done it. If she killed the doctor with the knife, she would have been wearing the gloves and there would be blood on them. She did not kill the doctor, and she didn't kill Jerry Whitehead either."

"What about the door entrance at the Medical Unit? The record of her chip?"

"I told you any digital record can be altered or faked. Sicarius taught me that craft, and I am not the only one who knows it. No electronic record is worth anything compared to physical facts."

Part of me relaxed. "Do you know where she is?"

"Yes. Malachi has her in the hab by the photovoltaic panel field. There will be two guards, both Pioneers and unarmed."

"Unarmed?"

"Yes. Malachi is very cautious about giving out the rifles. He will have armed guards around himself until he hears that I have taken you, but they will also be set to watch each other. Malachi knows better than to trust anyone around him with a weapon. That is how he was taken on Earth. Three of his subordinates made a deal and gave him up." Hiep paused for a moment. "May I get up now? This ground is wet and we should get started."

I let him get to his feet and then allowed him to collect the M8 he had been carrying. As strange as that felt, if he were going to harm me, it would already have happened. I was alive because Hiep loved Penny and she was all that mattered to him. Hiep slung the rifle and headed back to the rover. I followed him.

As I pulled myself into the front passenger seat, I said, "You didn't say it, but I take it that you agree with me that Malachi is the killer. At least, he ordered the killings and he's going to execute Penny to cover it up."

Hiep started the rover, then turned toward me. "You can be certain that there is at least one, and probably two, other pairs of hands between him and the actual killings." He shrugged. "Since the day Jerry died, I have thought it was Malachi. He had the most to gain from Jerry dying. When I saw Penny's gloves, I was sure."

"You were sure," I said. "You're usually armed, you're experienced with weapons, and you're around Malachi. You could have done something."

The rover started forward with a bump and a splash. Then Hiep said, "You are often armed and were a member of a fabled military unit. You could have done something."

That stopped me, because he was right. "Yeah. The old judge, jury, and executioner approach was never a good one, was it?"

"No." He drove a bit farther before he spoke again. "It is more than that. I could have shot Malachi, but what happens next? Does Loretta shoot me? If I am able to shoot her down, too, does someone else get me? Who will pick up the rifles you brought, and where does it end?"

"In a mess, like it always does." I sighed. "I should know better. Do you know who actually did the killings?"

"I think so."

"Who?"

Hiep shook his head. "I will deal with this, all of it. Once you have Penny safe and off the planet, I will deal with it and see justice done."

"What? Wait a minute. You just had me convinced that you shouldn't be a vigilante, now you're telling me that is your plan. What's going on?"

"The situation now is different than it was even a day ago." Hiep was looking straight ahead at where the rover was going. Not once did he look over at me. His words were harsh as he spoke them. "I know now what Malachi plans. He will have Penny flayed alive. He will make his Pioneer leadership team do it. You know how he will, a mixture of command and threat. Then he is going to have her cooked for them."

"What!" My stomach threatened to rebel. I had seen all sorts of horrors made commonplace during the Troubles, and I even saw the aftermath of cannibalism when we lifted the siege of Dushanbe, but this was different. This hit me hard. "Why is he doing this?"

"Because those who do it will never be part of the community again. There is no going back after something like that. Malachi will own them because they will know that if Malachi falls, the people will remember what they did. This is how Malachi creates a group that must support him, no matter what happens. There were always rumors about the Grand Company, that they did this to make sure certain people could never leave. I am sure, now, those rumors are true."

"When the spaceplane takes off with Penny on it, you are going to war. Is that right?"

"Yes," he said. "This is evil."

"What will be here afterward? What is your plan for after?"

"I don't know," Hiep said. "I think the colony will fail and we will all die. I am sorry for those who have no part in this. It is, what is the word, ironic. Malachi actually could make this colony work, I think. He is ruthless and can execute a plan. If he murdered two people but the colony survived, well, many great leaders have had more blood on their hands than that. I would have accepted that. But when he broke his promise to me, I learned also that he has given up on the colonists; he may no longer believe it is possible to make the colony sustainable. He intends to live like a king for as long as he lives with no care for what comes after. He told me I could do the same. That was his larger picture. As I said, this is evil. Penny could, I think, figure out how to save this colony. She is that smart and she would do it." Hiep sounded almost wistful. "But you must take her away. I will never see her again, never be able to touch her again, but it will be for the best. I will do what I must. There is a saying among Sicarii. Always save the last bullet for yourself."

CHAPTER THIRTY EIGHT

Hiep drove the rover across the soggy plain, and the two of us were quiet for a while. A stiff wind from the west blew out the last of the clouds. Two of the moons were overhead to light our way, set amid thousands of twinkling stars. I was lost in my own thoughts, and those weren't pleasant ones. I had grown up in a deeply cynical time, raised on the philosophy that anything that sounds too good to be true isn't. I had never bought in to the concept of the New Golden Age being the best period in the history of humanity, not really.

When I came back from the stars to the New Golden Age, I thought people repeated it too fervently, a mantra that, if they said it often enough, would be true. Still, I thought—hoped—that we had left the behaviors and horrors of the Troubles behind us. I guess not. Maybe Malachi was right about that. The Troubles had never gone away. They were a part of us, and we took them with us wherever we went. Depressing thought.

Thinking about the Troubles brought me back to the task at hand. I'd been a soldier in the Troubles—a good one—and I needed to be a soldier again.

"Does this rover have enough battery life to get us to Penny and from there to the LZ in the dark?" I asked Hiep. "I don't want to wait for recharge from the photovoltaics after the sun comes up."

"We'll make it," he said. "I would not risk any delay either."

"Good." Then I told him we needed to coordinate with Yong, who would already be at the spaceplane with the others.

If Hiep was surprised that we had already moved the rest of our crew to the LZ, he gave no sign of it. Maybe he would have been surprised if we had not. "You should hold off that call as long as possible," he said. "You can assume there is a network bot set to look for your phone, and it will issue an alert with your approximate location when you connect."

"I'm not going through the St. Peterstown network," I said. "The spaceplane has a separate system. I'll give you the ident and code."

That done, I called Yong and gave her a capsule summary of the situation. She wasted no time thinking about Malachi. "What is your plan when you reach the photovoltaic panel field?"

"We will need to figure out how to get in close," I said. "We need to assume that Malachi knows how to set up sentries at a base. They'll be chipped in through equipment at that hab. Kill them, and the chips will signal that. Even if we can get close to them and knock them out, a properly set up chip will signal the loss of consciousness even if the sentries don't send a notification. We used to set up chips to signal if a sentry went to sleep on duty." The damned chips were very good at that sort of thing, which had given rise to all sorts of real-life schemes to penetrate bases in disguise and even wilder versions in vids in the years after the Troubles. "It all depends on how skilled Malachi or one of his people is with setting chip alerts."

"It is safest to assume we will trip an alarm," Hiep said, "and that any way into the hab will be alarmed. We should get the rover in close, though. Penny still limps from that wound. The less distance we need to cover to get into the rover, the better. Let's do it this way. I'll drop you off, Leif, and drive to the front of the hab.

"I am chipped out, in any case. Malachi cannot know what happened at the lake, so he will not know about me. I can occupy their attention while you come up behind and take them down. We assume an alert goes out then, and we move as fast as we can. If I sense there is an alert about me, they will die fast and we move."

"Makes good sense to me," I said. Yong agreed as well.

Hiep drove the rover up to the back side of the panel field to let me off.

"Have you told Penny how you feel?" I said to Hiep before I got out.

"No, of course not." He did not look at me. "I am prepared to die. I am not prepared for her to feel . . . differently."

"Well, you should. Before something happens and you can't." I jumped out of the rover.

I'm a good one to be advising a guy about women.

I watched Hiep drive off so that he would come up to the hab as though he were coming from St. Peterstown. The panels were tilted toward the horizon to be nearly perpendicular to the sun as it rose. That provided a wall shielding me from the view of anyone at the hab. I worked my way through the forest of panels to the back side of the hab.

"Good luck, Leif Soldier Boy," Yong said on the private line we had established. "Flygirl will be here when you need her."

That stopped me for a second. Yong never referred to herself as Flygirl. She must be certain trouble was ahead of us.

I had thought one of the guards might be at the back of the hab—in which case, I would wait among the panels for Hiep to drive up and draw their attention to him—but I could see them standing together near the door and chatting. That let me creep close. One of them was yawning. Neither seemed particularly attentive. Maybe no one was monitoring their chips. Don't bet your life and your mission on it, I warned myself.

The hab had an inviting rear window. Was there a possibility of deactivating the alarm? Could I slip Penny out, with the guards none the wiser while we drove off into the sunrise? I dismissed the idea immediately. Penny's coordination wasn't great even without a gimpy leg. The likelihood of getting her out without alerting one of the guards by old-fashioned noise was very low. Don't improvise, I told myself.

As planned, Hiep drove up as if coming from the town. As soon as he stopped the rover right in front of the two guards, he jumped out and waved to them. That was enough. They both moved forward, eyes only on him. I moved in behind.

"Listen to me," Hiep said, "and listen carefully."

They did, and that was all the opening I needed. One of them was a little behind the other. I got him with a sleeper choke hold. He went out and down. No air got past the arm I had across his throat, but his falling made enough noise for his partner to turn around. That earned him a quick kick to his groin. His eyes bugged out and he doubled over. I grabbed two handfuls of hair at the back of his head and yanked down as I slammed my knee into his forehead. He was out before he hit the ground, blood from his smashed nose staining my pants.

"We're on the clock for the alarm now," I said to Hiep.

He gave a quick nod and we both went for the entry to the hab. The doors on these habs didn't have locks. I kicked it open anyway. Inside, Penny was sitting at the desk Malachi had used. Her head was down on the desktop, hands over her hair. The surprise on her face as we burst into the room would have been comical under other circumstances.

"C'mon, Penny, we're getting out of here," I said. "They mean to kill you. We need to go now!"

Even though I left out all the awful details, maybe I shouldn't have mentioned anything about being killed. She stood up, but I could see her start to shake. She didn't move away from the desk.

Hiep stepped past me, to Penny's side. He held his hand out to her. "Come with me, Penny," he said. "It'll be all right. I promise."

She took his hand. Her shakes stopped. I saw Hiep smile and she returned it.

"Come on, folks. We're not off to the goddamned prom," I said. "Let's go."

The guards were still down when we went out through the door, but one of them was starting to moan. We got Penny into the rover. More accurately, Hiep got her into the rover and I slipped into the driver's seat. I headed the rover east, past the south end of St. Peterstown and then angled in the direction of the LZ. The sky had already brightened by the time we started. It was going to be a clear day. The sun began to rise as we went, bright and red at the eastern horizon. We drove straight into the sunrise.

"I didn't kill anybody," Penny said as we were driving.

"We know that," I said, my eyes on where I was going. "Malachi knows that too."

"Then why is he going to kill me?" A plaintive question if there ever was one.

"It's a convenient way for him to cement his control here," I said. "And he is the one responsible for the deaths."

"Then what happens to me now?"

"Leif will take you to the spaceplane and back to the *Dauntless*." Hiep's voice was gentle in a way I had never heard it. "You'll be safe there."

Penny pulled herself forward so that her head was even with where we sat. "But that's no good for people here," she said. "There won't be enough food and you need me for that. I don't want you to die, Hiep."

"We all die sooner or later," Hiep said. "If we're lucky, we can die doing something worthwhile. I want you to live and be safe."

Penny didn't say anything right away. After a long silence, broken only by rattles from the rover as it bumped over the plain, I heard a soft, "Okay," from her. She sat back down in the seat and said nothing else.

For a while, we drove across the plains without any bother. I fantasized that we would make a clean getaway. Nobody had set any alerts on the chips. Everyone had chosen to sleep late. Daydreams don't last.

Where the plain had been wide open before us, all of a sudden I squinted into the rising sun and saw rovers, backlit against the bright sky. As we rolled in that direction, I became certain they were no mirage. The town's other rovers were between us and the LZ.

A call notice to me and Hiep flashed on my field. It was Malachi.

"Good morning, Leif!" I hate false heartiness. "As you can probably see by now, we are blocking your path to the spaceplane. I will tell you that seven of us are armed with the M8s you provided. This is not going to go well for you. But I have a proposal. You give me the girl and Hiep, and you can go to your spaceplane. Safe passage. I just want them."

I clicked off without a word. I hate spam calls.

"Malachi doesn't know me at all," I said when I saw Hiep watching me.

"He doesn't understand me either," Hiep said. "He assumes everyone will act as he would. He hopes that you would try to shoot me and then turn over Penny for your freedom, or that I would suspect you would do that and kill you. He dreams of winning without a fight, or having only one of us to face."

"Fat chance. However, he still has seven rifles to our one and my popgun." I patted the pistol in its holster. "Maybe if I loop farther south and then head for the coast, we can get around them and come down to the LZ that way. Do we have enough charge, and is this rover faster than theirs?"

Hiep leaned over to peer at the panel. "It depends on how far out of the way you go and how fast you push it. Maybe."

"Worth the try," I said. "Let me call Yong and let her know what is happening."

However, when I made the call with Hiep also on the private channel, Yong vetoed it immediately. "Stay on your current course," she said. "Do not close with them, of course, but keep the relative positions. I will provide air cover. Yang out." She clicked off.

"I don't understand," Hiep said. "The spaceplane isn't armed, is it?"

"No, of course not."

"Then this makes no sense," he said. "She can't do anything. And as it is, we have the sun right in our eyes."

I sighed and looked over at Hiep. "Hiep, I don't know what she is thinking either, but I will tell you something. Yang Yong is the most stone-cold killer I've met, and she was the best pilot China had in the Troubles. I've seen some of what she has done. I trust her with my life. We should do what she says."

Hiep locked eyes with me for a few seconds. "Okay," he said finally. "That's how we'll do it."

I drove the rover forward, directly at our reception committee. I could see people jumping out of the rovers ahead of us. I counted the seven with rifles, starting with Malachi and his bald head. Two Pioneers had rifles: Bjorn and Reality. Many more Pioneers and some *Daredevil* crew were in those rovers as well. Malachi was making them own what was about to happen, I assumed.

I gauged the shrinking distance between us and by eye chose a point to slew the rover sideways. "I'm accurate with an M8 from this distance," I said.

"So am I," Hiep replied, showing no inclination to hand over the rifle. He dismounted from the rover and took a position by the front end, opposite from our friends across the plain.

I shrugged and climbed out as well to take a prone position at the rear, with as much cover from the rover as I could manage. I could hit a man-sized target with the pistol at this distance, but it would be at a firing range and under perfect conditions. This was combat. Well, I could get lucky. Or spoil their aim.

Penny copied us in getting out of the rover but then stood by it, uncertain of what to do.

"Get down," Hiep and I said together.

Hiep didn't even notice I had spoken. His attention was on Penny, so I shut up and let him show her how to crouch so that she was even with the interior front panel of the rover. At our current range, that area of the rover ought to stop an M8 bullet.

"Keep your head down," Hiep said to Penny. "Below the side of the rover. Don't get up for any reason. Leif and I have some work to do."

I had to grin. Some work, indeed. "How good are they?" I asked. "Can they hit anything at this range?"

"Loretta can," Hiep said. "I think Malachi is almost as good. The others . . . no, not at all."

A broadcast call sounded in my ear. "Last chance for safe passage out, Leif," Malachi said. "If we have to come get you, you'll get the same as them."

Bjorn's chorus sounded out over the broadcast. "Pennywise, full of lies! Pennywise, not so wise! Pennywise, now she dies!"

Stupid. Come and get us. The problem, of course, was that they could. Some of them could put down covering fire while others advanced. If Loretta or Malachi were good enough sharpshooters, they could pick off Hiep if he exposed himself to try to stop an advance. I wouldn't be much of a factor with the pistol, not until they got a lot closer. I planned on leaving a number of them on the ground before I went down, but I don't think Malachi cared much about that. We wouldn't be able to hold them off for too long if they knew what they were doing. Maybe they didn't.

A series of cracks and spurts of flame from their positions announced the start of the attack. A couple of bullets whacked into the rover but did not come through it. I peeked around the rear to see if they were starting an advance, but no one was that adventurous. Yet.

A call came to me and Hiep on the spaceplane private channel. "This is Yang." Flat and cold. A killer's voice. "Target acquisition complete. Beginning my attack run."

What? I fought to tear my mind away from the flashback to Mindanao when I'd seen her bring her J-45 attack plane in against us despite a storm of defensive fire. I had no time for those memories. What was she attacking with here?

A buzz filled the air followed by a shrill whistle. Thirty pounds of drone at two hundred miles an hour dive-bombed out of the sun directly into Malachi's head. A cloud of pink spray blossomed where his head had been. The others behind their rovers looked in vain for the source of the attack, for where the threat had come from. They couldn't see it, because they had to look behind them, directly into the blinding sun. Three more drones followed in quick succession. Loretta and two others from free companies fell, their heads blown off.

"She's only got four drones!" I yelled to Hiep.

Hiep did not hesitate. He popped up, rifle leveled over the rover in firing position. Across the ground between us, the remaining free company man saw Hiep move, tried to aim his rifle. Hiep fired a single shot. The man's arms flung wide and he fell. Bjorn started firing, spraying bullets wildly across the plain. Hiep dropped flat. Three bullets hit the rover. I saw someone move toward one of the dropped rifles. I fired from a prone position and missed, but that was enough to freeze the movement and draw Bjorn's attention to me. Hiep was back up, rifle leveled. He fired. Bjorn's head snapped back, and he dropped. Reality never fired. She threw her rifle away and raised her hands. "Don't shoot me!" she screamed. "Please don't shoot me!"

Hiep shifted, sighted on her.

"No!" That shout was Penny's. She was standing up, eyes wide as she took in the scene. "Stop shooting! Stop the shooting! We can't keep killing each other!"

Hiep tilted his rifle up to the sky. He nodded. A broadcast notification flashed on my field.

I AM VO HIEP, SICARIUS. I CALL THE DEMOS TO DISCUSS THE MURDERS OF JERRY WHITEHEAD AND FRANCESCA BALBONI AND OTHER RELATED BUSINESS.

CHAPTER THIRTY NINE

It was a somber crowd that filed into the Community Dome at midday after the living had returned to St. Peterstown. All work had been canceled for the day, more of a consensus than anyone's decision. The enormity of what had been done—and almost done—had sunk in.

Ibiana sat at the Town Council table by herself. The empty chairs on either side of her seemed bigger than she was, a stark reminder of the morning's fighting. She fiddled with her fingers as people took seats, unsure of when, or how, to start. I stood off to the side, as usual. Yong and the others had come back to town from the spaceplane to join the meeting. Yong, standing next to me, was the focus of as many stares as Hiep, who sat in the front row. They both ignored the stares.

After what felt like eternity, Ibiana cleared her throat and spoke. "Vo Hiep. You called for the Demos to meet. Please speak."

Hiep stood and turned to face the crowd. He gave the formulaic introduction and then said, "I accuse Dustin Russell of murdering both Jerry Whitehead and Francesca Balboni on the orders of Malachi Oates."

"What!" Dustin jumped up from where he was sitting in the very last row. I could see his face was red from where I stood. "You're the hired killer, not me! You don't know what you're talking about!"

"Yes, I do," Hiep said. "I know why you did it and how. Loretta and Malachi gave you what you wanted: no hard work outdoors, access to whatever you wanted. And they were going to give you your fantasy, what you wanted to do to a woman. That's what they dangled in front of you. I will not say the details here, but I know them. If you had done it, I would have killed you.

"I know what you did do. I told Leif before that the door entry record at the Medical Unit had been faked. The record of Penny's entry and exit was changed from when she came in to have her leg looked at, and it was changed at the same time the exit time for the unidentified person was faked. I am, as you said, a hired killer. I know how this is done and what to look for. I also know that an exit time can be faked, not to change the time of exit but because there was no exit. Not through the door. There is a window at the back of the unit that is screened by the privacy wall. There were no footprints on the ground below the window, which would be there if someone dropped to the ground, but there is framing at the edge of the roof where it extends beyond the wall of the building.

"Someone can stand in the window, grab the framing, and pull themselves up to the roof. From there, they can jump to the top of the privacy wall and drop down the other side. Leif gave me that idea when he escaped the school building. This would be difficult to do because of the overhang, impossible for almost everyone here except maybe me and Leif. And except for you, because you are a top gymnast. That's how you left the Medical Unit after you killed Francesca.

"I believe Malachi fixed the door records, but not very carefully, because he was rushing and he was not expert in that kind of thing. Loretta probably got rid of your clothes and those fancy shoes that had blood on them. Penny never took your shoes and boots. You set it up to look that way and also hid Jerry's case in her bedding. You gave Jerry the poisoned joint because he would take something from you that he'd never touch from Loretta or me or Malachi. You took the case when you left and turned on the air system. That's how it happened, isn't it?"

"No!"

Dustin turned as though he was going to flee, but Hiep's M8 was in his hands and aimed before Dustin could take a step away from his seat. At the sight of the barrel trained on him, Dustin froze.

"Penny said no more killing, but if you try to run, I will leave you crippled," Hiep said. "Now answer my question. In front of the Demos."

Dustin looked left, then right. He searched the faces staring at him and found no support or sympathy. The yes came out in a whisper. Then he broke down and started talking, almost babbling.

"It was all Loretta. She told me what Malachi wanted me to do with the joint, how to get Jerry to take it. That I should take the case with me so that we were sure he smoked what I gave him. She told me how to use the air system and get out of the hab so that I would be okay. She said she would make sure there was no one outside to see me. She said I'd get a position from Malachi afterward, I'd get treated right. Not what you said. I said yes. I only said yes so I could take care of Penny. This was all for her, all because of her."

Shouts of "Bullshit!" from across the Dome and the sight of Penny's face put a stop to his claims.

At a gesture from Hiep's rifle, he started up again. "Loretta told me there was a mess with Francesca. I had to clean it up. She said to make it look like Penny did it; that I would know how. What could I do? Yes, I stole Penny's knife. It was easy; I knew where she kept it. I left the sheath and put it in a plastic clip-on case. I hid Jerry's joint box there when I did it. It was easy to have some crumbs of thistle leaf in it. Loretta took the knife afterward. Loretta got rid of the bloody clothes and she took my Specials, too, because the blood wouldn't come off. That's why I went back and pretended to find my boots in Penny's hab, so I could say she also had my Specials. What else could I do? Loretta said I had to. What else could I do? It's all because of Penny. That's why it started. Because of her. What else could I do?"

The only word I could think of for that litany of "What else could I do?" was *pathetic*. He stood there, when he ran out of words to say, with his head down and the front of his pants soaked. He was such a sorry sight, no one even laughed.

"Well . . . I think . . . uh . . . we know what happened," Ibiana said. "What do we do now?"

"Take him out and shoot him!"

I didn't see who said that, but others in the Demos took up the cry as well.

"No!" Penny was on her feet. She marched to the front and turned to face the Demos. For the first time, in front of people, I did not see her trembling. What I saw was anger in her face and I heard it in her voice. "We are not shooting him or anyone else. Hiep, you can aim that damned gun at the floor. What do all of you want to do? Keep shooting each other until there's no one left? What *are* you?"

"What should we do?" Ibiana asked. "What do you want us to do?"

Penny shrugged. "I don't know the right answer. If you ask me, I'd say let him work. There's plenty of work that needs doing, the kind of work people don't like. He can do it. Or he can leave and it's on him what happens after. He is not part of the Demos anymore and he can't vote, he keeps his hands to himself, and he stays far away from me." She raised her hands in the air and let them slap down against her sides. "That's all I can think of."

It passed by acclamation.

"Should we adjourn now?" Ibiana asked.

Before they could vote on it, even before anyone could second it, a shouted, "No!" came from the last full row. Reality was standing there, twisting her hands together in front of her.

"Reality Busby, Pioneers. I have to speak. Oh my God, I have to speak. Especially now. Listen to me. Penny, listen to me. I'm speaking but I'm speaking for all the Pioneers. We all talked about it after we came in, and it has to be said, and we decided I have to be the one to say it. All of us know what we did was wrong, what we did to *you* was wrong. Worse than that." She hesitated and tears started to flow. "We didn't like you, none of us did, even though you never gave us any cause. We made fun of you because you're smart and you say what you think and it was easy to pick on you and it was funny. Until it stopped being funny . . . I guess it never was funny. That's on all of us. My God, we nearly helped kill you and then . . ." She gagged. "There'd be no return from that. I don't know how you didn't tell Hiep to keep shooting and kill me and the rest of us. I would have, but that's just another way you're better than I am. We're not asking you to forgive us. I don't know how you could. If it was me, I couldn't, but we all decided this had to be said, in public, in front of the Demos. Like I said, we don't see how you can forgive us but here's our promise, as long as we survive here, nothing like this ever happens again. Not to anyone.

If we live to have children, we will teach it to them and to their children. We promise. I promise."

"Miroslav Petrovic, Pioneers." He was on his feet even before Reality finished, his stare fixed on her. "I don't buy it, Reality. Not from you. I really don't, and I'd be surprised if anyone else here does. We all saw you vying with Bjorn to be Malachi's favorite when it looked like Malachi was going to be dictator. The only person your stupid competition with Bjorn helped was Malachi. You helped frame Penny. I know it and so do a lot of others. I got whipped and damned near crippled and I didn't see you do anything to stop it. So, fuck you, Reality."

"I wasn't part of the whipping, and what could I have done at that point?" Reality said. "I'm the one who got you down after and got you to Medical."

"Yeah, I'll give you that," Miroslav said. "But you were part of what nearly happened this morning. Plenty of others there, too, but you were carrying a gun. What would you have done if Yang hadn't blasted Malachi?"

"You don't think I know all that!" Reality was screaming. "I know what I did! I know why I did it! I know I was wrong! Wrong! Wrong! Wrong! How many times do I have to say it? None of you were saints in this either. I've got to live with that the rest of my life."

"Good for you. If you want me to believe you've suddenly opened your eyes and changed your life, you're going to have to show us. You have to prove it."

"Miroslav, I have to be able to start over. We all have to be able to start over. If we can't start over, we're all going to die." Desperation sounded in Reality's voice.

There was an uneasy stir in the crowd. Reality was bawling, tears running out so fast they dripped off her cheeks.

I considered the situation while I watched Reality on the verge of a complete breakdown as Miroslav made it clear what a shit she had been. The problem was, it wasn't just Reality. Did I really believe the Pioneers and the *Daredevil* crooks had just had a kumbaya moment and would now get along fine and pull together to save the colony? I wasn't even sure this crowd of misfits *could* do it. Out of all of them, there were only two I really cared about. Penny looked at me and at Yong. She didn't know what to say.

So, I spoke. "I'm glad to hear what the two of you said, but the situation still is what it is. Pilot Yang and I have a way forward. We will take Penny and Hiep back to Earth with us on the *Dauntless*. I think that's fair and it's a reasonable solution. You can do whatever you want here."

I saw a ghost of a smile on Penny's face, then a quick shake of her head. "Thanks, Leif, Pilot Yang, but no thanks. Hiep, I heard you say that we all die but if we're lucky, we get to die doing something worthwhile. I've learned that trying to be safe all the time is just a way of dying without doing anything. I can figure out how to farm here. I know I can. I can run the hydroponics and the cell foundries. I can have my farm here, what I could never have on Earth. I'll grow the food, and raise the animals, and I can teach other people if they want. And I'll learn how to watch my mouth." She was smiling.

Maybe I wasn't surprised. She looked relaxed for the first time since I had met her. Maybe there is something to the idea of destiny after all. "Okay," I said, and turned to Hiep. "What do you say? The offer is still good for you if you want to come."

"No, thank you," Hiep said. "I appreciate it, but no. I'm going to stay here. With Penny. If she will have me."

Penny's mouth fell open as she realized the meaning of his words. Then, so help me God, Hiep went down on one knee and asked her. I was afraid she would faint before she got out the word *yes*.

The assassin and the polymath. Who would have thought?

"You don't have a mayor here at the moment, but I think I have the authority to officiate." Yong was actually grinning.

Hiep stood up at that and said, "That's one more thing we should do as the Demos. I think Penny should be mayor. Who agrees with me?"

"No, no, no," Penny said. "I don't know how to do anything like that. It should be Sonal. That would be right."

"No, it should be you," Sonal said as she pushed through the now largely standing crowd to reach the front. "You're the one who knows what to do and you're never afraid to say it. I'll help you, along with Ibiana, we can be the rest of your Town Council, but you have to be the mayor."

The scene was giving me mental whiplash. Maybe. Maybe this could be done. Penny had the smarts and the drive. Hiep, well, Hiep was with Penny, and that would be enough to keep people from turning on her when there were hard times, or when she shot her mouth off. Sonal was pretty good with her organizational psych stuff, and if she didn't need to be a leader, could help people hold together. Ibiana would help with the *Daredevil* colonists. Maybe they could start over and maybe it could work.

The mayor was elected by acclamation.

Then we had a wedding.

CODA

Fare thee well! and if for ever,
Still for ever, fare thee well.

Lord Byron, "Fare Thee Well"

CHAPTER FORTY

We stayed to help out for nearly three months. It was a busy time. Penny and Hiep did set up their farm in Happy Valley. I spent a lot of time hauling hab material and photovoltaic panels from St. Peterstown to Happy Valley and then helping with construction. Penny picked crops for the unrelenting hot weather and put them in. Shellhound shit did turn out to be magic fertilizer for Earth crops. Terrestrial root systems and Heaven worms appeared to get along well. We were able to enjoy Heaven-grown sweet potatoes and eggplant, for starters. The bamboo grew fast and tall and the sugarcane also did well. The mango and banana trees looked like they would grow but, of course, wouldn't bear fruit fast enough for us.

The embryo tanks were put to use. Penny got her Australian cattle dog puppies. Dogs are not really my thing, but as Penny put it, these were wicked cute. They yipped at the shellhounds and ran around them and took ownership of the farm. Chickens grew well, so there was a lot of clucking around the grounds. There would be eggs for breakfast in the future, but the hens wouldn't be ready to lay in the time before we left. Lambs and goats were due to follow the chickens, but again, we would not be around long enough to see them. We also would not be around to see the child Penny informed us she was expecting. She said that if the child was a boy, he would be named Leif, and a girl would be Yong. That made me excited and sad at the same time. I would never know.

Sonal and Klaus decided they would try their hand at farming, too, so we all pitched in and set them up a short distance from Penny and Hiep. As Penny's little farm grew, I heard others discuss making the same move. It turned out that Klaus knew how to make bricks, and the mud along Happy River was suitable. Concrete and glass would need to wait, but he was already making plans for them.

Jorge told us that he would not risk another voyage in hib and would stay on Heaven. The colony didn't need a starship pilot, but Jorge was good with IT and the town could use help with that. His first job was going to be removing the programming that required the chip settings for the habs and allow manual control. Actually, that was his second job. He commandeered Dev, who was complaining of boredom, and they stripped most of the controls and circuitry out of the nuke. That reactor was dead and would never be revived, but with the equipment they salvaged, they set up an accessory node in the valley. That would be useful in the years ahead.

Jing decided that if Jorge was staying, she was staying with him. The town did need a real doc, so that decision was greeted with cheers and sighs of relief. She took charge of Yuki and the other Pioneer who had a nursing background and started training them in how to handle babies in rural settings. That struck me as a good idea, because with contraception stopped, it seemed like two out of three couples, whether formal or informal, were expecting. Jing posted a big sign outside the Medical Unit. SONG JING, MD. WALK-INS OKAY. Then we had another wedding. Penny discovered that, as mayor, she was expected to officiate. Red faced and stammering, she got through the few lines she had to say and we all cheered Jing and Jorge's kiss. We all took pictures, making sure to capture Jorge's immaculate hair, every strand in place. He loved the pics, but said, with sorrow, that with Heaven's weather he had used up almost all his hair products.

"You could always shave it," I suggested. "Start marriage with a clean slate."

"Your jokes still aren't funny, Leif," Jorge replied.

Some people have no appreciation for fine wit.

A conversation I hadn't expected was with Reality. She came to see me dressed in her uniform, as cleaned as it could be, complete with her kerchief and armband. She told me that she had actually been trained as an early childhood teacher.

"I wasn't good enough for one of the programs that would get me to a top administrative job." Her face sported a rueful grin. "That's why I'm here. I talked myself into believing I could be best among the second best. We all know what happened with that. I do know how to work, though, and I know how to change a diaper. Miroslav said I have to prove I meant what I said, and maybe if I spend a few years up to my elbows in shitty diapers, that will be a start. The town will have kids soon. What do you think?"

I told her that was a conversation she needed to have with Penny. One-to-one. I don't know what was said between the two, but I do know she started to put the school building in shape to have a day care on the ground floor. The town was going to need it in several more months.

Oh, what about Dustin? There was a loud argument in the dining hall one evening, and he did hit one of the women. We were going to hold a trial in front of the Demos, but the next morning, he was gone and never seen again. I must admit, we didn't search very hard.

Other than that incident, it was a very pleasant time. I'm not pretending everything was sweetness and light. People are people. We had other arguments. Sonal and Ibiana spent a lot of time cooling folks down and keeping them on task. They were successful, most of the time. Two of the Pioneers got into it one afternoon and Jing had to fix a busted nose, but I figure if that's the worst you need to deal with, you're in good shape. Hiep locked up the M8s in the old reactor control room. He occasionally needed one to deal with one of the gators from the river, or a sawtooth roo, but that was about it. People forgot the rifles were even around. Weapons are funny things. When you need them, you can't live without them, but if you don't need them, they can make living a difficult matter.

All in all, I liked it on Heaven. I don't mean that I ever came to terms with the weather, but I learned to coexist with it. It was peaceful, and peace has a lot going for it. On that, Yong was in complete agreement. We ventured down to the beach one day, just the two of us, and spent a couple of hours sitting on the sand watching the waves roll up. Yes, we held hands. Yes, we did more than hold hands. That beach is a beautiful setting, but the sand is hot.

All things come to an end, however. In our case, the timing was dictated by the supplies on the ship we would need to sustain us in our SFOR awake time on the way home. St. Peterstown was in no position to give us supplies. They were going to survive, but we couldn't take anything from them. Even if we could, we lacked the means to pack and radiate food so it would last the four-plus SFOR years the trip would take. Reluctantly, we broke the news that it was time to go and we said our goodbyes.

Penny and Hiep drove out to the LZ with us on takeoff day. We stopped at a safe distance from the ship and embraced; then Yong, Dev, and I went up the ramps to the cabin and cockpit. It was strange, being in the spaceplane again, preparing to head back into space. I strapped into the right-hand cockpit seat next to Yong. Through the cockpit windows, I could see Hiep and Penny, hand in hand, waving to us. I waved back, not knowing if they could see it.

Yong went through her checklist and then started the engines. Slowly, the spaceplane crept forward across the ground as the friction sections of the skids retracted. We bounced and rattled forward on the frictionless skids as the speed picked up. The vibrations stopped as we rose into the air.

Yong brought the spaceplane around in a wide loop so that we overflew Hiep and Penny. I could see them on the ground, Hiep now with an arm around her shoulders and Penny with one around his waist. They were still waving. Yong gave a waggle-wing salute with the spaceplane, an official goodbye wave, as we passed over them. We would never see them again. By the time we returned to Earth, they would have lived out their lives here on Heaven and we would never know how those lives turned out.

I wiped away some moisture I felt at the corners of my eyes and gazed at the white clouds as we rose past them.

"Flygirl, let's go home."

ABOUT THE AUTHOR

Colin Alexander is a writer of science fiction and fantasy, who has had a career as a physician, biochemist and medical researcher. He now lives in Maine with his wife where he also studies and teaches taekwondo.

Murder Under Another Sun is the second of the Leif the Lucky novels. The events of this story take place directly after the ending of the first book, *Starman's Saga: The Long, Strange Journey of Leif the Lucky*.

Find Colin on the web at:
www.afictionado.com
www.facebook.com/ColinAlexanderAuthor
www.goodreads.com/colinalexander